Report #11

by

Hugh Chare

Publication Data

Report #11 ©Hugh Chare, 2025

Book and cover design by Hugh Chare using a NASA image of the Earth.
ISBN: 978-1-940012-75-9

 Kilihune Books

www.kilihune-books.com

<u>The James Martin series</u>
African Encounter
Across the Zambezi
Just off the Great North Road
Well, there you go!
Back to Africa
We don't make glass
The Sagitta Mishap
Carbon Copy
Flight 5 to Johannesburg

<u>Marieke Englebrecht mysteries</u>
Death in the Mopane
Revenge after twenty years
Death in a Bush Camp

<u>Other books</u>
The journal of Jan Englebrecht
British Spy in the Bushveld
Federica
First to the Cape
Report #11

Preface

This is a work of fiction. Any resemblance in the featured characters to actual persons, living or dead, is purely coincidental. The classification of stars and planets in this novel is that used by the fictional visitors to Earth, not necessarily those in common use on Earth. The use of an image of the Earth on the cover of this book in no way implies endorsement by NASA of this work or the ideas presented.

Contents

Your next assignment

"Tiye reporting as requested, Elder Bastet."

"Ah, good, we have your next mission," Bastet said. "We have been following the development of Geb, a small planet in the Memphis system; it would seem that our routine check is overdue. One of our patrols has picked up a device that originated from Geb; it seems that they have made significant technological advances since our last check."

"What do we know about Geb?" Tiye asked.

"It is a class Reff satellite of a class Ghi star. The first visit of the Hemsut was some 100,000 renpet ago, and they determined that Geb was the only one in the system that would support our type of life, which is why it was seeded to support the existing beings that were there. They made another visit 50,000 renpet ago to check on development, then 25,000, 12,500, 6,2500, and 2,550. On that visit, we were allowed to go with them. Since then, we have made 10 visits on our own, about every 250 renpet, and our information shows an increasing population and an increase in the rate of technological development," Bastet recited. "It seems probable that we are at the point when we have to once again decrease the amount of time between visits."

"What did we pick up?" Tiye asked.

"A primitive device with some form of communication attached," Bastet replied. "We removed it and were able to decode it. It included images of their civilisations, languages and clues to where they are. It had left their system and was moving further into deep space. It clearly indicates that they have developed the ability to launch things from their planet into outer space."

"If they have developed technologically enough to be able to do that, then perhaps they'll have the ability to detect us if we approach. What are your instructions?" Tiye asked.

"Contact them if you can, if they are amenable, then we might agree to more frequent visits and perhaps technical assistance," Bastet said.

"And if they are belligerent?" Tiye asked.

"Take whatever steps you need to protect yourselves," Bastet said. "You have authority to use whatever weapons you choose should they try and attack you. I want to see you all back alive and well."

"If they contact us and request that we bring volunteers back with us?" Tiye asked.

"That has not really worked on previous visits," Bastet said sadly. "But perhaps they have advanced sufficiently not to be terrified by what they see here. Inanimate objects bring back by all means, it helps us see how far technologically they have progressed."

"Even orbiting objects?" Tiye asked.

"Especially orbiting objects," Bastet said.

"On our visit to Bearace, we found that they had so littered the orbital space around them that it was almost impossible to find an orbit for a new satellite that would not collide with something. If Geb has done the same, have you instructions?" Tiye asked.

"Clean up the place," Bastet said. "I like orbits to be clear of debris, so take sweepers and tugs with you and clean up the skies if necessary."

"And if they don't like us doing that?" Tiye asked.

"Then take whatever measures you need to protect yourselves and clean it up anyway. If they are really belligerent, then take everything and let them start again. This is our experiment, or at least it's the Hemsut's latest, so it may need putting back onto a better path," Bastet said. "If you are able to communicate easily with them, then make a condition of assistance from us contingent upon their behaviour."

"Very good, Elder," Tiye said. "And after this mission?"

"Then I think you will have all earned some leave," Bastet said.

"Is there anything else?" Tiye asked.

"Yes, it seems that Geb has advanced more than we thought likely. If you are able to make contact, report back as soon as you can, and we will send an Elder to advise," Bastet said.

"Do you think that likely?" Tiye asked.

"I see it as a distinct possibility, and I want no heroics," Bastet said. "Take care and report back when you return, or sooner if necessary."

Tiye left and gathered her crew.

"We are to go to Geb for a routine check on progress," she told them. "When can we leave?"

"We'll be ready in four auns," Menhet, her second in command, said.

"Good," Tiye said. "Let's get this done, and we can then take some leave. You should know that Geb has now developed launch capability, and we have obtained a probe that they sent off into deep space and from that the Elders have decoded these images."

"What does Isis have to say?" Menhet asked.

"Isis, remind me what we have on Geb?" Tiye said.

"It is a class Reff satellite of a class Ghi star, it is one of eight larger natural satellites of the star, there are also another five lesser natural satellites, plus innumerable small objects in distant orbits. Our data gathered over time indicate that they measure time based upon one revolution of their satellite upon its own axis and upon one orbit of the satellite around their star. Based on our last visit we know that one of the cultures calls one revolution a day and that is divided into 86,400 seconds, or more precisely, hours, minutes and seconds, each a factor of sixty of the other, and one orbit is approximately 365 of their days, called a year, not exactly, so they have to make adjustments on occasion. The first visit of the Hemsut was some 200,000 of their years ago, and they determined that Geb was the only one in the system that would support our type of life, which is why it was seeded to support the existing beings that were there. They made another visit 100,000 years ago to check on development, then 50,000, 25,000, 12,500, and 5,100. On that visit, we were allowed to go with them. Since then, we have made 10 visits on our own, about every 500 of their years, and our information shows an increasing population and an increase in the rate of technological development. From our last visit, we have language that is similar to some of that on the probe. The probe included these images that show that they have now developed the ability to travel in air and have developed chemical propulsion to leave their satellite," Isis intoned, repeating some of what Tiye had been told earlier and adding a few more details.

"They don't seem to have mutated far from the original seeding," Tiye said, studying the images from the probe and the history files. "There is just more colour variation in skin tones, but I suppose that is to be expected as they moved into more extreme climatic zones. They still seem to have ten fingers and presumably toes, and the rest of their physiology, based on the diagrams and images, appears to be similar to ours. What else is in the record about this place, Isis?"

"It is a satellite with abundant water, it has a breathable atmosphere, its gravity is a little less than the home satellite. At each visit, warfare was noted between different groups of the inhabitants. It has cold regions that they call polar regions, which are on the axis of rotation, towards the centre of the body, temperatures are much warmer," Isis said. "My projections on the rate of development are that they now probably have multiple artificial satellites, many of which probably no longer function, leaving open the possibility of scavenging. My analysis suggests that they are still using chemical means to leave their satellite, so have not yet developed any of the drive systems we use."

"Noted," Tiye said. "Isis, have the systems online and ready to go in four auns."

"All set?" Tiye asked when they assembled to leave. "Isis, take us through wormhole 5."

"Done," Isis reported a little while later.

"How far away is Geb now?" Tiye asked.

"Based on the velocity that the probe was travelling when we intercepted it, I calculate that at the speed of light, it would take us 40.356 auns to put us in a low orbit," Isis stated.

"So, if we go sub-light, say 400 auns, we may need longer than that to put a plan together. If they put a probe into space some 40 of their years ago, they probably have technologies to detect our presence. We can't do what the reports say we've done in the past and just park in orbit and visit as we wish, observe and then make our report. What about the other natural satellites? Is there anything on them worth scavenging?" Tiye asked.

"Our records indicate that only Geb has developed and only Geb would have materials that we may wish to acquire easily," Isis said.

"Let's move a little closer and take a look and listen," Tiye said. "Semat, see what you can pick up in the way of signals from Geb and see if we can work out what's going on there now and what we'll have to report and if they have discarded and broken artificial satellites that we might scoop up for analysis and recovery."

"I wonder if the life forms there now are still compatible with us, I know they look like us, but are they really still like us, or have they developed diseases that would make contact inadvisable?" Menhet thought aloud.

"That is a good question," Tiye said. "Based on these images, I would say that they are quite compatible; the trick will be to find out what diseases they might bring with them that we have no immunity to, or cannot quickly identify and develop antidotes for."

"Pardon me," Isis said. "My analysis of the data on the probe we captured indicates markings that are consistent with the numbers and language of the people that inhabited this land when we last visited." Isis brought up an image of Geb and indicated the area that was known by the people of Geb, Earth, as the British Isles. "I have also isolated all the materials used in the probe, and there is a wide variety, but not much mass. If you want to acquire materials that have value and not just submit a contact report to the Hemsut, we would have to investigate further."

"What's the probability that they have multiple artificial satellites?" Tiye asked.

"Ninety-nine per cent," Isis said. "This probe tells us that they have the capability to launch, and the images show technology that is low level, and the probe has been travelling for 42 of their years. My projections are that in the intervening time, they will have moved up to almost a mid-level of technology, and will have communication, observation, and other artificial satellites."

"And we know that they all have lives, so there must be some dead ones floating around; they should be happy for us to clean up their orbital paths for them," Menhet laughed.

"Tiye, I've been scanning signals from Geb, and they are emitting a wide variety of signals; they are all weak, but that is not surprising," Semat said. "I've filtered a lot of signals out, and it breaks down to a few dominant languages and many minor ones. Some of the signals are audio only, some include images. I'll put up one of the complete signals I received." She put up the signal on a display, and they were watching a news broadcast in English of missile launches in what they knew from previous reports as the Great Josean State.

"So, they are still using chemical energy to leave Geb," Menhet said.

"Isis, can you interpret this for us?" Tiye asked.

"Based upon the language files we have, this is what I project is being said," Isis replied. Isis then played a recording in the language of Tiye and crew that archæologists would note had great similarities to ancient Egyptian.

"We need an analysis of the current languages and which one is in the widest use, and develop a learning program for us," Tiye said.

"I'll take care of that," Semat promised. "It would help if we moved a little closer and got stronger signals."

"Let's do that," Tiye said. "There are eight large natural satellites, and Geb is the third one from the star, so Isis put us behind the fourth one and deploy a relay probe so that we can listen without being seen too quickly. Now, let's do a further risk analysis. Isis, get me Kapes."

"What's up?" another voice said.

"Kapes, we've picked up a probe from Geb, and we're going to take a closer look," Tiye said. "If we start collecting more materials, we'll need to know that we're safe, so could you look at risks for us?"

"Of course," Kapes said. "Did our scans pick up anything off the probe?"

"No," Menhet said. "No life forms, no bacteria, no viruses, nothing."

"When we get closer in, we may find some," Kapes said. "Remember the asteroid that Hemetre and her crew picked up, that nearly killed them all; they were lucky to be able to isolate the bacteria and develop an antidote for it."

"Let's get ready for Geb," Tiye said. She pressed a button and broadcast to the ship, "Attention, we are moving to examine the satellite Geb, all hands should be ready in 400 auns by which time we will be behind the adjacent satellite listening in to them. We will deploy some probes, and I want a full analysis of potential contact with the people there and what their reaction may be. There may be artificial satellites that are no longer functional that we will be able to recover and scavenge. Isis has background on Geb. Please review it all before we get there."

"I have taken us to an appropriate velocity to put us behind the fourth satellite in 400 auns," Isis said.

"Let's look through those images again," Tiye said. "If they contact us, then I don't want them to panic and start throwing atomic weapons at us."

"I don't know," Menhet laughed. "That might be a good way to pick up some materials. I'm sure that whatever mechanisms they have on any weapons to cause them to explode, we can disable."

"Nefertiti, could you join us on the bridge?" Tiye said. Her request was picked up by Isis and relayed, and the response was almost immediate.

"On my way," she said. She arrived shortly thereafter.

"Nefertiti, take a look at these images we picked off this probe and give me your analysis," Tiye said. Nefertiti scanned through the images quickly.

"Well, anatomically they're the same as us, same reproduction, same probable size, two sexes, I've seen some of the old images from Geb and fashions in clothes have changed a lot, they've also changed weights and measures since the last visit, these new ones are centimetre, metre, kilogram and my analysis suggests that the linear units are based on the diameter of the satellite and the weights on their gravity and the mass of water. Time, as we know from previous reports, is based on the rotation of the satellite and star's orbit. There's not much there about their organisational structure, so we can't tell if they're a unified population or still in the stage of establishing a decent system," she replied. "I would guess from the images that their society is male-dominated, but that is only a guess. The biggest unknown that we have to work out before we contact them is their system of government, are they one or are they fractured?"

"Look at this," Menhet suggested, and she called up the news item they had just been looking at of the rocket launches. "The people who are talking about this don't seem too happy about it."

"Will they unite if we contact them?" Tiye asked.

"That remains to be seen," Nefertiti said.

"Semat is doing some signal analysis," Tiye said. "Take a look at what she finds and see if you have any suggestions."

"Could we get some new blood out of this?" Nefertiti asked.

"We'll see," Tiye said. "Whereas they look compatible, I'm concerned about disease; I wouldn't want to take on passengers and have them kill us all off."

"Tiye, we've done a complete analysis of the probe that was captured," another crew member by the name of Abar said. "The technology is fairly primitive, but the probe did have cameras and sensing devices; it also had a system for relaying data back to its home world."

"So, they'll know in about 40 auns that something has happened to their probe," Tiye said. "When they no longer get signals, then for them it will mean either their systems failed, or the probe crashed into something and destroyed itself, or was picked up by someone. Which do you see as most likely?"

"That their systems failed," Abar said. "That's the most likely scenario anyway; something fails, and they lose communication."

"So, what will they try and do?" Tiye asked.

"Reestablish communication," Abar said. "I'm sure that they have a set of commands to turn on and off basic functions. Isis, what do you make of the computer on this probe?"

"It is a crude system," Isis replied. "It has the capability to turn the imaging system on and off and perform some other basic functions. The power system is a radioactive system with quite a long half-life; it has lost the ability to produce all the power it could when it was launched, but it still has enough for some time to come for basic functions."

"Can we use the elements?" Tiye asked.

"We can," Isis said. "The Elders disassembled the system completely and recovered what they could."

"I need something to eat," Tiye said, mostly to herself. She left the bridge and went to the crew area and found herself some food. That set her thinking, she wondered what the people of Geb ate and if it would be safe for her crew to eat the same. Having something fresh for a change would be nice. Living off deep-space rations was fine, but it lacked variety. She sat pondering the possibilities of scavenging from the orbit of Geb, wondering how much they could realise from whatever they picked up. She was joined by Nefertiti.

"What do you think, Tiye?" Nefertiti asked.

"It's worth a close look," Tiye said. "It'll be interesting to see how far they've developed since the last visit. I need to read the files and see what I can learn about their system of government. I wonder if it's changed much?"

"I have some information," Semat said, joining them. "Based on signal analysis, I've isolated five languages most widely spoken, not the most spoken, but the most widely spoken, I've also worked out what they call them, so the first is English, and we can fit much of it to our last visit, next is putōng huā, also matches up well to our last visit, then Hindī, then Español, then Français. Español and Français are related languages; you can find common roots in them. English shares some commonality with Français but obviously has been influenced by other languages. Putōng huā and Hindī are unrelated to the others. There are hundreds of other minor languages, but I think we should focus on the top five and then, more so, on English, which seems to be the technical language. There is a lot of signal traffic that we're looking at still, and I expect more as we get closer. I've also noted that there are many artificial satellites orbiting Geb, some active and some dead. There is also an amazing amount of debris orbiting; it looks as if they have been careless with their skies."

"Thanks, Semat," Tiye said.

"Can you pick out where on the satellite the signals are coming from?" Nefertiti asked.

"Not yet," Semat said. "But when we get closer, I expect to be able to pick out the transmitters and map them so we'll have a good idea who the most developed people are."

"I'm going to get some sleep," Tiye said. "Isis, wake me when we're behind the fourth satellite."

"I will do," Isis said.

"We have arrived," Isis said, after sending wake-up tones. "We are positioned behind the fourth satellite, and we will remain with the fourth satellite between us and the third. And we have deployed relays and probes to collect information on Geb."

"Thank you, Isis," Tiye said. She got up, cleaned herself, dressed and went back to the bridge. "Can we see Geb yet?"

"Just," Menhet said. "I'm using the long-range scanners that we have on the relay, and there it is."

"Pretty looking place," Tiye said. "What do the files say about the atmosphere?"

"Quite breathable," Menhet said. "Slightly more oxygen than we have, but not much."

"Enough extra to cause problems?" Tiye asked.

"No," Menhet assured her.

"We have a better analysis of language now," Semat said. "I've put together a learning program for the English that they speak, and have also isolated their names of the star and the natural satellites; the names have changed over time and vary by language and culture. The people who speak English call their star the Sun, then the satellites working out are Mercury, Venus, Earth, Mars, Jupiter, Saturn, Uranus and Neptune; many of those satellites have their own satellites that they call moons. Earth has a large moon, which, believe it or not, they call the Moon. So, we're parked behind Mars, and our target is Earth. Why anyone would call their home world after soil or dirt is a mystery to me."

"So, Geb is Earth," Tiye mused. "Have we sent any probes yet to take a look at the place?"

"I sent a swarm as soon as we arrived here," another crew member by the name of Merti replied. "We're getting data and images back now. I'll have a complete map soon. I also sent a swarm around this satellite as well, and now have a map of here, and I noticed what looks like remains of probes on the surface, and there are active artificial satellites in orbit, and a couple of active probes on the surface. I've sent another swarm to look for metallics and other debris. It looks like the people from Geb have been venturing out."

"Pick up whatever you spot," Tiye said. "We need to make something on this trip. I think it's time for a crew meeting, Isis. Please get everyone up here." The rest of the crew assembled quickly and waited for Tiye.

"You all know that we picked up a probe from Geb, or Earth as they call it, we're going to take a look so that we can fulfil our mission and report back, make contact and assess the stage of their development, and potentially pick up some defunct artificial satellites as salvage. Abar is doing a technology evaluation of the probe that was picked up, and it looks like we may get some more probes off the surface of this satellite, which they call Mars. Betrest, I'd like you to make sure that all the capture tugs are in working order. I don't want to grab some object and not be able to get it back. Henuttawy, it's a possibility that the people on Earth may not like us taking their junk, so we need the defensive systems up, data back from an early probe we sent out shows that the atmosphere has been polluted by the use of atomic weapons, so it's possible that they may try and use one against us, so we need long-range sensors up to disable firing mechanisms, Iset, ramp up the bays for disassembly and recovery, Kapes is looking into life form risks from bacteria, we don't want what happened to Hemetre happening to us, Menhet will manage the approach when we go and put us into the right orbits, Merti has sent out probes and will give us a better picture of the place when she has all the data, Nefertiti will handle communication with these people when we make contact, Penebui can you prepare some isolation quarters, we'll see if we can get any beings from Earth to join us, Semat is analysing their communications and has isolated primary languages, she has a learning program for the one we'll use. Anything I've forgotten?" Tiye asked. There was a buzz of conversation, but it was mostly speculation about what they might find and what value it would have.

Isis set off an alert and noted that some artificial satellites orbiting Mars were relaying signals from the surface to Earth.
"Do we pick up all the devices on the surface?" Menhet asked.
"I don't think so," Tiye said. "Let's not alert the people on Earth to our presence yet. We'll pick up the active devices here on our way home. Anything that is dead we'll take now."
"I've noted in orbit six dead artificial satellites and 11 that are active. On the surface, we've detected 12 objects that are dead and five that are active," Menhet said. "So, I'll sweep and pick up the dead satellites and the junk from the surface. These people really are a messy people, they just leave junk lying around all over the place."
"We were like that once," Tiye chided her gently. "These people just haven't learned how to launch simply and how to bring things back."

11

"I estimate that we could pick up nine mega deben of material between the surface and orbital junk," Menhet said.

"That's a start," Tiye said. "Given that they've sent probes to look at this Mars, I wonder if they sent probes to what they call the Moon, and how much junk is there?"

"When we move closer, we should stop and have a look," Menhet said.

"I think we'll do that," Tiye said.

"I'll start with the orbiting bodies," Menhet said. "I'll send out a tug and start bringing them back. It shouldn't take long; there aren't that many. For the stuff on the surface, looking at where it's spread out, I'll send down two tugs and sweep everything up that's dead."

"Our sensors have detected water on this satellite," Isis intoned.

"Where is it?" Tiye asked. Isis brought up images of Mars and indicated where the water, in the form of ice, was most abundant.

"I'll send a tug and get enough to replenish our stocks," Kapes said. "I'll check it for organisms and clean out anything that I find."

"Good," Tiye said. "We don't want to kill ourselves by picking up something in the water."

For about an Earth week, Isis stayed behind Mars while ice was mined and the dead objects, both orbiting and on the surface, were collected and brought back. Inside the ship, the automatic systems went into action, the ice was cut into easily stackable blocks and stowed, and the satellites and probes were dismantled and the various materials sorted out and consigned to storage areas.

"Did we learn anything from these objects, Isis?" Tiye asked.

"An analysis of the markings and emblems would indicate six entities that have sent probes here," Isis said. "Cross-referencing with signals we have picked up and analysed, we name them as the United States of America, the Union of Soviet Socialist Republics, a now-defunct political entity, the People's Republic of China, the United Arab Emirates, India and the European Union. The latter has only two objects here; the rest are from the first five. We have identified on screen where these entities are." Isis put up an image of the Earth with the countries marked. "Images of the devices active on the surface put them as coming from the United States of America, and for those in orbit, there are objects from the United States of America, India, the European Union in combination with Russia, which we have concluded is the surviving political entity once called the Union of Soviet Socialist Republics, China, and the entity calling itself the Emirates. Most of our probes that we sent to map the satellite Earth are back, and we now have current maps of all habitations. They are on screen now."

Tiye looked over the images and worked the controls to spin the globe, zoom in and zoom out, and alter the wavelengths of the images to see visible light, infrared and ultraviolet.

"Have you an estimate of population, Isis?" Tiye asked.

"9,500,000,000 and growing exponentially," Isis said.

"How did they get themselves in this fix with too many people?" Tiye speculated.

"They appear to have little or no control over population growth," Isis said.

"So, they may be actively looking for somewhere else to colonise," Tiye thought. "I don't think we want to encourage that. Can this satellite support the population?"

"Difficult to say," Isis said in a rare moment of uncertainty. "They are destroying their natural habitat and are polluting their atmosphere with large amounts of products of combustion."

"So, where we were a while ago," Tiye said. "I think we can start to move closer to Ged now, take us to a velocity that will get us there in two weeks of their time. I'm sure that at some point they will detect us, so it will be interesting to see what their reaction will be, to try and communicate or to attack, so make sure all our defensive systems are active. Menhet, have you any views on the orbiting artificial satellites they have?"

"They have a lot," she replied. "There are many derelict objects, both large and small. We will need the sweepers just to clean up all the small objects that are too small for them; they really have been messy in their placement of their artificial satellites."

"Is the orbital plane consistent?" Tiye asked.

"There are some patterns, typically what they would call equatorial or polar orbits," Menhet said. "I think we can deploy the sweepers and pick up a lot of the small debris in a few orbits. Their low orbit would mean that we could make at least ten orbits for one of their days, so we could sweep up the small objects quite quickly."

"What do we do if they object?" Tiye asked.

"I'm presuming that you've already decided to scavenge what we can, no matter what they think," Menhet laughed. "If they object, tell them too bad and continue, then have our defensive systems up for kinetic weapons, light weapons and atomic weapons."

"Isis, is there any indication whether these people are united or in factions?" Tiye asked.

"Analyses of signals suggest a high degree of factionalism," Isis reported. "Whether or not they will unite when we are detected, I cannot predict."

"How many objects are in higher orbits that put them stationary with respect to their Earth?" Tiye asked.

"Quite a few," Menhet said. "Our count is 556."

"And in low orbit?" Tiye asked.

"Some 11,500 objects of some size and over 1,500,000 very small particles, that's what the sweepers would go for, plus much of the 11,500 objects, there are a lot of pieces that by the look of things have either been detached, or be the result of the placement, or the result of collisions," Menhet said.

"If we clean up this mess for them, they ought to be happy," Tiye said.

"They ought to be," Menhet agreed. "But, if our experience with other cultures is anything to go by, they will object just to object."

"Do any of the artificial satellites have life forms?" Tiye asked.

"Our analysis shows two large objects that do have life forms," Isis said.

"What kind of life?" Tiye asked.

"Life that is compatible with you," Isis said. "I also have temperature maps of Earth now, and you can see where the hot and cold areas are. Most of the population is to be found in the temperate zones.

"I've mapped signal transmitters," Semat said. "It correlates with the nighttime images that show artificial light. Population density varies a lot; I have marked those areas with what we project are the highest densities. I've also detected air transportation. I've put a pattern together with the most trafficked areas."

"I wonder what they eat?" Tiye said.

"Analysis suggests that they grow large amounts of herbivorous crops," Isis said. "Whether or not they are in any way carnivorous, I cannot tell yet."

"It looks as if they've been getting images of us," Menhet said. "We've detected cameras being moved to focus on us."

"So they know we're here and they probably know what we look like," Tiye said.

"I wonder what they're thinking?" Semat said.

"I would be wondering if we're invading or just visiting," Menhet said.

"So, how will they react?" Tiye mused.

"Hard to say," Semat said. "It depends on their culture. My sense from what we've seen on scanners and from the probes is that they're a fractured society, probably constantly warring with one another, so their first instinct is to attack, so, we should be prepared for them to throw something at us. Reading the contact report from the last time we were here, we were able to infiltrate without revealing our identity because they had no way to detect us. Now it seems that they do, so our approach will have to be more direct."

"Henutawy, are we all up and ready?" Tiye asked.

"We are," Henutawy replied. "I've got shields up, I've got long-range scanners looking for kinetic and light weapons. If they throw something at us, we can always outrun it if we can't deflect it or redirect it. If they try high-intensity light or other wavelengths, we can mirror them back to the source and take them out."

"Let's wait a bit and see if we hear from them," Tiye said. "If we get a friendly greeting then let's move closer, say, take about two weeks of their time. I don't want to go too fast, they might think we're attacking and I want them friendly enough that they'll be happy for us to clean up their junk."

"It would seem that they have done a fair amount of exploration of Earth," Semat said. "When we were last here, this place, the United States of America did not exist, there were just small colonies of people from those they called English, French and Spanish and some people who were already there and not part of a colonising effort. When we were here last, there were no systems of transport powered by combustion, but they did have crude explosives, mainly used for warfare."

"It's interesting how warfare seems to stimulate and propel technology," Tiye said. "I suppose that if they have chemical systems for launching satellites, then they've used the same technology to launch projectiles at each other."

"That would be logical," Henutawy agreed. "Geb is far advanced compared to that place we were a while ago, where they had just started to use bronze for weapons and tools. We haven't been to a society yet that doesn't have metals, that would be interesting to see how they develop tools for rocks, wood and animal parts."

"The old reports that we have show that Geb went through those eras," Tiye said. "From stones, to bronze, to iron."

"How long are you going to do this, go from place to place looking at the work of the Hemsut?" Semat asked.

"I think I will give it up after this trip," Tiye said. "The adventure of going somewhere new is nice, but I don't want a life that is just travel to the far reaches of our galaxy. The Hemsut can find a new leader easily enough. What about you?"

"I like the travels and I like to see how societies develop," Semat said. "It is something that I enjoy studying. There seems to be almost a universal nature to the development cycles; human nature cannot be escaped, no matter how technological the society."

"So, you're becoming a philosopher?" Tiye asked.

"Perhaps," Semat said. "Perhaps that is what we need to evaluate progress in the societies that the Hemsut have intervened in. What we have not been allowed to do yet is explore and find developing beings that the Hemsut have not taken a hand in moulding. Have you ever met any of the Hemsut?"

"Twice," Tiye said. "It was interesting, they have developed far beyond us, and they entered my mind and we communicated without me saying one word aloud. It was fascinating and disturbing. We have a long way to go to be at the stage of development that they are."

Lost contact - 13:33 PST, March 5th, 2029

"We've lost contact with Voyager 1," Jim said to the others in the control room of JPL, the Jet Propulsion Laboratory of NASA in Pasadena, California.

"Nothing?" Dave, one of the others in the room, asked.

"Nothing," Jim said. "I was getting a dump from it when the signal just stopped."

"Any ideas?" Dave asked.

"Not right now," Jim said. "I've sent a couple of commands back to see if I can get things turned on again; maybe it got hit by something."

"Possible," Dave agreed. "So, we have to wait almost two days to find out if you get anything back."

"Bitch, I agree," Jim said, then he went back and pulled out all the manuals and started to go through the possible failure modes to see if he could get any ideas as to why the signal just stopped and if it might be possible to get it turned back on. That would take a while and on top of that, the time for the signal to reach the probe was about 24 hours, so 48 hours before he might have some idea of what went wrong. Jim waited and waited, and nothing came, he tried different signals, then waited, but still nothing.

"Still nothing from Voyager?" Dave asked after two weeks had elapsed.

"Nothing," Jim said. "I'm beginning to think that it really is dead."

"That's too bad, but we still have Voyager 2," Dave commented.

"I'm just hoping that doesn't go offline too," Jim said.

"While you're thinking about that, take a look at these images," Dave said.

"Wow," Jim said. "That's new and it's moving pretty damn fast, wait, where the hell did it go?"

"Behind Mars," Dave said. "It appeared in the sky, came towards us at a damn good rate of knots, then disappeared behind Mars."

"Do you think it hit Mars?" Jim asked.

"Well, it was there before and now we don't see it, all we see is Mars, so it's not an unreasonable inference to draw that it actually hit Mars," Dave said.

"Any idea how big it was?" Jim asked.

"Pretty big," Dave said. "We didn't get any good images, but we think it's somewhat cylindrical, about 700m in length by about 100m in diameter."

"Good size, how fast was it going?" Jim asked.

"Our best guess, about one-tenth light," Dave said.

"We should get one of the satellites around Mars to start looking for a bloody big hole," Jim said. "At that speed and that big, it would have been a hell of an impact."

"That's the problem," Dave said. "There's no impact crater anywhere on Mars."

"Well, it can't have burned up, there's not enough atmosphere for that, what's your theory?" Jim asked.

"We have to consider the possibility that it's a vessel under control," Dave said.

"Oh shit," Jim said. "Have you sent this up?"

"I sent up the notice that we had a new object and that its trajectory would make it a Near Earth Object, then I sent up the details that I had, including the fact that we could no longer see it," Dave explained. "The other interesting thing is that it came from the same direction as Voyager 1 and appeared not that long after you first lost signal."

"You think someone found Voyager 1, read the message and is coming to have a look?" Jim asked.

"It was looking that way until it disappeared behind Mars," Dave said.

"What if, and this is just really wild speculation, it's hiding behind Mars, getting a better look at us before coming closer?" Jim asked.

"There's more," Dave said. "In the last couple of days, we detected a whole swarm of small objects that came close, orbited a few times, then went back off, towards Mars, would you believe."

"Probes sent to look us over?" Jim asked.

"I think we should send out an alert that we think we're being looked over, by what or whom we don't know," Dave said.

"We'd better get whatever telescopes we can to focus on the Mars neighbourhood," Jim said. "Can we get any of the Mars rovers to turn their cameras skywards and see if they can see anything?"

"I'll talk to the team," Dave said. "You realize as soon as this goes up, that we're going to have military guys all over the place."

"I know, standard response, give it to the military. I wonder if they even get the idea that if there is something there and it is a vessel of some kind that can do one-tenth light then they have technology far beyond anything we have, and they probably have defensive systems to counter anything we might throw at them," Jim commented.

"Let me go and talk to the rover guys, tell them what we've seen and see if they can swing a camera up and take a look," Dave said.

"Good morning gentlemen, I am General Hopkins of the US Space Force, and we are taking charge of this investigation," was how Jim and Dave were introduced to their new supervisor. "Any and all images, data, telemetry or other signals relating to this object are now classified. Any questions?"

"Have you seen the images from the rover camera?" Jim asked.

"That's why we're taking over," Hopkins said. "We don't know who these beings are or what their intentions are, and we need to start preparing possible responses. Colonel Williams will be your immediate liaison. Now, what can you tell me about this object?"

"You can see that it's a large manufactured vessel," Jim said. "We put the length at about 700m and diameter in the widest point at 100m, about twice as big as an aircraft carrier, looks like a bunch of modules strung together. It looks like it's got communication antennae, and what look like doors of some kind here and here."

"Who are they? Where are they from?" Hopkins asked.

"We have no idea," Jim admitted. "We speculate that they may have encountered Voyager 1, read the message that was on it and come to have a look."

"I always thought it was a big mistake to put that damned message on those probes," Hopkins said. "Now we may be faced with a real alien, and we don't know if they're friendly or are sitting out there waiting to blow us all to kingdom come."

"Have we received any kind of communication from them?" Williams asked.

"Not yet," Jim said.

"Looks like something right out of Hollywood," Hopkins said. "Are we sure the Russian or the Chinese are not spoofing our signals?"

"They have been getting images as well," Dave said. "I know one of the Chinese guys, and he sent me a text."

"That stops right now," Hopkins said. "No communication with the Russians, Chinese, Europeans, Indians, Emirates, anyone."

"So, if we're not getting a spoofed image and it's real, what kind of vessel is it?" Williams pondered. "Is it a vessel of war or what?"

"We've no idea," Jim admitted. "What would a space frigate look like, this doesn't look like a Star Wars Imperial Cruiser."

"I would have thought that there'd be some sort of weapons that we could see," Williams said.

"There may be," Jim said. "We just don't know what we're looking at. Hollywood has provided us with their ideas of what a warcraft in space would look like, but we've really no idea. Let's face it, everything we dream up is influenced by our experiences, so it's very difficult to come up with something truly alien."

"So, no Star Destroyer?" Williams said.

"Who knows?" Dave said.

"Why are they hanging back behind Mars?" Hopkins asked.

"Again, we've no idea, but we speculate that they're looking us over, that swarm of small objects that came and went, we thought might be probes to map us," Dave said.

"If we're really talking about aliens, I wonder what they look like?" Williams said.

"Little green men, or Chewbacca?" Jim mused.

"Maybe even the Alien," Dave added. "Or the Predator, the Blob or something we can't even see, like the Midwich Cuckoos."

"We need to get all our air defence systems up, radar, imaging, radio telescopes, anything that can give us better images, is Hubble still online?" Hopkins asked.

"It is," Jim confirmed. "It was fixed about two years ago, so it's back operational now."

"I want it repositioned so that we can see Mars and this thing, if and when it comes out from behind Mars," Hopkins said.

"That's not my call, you'll have to talk to the Hubble team," Jim said. "That will mean telling them what you're looking for."

"Can we re-task the Webb telescope?" Hopkins asked.

"We'd have to call those guys and tell them why, but remember it's an infrared scope, so may or may not see what we're looking for," Jim replied.

"I'll take care of that," Hopkins said.

"Don't you have some surveillance birds that you can re-task?" Jim asked.

"We need to keep them on task to see what the Russians, Iranians, Chinese and North Koreans are up to," Hopkins said. "Besides, the cameras are not really good for objects that far away; we need to get the big telescopes to look in that direction as well."

"That's your department," Dave said. "If you want all the big telescopes in Chile, Hawai'i, Arizona, Texas, South Africa and Gran Canary, you're going to have to make the calls. My guess is that they've already heard and that they're looking to see what they can find right now."

"I wonder what they really want?" Jim mused.

"That's always the question about visitors and invaders, isn't it?" Dave said. "I'm sure the natives here wondered about the Pilgrim ships when they showed up, friend or foe?"

"So, what kind of technology do they have?" Hopkins asked.

"We estimated earlier that they were moving at about one-tenth of the speed of light, say 29,600 km per second, give or take, the fastest we've been able to go to date in space is 73 km per second, so they're orders of magnitude faster than us and we have only speculation as to how they achieve those velocities," Jim said. "The other thing to consider is that they decelerated from that speed in a relatively short distance, so this is not solar wind kind of stuff; they can turn their drive on and off. One other thing to consider is at those speeds, if you hit anything, even something really small, it would go straight through any structure we could build, so we have to consider that they have some kind of shielding system that brushes aside objects, plus accelerations and decelerations at those speeds would be a real problem for us, so if they can do that, they must have some magic technology that protects them, if in fact there's any life aboard and it's not just a robot ship."

"I'll bet a nuke would take them out though," Hopkins bragged.

"I wouldn't be so sure," Dave cautioned. "We've no idea what their capabilities may be, to fire a nuke at them we have to launch it from Earth, they'd see it coming and for all we know they have light or kinetic systems that could take out our launch vehicle before it even leaves the atmosphere, then we've got a weapon coming back at us, would it just burn up, or would you get an EMP out of it?"

"Are we that helpless?" Hopkins asked.

"The simple answer is we just don't know," Jim said. "It may be that if they land, then the War of the Worlds happens, and bacteria take care of them, but if they don't land, we'll have to try and work out what they're up to. Do you want to try and communicate?"

"We could try, but what the hell do we say, what kind of message do we send, sounds, images, tones, what?" Hopkins asked.

"If they have picked up the Voyager 1 message, then just send the audio from that," Jim suggested. "That way we'll confirm that we sent it, but my guess is that they already know that."

"How do you send it?" Hopkins asked.

"Use a broad spectrum of frequencies," Jim suggested.

"I should brief POTUS," Hopkins said. "It's frustrating that we don't have much solid information. Williams, let me know if anything new happens."

"Sir," Williams said.

"General Hopkins to see POTUS," he said when he made his way to the White House very early the next morning, having flown overnight back to the East Coast.

"Come with me, Sir," one of the aides said. He was led straight to the Situation Room, where he joined the Attorney General, James Black, and the Secretaries of Defense, John Madison, Homeland Security, Madeline Wilson, Agriculture, George Grant, Energy, Helen Cortez, Health and Human Services, Miho Yamamura, State, Andre Romero, Commerce, William Botha, and the Joint Chiefs and the heads of the NSA, FBI, CIA, NASA, FDA, CDC and EPA. They waited about three minutes, then the president, Jane Adams, and vice president, Brian Taylor, joined them.

"So, General Hopkins, what do we have?" POTUS, Jane asked.

"Frankly, we don't know Madame President," Hopkins said. "We have these images of a vessel parked on the back side of Mars. Some are from our rover, some are from our orbiters and some we lifted from the Chinese, European, Russian and Emirati orbiters. It's big, about twice as big as an aircraft carrier."

"How many men can you get in a carrier?" she asked.

"The crew of one of our carriers is about 5,000," Madison said. "We also have planes on board."

"So, if whoever these beings are is about the same size as us, nowhere near enough to conquer the Earth?" she suggested.

"We don't know Madame President," Hopkins said. "We don't know what their capabilities are, their weapons systems, if this is just a scout vessel for a larger fleet, we are in the dark."

"We've had no indication from them what their intentions may be?" she asked.

"We've had nothing direct, Madame," he said. "We're fairly sure they sent some probes that orbited the Earth, then went back; we surmise that they were looking us over, perhaps testing our weaknesses."

"How is it that we didn't see this thing earlier?" she asked.

"Apparently, it was moving very fast and the interval between images was such that it moved out of the frame before they had time to compare images, Madame," he replied.

"Have we tried to communicate with them?" she asked.

"Not yet, Madame," he said. "We're waiting to see what they might do. We're thinking that perhaps sending out the audio from the Voyager Mission might not be a bad idea."

"What did that say?" she asked.

"Essentially, hello, how are you, in 55 languages," he said.

"I understand that the object is currently behind Mars, but I have to presume that they have the means to listen to us. Why not send it now and see what happens?" she asked.

"We can do that, Madame," he said.

"How long for us to send a message to them?" she asked.

"About four minutes, Madame," he replied.

"Do it," she instructed.

"May I call and tell them to go ahead?" he asked.

"Please do," she said. Hopkins picked up the telephone on the desk and gave the operator the number.

"JPL, Jim speaking," was the reply.

"Jim, this is General Hopkins. Go ahead with the broadcast of the Voyager messages," Hopkins instructed.

"I'll do that," Jim said. "And if I get a response?"

"Relay it to me immediately," Hopkins said.

"So, what risks or threats might there be from these beings?" Jane asked.

"They may be a precursor to an invasion," Madison offered. "They're just here to probe our defences and our weaknesses."

"If they are peaceable and we let them land, then they might bring disease that is far worse than the pandemics of 1918 and 2020," Yamamura added.

"So, what defences do we have against them?" Jane asked.

"We can use nuclear weapons," Madison suggested. "That would blast them out of the sky."

"If they land and bring an unknown virus or bacterium, then we have none until we know what it is, so I would recommend that even if they are peaceable, we don't let them land," Yamamura added.

"And if they just brush aside all our air defences and land?" Jane asked.

"Then we'll have to bring in the army and establish a perimeter around them and see if we can contain them," Madison said.

"What does NSA have to say, have you picked up any transmissions from them?" Jane asked.

"Not a thing, Madame," Tom Price, the NSA man, replied. "Our signal gathering is mainly focused on our adversaries."

"Well, what do they have to say about this thing?" she asked.

"They seem as confused as we are," Price replied. "Everything we've decoded tells us that they are having the exact same conversations that we are, what their intentions might be, how to counter a threat and what to do if they land. That's true for the Chinese, the Russians, the Indians, the Brits, the French, the Germans, the Emirates, the Iranians, even the North Koreans."

"There is potentially a problem with launching a missile against them," Hopkins said. "The JPL guys said that they estimated that when the object entered the solar system, it was doing about one-tenth of light speed, and they seem to have the technology to accelerate and decelerate at will, so at those speeds, they can just outrun anything we launch."

"Even with a surprise launch?" Madison asked.

"Speeds on launch are relatively slow," Hopkins said. "If we presume that they can detect launches, as we can, then all they have to do is run around the other side of the world, or worse still, orbit so that anything chasing them goes into a decaying orbit and comes right back at us."

"You are full of good news," Jane said.

"I'm sorry, Madame," he said. "But we're dealing with technologies here that we just don't understand."

"We're sure that there are beings on this object?" she asked.

"It certainly seems to be under control," Hopkins said. "So, either there's a very sophisticated computer system managing things, or there are beings."

"What if we have a HAL?" Madison asked.

"A SciFi mad computer?" Hopkins mused. "I would doubt that, but at this time, we cannot dismiss anything."

"From the image, can you hazard any guesses as to what a being inside it might look like?" she asked.

"We've blown up the images and we've picked out two sizes of what we think might be accesses, one is big enough for some kind of space shuttle, certainly big enough for our old shuttles, the other is smaller but big enough for humans, so our surmise at this time is that they won't be giant anything, be it Wookies, ants, the Predator, Aliens, E.T., or even humanoids," Hopkins said.

"I'm thinking we should convene a Security Council meeting," Jane said. "As a world, we need to have a united front in case we really do have to defend ourselves."

"I'm surprised that the Secretary-General hasn't done that already," Romero said.

"Maybe he hasn't been fully briefed yet," Wilson suggested.

"We'd better get on this quickly," Jane said. "If we don't, chaos will ensue. How long before it hits the mainstream media?"

"My guess is as soon as they send a signal, if they do," Hopkins said. "There are just too many ways to pick up signals, so everyone with an antenna will pick it up."

"Will they respond?" Madison asked.

"I've no way of guessing," Hopkins said. "I know this is a scenario we're supposed to have practised and reviewed, but somehow it's different now it's real."

"Who will attack first?" Jane asked. "The Russians or the Chinese?"

"I think the Russians or the North Koreans," Madison said. "Their answer to everything seems to be attack, then ask who and what."

"I'll bet that there are more than a few regimes around the world that are concerned about their survival," Romero commented.

"Most probably don't know that they're here yet," Hopkins said. "We only know because we're looking at images sent from our Mars Rovers and orbiting satellites."

"Wait until the various religions get wind of real aliens," Romero said. "Then see what happens."

"As a precaution, let's go to DefCon 3," Jane said. "We may have to increase readiness soon, depending on what the visitors do."

"I'll give the order, Madame," William Brant, the chairman of the Joint Chiefs, said.

"What else?" she asked.

"We wait," Hopkins said. "I know that's not what everyone wants to hear, but anything we launch at them from here will take months to get there."

"How fast did you say they could be here?" Yamamura asked.

"At the speed at which they were first detected, about fifty minutes," Hopkins replied.

"So, do we expect our visitors to be showing up in orbit soon?" Yamamura asked.

"I've no idea," Hopkins admitted. "I would have thought that if this were an attack that they would have been here already and taken out much of our defensive systems, so my surmise is that they're looking us over."

"Do they know that we know that they're there?" Romero asked.

"Again, I don't know, but my surmise is that yes, they've probably detected the camera movements of the rovers," Hopkins said.

"You're the Space Force," Romero said. "What do you have to use against them?"

"We have some lasers that we can re-task," Hopkins said. "But much of our capability was designed around protecting our birds and possibly taking out the other guy's birds. One thing the JPL guys pointed out to me was that at the speeds they were going, they have to have some kind of protection because at those speeds, anything they hit is going to go right through them."

"How are those speeds possible?" Madison asked.

"We don't know," Hopkins said. "We have theories and models, but how one actually achieves those kinds of speeds, apparently at will, is beyond us."

"Could they defend against lasers?" Madison asked.

"We don't know," Hopkins admitted. "Lasers are just light, but the light wavelengths vary a lot depending on the laser. Whether or not they could defend against lasers, I don't know. If I had to hazard a guess, I would say yes, because anyone who can devise a propulsion system that takes them as fast as it does can probably develop other systems as well."

"So they truly have technology that is beyond even our experimental systems?" Jane asked.

"I believe so, Madame, even beyond our theoretical notions," Hopkins replied.

"I see the biggest challenge we're going to have is avoiding mass panic when the news breaks," Wilson commented. "We should be prepared to call out the National Guard in all states."

"Put together a briefing for all the governors," Jane instructed. "Have them online in an hour, all hell might have broken loose by then, but perhaps not; it'll all depend on whether or not E.T. phones home. General, you said that it would take about four minutes for a message to get there, and presumably back. We haven't heard from them. Is that good or bad?"

"They may be trying to understand what the message means," he said. "We have no idea if greetings actually have any meaning to them."

"I watched *Arrival*," Jane said. "I liked the way Hollywood made the Chinese the bad guys, by having them interpret knowledge as weapon."

"This all does rather have the feel about it of a second-rate movie," Romero said. "If it weren't so serious."

"So, what else can we do?" Jane asked. "We're going to DefCon 3, we're calling up all the National Guard, do we pull people back from our bases in Germany, Korea and Japan?"

"It might be a good idea to do that," Madison said. "It will take days to do that, by which time it might be all over, but I'd rather have our troops here defending the States, not some other place."

"We should be careful," Romero cautioned. "If we pull our guys out of Germany, the Russians are just as likely to try and move in, same is true in Korea, if we pull out then the North will move, and to round it all out, the Chinese may take advantage of the focus on the object to further their advances in the South China Sea and in the Himalayas."

"If the aliens land and bring in viruses or contagions that are new to us, how long before we could isolate and analyse them?" Jane asked.

"Our experience with the 2020 pandemic taught us a lot," Dr Tamara Park, the head of CDC, said. "We could probably get some idea of what we were dealing with fairly quickly if anyone got sick, and we were able to tie it back to aliens, whether or not we could deal with it is another matter."

"It's also possible that we could have a longer-term problem," Cortez added. "We tend to think of contagions in human terms, but if there was some kind of blight that we did not understand and it got into our food supply around the world, we could face longer-term starvation."

"Do you have the capabilities to check?" Jane asked.

"We have some," Cortez replied. "CDC and EPA have labs; the CDC labs are best equipped for pathogen detection."

"I expect you to work together," Jane said. "There will be no political pressures, no posturing, you need to do your jobs and tell us from a scientific point of view what we're dealing with, not what looks good in the polls. I want real science on this, none of your pseudoscience, no weird ideas from conspiracy theories; we had enough of that in the last decade. Science is what we will need to win this thing, so it's not a dirty word, no matter how much some of our politicians would like us to believe, the Bible is not going to get us out of this one."

"Yes, Madame," Cortez replied.

"What food stocks do we have?" Jane asked.

"We have the pre-positioned disaster supplies," Wilson said. "Plus the military has some, we could probably feed the nation for two weeks if the entire food supply chain were disrupted. Some folks, particularly in places like Utah and Idaho, have long-term stocks, but the vast majority of the population lives day to day, or at best, week to week."

"Water," Jane asked.

"Water supplies are always an issue," Wilson said. "We've got plenty, but not where the people live. Demands on the Colorado have made living in California a challenge, but Michigan, Minnesota and Wisconsin have plenty from the lakes. The problem we have is that we've no means to move the Great Lakes water to high-demand areas, like California. That all assumes that the aliens don't mess with the water supply."

"So, from a threat point of view, we have direct attack with some kind of weapons that kill us, we have potential disease, we have potential threats to our food and water, anything else?" Jane asked.

"EMP," Madison said. "An electromagnetic pulse above the Earth that takes out our communications systems and leaves us blind doesn't affect us as humans, but pretty much anything electronic is toast, including most cars, all cell phones, computers, the works. We have some shielded communication networks, but cell phones would be out, and so would all the household appliances that have electronics. Highways would be a mess because cars would just die; the only ones running well would be old gas and diesel that had no electronics."

"So, EMP, weapons attack, contagions, threats to food and water, anything else?" Jane asked.

"I suppose there's always the possibility of climate manipulation," Hopkins added. "If they can do that, then we're rather at their mercy. Plus, a few well-placed large explosions in the oceans could send tsunamis that would take out all the world's major seaports and quite a few cities to boot, this one included."

"I wonder why they haven't responded to our signal," Madison said. "What's holding them up?"

"Maybe they're still trying to figure out all the various languages," Hopkins said. "It's a pity space on the disk was limited; it might have been better to have videos of people saying the greetings. Maybe they're formulating a reply, maybe they just don't want to talk to us."

"And you say any pre-emptive strike on our part would fail because where they are, it would take seven months for anything to get there?" Madison asked.

"About that," Hopkins confirmed.

"Can we zap them with a laser?" Madison asked.

"We can't see them from here," Hopkins said. "Lasers are line-of-sight weapons, and if we can't see them, we can't hit them."

"Damn, I hate this sitting around waiting, waiting to see if the next thing we hear from them is a bomb or else some kind of a friendly greeting," Madison complained.

"We should get the leaders of the House and Senate over here and brief them," Jane said.

In their own sweet time, the Speaker, John Harris, the leader of the minority in the House, Donald Trent and the leaders of both parties in the Senate, Bill Evans and Mitch Decker, arrived and were shown into the Situation Room.

"Gentlemen, thank you for coming. We have a situation," Jane started. "We have detected what looks like an alien spacecraft that is currently on the back side of Mars. JPL detected it and NASA has got some images from the Rovers we have on Mars and from orbiting satellites. This has all come in in the last few hours, so is very fresh and not completely analysed. You can see from these images we just got back from Mars that it's pretty big, but doubtful that it's big enough for an invasion force unless it's a scout ship for a main party."

"Why weren't we briefed earlier?" John Harris complained.

"We called and told you that we had a situation that we should have briefed you on three hours ago," Jane replied.

"We had no idea what it was about," Bill Evans complained.

"It's not the kind of information that gets bandied about," Jane said. "Cell phones can get hacked easily enough. You need to get with your constituents and be prepared for what may come. I will be briefing the governors soon."

"Who are they? Where are they from?" Harris asked.

"We have no idea," Jane admitted. "JPL tells us that going back over earlier images of that part of space, it showed up, but was travelling so fast that it was out of frame quickly and difficult to detect. Once we lost it behind Mars, NASA retasked their landers and satellites to look for and at it, so we have these images and we've pulled these from the Chinese, the Russians, the Europeans and the Emirates."

"It's real, it's not the Chinks trying to spoof us?" Decker asked.

"Not that we can tell," Jane said. "NSA analysis of their traffic shows that they are as uncertain as we are."

"Can we just blast them out of the sky?" Trent asked.

"JPL speculates that they have technologies that we cannot imagine, so they may well have counters to anything we may throw at them. That being said, we need to be prepared, so I'm briefing the governors next and they can activate their Guard units both for maintaining order and for possible protection against invasion," Jane replied.

"Holy cow," Harris said.

"JPL lost contact with Voyager 1 at about the same time this showed up, and it came from the same direction that Voyager was headed," Jane added.

"So, someone read the message on Voyager?" Trent asked.

"We don't know, but have to consider that as a possibility," Jane replied. "We sent out the Voyager message again on several frequencies. It will be interesting to see if they respond."

"Why send them messages? We don't know their intentions?" Harris asked.

"If they're anywhere in our neighbourhood, they're picking up all kinds of broadcast transmissions, from old *I Love Lucy* reruns to the latest news. It's about a four-minute delay for signals to get to Mars," Hopkins explained.

"How is that possible?" Evans asked.

"It's basic physics," Hopkins said, thinking again how appallingly ignorant these supposed leaders were. "Electromagnetic radiation signals just go out into the ether and can be picked up by anyone with a scanner and receiver."

"What are the risks to us?" Decker asked.

"We've talked about that and have risks from attack with weapons, some we may not even have thought of, risks from pathogens harmful to us as a species and to our food and water supplies, EMP that could knock our communications and computers, and a few more. We'll have a briefing paper later today," Jane replied.

"Goddamn," Trent said. "Never thought I'd see the day. Hollywood is going to have a blast rereleasing all the old space invaders movies. There'll be a run on food and guns, we'll have some nutcases running around shooting into the air at nothing, when will we be able to see them with the naked eye?"

"We've no idea," Jane admitted. "We don't know how long they'll sit behind Mars, or if they'll just leave. I wouldn't have thought so. Why come all the way here and not make contact, be it good or bad?"

"Just keep us informed," Harris said. "We need to go back and brief our defence and intelligence committees."

The meeting with the governors was convened, and Jane gave them the news.

"What does it mean for us?" Texas asked.

"We don't know yet," Jane admitted. "We don't know if they're friendly, or at least not overtly hostile, we don't know if this is a lone vessel, or if it's a precursor to an invasion, we don't know if we can even communicate."

"I'm calling out our National Guard," Florida said.

"I've already given the orders to federalise the National Guard," Jane said. "Your commandant should have told you."

"Right, he did mention something about that. I've been focused on other things like the hurricane that's about to hit," Florida said.

"What can we do?" California asked.

"Be prepared for mass panic," Jane replied. "We may all imagine what we do in the event of an alien, but reality is a little different."

"I'll bet the religious groups will have a field day," New Mexico added.

"Our beliefs will carry us through," Texas said defensively.

"Thank you, ladies and gentlemen, I will brief you again when I know more," Jane said, not willing to listen to the harangue that usually followed anything that challenged the Texas Taliban, as she privately called the so-called Christian Nationalists who held sway in Texas and some of the other southern states. Well, they might just get to see the Second Coming, and it might not be what they hoped for.

"So, what's the story?" Jane's husband asked when she joined him in the private rooms of the White House, after a long day of briefings and more briefings.

"It looks like we have a visitor," she said.

"From where?" he asked.

"We've no idea," she said. "All we know is that an alien craft showed up in our solar system and is now sitting behind Mars, whether they're just looking us over, or waiting for the rest of the gang, we've no idea."

"Really?" he asked.

"Really," she confirmed. "Whoever they are, they have technology that we can't come close to; they could be here in hours, where it would take us seven months at the minimum."

"So I suppose there's lots of theories being bandied about?" he asked.

"There are the biggest issue is going to be panic," she said. "At some point, we're going to have to go public. I imagine that there will be a run on the gun shops, the supermarkets and the banks."

"What do you think?" he asked.

"I'm waiting to see what they do next," she said. "We raised things to DefCon 3 as a routine precaution. I've briefed the weasels in the House and the Senate and the governors, and they all said that at the first sign that this will go public, they'll call out their National Guard units in case of mass panic. I pre-empted them on that and told them that I'd already federalised the National Guard and was calling them all up."

"Why do people panic?" he asked.

"I think the unknown," she said. "If there's a hurricane coming at you, you don't tell the people that it's just a small storm; you tell them that it's a hurricane, and then you tell them what to do. That's what people want to hear, What do I do?"

"So, the big pandemics of 1918 and 2020 were classic examples of how not to manage and lead because in both cases the government said that they didn't want to cause panic, so essentially did nothing?" he asked.

"I think so," she agreed. "In both cases, it was bad, and in both cases, the impacts could have been reduced dramatically if the government at the time had taken a true leadership role, told people that it was bad, but also told them what to do. The problem I'm wrestling with is that I don't know if this is going to be bad, and if it is, what do I do, give a Churchillian speech about fighting them on the beaches, or go underground and wait, or perhaps it's not an attack at all, so do we say hello, nice to see you, what can we do for you?"

"So, no indication at all what their intentions might be?" he asked.

"Not a bit," she said. "The other issue is watching the Russians and the Chinese to see if they try and grab more territory while focus is on the aliens."

"If they attacked, could we defend?" he asked.

"That would depend on the mode of attack," she said. "If you follow Hollywood, then they'll show up in massive ships, shoot up everything and take what they want, but what if it's more subtle, they release a pathogen that is completely unknown to us, that's as deadly as Ebola or worse, they do it worldwide so the death toll is high and immediate, we can't respond, so humans die out leaving the rest of the planet intact? If you're an alien, you then wait for the pathogen to burn itself out, then walk in with infrastructure largely intact, insects, birds and animals all still here, and have yourself a nice new world."

"We've only seen one ship so far?" he asked.

"JPL reports only one," she confirmed. "They said it came into our system at an amazing speed, then just stopped and hid behind Mars. We're getting images from the gadgets we have on Mars now and the orbiters we have whizzing around Mars. It looks like a big collection of separate modules all strung together; it's about twice as big as an aircraft carrier."

"So, what do you do now?" he asked.

"We wait," she said. "It's always possible that they'll just go away, but my guess is that they'll come closer for a better look, so expect a busy next few days."

"Do we have stocks of food and water here?" he asked.

"There are the emergency supplies in the basement," she said. "Probably enough for quite a while, and if we decamp to the emergency bunker, then there's enough for a year or two, pretty boring after a while, but enough for survival."

"What's the good of us surviving if all the skills we really need to rebuild are gone?" he asked.

"That's always been the flaw in the system," she admitted. "We do all we can to protect the government, but when we come out of hiding, can the congressional representatives grow crops, can they make tools, can they do anything really useful?"

"I suppose the systems were put in place in case of nuclear exchanges between us and the Russians," he said. "In that case, I could probably make a case for keeping some form of government, but what might they have to govern?"

"Perhaps something, perhaps nothing," she said. "Better to shelter true farmers and artisans, people who know how to do useful things, people like you, honest to goodness farmers. Not people who sit around, posturing and pontificating, let's face it, most of us in government are lawyers, and few of us have actually done anything useful from the point of view of growing crops and making things."

"How long before mass panic sets in?" he wondered.

"I suppose that will depend on the message that we send and how the media portrays this," she said. "I'm sure that the general public is not ready for the notion of alien visitors, any more than I am, but if they start communicating, then word will get out and honesty and full disclosure are probably then better than obfuscation and cover-ups. I have to decide that if and when we do have to go public, what do I say?"

"Telling people not to panic doesn't work," he said. "I think just the facts, an alien visitor, size and type unknown, intentions unknown, but unlikely to be hostile, or we'd all be dead by now or in a fight for our lives. If they communicate with us, then I see that as a good sign; if they're going to attack, why communicate?"

"That makes sense," she agreed.

"We're sure there's only one ship?" he asked.

"We've only seen one," she confirmed. "There may be more waiting in the wings, but the military all see that as unlikely. Why signal your presence with one? If you are an invasion fleet, then you come in quick and hard."

"What if they're a remnant group of another planet escaping from their own disaster, or their own invaders?" he asked.

"Anything's possible," she agreed. "We'll just have to wait and see."

Message

"They've sent us a message," Semat reported.

"Can we interpret it?" Tiye asked.

"It is the same message or messages that were on the artefact," Isis reported.

"So, we know certainly that the probe came from there. How should we respond? Should we respond?" Tiye pondered.

"Do we trust them?" Hennutaway asked.

"Only so far," Tiye said. "Who did we hear from?"

"The signal came from the place that calls itself the United States of America," Semat said.

"Nothing from anywhere else?" Tiye asked.

"Not yet," Semat said.

"I'm trying to decide if we wait a little while and see if anyone else wants to try and talk to us, or just send a basic message now and see where it leads," Tiye said. "What are their probes and satellites here doing?"

"Trying to get a good look at us," Abar reported. "I've seen cameras move and all pointed at us; they must have many images by now."

"Should we blind the cameras?" Semat asked.

"Not much point now, let them have the images, it'll give them something to speculate about," Tiye said. "Let's think about how to respond to the message."

"I think we should reply in our own language," Abar said. "That will make them all scurry about trying to work out what we say."

"If they have any historians, they may be able to work it out," Tiye said. "Do we just send an audio message or include an image as well?"

"I think we should get Nefertiti to dress up and make a formal address," Semat said. "From what we've seen, their society seems to be male-dominated, and to have Nefertiti send a message will send another message as well. That will have them all busy trying to understand who we are and what we want."

"What do you think, Nefertiti?" Tiye asked.

"I'll do it," she agreed. "Give me a little while to put on formal clothes and makeup; meanwhile, think about what we want to say to them."

"Good," Tiye said. "Now, I was thinking of something along these lines. *Greetings, people of Geb, we are delighted to be returning after so many of your years and are impressed with the advances you have made, but are distressed that you do not seem to have advanced enough to stop warring among yourselves. We would be interested in talking to your leaders, if in fact there are any that may speak for all the people. We have no interest in becoming embroiled in petty squabbles between neighbours. We await your response.*"

"That sounds good," Abar said. "I like the bit about petty squabbles. If they respond and ask us where we are from, what do we tell them?"

"We're vague," Tiye thought. "I don't like telling people where we're actually from, even if they're not likely to get there in the near future."

"Do we show them an image of our star system?" Abar asked.

"Let's look at what we have and decide," Tiye suggested.

"We have another signal," Semat said. "It looks as if it came from the area known as China."

"Can we interpret?" Tiye asked.

"I can," Isis stated. "It includes the atomic numbers for what they call helium, hydrogen and oxygen, plus models of atoms; it looks like they're trying to form the basis of a common language."

"How do we respond?" Semat asked.

"We'll wait until Nefertiti is ready, then the message we'll send will be seen by many, and they can draw their own conclusions," Tiye said.

"I wonder how they'll react when they realise that we say we're returning?" Abar said.

"I suppose once they work out what language it is, then they'll bring in every scholar they can find," Tiye said.

"You don't just want to send them a message in the language they call English?" Semat asked.

"I'd rather string them along a while," Tiye said. "See what we can pick up on their chatter."

"There's another signal," Semat said. "This one originates in the area they call Russia."

"What's this one, Isis?" Tiye asked.

"It seems to be a language code," Isis reported. "It starts out with dots and relates them to numbers, then there's an image of their system with names of the star and the satellites, then there's an image of a male and female, and words for them."

"Interesting to see how they're all trying to build some bridge for communication," Tiye said. "I'm a little surprised that the signals we've been getting have been from different places and with different ideas. I would have thought that there would have been some cooperation between the various parts of this satellite. It really looks as if they're all trying to gain advantage over each other by being the first to establish some form of communication."

"I'm ready," Nefertiti announced as she came back to the bridge.

"Where to put you?" Tiye mused. "I think here with the images in the background of Mars and Earth, let them know we can scan them."

"I like the dress," Abar said.

"I thought traditional, but in keeping with a past era that most closely fits our own culture," Nefertiti said. She was dressed in a loose-fitting white dress, with a scarab pendant and a simple gold circle on her head, looking very regal.

"Looks good," Tiye agreed. "So, are you ready?"

"I'm ready," Nefertiti said. She then launched into her prepared words.

"*I am Nefertiti of Isis, greetings, people of Geb, we are delighted to be returning after so many of your years and are impressed with the advances you have made, but are distressed that you do not seem to have advanced enough to stop warring among yourselves. We would be interested in talking to your leaders, if in fact there are any that may speak for all the people. We have no interest in becoming embroiled in petty squabbles between neighbours. We await your response.*"

They recorded that, played it back, suggested changes, tried it again, in fact, four more times until everyone was happy.

"Okay, Isis, send it," Tiye said. "Send it back on the frequencies that we received signals on, and on all the major frequencies that we noted that they use for their general communication, send it out with enough strength that it pre-empts anything that may be broadcasting."

"Signal sent," Isis said.

"So, now we wait to see what they'll do next," Tiye said.

"We're picking up lots of signals," Semat said. "They seem to be broken down by language, and much of it is communication between military groups. I think they are uncertain as to our intentions; some want to attack, some want to wait and see."

"What have we learned from the probes that we collected on this satellite?" Tiye asked.

"They seem to have spent a lot of time looking for water and life," Semat said. "The probes are quite clever, and we have been able to salvage quite a lot from them. There are also pieces of debris lying around. I suspect that some of the probes failed on landing and others just died. This satellite does have dust storms that are quite intense; you can see one here, and another here," she said, pointing to a screen."

"Well, we cleaned up their mess," Tiye said.

* * * * *

"Holy shit," Jim said at JPL. "Are you seeing this?"

"I am," Dave confirmed. "And I'm recording it. I wonder if that's what they really look like. Look, based on her hair and the way it hangs, they seem to have some form of artificial gravity."

"All I got out of that was Nefertiti and Isis, they're Egyptian, I wonder if Amal can tell us anything," Jim said, referring to his friend Amal al Bayoumi, who was a graduate student at UCLA and an expert on ancient Egypt.

"Call her," Dave said. Jim did, and when Amal answered the telephone, she was agog with excitement.

"Did you hear that Jim?" she asked.

"You heard it?" Jim asked.

"It's on all the networks, it broke in over the broadcasts, even on my phone and my tablet, played three times then stopped," she explained.

"What did she say?" Jim asked.

"I'll have to go back and listen a few more times because it's like listening to Elizabethan English and I'm more used to interpreting written language not listening to it, but essentially, I'm Nefertiti of Isis, don't know whether Isis is a place or what, one thing I am sure of is that it has nothing to do with the whack jobs that called themselves ISIS and wanted to establish an Islamic Caliphate, then she said something about being here before and wanting to talk to our leaders if we have any," Amal said. "I'll listen to it a few more times and get the others here to do the same, and we'll see if we can't get you a full translation."

"Thanks, Amal," Jim said. "Anything significant in Nefertiti or Isis?"

"It certainly suggests previous contact, or is an amazing coincidence," Amal said. "I wonder did they get Nefertiti from Egypt or vice versa. Isis, goddess of the dead, don't know what to make of that. Is Isis a place, or do they worship Isis?"

"Thanks, Amal," Jim said.

"I'll go over this a few more times and compare notes with others and get back to you," she said. "This is so exciting, does this really come from outer space?"

"We identified an object that moved and parked near Mars," Jim said. "This signal seems to come from that."

"This must be amazing for you, Jim," she said.

"It is, I'll call you later, Amal," he said.

"So, what did she say?" Dave asked. Jim relayed the conversation and then said. "We'd better call Hopkins."

Dave picked up the telephone and called the number he had been given.

"I'm looking at it," Hopkins said when he picked up the telephone. "It's on all the networks and social media. Any ideas about the language?"

"Jim has a friend at UCLA who says it's related to ancient Egyptian," Dave replied.

"God, that's all we need, all the ancient alien types are going to love that," Hopkins lamented. "Any idea what she said?"

"According to his friend, Amal, hello, I'm Nefertiti of Isis, we've been here before and would like to talk to your leaders," Dave relayed. "I'm sure that there's someone at the Smithsonian who can get a translation for you."

"Okay, keep listening," Hopkins instructed.

"General, is there any way we can confirm that the signal actually came from the aliens, or are the Russians or Chinese trying to spoof us?" Jim asked.

"I had the same thought," Hopkins said. "I'll ask around, but my sense tells me that the alien craft did send this. I don't see the Russians or Chinese as being likely to round up an ancient Egyptian speaker and putting the message together."

"Well?" Jane Adams asked.

"Madame, it seems, according to someone at UCLA, that it's related to ancient Egyptian and essentially says that they've been here before and want to talk to our leaders," Hopkins summarised. "JPL suggested we get the Smithsonian to help."

"Call them and get the best linguist they have on Egyptian to come over here, better still, send some people over and bring back the best Egyptologist that they have," Jane instructed.

"Yes, Madame," Hopkins said. He called the switchboard and relayed the instructions.

"I wonder if that's what they actually look like, or if they've concocted that image to lull us into a false sense of security," Madison said.

"We need to do a full analysis of those images, there was the speaker and behind her, it, whatever, it looked like more figures," Tom Price said.

"What can you learn from the images?" Jane asked.

"It looks harmless enough," Madison said. "The figure doing the talking looks humanoid, but is that real or just an avatar to make us feel secure. It certainly looks like they have some kind of images behind her of Mars, and here, I counted the images of four others there, including those reflected in the screens behind."

"Age of the one we saw?" Jane asked.

"If, and it's a big if, she, it, truly is humanoid, then under thirty, but who can say," Tom said.

"Size?" Jane asked.

"In proportion to the objects in view, but if it's all in proportion, then hard to know if we're talking three feet or eight feet, but based on the apparent size of what look like access doors, I would have to guess less than six more than five," Tom replied.

"Anything else strike you?" Jane asked.

"Judging by the hair, and I'm presuming here that it is stranded hair like ours and not some kind of headdress, and the drape of the clothes, they would appear to have some form of artificial gravity," Hopkins said.

"Comments on the mode of dress?" Jane asked.

"The speaker's looked nothing like a uniform as we know them, but, again, we don't know," Yamamura said. "It looks like linen, the way it drapes, and if we zoom in a bit, we can probably get some sense of woven, knitted or rolled out like a plastic."

"What looks like jewellery, what do you make of that?" Jane asked.

"Looks like a scarab pendant and the thing on her, its, head, some kind of simple circle, maybe gold," Yamamura said. "We didn't see feet, but the hands look like ours, and I saw no rings or bracelets."

"She, it, reminds me of someone?" Romero said.

"Patricia Velásquez," Yamamura said.

"Who?" Madison asked.

"Patricia Velásquez, actress, played in The Mummy, Fidel, Zapata and The Curse of La Llorona, before your time," Yamamura explained.

"God, now we'll have the movie buffs all atwitter," Madison said. "It could still be a contrived avatar, even our AI is pretty good and could probably create that."

"The JPL guys asked us if we can confirm that the signal actually came from the alien craft, and it's not the Chinese or the Russians trying to spoof us," Hopkins said. "I've got my Command looking into that."

"Excuse me, Madame," an aide said, interrupting things. "We have Professor Hunter and Professor Mills from the Smithsonian."

"Come in," Jane said. "You've seen the images we picked up earlier and heard the words. Any comments?"

"Amy," Mills prompted.

"Well, Madame President, the language is certainly related to ancient Egyptian, whether they learned it from the Egyptians or vice versa will be debated for years to come," Amy Hunter said.

"What does she say?" Jane asked.

"*I am Nefertiti of Isis, greetings, people of Geb, we are delighted to be returning after many of your years and are impressed with the advances you have made, but are upset that you do not seem to have advanced enough to stop warring among yourselves. We would be interested in talking to your leaders, if in fact there are any that may speak for all the people. We have no interest in becoming involved in petty squabbles between neighbours. We await your response,*" Amy quoted. "I may not have got some of the meaning exactly as they intended, but that's the gist of it. A quick note here, Geb was the old Egyptian word for the Earth. What is exciting is that it probably gives us a good idea of what ancient Egyptian sounded like, we've only been guessing to date. When she talks about being of Isis, I have no idea if that's what they call their home world, if it's a society, I have no idea."

"Do you attach any significance to the name Nefertiti?" Jane asked.

"It clearly is similar to an old Egyptian name," Amy said. "That perhaps lends credence to previous visits, whether they took the name from Egypt or Egypt from them, we don't know."

"What about what she's, and we're all assuming here that the being we're looking at is as it is and female, wearing?" Jane asked.

"It looks like a typical linen tunic or dress that would be typical of the early dynasty, that would fit with the scarab pendant and the simple crown, probably gold. You'll note that it's tied at the back and has some jewels embedded, typical of the early era," Amy reported.

"And the others we can see bits of in the images?" Jane asked.

"Not as dressy," Amy said. "Almost as if they're in work clothes and she's dressed for the message. I can't say too much about what the others might be wearing, but it seems to me to be similar fabric, and what is interesting is that as far as I can make out, they're all apparently female."

"So, any credence to their claim of a prior visit?" Madison asked.

"Do you know when they first entered the solar system, and where are they now?" Amy asked.

"We first picked them up about a week or so ago, and they appear to be parked behind Mars," Hopkins said.

"In that case, I doubt that they've been here long enough to find sources for the ancient Egyptian language, so it certainly suggests prior knowledge," Amy replied.

"So, who do the Russians and Chinese have that can translate this?" Romero asked.

"Quite a few," Amy said. "The best are probably at the British Museum, but the Russians and the Chinese have their share of Egypt scholars. The message probably caused a stir in Cairo as the Copts still speak a modified version of the language; to them, it would be like us listening to Chaucer English. They would recognise it, even if they could not fully understand it."

"So, no chance of keeping it under wraps?" Madison asked.

"No," Amy said. "We all heard it on multiple channels, so we can assume that everyone in the world with any kind of TV, radio, smartphone or tablet picked it up. It even made its way onto Facebook, Instagram, X and other social media platforms. Don't know how they did that, they must have done it through the satellites and microwave relays that are out there."

"Great," Madison said. "Now we're going to have mass hysteria and all the religious groups arguing about whether this is a weird Second Coming, or if the traditions of the main monotheisms are even valid."

"Perhaps not," Amy said. "In times of uncertainty and crisis, people tend to turn to their religion for support."

"Anything about what she says about our leaders?" Jane asked.

"It suggests that they're either very cynical, perhaps based on their own experience, or that they've watched us long enough to pick up on the issues between us and the Chinese and the Russians," Amy suggested.

"How do we respond? Do we respond?" Jane asked.

"I think we should," Amy said. "It might be useful to see if we can get a sense of whether or not they were really here, or have picked up some knowledge from somewhere, maybe they've hacked computers."

"So, how do we do that?" Jane asked.

"Ask them who the pharaoh was when they were last here," Amy said.

"Can you put that into words for us?" Jane asked.

"Of course," Amy said. "It might be best if I just recorded the words and then you could send them when and how you like."

"Is there anything else that you can pick up from the images?" Jane asked.

"If we assume that the image we're seeing is real and not an avatar, then she is well-formed, has delicate hands, just like ours; you can see the hand bones in a couple of her gestures. Can we get an enlargement of the image?" Amy asked.

"Coming up," Tom said. He zoomed in on the image and her face.

"The circlet on her head is typical of the First Dynasty," Amy said. "She wears makeup like most did then. Dentition, from what I could see, is good, same as ours; her teeth are the kind that would put our orthodontists out of business. Interesting that from what I can make out of the others, none of them is wearing any makeup."

"I never noticed that," Hopkins said.

"Can we pan down a little?" Amy asked. "High-quality woven linen, by the look of it, either machine-stitched or done by a very good seamstress. The scarab pendant looks like steatite and is set in what looks like silver. Pan down to her hands, please. Nails nicely trimmed, not broken at all, polished but not varnished, if we were talking about someone from here, I'd say money and enough that she doesn't have to let you know she has money, the dress, circlet and scarab here would all be expensive, the same would have been true back in the First Dynasty, that all assumes of course that we are looking at a real being and not an AI-generated image."

"Do you think she came here at that time?" Hopkins asked.

"That would suggest time travel," Amy said. "Not my field at all. I think it's more likely that the clothes and jewels we see are just part of their culture, and that they have historical records of earlier visits. I would also suggest that they use numbers to the base of ten, they have apparently ten fingers as we do."

"Excuse me, Madame President," an aide said. "The Secretary-General is on the phone."

"Mr Secretary," Jane said. "I presume you've seen the images and message from our visitors?"

"I have," he replied. "I think it would be prudent if the heads of state of the permanent members of the Security Council met to discuss this."

"Have you a translation of what they said?" she asked.

"I do," he said. "I'm particularly interested in their statement that they've been here before, and wonder when, and that they ask, rather cynically, if we have leaders who can speak for all."

"Have the others agreed to a meeting?" she asked.

"They have, they're on their way, so expect to hear from them soon; they will be flying into JFK," he said.

"We'll be ready," Jane said, nodding to Madeline Wilson, who nodded in response and went out briefly to make her own calls.

"I've called the meeting for ten tomorrow morning," he said. "Please bring whoever you regard as your top Egyptologist."

"I will," Jane said, nodding to Professor Hunter.

"Thank you, Madame President, these are interesting times," he said.

"They are indeed, Mr Secretary. I look forward to seeing you tomorrow," she said. She hung up the telephone and looked at Amy. "Who will the others bring?"

"My guess, based on reputation and standing, the British, Gerald Thorndyke, the French, Marie Molière, the Russians, Igor Spassky and the Chinese, Lao Xi Ming. If they bring anyone else, look to that person being more from the intelligence community than the academic," Amy replied. "It struck me from the message that we may be placing too much emphasis on the Egyptian thing; they may have been here multiple times and have merely selected the Egyptian era to see if we can dig into our history and work out the language they used. For all we know, they may have been here more recently."

"As much as it pains me to ask," Jane said. "Who's the most credible of the ancient alien theorists?"

"Geoffrey Miller," Hopkins said. "He's a Brit, but he's rational and has some reasonable arguments as to when and why we may have been visited before."

"Where is he?" Jane asked.

"In LA," Hopkins said.

"Can we grab him before he hops back across the pond to talk to the Brit government?" Jane asked.

"I'll get right on it," Madeline said. She slipped out again and was back quickly.

"Okay," Jane said. "Tom, are we picking anything useful up from the Russians or the Chinese?" she asked of the NSA chief.

"Lots of traffic, but not much more than we have," he said. "The Chinese sent a message to the aliens, they sent information about atoms, and the Russians sent one about numbers, and our star system and what the names of the planets are, in Russian, of course."

"But, the only reply back was in this Egyptian?" Jane asked.

"Yes, Madame," Tom said. "It was almost as if they were in a polite way telling us to quit all trying to one-up the other and get on the same page. By picking a long-dead language, they've caused us all to rely more on scholars than defence chiefs, sorry Dave."

"Interesting," Jane said. "Okay, do I address the nation?"

"I don't think you have a choice, Madame," Madison said. "Everyone with a TV, radio, tablet or smartphone has seen the message, and you need to tell people what we think it says."

"Do I give all the message?" she asked.

"I think you have to," Hopkins said. "There are too many out there who can get a pretty good idea of what was said, and if you leave anything out, they'll speculate as to why."

"Okay, call the networks, we'll do a major press conference at two this afternoon, have the Russians and Chinese told their people yet?" she asked.

"Not that we've picked up," Tom said.

"Anyone else?" she asked.

"The European channels all have talking heads, and they're all busy pontificating and speculating, but so far, no government has come out and made a statement," Tom reported.

"Probably all trying to work out what to say and how that's not going to land up as political suicide," Jane said. "What's the downside?"

"We will get some reaction from the ultra-religious groups," Hopkins said. "They're not going to want to hear about another race of people, but if they can connect them to us somehow, they're probably going to identify them as the lost tribe of Israel, saying that they fled from the tyranny of Egypt and found a way to get off planet."

"That's a bit far-fetched, isn't it?" Jane asked.

"True," Hopkins agreed. "But for a religious zealot, the facts could be manipulated to fit the beliefs."

"I never pegged you as a real cynic, Howard," Madison said.

"Okay, apart from telling people that analysis leads us to believe that the message is genuine and what it says, what else, we're meeting with the UN and other world leaders to discuss a response, we don't know what their intentions may be, we don't suspect any kind of invasion because we've only detected one vessel, do we show an image of it?" Jane asked.

"I would," Hopkins said. "I'd also give an estimate of size."

"Okay, we'll have to say we've no idea where they come from," Jane said. "Then finish up with the usual no need to panic, no need to rush out and buy up the store, not that that ever stopped anyone, there'll be the usual run on gun sales, maybe even telescopes, the preppers will be in seventh heaven, all full of I told you so. I just wish we had some idea of where they were from and what they wanted."

"If, and I know it's a big if, they are peaceable and want to land and visit, how do we manage interaction so that they don't infect us with any weird space virus?" Dr Park from the CDC asked.

"We'll set up a facility that permits separate accesses and maintains a screen between us and them, we can probably also fix up something like a jetway so that they can go from their vessel to the room without going outside, we'd need to know a lot more about them before we could do too much, but it's possible," Madison said.

"If I were them, I wouldn't land," Romero said. "Too risky for them, I'd do all my communicating remotely."

"What do we do if they want something from us, like water?" Cortez asked.

"I suppose that would depend on how much and fresh or salt," Hopkins said. "If we give them water, do we ask for a trade? If we do, I'd really like to know how their drives work so that they can achieve the speeds that they do, I also wonder how they got from their home world here, even at light speeds, it would take æons to get here from the closest star, so do they have the technology to warp space, are there really wormholes, just how did they do it, or are they just wandering around in space?"

"Do you think they'd tell us?" Madison asked.

"Good question, if it were me, I wouldn't tell us, but maybe they're more generous," Hopkins said.

"Excuse me, Madame President," Tom said. "I've just got a text here and it tells me that our best analysis of the image is that it is real and not a construct, so the aliens may actually look like us, or it may just mean that their image processing capability is better than ours."

"Anything on the others that seem to be around?" Jane asked.

"As far as we can tell, all female," Tom said. "Which may or may not be significant, it may be that the crew is female, or it may be that that's just the watch that happens to be there, or there may be males in the wings that we haven't seen yet."

"Okay, let's grab something to eat quickly and then get set up for a press conference at two," Jane suggested.

"Oh, before we all go," Hopkins said. "I've just got this from the Space Force, they analyse the signals as not spoofed Russian or Chinese, but from a transmitter near Mars, so probably the aliens are using a relay."

"Thank you, General," Jane said.

"We're ready, Madame President," Jane's chief of staff, Barbara Edwards, said. Jane walked out into the briefing room, followed by the members of the cabinet.

"Ladies and gentlemen, good afternoon," she started. "You have all heard and seen the message that came to us this morning. We have every reason to believe that this is truly a message from another civilisation. What was said was this: *I am Nefertiti of Isis, greetings, people of Geb, we are delighted to be returning after many of your years and are impressed with the advances you have made, but are upset that you do not seem to have advanced enough to stop warring among yourselves. We would be interested in talking to your leaders, if in fact there are any that may speak for all the people. We have no interest in becoming involved in petty squabbles between neighbours. We await your response.* We have determined that Geb is their word for Earth, and that the language used is very similar to ancient Egyptian. The Secretary-General of the United Nations has called a meeting of the Security Council and the General Assembly tomorrow, and we will discuss our response. We have no knowledge about where these beings may have come from. Our best assessment at this time is that they are peaceable, if we were going to be attacked, we feel that that would have already happened. They clearly have technologies that far exceed anything we have. I ask you to remain calm and to go about your business as usual, difficult to do I grant you, given what we are seeing. This is an image of their vessel that we took from the Mars Rover. We estimate its size to be about twice that of an aircraft carrier, large, but nowhere near large enough for an invasion force. We suspect that they found the Voyager 1 spacecraft and read the message that was included in it. I will have another briefing tomorrow after the UN meetings. I will take questions now."

"Madame President, who first spotted this vessel?" CNN asked

"The scientists at the Jet Propulsion Laboratory in Pasadena, California, first brought it to our attention. They also noted a loss in signal from Voyager 1," Jane replied.

"How do you know they're not hostile?" VCN asked.

"We do not," Jane replied. "But any element of surprise for an attack has long gone, so it seems to us unlikely. As a routine precaution, we have raised our readiness level and have also instructed the state governors to call out their National Guard."

"Why can't we just send a rocket and nuke it out of the sky?" VCN asked.

"The vessel is currently in the vicinity of Mars; it would take seven months for anything we send to get there," Jane replied.

"So, we can expect them to be here in about seven months?" CBC asked.

"Our analysis of their entry into our solar system suggests that they have the technology to attain speeds that we can only dream of, so they could be here much earlier than seven months, in a matter of hours if they so choose," Jane replied.

"What do you intend to ask them?" NBC asked.

"We would like to try and open a dialogue," Jane said. "We would like to know where they come from and what their intentions are."

"How much credence do you give the statement that they've been here before?" VCN asked.

"We're treating that as if it were true," Jane said. "We cannot explain the language except in the context of previous contact."

"How many people, beings, things, are on this vessel?" ABC asked.

"We don't know and have no way of telling," Jane said. "Our analysis of the message sent suggests six others in the same area as the speaker."

"Who interpreted the message?" The Washington Post asked.

"Professor Amy Hunter of the Smithsonian," Jane said. "Professor Hunter is here if you have questions for her."

"Professor Hunter, how do we know that you accurately translated the message?" CNN asked.

"The language is consistent with ancient Egyptian," Amy replied. "I, and several colleagues, concur that we have it correct. Tomorrow at the UN, there will also be experts from the other Security Council nations; we will compare notes."

"I was thinking more along the lines of nuance," CNN commented. "I'm thinking of the old Twilight Zone episode where To Serve Man has more than one meaning."

"There is always the possibility of a language nuance that we may not understand," Amy agreed. "But we are confident that this message is simple enough. Time will tell with future communications if anything else is intended."

"What do you think they meant by, we would be interested in talking to your leaders, if in fact there are any that may speak for all the people?" ABC asked.

"We assume that they mean just that, we have 193 members of the United Nations," Jane said. "I would not presume to speak for all those nations, so who does? The Secretary-General is perhaps our best spokesman."

"But, would he represent our interests?" VCN asked.

"That is why we are meeting tomorrow," Jane said. "We need to try and develop a unified response."

"How do we know that this vessel is not just a scouting party for a main invasion fleet?" VCN asked.

"We don't," Jane said. "There is always the possibility that they are testing our defences and evaluating our capabilities, but we would have thought that if they were doing that, then they would have been a little more secretive about it."

"What if this is all just to lull us into a false sense of security, then the main body shows up and takes us all out while we're all peace and love?" VCN asked.

"That is a possibility that we have considered," Jane replied. "No matter what happens in the next hours, weeks and even months, we will not let our guard down."

"What should we all do now?" CNN asked.

"Go about your business as usual," Jane said. "I know that's easy to say and very difficult to do. I know that there will always be people who will take advantage of the situation and look to make personal gains, which is why the governors have all called out their National Guard. We will not tolerate looting, profiteering or other activities designed to take advantage of uncertainty."

"Have you talked to religious leaders?" the Christian Science Monitor asked.

"We only received this message this morning and have spent time formulating our immediate plans. I am sure that the leaders of the major religions will all have questions, and we will do our best to answer those questions," Jane replied.

"Where is Isis?" NBC asked.

"We don't know whether Isis is the name of their home world, or a family, or an organisation," Jane said. "Professor Hunter, any thoughts?"

"Isis was one of the ancient Egyptian goddesses, so it's possible that these beings worship her, or it may be simply the name of their planet," Amy added. "We don't know."

"The image we saw in the message appears to show someone who looks like a human," CBS said. "Do we know if that is what they look like, or have they taken images from here and constructed their own?"

"We don't," Jane said. "Our best analysis of the images in the message would indicate that the images are real and not constructed, but that's with our technology; they may have more advanced techniques that can produce a very lifelike image, even better than our best AI-generated images."

"So, for all we know, they may be giant ants?" CBS asked.

"That is always a possibility," Jane said.

"You don't appear to know much," VCN commented.

"If you know more, Mr Charles, I would be delighted if you'd share your knowledge with us," Jane said.

"I've been told that this is in fact, a Chinese vessel that they've been secretly building," VCN said. "I've been told that the Chinese have a super weapon on board to threaten us."

"Then the Chinese have made strides that have left the rest of the world in the dust," Jane said. "I will ask the premier tomorrow if he intends to threaten us. The JPL people estimate the mass of this object to be several thousand tons; to have put that much material into space would have required thousands of launches, and I am sure we would have noticed that."

"I still think we should blast them out of the sky," VCN said.

"I have been informed by the JPL people that these beings have the ability to attain such speeds that no missile we would launch could ever catch them," Jane said. "If we launch at them, and they have a tracker on the missile, they simply have to lead the missile along, get it into a decaying orbit and then it would come right back at us."

"Doesn't the Space Force have lasers that can zap them?" VCN asked.

"I have been told that at the speeds that they seem capable of, then any object they might hit would pass straight through them causing damage, so we presume that they have some kind of shielding, if they can do that, they can ward off any light weapon we aim at them," Jane replied.

"When they say they've been here before, do we know when?" ABC asked.

"No," Jane said. "We have made the assumption based on the language they used, that if, in fact, they have been here before, at least one of their visits was in the era of the First Dynasty of Egypt, say 5,000 years ago."

"Have they been back since?" ABC asked.

"We don't know," Jane said. "I'm sorry, ladies and gentlemen, we know very little at this time, and all we can do is speculate and make plans accordingly. There will be another press conference after the meeting at the UN tomorrow."

"Why is it that the VCN people are all conspiracy theorists?" Jane asked when they were all back in the situation room.

"They can't help it," Madison said. "I wonder which of their tame idiots came up with the Chinese space warship idea?"

"Anything new from JPL or anywhere else?" Jane asked.

"Nothing, the aliens seem to be just sitting there waiting for our reply," Hopkins replied.

"The Japanese, the Chinese and both the Koreas have just made broadcasts to their people," Tom reported. "It sounds very like the message you delivered, Madame. The only weird one is North Korea; their message is to stand and fight against the imperialist aggressors."

"Typical, I suppose the clock is not right for the Russians and Europeans," Jane thought. "Look for the Indians next, then the Middle

East, then the Europeans. Any sense of when the Chinese and Russians will be landing?"

"We estimate at about seven tomorrow morning," Madison said. "We'll keep track of them and make sure there are no issues."

"My guess is that the five of us will meet with Sharma, then he'll call in the rest of the Security Council, then the General Assembly, so tomorrow could be a long day," Jane thought. "Who's the best linguist we have for Russian and Mandarin?"

"Elizabeth Gabbard," Romero said. "She's equally good with Russian, Mandarin and French."

"Good, I'll take her with me tomorrow as well as you, Professor Hunter; we might as well have our own translation of what the Russians and Chinese say," Jane said.

"You don't trust the UN interpreters?" Amy asked.

"They'll do a good job," Jane said. "But I want to pick up on any nuances from body language as well as what's said. The interpreters don't always have the best view. Amy, is there anyone you want to consult with before we go tomorrow?"

"I'll meet with the rest of the Egypt Department tonight and we'll go through the message again and look for anything we may have missed," Amy said.

"Any comments on the messenger's body language?" Jane asked.

"If she's human, then controlled, not giving anything away, used to negotiating, no tics or tells that I could spot," Romero said. "I'd say this is not the first time she's delivered a message."

"Anyone else?" Jane asked.

"I thought I saw what could be some kind of recording device mirrored in one of the screens behind, perhaps the message was recorded, then sent," Tom suggested.

"Could be," Jane agreed. "Why?"

"Maybe the language they picked isn't their language, but one they picked that they thought we could understand. Let's face it, 5,000 years ago, Egypt was the centre of Afro-European power, so it would be reasonable to assume that their language still predominated," Yamamura suggested.

"Where was China 5,000 years ago?" Jane asked.

"It would have been the Bronze Age," Amy said. "Back then, China was not a consolidated country but a collection of smaller kingdoms. India was at that time also a collection of cities, but no unified state. The Europeans were developing, there was a fairly wide trading network in the Aegean, but no significant power."

"Who would have thought when I took the oath of office two months ago that we'd be facing this?" Jane asked.

"It is rather unprecedented," Romero said. "We've all read the playbook for extraterrestrial encounters, but somehow it doesn't seem to apply."

"What does NASA say, John?" Jane asked John Busateri, the head of NASA.

"JPL is on top of things," he said. "We've re-tasked the Hubble Space Telescope and the Webb Telescope to see if we can get any images when they come out from behind Mars. Right now, our best images come from our Mars lander and those of China and Russia and from the various orbiters. I have a file just sent to me of the latest images, ours and the others."

"Big looking thing, isn't it?" Jane commented as they looked over the images. "Any ideas about the design?"

"No, I suppose it looks very much as we imagined a deep space vessel to look, but let's face it most of our ideas of what a deep space vessel would look like come from Hollywood, our own spacecraft tend to be limited in size and shape by the need to launch from here on top of a rocket, the ISS, the old Mir and Tiangong and probably closer to reality than most things, but they were designed to orbit not travel," John said. "There are parabolic dishes that could be for sending or receiving signals, there are other things that look as if they could be some other form of antenna, there are no solar panels, so whatever their power source is, it's all internal to the vessel. We'll be analysing these images for some time to come."

"Okay, there's not much else we can do today, we'll reconvene tomorrow at seven, and then I'll fly up to New York and the UN," Jane said. "While I'm in New York, keep an eye on Chinese and Russian troop movements."

"We will, Madame," Madison confirmed. "We'll also be watching the North Koreans and the Iranians."

"That was unexpected," Tom said when Jane returned to the private rooms of the White House.

"It was rather, wasn't it?" she agreed.

"What language was she speaking?" he asked.

"Ancient Egyptian, or at least a language that is very similar," she replied. "We had a prof come over from the Smithsonian, and she gave us a translation."

"Do you think they really look like that?" he asked.

"I don't know," she admitted. "They could do, or it could be that they just picked a face to disguise what they actually look like so as not to alarm us too much, let's face it, even we with AI can gen up images and videos that look real enough."

"You'll have all kinds of applicants wanting to go and volunteer to make contact," he said.

"I wonder if we'll ever actually meet?" she said.

"Why not?" he asked.

"There's a risk to us of unknown pathogens, and it may be just as big a risk to them," she said.

"Sort of *War of the Worlds?*" he suggested.

"That's a possibility," she agreed. "I think if I was going to visit, I'd keep a healthy distance, and a screen, something like the tanks in *Arrival*. But, even then, we wouldn't know what might be brought in on the surfaces of their vessel, particularly if they have some drive system that allows them a controlled descent and they don't get the extreme heat of re-entry."

"That's true," he agreed. "What did they discover with the last pandemic, that the virus could live for days on hard surfaces? Whether or not an organism could stand the temperatures of space, I doubt, but then I'm no expert."

"It could also be a type of pathogen that we've never encountered before," she said. "Then we'd have no idea what to do about it. I was thinking of the *Andromeda Strain*."

"It's funny, isn't it," he said. "All the big blockbuster Hollywood movies have aliens with guns of some type, things we can identify with, even if they portray weapons systems that haven't been invented yet."

"I think that's because we have a difficult time dealing with things we've never encountered before, we've no frame of reference, we've no way of categorising them," she said.

"Well, it's going to be interesting," he said. "Good luck at the UN."

UN

"Anything new?" Jane asked when the cabinet reconvened the next morning.

"Nothing, Madame," Madison said. "Some riots in some cities, but the National Guard quickly quietened them down. The multitude of white supremacists are out in force, waving their guns around and shouting that we should take out these aliens as soon as possible, they're blathering on about it's bad enough that we've got immigrants coming up from the south, we don't need them coming from outer space as well."

"Well, no wall will keep these aliens out," she said. "Nothing more from the aliens?"

"No, Madame," Hopkins said. "It really does look like the ball is in our court and the next move is up to us."

"Okay, if Professor Hunter and Liz Gabbard are here, I'll leave for New York," Jane said. She left with her small entourage and was driven out to Andrews Air Force Base. She took a small plane, not the huge Boeing that usually functioned as Air Force One, and they flew into the LaGuardia airport in New York. From there, it was a short helicopter ride to the UN headquarters. They actually landed on a grassy area adjacent to the building, where they were met by Nicole Edwards, the US Ambassador to the UN.

"Good morning, Madame President," the Secretary-General said when they were shown to the chamber. "We are all here, so I see no reason to delay our discussions just to start at ten. Are we all agreed on the contents of the message?"

"Professor Thorndyke has a couple of minor quibbles with the version that President Adams relayed," the British Prime Minister said. "He translates the message as: *I am Nefertiti of Isis, greetings people of Geb, we are delighted to be returning after so many of your years and are impressed with the advances you have made, but are distressed that you do not seem to have advanced enough to stop warring among yourselves. We would be interested in talking to your leaders, if in fact there are any that may speak for all the people. We have no interest in becoming embroiled in petty squabbles between neighbours. We await your response.* I know the changes are minor and in no way affect the overall meaning of the message."

"So, the only changes you see are the addition of so, giving us, so many years, changing upset to distressed and embroiled instead of involved?" the Secretary-General asked.

"That's it," the PM agreed.

"We have nothing to add," the French president said.

"We accept the translation," the Premier of China said.

"We accept it," the tsar of Russia added.

"So, what does it mean?" the Secretary-General asked. There then followed a lively discussion, but the consensus was that there really was an alien vessel parked near Mars and that they had technologies far exceeding anything any of them possessed. Then there was a long discussion about how to reply and the consensus was, who are you, where do you come from, what are your intentions, and as an afterthought to see if they could verify that the aliens had in fact, been in the past, who was the Pharaoh when you were last here. The linguists were then tasked with translating that into Egyptian, which Geoffrey Thorndyke quickly did, and then he passed it to the others for comment. There was a short debate about a couple of the words, but essentially, they agreed on what he had proposed.

The message ready, the Secretary-General was coached on how to actually pronounce all the words, so that his message sounded reasonable. They also made it easier for him by providing a phonetic approximation of the words, using accepted phonetic notations. That ready, the rest of the Security Council was called in and the gist of the discussion relayed to them as well as the proposed message. India suggested that they add, how long did it take you to get here, which was accepted and added to the message. Finally, the General Assembly was convened, and again the message to be sent back was read out, first in English, then in Egyptian, and then discussed. There was actually very little to discuss; what else did one say to visitors from another world? What everyone really wanted to know was, what were their intentions. All the questions that everyone wanted to ask could wait until some form of dialogue was established. There was agreement reached that member states would not try sending their own private messages in Egyptian, which would cause confusion and could lead to serious misunderstandings, with who knew what kinds of reaction from the visitors. The biggest debate then was from which country should the message be sent. The UN actually had a big dish antenna, so agreement was reached that the message should be sent from the UN itself. The Secretary-General read out the message again so that all could hear, then he asked the linguists for comment, and they all focused on two words that needed work. The Secretary thanked everyone for their patience and said that as soon as he had the message down then he would send it and let them know that it had gone. The linguists from the permanent members of the Security Council stayed with the Secretary until he had recorded the message and until it was sent.

They used a studio that the UN had and arranged things so that Amir Shamir, the Secretary-General, was placed in front of a backdrop that was the UN flag and had him seated behind a desk. They used a teleprompter to remind him of the message and ran through it a few times until the linguists were happy that it sounded right. When everyone was happy, then the message was sent and also broadcast to the various Earth networks. That done, Shamir reconvened the General Assembly and let them hear the message that had been sent. There was some discussion about the way they heard it, particularly with reference to the message from the visitors. Shamir had some problems to start with, as word sounds used facial muscles he was not used to using, which did not surprise the linguists; many cultures had some difficulty with intonations not familiar to them, and even heard words the same, even though they were quite different to the native speaker. The Egyptologists were able to assure them that they were all in agreement that Shamir had done the best job he could of relaying the message.

"Okay, do we stay here and wait for an answer, or do we go back?" Jane asked her people.

"I would doubt that we will hear back immediately," Amy said. "If I were them, I'd take some time to formulate a reply."

"Fine, we'll go back to DC and wait, Nicole, if you don't mind, stay here and keep your ear to the ground and pick up what you can about the attitudes and intentions of Ivan and Zhou," Jane said. She and the others walked back to the helicopter. The flight back to La Guardia was short, and they were soon back in the air on the way to Andrews Air Force Base. One of the privileges of being president was that one got priority when it came to take-off slots. At the White House, Jane told Amy to go home, or back to the Smithsonian, she would call if there was anything.

"So, Liz, any byplay between Premier Zhou and his people?" Jane asked.

"They're wary of the Russians," Elizabeth replied. "I think that they think that Tsar Ivan has got his eyes on some more territory in the east."

"When is Zhou going to follow Ivan's lead and declare himself Emperor?" Jane asked.

"In the next five years or so, I would think," Elizabeth said. "He's consolidating power right now in the same way that Ivan did."

"What is with people and power?" Jane asked, mostly of herself. "We've got two nations who were communist, essentially reverting to rule by divine right, rather smacks of Roman History. The Russians should never have given Ivan extraordinary powers; once people like him have power, they won't give it up. He did what most pretenders to the throne have done in history: did away with the old leader and all his family, and then confiscated his fortune, which was considerable. So, what do the Chinese and the Russians want from the E.T.?"

"I'm sorry, Madame, E.T.?" Elizabeth asked.

"Our visitors from outer space, old movie from the early 1980s," Jane explained.

"I think what we probably all want, the secret of their ability to travel in space," Elizabeth said. "The Chinese will take a long view; they'll be happy for the dialogue to go on and on, the Russians will want the answer now or sooner."

"Is either one of them mad enough to try and threaten the aliens?" Jane asked.

"Both are," Elizabeth said. "But, I see the North Koreans or the Iranians trying it before the Chinese, but in the long run, the Chinese will be a greater threat, and they will also look to expand in the South China Sea while attention is on the visitors. I wouldn't be surprised to hear that they've invaded Vietnam, or come to think of it, Indian Kashmir."

"What about Russia, who do they take?" Jane asked.

"I wouldn't be surprised if they didn't pressure some of the stans to come back into the fold, citing the need for security, they've already got Belarus and Ukraine to face off the Europeans, if they get Kazakstan, Kyrgyzstan and Tajikistan back into the fold, then they'll be facing off China, look for some byplay there," Elizabeth said.

"And Mongolia?" Jane asked.

"That's interesting," Elizabeth said. "Ivan's not a White Russian, he's actually a Mongol from Novosibirsk, the past president made the mistake of making him the head of the security services; he's ruthless, has all the hallmarks of another Genghis Khan, and would be happy to add Mongolia to the Tsarate."

"So, on top of our visitor showing up, we've got two giants in the east both flexing their muscles and looking to expand," Jane said.

"That's only as I see it, Madame," Elizabeth said. "I'm sure that the experts at the CIA and at State would have a more nuanced view."

"Perhaps," Jane said, intrigued. Elizabeth Gabbard had a different view of things and would be worth talking to from time to time.

"Is there anything else, Madame?" Elizabeth asked.

"No, thank you for your time. I may call upon you from time to time," Jane said.

Back in the Situation Room with her Cabinet, Jane quickly ran through the discussions at the UN and read them the agreed-upon message. Then she called in the House and Senate leaders and read them the message.

"Do we call a press conference?" Romero asked.

"I said that there would be one, so let's set it up?" Jane replied.

It took about an hour, and when all the network people and reporters were assembled, Jane went in to talk to them.

"Good afternoon, Ladies and Gentlemen," she said. "After deliberation, the UN agreed upon a communication that was sent to the visitors. It was translated into the same language that they used, and I have a recording here if you are ready?" She played the recording and noted that they had all held up cell phones or other recording devices.

"As to what it says, the English translation is: *Welcome to Geb, I am Amir Sharma and I speak for all the people here. Please honour us by telling us what you call yourselves, what star system you come from, and how long did it take you to get here? We would also like to know who was Pharaoh when you were last here. Is there anything we may help you with, or are you merely passing?* We all agreed that their reply to that message would set the tone for further messages. We also all agreed not to send private messages so that we do not create confusion by sending disparate signals. I'll take questions now."

"Isn't that rather wishy-washy?" VCN asked.

"We felt it more diplomatic than to just ask who are you and what do you want. This, after all, is not a robocall," Jane replied, causing a titter of amusement among the reporters, all of whom had been plagued by unwanted computer-generated telephone calls in the past.

"When was the message sent?" CNN asked.

"About three hours ago," Jane said.

"And we've had no reply?" CNN asked.

"None yet," Jane said.

"What do you expect them to do?" ABC asked.

"I really don't know," Jane admitted. "How we proceed from here will depend very much on the tone of their response."

"Have they moved at all?" CBS asked.

"We have nothing from JPL that indicates that they have moved; the Mars Rover images still show them as sitting behind Mars," Jane said.

"Do we have any idea what they are waiting for?" CNN asked.

"We don't," Jane said. "We, and I include in we, the Russians and the Chinese, speculate that they're trying to decide what to do."

"How long does it take messages to get to them?" VCN asked.

"About four minutes," Jane said.

"So, they've had plenty of time for an honest reply," VCN said. "My information is that they're not there at all, but are behind the moon."

"Perhaps you would favour NASA with your sources so that we may be better equipped," Jane suggested.

"Well, my sources are sure that's where they are," VCN said.

"The Russians and the Chinese and the ESA all have images of them in the vicinity of Mars that are less than thirty minutes old, when were they supposed to have been spotted behind the moon, and by whom?" Jane asked.

"Well, you can't trust them," VCN muttered.

"Do we know what these aliens really want?" ABC asked.

"We don't," Jane replied. "One can speculate about intentions, but without more clues, it's hard to guess. It would seem that invasion is unlikely; the element of surprise is gone, it is possible that they may have designs upon our planet, but as yet we just don't know."

"What's the closest potentially habitable planet?" CBS asked.

"General Hopkins," Jane said.

"Our best guess is Proxima b, which orbits Proxima Centauri, which is a little over four light-years from our sun," Hopkins said.

"So, do these aliens come from there?" NBC asked.

"We have no idea," Hopkins replied. "We also only have speculation that Proxima b is even habitable."

"So, if these aliens have achieved light speeds, it would take over four years to get here?" CNN asked.

"At light speed, yes," Hopkins confirmed.

"How fast was the alien craft going when we first spotted it?" CNN asked.

"About one-tenth light," Hopkins replied. "So, if they travelled at that speed, it would take forty-plus of our years to go from Proxima b to here, but we don't actually know how fast they can go, and we don't know where they come from."

"Any further questions?" Jane asked.

"How do we know that there is only one vessel and that they're aren't others that are shielded from our systems that are sitting right on top of us now, while we focus on the one that's supposed to be near Mars?" VCN asked.

"If they have shielding or cloaking technology, then we don't know," Jane replied. "We are staying vigilant, and anything untoward anywhere on the planet will be reported as soon as it happens."

"What are the risks to us?" ABC asked.

"Apart from invasion, there is always the possibility that they may bring with them a pathogen that we are unfamiliar with and to which we have no counter. Similarly, we may have pathogens here that are unknown to the aliens and may cause them harm," Jane replied.

"Sort of *War of the Worlds*?" ABC asked.

"Indeed," Jane confirmed. "We are considering every possibility and, to the best of our abilities, planning for them."

"When will you hold another briefing?" CNN asked.

"When there is something to discuss," Jane said. "I anticipate that that will be as soon as we hear back from them. Thank you, Ladies and Gentlemen."

"Are those VCN people deliberately perverse, or is there another vessel we haven't spotted?" Jane asked her cabinet after the briefing.

"We have no evidence of another vessel," Hopkins said. "The Chinese have a lunar satellite and it's been sweeping the skies of the moon since the aliens showed up behind Mars, in case there was more than one, nothing there."

"Given VCN's history of inventing the news, I'm surprised we haven't seen faked-up images of spaceships and the aliens from them," Romero said.

"Well, they are what they are," Jane lamented. "Let's raise the DefCon level to 2, we need to be prepared, in case the Russians or Chinese do something stupid, and in case VCN is right for once and some Klingons or Vogons are sitting over Antarctica while we study Mars. Anything of note that I've missed?"

"We might put the CDC and FDA on full alert," Madison suggested.

"Good idea," she said. "Emily and Tamara, can you attend to that? While we're at it, let's invoke the War Powers Act and ramp up our supplies of medical equipment. We could get another pandemic just from panic behaviour, riots or a genuine crisis if the aliens land and brings a pathogen with them."

"Do we evacuate cities?" Madeline Wilson asked.

"And go where?" Jane asked. "If people leave the cities, they'll just take the centre of gravity of population to another place, and at the moment, there's no evidence that the aliens are going to attack cities. As far as possible, I'd like to see life carry on as normal. I know that's a hard thing to do, but until we know more, why create panic where none is necessary. Have we seen any uptick in travel?"

"We have," Madeline said. "All the airlines are reporting increased travel; looks like people are getting together as families again, the same is true for Amtrak and on the highways."

"Thank you, Madeline," Jane said. "I want us to be aware of what is happening; it's a balance between telling everyone all we know and doing a *Don't Look Up* and sticking our heads in the sand."

"The difference between that scenario and ours is that that was an asteroid the trajectory of which could be calculated; this is a vessel that is, as far as we can tell, under control," Hopkins said.

"Are you going to evacuate to the secure location, Madame President?" Madeline asked.

"I see little point," Jane replied. "We're not under attack. I may be sticking my neck out here, but I don't see an imminent attack, so why would I run away?"

"The North Koreans have been moving troops around, and it looks like they're getting ready to do something at one of their missile launch sites," Madison said.

"Keep an eye on them," Jane said. "What is it with the North Koreans?"

"They really are intent on taking over the whole peninsula," Romero said. "It's been a goal of the state since the armistice in 1953. They may see this as a good a time as any, while we're all busy talking to the aliens, they move across the border and at the same time provide cover by taking out some of our assets in Guam."

"If they fire anything at Guam, I want their navy sunk," Jane said. "In fact, anything on the seas that has a North Korean flag, or is leaving or arriving at a North Korean port, sink it."

"Isn't that rather drastic?" Romero asked.

"Not if they've fired upon Guam," she said. "And I don't care if it's an errant missile that's gone off course, I don't want them shooting anything at or near us. Admiral Wilson, can that be done?"

"Yes, Madame," the admiral said. "We've got an attack boat behind each of the North Korean submarines, and we have a carrier task force not far off Guam. Any overt attack by the North Koreans and I will order unrestricted warfare against any and all North Korean navy or shipping."

"If we do that, then I'm sure they'll open up on South Korea," Romero said.

"Then the South Koreans had better be ready," Jane said. "We're facing an unknown situation which may or may not mean the end of our civilisation, and we've got nations looking to take over others, what if these aliens see that and disapprove?"

"So, even though they come in peace, they may take exception to opportunism?" Madison asked.

"They might," Jane said. "Who knows, maybe these people see themselves as the guardians of the galaxy and are tasked to stop fighting, what did she say in the message, your petty squabbles?"

"That does rather suggest that they would take a dim view of warlike actions taken while they're here," Madison agreed.

"There's little more we can do now, let's reconvene tomorrow at nine, whether or not E.T. has phoned home," Jane said.

When everyone had gone, Jane went back up to the private section of the White House.

"So, what's new?" her husband asked.

"We sent a message from the UN," she replied.

"Are they peaceable?" he asked.

"Don't know," she admitted. "My feeling is yes, if they were intent on some kind of attack, I think they would have just come in fast before we could react in any way and do what they came to do."

"So, we don't evacuate?" he asked.

"I see no point at this time," she said. "When they're sitting right on top of us, I might want to eat those words, but for now, we sit tight. How are you?"

"I've been busy," he said. "The stock market is going nuts, defence stocks are through the roof, transports are down, as is the hospitality industry. New fashions have appeared, mimicking the ones we've seen on their broadcasts. So, the first clothing outlets that had them are raking it in. The supermarkets are being besieged by shoppers, the banks are running out of cash, it's chaos."

"Sadly, there's not a lot we can say that will calm everyone down, because they broadcast their messages, we can't manage what the public sees and hears, so we have to react," she lamented.

"So, we wait?" he asked.

"We wait," she confirmed. "But I think, as far as possible, we should ramp up production of defensive missiles in case we do get into a shooting war with flying or land machines. I've seen data from the Gulf War, the invasion of Iraq and our actions in Afghanistan and those of the Russian Ukraine war, and it amazes me how quickly we went through those things. We've already invoked the War Powers Act to ramp up medical protective gear; there's not much we can do about food, we can't accelerate the growing cycle."

"What about oil and gas?" he asked.

"Good point," she said. "I'll get Energy on to it tomorrow to start doing what they can for the Strategic Reserves. It's a bit late, but we should do what we can."

"Water?" he asked.

"We've got huge supplies in the Great Lakes, but no real way of moving it. The pipeline that just got completed from the Mississippi to Arizona will move some, but not all that the big southwestern states would need," she thought. "I really question the logic behind that Arizona pipeline. We screwed up the ecosystems all along the Colorado by pulling too much water out; now we're going to do the same to Iowa, Wisconsin, Illinois, Missouri, all the way down to the Gulf."

"I wonder if Hollywood has got anything right in their portrayal of aliens?" he said. "I know we've seen all kinds in the past and all kinds of technologies, some of which we've seen in real life."

"I think inventing a flip phone isn't quite the same as trying to imagine an alien," she said. "Are we dealing with genuine humanoids, or things more like the big-headed beings that the supposed abductees talk about, or something really like the creatures in *Alien* or *Predator*?"

"The image we saw of this Nefertiti, is it real?" he asked.

"As far as we can tell," she said. "But that's only what we can tell; who knows what kind of technology they may have to manipulate images and make us see what they want us to see? Our own AI will give us believable images and voices."

"So, I wonder how long we'll have to wait until we get some more answers?" he mused.

"That nags at me too," she said. "I can't decide whether I'm terrified or excited. Part of me sees these aliens as a threat to us, and I feel helpless not being able to do much about it. Part of me is curious about where they come from, who they are, what do they want and can we learn anything from them."

"Perhaps we'll get some more answers tomorrow," he said.

"Perhaps," she echoed.

Dialogue

"We have a reply," Semat said. "They must have found people who had studied languages."

"I see," Tiye said. "Comments?"

"It looks like an older male of the species," Semat said. "Looks as if the message was recorded in some kind of building, no others around that are visible. What is the import of this emblem behind the male?"

"Isis, any comments?" Tiye asked.

"Based on signals analysis, Amir Sharma has the title of Secretary-General of a group that calls itself the United Nations, the emblem that is behind this Sharma is the emblem of this United Nations," Isis replied. "Our reading of their signals suggests that the leaders of many of their societies met and formulated a reply."

"Anything else?" Tiye asked.

"We picked up messages in many languages. I isolated the most widely spoken ones and translated them; they all convey much the same, we are here, they don't know who we are and where we come from, we appear not to be warlike, at least not yet," Isis elaborated. "There was an interchange between the one who appears to be the leader of the society that calls itself the United States of America and some others, and I isolated two words that should cause us to remain vigilant, they were Nuke, by which I infer they mean fission weapons and Laser, which I infer to mean light weapons."

"I noticed that," Henuttawy said. "I've got the appropriate scanners and defensive systems up and ready. If they throw anything at us, I'll either capture it or negate it."

"One item that is worth noting, there are only four of the major societies that are led by females of their species, the others are all led by males," Isis added.

"So, opinions on this older male?" Tiye invited.

"He looks formally dressed in some kind of uniform," Nefertiti said. "Not very colourful, grey, white and red. I would guess if they age the same way that we do, that he is well into the later period of his life."

"He was reading something," Abar said. "I watched his eyes track as he was talking; this was a prepared message."

"He's unsure how to manage this," Menhet said. "He read the message, but he's only the messenger; there are others who are directing."

"So, how do we reply to this old male?" Tiye asked. "Given that some of their society is already thinking how to attack us."

"Analysis suggests that the calls for attack are in the minority," Isis said.

"Maybe, but when we start scooping up their dead satellites, that may become more universal." Tiye thought. "So, back to their questions. Who are we, simple enough, where are we from, we'll think about giving them our name for our system, how long did it take us to get here, enough time, what do we want? Oh, and who was Pharaoh when we last here? Let's take the last first, switch languages to English, not the English spoken last time we were here, but the more current version that Isis has picked up and analysed, then tell them that the Pharaohs had fallen and they were at the time of our last visit ruled by Mehmed III, it was also the time of Elizabeth, Henri IV, Boris Godunov and Zhu Yijun. That should keep them busy for a short while, working out the possible time period."

"Do you want to switch messengers?" Nefertiti asked.

"Why not?" Tiye said. "Why don't we have Penebui send this one?"

"I can do that," Penebui said. "But, I don't want to wear the awful clothes that were worn in the time and place of Elizabeth, which I found images of in the report on the last visit."

"Why don't we take a look at the images we've been picking up and decide from there?" Tiye suggested.

"Agreed," Penebui said. "Of course, we could always shock them and wear nothing."

"I don't think they're ready for that," Tiye laughed. "No, for now, keep it subdued. When we leave their system, we'll send a farewell message that will keep them talking for a while. Okay, who are we, we're of Rahotep, we'll see how long it is before they ask us for a star map that we use, so they can compare it with theirs and work out what they call our star."

"What about telling them how long it took us to get here?" Semat asked.

"We tell them that we took advantage of a natural phenomenon," Tiye suggested. "We can claim ignorance of the precise details. We'll just say that we followed standard procedures and used information given to us by the Elders."

"What about what we want?" Semat asked.

"I think just tell them that we're interested in learning more about them," Tiye said. "We can suggest that we might move closer, but that we've noticed an alarming number of objects orbiting where we might place ourselves. That will give us the opening to suggest that we clean things up for them a little. How are you, Penebui with the English language?"

"I've been listening to the subconscious tutorials that Isis created. I think I could manage it fairly easily," Penebui replied.

"Just Penebui in the view?" Semat asked.

"No, let's include Nefertiti," Tiye thought. "Let's eat, get some rest, then we'll get things set for you to send the message."

"Just send it, no pre-recording?" Penebui asked.

"Do you think you could manage that?" Tiye asked.

"I can," Penebui agreed. "Nefertiti, come and help me find something for us to wear."

"When do we send it?" Abar asked.

"Let's send it one of their days after they sent their message to us," Tiye suggested.

"What shall we wear, Nefertiti?" Penebui asked.

"I think just our normal clothes," Nefertiti suggested. "I got dressed up before, but now let's get more practical."

"Isis, what are your projections for the possibility that these people will attack us?" Tiye asked.

"At the moment, my analysis indicates a forty per cent chance that one of them will try," Isis responded.

"What is the rate of technological development?" Tiye asked.

"Without more data, that is hard to predict," Isis responded. "There have been significant changes in the past, but those were the moves from stone to bronze to iron; there has clearly been an acceleration of development since Report #10."

"I think that's the first thing to go into Report #11, we need to visit far more frequently, possibly every two to five of their years," Tiye thought. "Isis, start my official report. This is Tiye of Isis, with Report #11 on the development of Geb. We have made contact with the people of Geb, who have advanced enough to be able to launch artificial satellites from their planet. We have opened communications, indicating that they have mastered some aspects of electromagnetic theory. We will proceed with caution and try to establish a dialogue before we move closer. Our first encounter was with a probe that had been launched some time ago and which contained a message, apparently meant for any society that would find the probe as it left their system. They have moved out from their home natural satellite and have started to explore other natural satellites in their system. We have collected satellites and surface probes that are not functional and have started the process of analysing them, looking for levels of technological development. We have sent one message and received one back, both appended and will be sending another soon, also appended. Got all that, Isis?"

"It is logged and recorded," Isis confirmed.

"Good, now time for something to eat and some sleep before we reply to Geb," Tiye said.

They reconvened and got themselves ready for the message. Tiye staged the area to show Nefertiti and Penebui but kept the rest of the crew out of the camera angle. She sat them on chairs side by side and aimed the camera to take in all but their feet. They did two trial runs before everyone was happy, then Semat turned on the transmitters, and they ran the broadcast. Penebui breezed through it as though she had been speaking English her whole life. Tiye also decided that it was now the time to start moving toward the Earth. She instructed Isis to take them from behind Mars and to start accelerating to a speed that would put them in low Earth orbit in two Earth weeks. That would leave plenty of time to continue the dialogue before they got too close. They said goodbye to Mars and started on the journey to Earth, a journey that had taken the various probes sent to Mars from Earth about seven months, but which they could do in minutes; but Tiye wanted time to assess the reaction and behaviour of the people on Earth. She reasoned that a really fast approach might seem threatening, so elected to go a little slower to give them more time to observe Earth and its people.

* * * *

"We have a message, Madame President," Barbara said, interrupting her thoughts as she tried to work out just what the visitors might be doing.
"What do they have to say?" she asked.
"We're recording it, but it's still playing," Barbara said. Jane turned on the television, and it was a different messenger, and to her surprise, this one was speaking English. She came into the message partway through, so what she heard was: "…*we made use of natural phenomena, the technical details I leave to the navigators, we are interested in learning more about your culture and would move closer, but the place where we would like to position our craft, we note, has many objects that appear to be uncontrolled. We look forward to hearing from you how we may safely position ourselves above your planet.*"
"Did you get the complete message?" Jane asked.
"I did," Barbara confirmed.
"Please call together the cabinet for me," she said.
"Yes, Madame," Barbara said.
"So, let's hear it all," Jane said when the cabinet was convened.
"*Greetings, people of the planet you call Earth, I am Penebui of Isis, you will remember Nefertiti of Isis, who is here with me. We are of Rahotep; we have no knowledge of your current name for our star. You asked the Pharaoh when we last visited. The Pharaonic era had ended then, and those people were under the rule of Mehmed III; it was also the time of Elizabeth, Henri IV, Boris Godunov and Zhu Yijun. To get here, we made use of natural phenomena; the technical details I leave to the navigators. We are interested in learning more about your culture and would move closer, but the place where we would like to position our craft, we note has many objects that appear to be uncontrolled. We look forward to hearing from you how we may safely position ourselves above your planet.*"
"Any observations?" Jane asked.
"It's in English," Romero said. "So, were they stringing us along with the Egyptian, or are they fast learners?"

"Let's see what Google has to say about dates," Yamamura said. "Okay, according to them, their last visit was between 1598 and 1603."

"That's a pretty tight window," Madison said.

"It's the period when all the rulers overlap," Yamamura replied.

"Well, a lot has changed since then," Jane said. "What about their skirting the issue of how they got here?"

"They could be referring to wormholes, space warps or parallel universes," Hopkins said. "We don't know, and she, it, was vague."

"What about uncontrolled objects?" Jane asked.

"That's true enough," Hopkins said. "There's probably well over a million bits of stuff floating around in low Earth orbit, so finding a place to park without being hit by something is always a challenge."

"Would someone call Dr Hunter at the Smithsonian and ask her if there's any significance to the name, Penebui and what she can tell us about Rahotep?" Jane said. "Any comments on the fact that she says they are of Isis but also says they are of Rahotep?"

"I wonder if Rahotep is a planet or a star system and Isis is a planet within that system," Hopkins speculated.

"Any ideas on the clothes, and do we see the same background as before, is it a backdrop or does it look live?" Jane asked.

"We'll have to do some image analysis," Tom from NSA said. "But, to me, the background looks the same, but I would say not a backdrop, I note slight changes from the last message."

"Clothes, it looks almost as if they've been watching our television and have picked out clothing more suited to our times," Yamamura said. "The styles are similar to the seventies or eighties, but nothing too outlandish. The clothes are certainly not of the era of Elizabeth and Boris Godunov. Can we zoom in? Okay, no crowns or headdresses today, hair, looks natural, but with computer-generated images, one can add strand by strand, it looks like hairstyles are short, facial features, we have Patricia Velásquez back, and the new one looks like Shannyn Sossamon."

"Who?" Madison asked. "Who's Shannyn Sossamon?"

"Actress, from the early 2000s," Yamamura explained. "Both wearing makeup, still in the style of old Egypt. For the clothes, looks like an upper garment, like a shirt made of linen again, dyed this time, Velásquez has on blue, French blue or something similar, and Ventura,

Burgundy, so they have the technology to weave and dye fabrics. Like the other message, I would guess that the fabric is linen. Lower garment, trousers, also linen by the look of them, I can't make out what type of closures they have, zips, studs, or something completely different. Can't see the feet, so have no idea what they may be wearing. No evidence of anything we would recognise as a weapon, but then the Secretary-General didn't have one, but we know that there are people close by him who are armed."

"This message looks live, not recorded," Tom said. "No teleprompters there, no eye movement at all tracking anything."

"Eyes, anything weird about the eyes?" Jane asked.

"Let's zoom in and have a look," Tom said. "No, both have brown eyes, eye structure with lenses and all, look like ours."

"Or, maybe ours look like theirs," Hopkins added.

"Are these avatars, or is this really our visitor?" Jane asked.

"I'm leaning more towards this is the visitor," Tom said. "Either that or they have image processing capabilities that Hollywood would kill for, even surpassing our best AI, which is pretty good, if they are avatars, I wonder what these visitors actually look like."

"We haven't seen anyone, anything, that looks like a male yet," Romero said. "Is that significant, and do we need to think about that in our dealings with them?"

"Perhaps in their culture, they are not dominated by males," Yamamura said with a grin.

"That won't go down well with quite a few cultures here, and those we've seen so far would be classified here as brown-skinned people," Romero said.

"You're right, the white supremacists are going to hate this; they'll see it is another threat to their superiority," Yamamura said.

"Back to the message," Jane said. "Let's look at it line by line."

"First line innocuous enough," Madison said. "Only change they made is that now we're Earth, not Geb."

"I am Penebui of Isis, you will remember Nefertiti of Isis, again, nothing there, just this is me, and you'll remember Nefertiti, who you saw before, maybe Isis is a society," Tom said. "They give us some

76

continuity of messenger, but are letting us know that they can master languages. We didn't hear Nefertiti say anything in English, so we don't know if they can all speak it, or if they have experts for the cultures they accessed in the past, so they may have a Mandarin speaker, a Russian one, maybe French, maybe Hindi, who knows."

"But the English they may have picked up in the time of Elizabeth would sound archaic today, so it looks as if they've been analysing our various broadcasts," Tom said.

"We are of Rahotep, we have no knowledge of your current name for our star. We're going to have to ask for some help there, but it does suggest that they call their star Rahotep, so perhaps Isis is a world orbiting this Rahotep, and they say current name, does that suggest we knew what it was in the past," Hopkins said. "On Voyager, we put markers to pulsars that would let someone triangulate back to Earth. We would need the same kind of information to let us work out where this Rahotep is and what we would call it. Rahotep sounds very Egyptian to me, so it's beginning to look more and more like they did come 5,000 years ago or more and left their mark."

"You asked the Pharaoh when we last visited. The Pharaonic era had ended then, and those people were under the rule of Mehmed III; it was also the time of Elizabeth, Henri IV, Boris Godunov and Zhu Yijun. I think more evidence that they really have been visiting," Madeline Wilson commented. "To have the names of the leaders of England, France, Russia, China and the Ottoman Empire so handily either suggests that they've tapped into some computer database here and worked fast, or that information is from their own historical archives."

"To get here, we made use of natural phenomena, the technical details I leave to the navigators: I think a bit of obfuscation here," Hopkins said. "I think they don't want to give us details of how to travel in space, if I were them, I would want to keep my home address and how to get there to myself until I knew us a little better. As I said before, they could be referring to wormholes, space warps or parallel universes, all of which are theoretical constructs for us, but none of which we know how to access."

"We are interested in learning more about your culture: fair enough," Madeline said. "I think they want to see how far we've advanced, they know that we can put satellites into space, and if they caught the North Korean launch recently, they also know that we're using chemical rockets. My guess is that they're far beyond that, so I think they want to see just how close we are to alternate launch technologies and can we in any way threaten them."

"Would move closer, but the place we would like to position our craft, we note has many objects that appear to be uncontrolled: my guess is here they're playing for time," Hopkins said. "They are right in that low Earth orbit is littered with junk, but we can find safe orbital paths, so I'm sure they can. Maybe they have the technology to clean things up a little."

"We look forward to hearing from you how we may safely position ourselves above your planet. There's a challenge for us," Madeline said. "Give us the orbital paths of the junk we have floating around, and we'll pick a route for ourselves. What did you say, Howard, over a million bits of stuff out there, even if we were sure that they could interpret our data, that's still a big file to upload."

"As I said, I think they're just playing for time," Hopkins said.

"Excuse me, Madame," Barbara said. "There's a telephone call for General Hopkins." Jane waved at a telephone, and he pressed the button to put it on speaker. "Hopkins here," he said.

"General Hopkins, this is Jim Ekstrom from JPL. The visitors are on the move," Jim said.

"What have you seen?" Hopkins asked.

"We're tracking them and they've moved out from behind Mars and are heading towards us," Jim said.

"How soon will they be here?" Hopkins asked.

"Unless they speed up a lot, in about two weeks," Jim said. "We'll keep tracking and make the best calculations of speed, but right now it looks like ETA is two weeks."

"Thank you, Dr Ekstrom, keep us informed of any changes in speed and apparent trajectory," Hopkins said.

"Will do," Jim replied. "Oh, and one more thing, it looks like the visitors picked up the dead satellites that were orbiting Mars, and the crashed and defunct probes that were on the surface. They did leave all the active devices, both in orbit and on the surface. Rather nice of them to clean up the place a little, but it does give them the opportunity to examine the various probes and get some indications of the state of our technological development."

"So, our visitors have decided to move a little closer," Jane said. "We'd better have another press briefing and tell them what we know. How are things in the country now?"

"We've had some demonstrations," Madeline said. "Some, welcome to Earth; some go home, some accusing us of withholding information; some accusing us of inventing the whole thing. So far, there's been only a little violence and looting, which may go up, if and when people can see the vessel for themselves."

"Well, we don't need to tell the governors how to run their states, and they've all already called out their respective National Guard, so they've got plenty of boots on the ground," Jane commented. "So, back to the message, what else?"

"I think we've covered it, Madame," Madison said. "We're not much the wiser than we were before, but it's beginning to look more like they're not intending to attack. If I were going to attack, I'd come at us fast, really fast, so that we didn't have time to react. They're not doing that; they seem to be taking their sweet time about getting here."

"Do you think they'll park themselves in a low enough orbit that we'll be able to see them?" Jane asked.

"If they're in low Earth orbit, we'll be able to see them with the naked eye," Hopkins said. "But, they'll still only be a dot in the sky, a biggish one I grant you, but still only a dot. I know Hollywood likes to portray invaders as just hanging there, but gravity is gravity, and unless they've got some antigravity type of system, they'll have to orbit the Earth to counter our gravity, and the lower they are, the faster they'll have to go."

"How fast?" Jane asked.

"Well, the first satellite, Sputnik 1, was at 359 miles and the orbital velocity was 18,020 mph, once around every 96 minutes," Hopkins said. "Better to stay higher up, maybe even high enough up to be in a geosynchronous location, talk to us, formulate a plan, then come down, or send a smaller craft down, if they have any."

"What do we read into their collecting all the dead satellites and probes from Mars?" Jane asked.

"I'm not sure," Hopkins said. "That'll keep lawyers arguing for years, do marine salvage laws apply to space, and what can they learn about us by examining the dead satellites?"

"I would think a fair amount," Madison said. "All the birds we and others sent would have had the latest technology available at the time, so they could pick up quite a bit about our computer technology, our communications capabilities and our engineering skills."

"Maybe they'll just say that they're cleaning up the neighbourhood," Madeline suggested.

"Maybe," Hopkins agreed. "We have to admit, we've not really thought too much about that. We launch to the Moon and Mars and just leave all the debris lying around."

"Madeline, is there much hoarding of food and other supplies going on?" Jane asked.

"Yes, Madame," Madeline replied. "There has been a run on Costco, Sam's Club and the other big box stores. Gun sales, as usual, are up; it seems a fairly typical reaction to a potential impending disaster."

"I don't suppose there's much anyone can do to convince everyone that hoarding isn't helpful," Jane commented. "Okay, let's get ready for the press conference."

"Good afternoon, Ladies and Gentlemen," Jane said. "I'm sure you will have all seen the latest message from our visitors. It was a surprise to us that they shifted languages, which caused us to speculate whether or not they had knowledge of English before they sent the last message, or whether they learn very quickly. The import of the message seems straightforward enough. To know which star system is theirs, we will need clues, probably similar to the ones we provided on Voyager 1, to pinpoint our system, by providing directions to identifiable pulsars. As to their comment about uncontrolled objects in orbit around Earth, sadly, that is true. Low Earth orbit is littered with old satellites, debris from collisions, pieces that have been lost over time, well over a million objects greater than 10mm in size. I will be talking to the Secretary-General of the UN shortly to discuss our next communication. I have also been informed by the scientists at JPL that our visitors are moving and that, at current speeds, they will be in the position to be in low Earth orbit in about two weeks. I will take questions."

"Do we have any idea where this Rahotep is?" VCN asked.

"Not at this time," Jane said. "As I said, we will need some clues to be able to compare our star map to theirs and work out which star may be theirs."

"It would seem that they claim to have been here in the late sixteenth or early seventeenth century," ABC said. "Do we have any evidence that they did indeed visit during that time?"

"I'm sure that historians the world over are looking at records to see if there are unexplained events that might relate to a visit," Jane said. "As I am sure you are well aware, we were just a settlement colony then, intruding into the domain of the Native Americans."

"Why do you think they picked English?" CNN asked.

"English is not the most spoken language, but it is possibly the most widely spoken language, understood by leaders and scientists around the world," Jane said. "It may be that they have monitored our broadcasts and analysed the results and come to that conclusion."

"What will our next message to them say?" NBC asked.

"That has yet to be determined," Jane said. "We will be discussing that later today."

"Is there anything significant to the fact that a second messenger was used?" CBS asked.

"That we can only speculate upon," Jane said. "It may simply be that this Penebui is more skilled in English than the one called Nefertiti, or it may just be that they wanted us to see another of their kind."

"Do you think we're seeing them as they are, or are these clever avatars?" VCN asked.

"Our best analysis indicates that the images are in fact real, but they may have better image generator systems than we do, in which case I'm sure that the people in Hollywood would love to talk to them," Jane replied, to general laughter.

"Are we in any danger?" VCN asked.

"My instincts are no, but I could be wrong," Jane admitted. "If they were a threat to us, then I would have thought that they would have made their move by now, unless, of course, the conspiracy theorists are to be believed, in which case they are just the scout ship waiting for the real invasion fleet to arrive."

"What can we do if that's the case?" VCN asked.

"I'm afraid very little," Jane said. "We have no idea how to defend against someone who appears to have the ability to travel at will in space."

"Do we know how they can travel in space?" the Washington Post asked.

"Frankly, no," Jane said. "There are theoretical models that suggest wormholes, space-time warps and parallel universes, which of these our visitors have perfected and use, we don't know."

"How long does it take us to get to Mars?" ABC asked.

"Depending on where Mars is relative to us, anywhere from six to eight months," Jane replied.

"So, how can they be here in two weeks?" VCN asked.

"Clearly, they have technology that is far more advanced than ours," Jane said.

"What should people do?" CNN asked.

"I think go about their business as normal. It may be prudent to make sure that they have two weeks' worth of supplies on hand, in case our food distribution system is disrupted," Jane said. "For many who live in earthquake or hurricane zones, they probably already have that."

"Have we seen any evidence of disrupting our communications?" ABC asked.

"Not that we have detected," Jane said. "We speculate that they are monitoring communications, but so far they have not interfered in any way with any of our systems, except to broadcast their two messages."

"So, they have transmitting capability?" VCN asked.

"That is evident," Jane said. "We also note that their broadcasts were done on a fairly wide spectrum of frequencies."

"Have you raised the readiness level of our military?" VCN asked.

"That was done as a routine precaution when they were first detected," Jane said. "Any perceived threat that is unidentified calls for us to raise the readiness level. In all probability, we will raise it further as the visitors near."

"What do the Russians and the Chinese have to say?" the Times asked.

"They're as much in the dark as we are," Jane said.

"I heard that the Chinese are thinking of launching a nuclear strike against them," VCN said.

"Then you have information that I do not," Jane said. "I cannot see where it would be in their interests to launch any kind of strike. As I said before, any launch we make now will take months to intercept the vessel, if a nuclear strike is made with the vessel in near-Earth orbit, the resulting debris would likely take out most of the satellites orbiting in that area, ours, the Russians, the Chinese, and the others. This vessel is double the size of an aircraft carrier, and destroying it in orbit around us would hardly seem an intelligent thing to do."

"But what if they intercept it halfway between here and Mars?" VCN asked.

"It is hard for me to imagine that the visitors would not be able to detect an incoming threat," Jane said. "How they would react to such an eventuality is the subject of much speculation."

"So, you've thought about it?" VCN asked.

"We have been through what seems at times an endless variety of possible scenarios, actions, reactions and outcomes. We are as prepared as we can be, dealing with a completely unknown quantity," Jane said. "Thank you all for coming. I will hold another briefing tomorrow."

"The VCN guy is getting on my nerves," Jane said to her cabinet after they had left the briefing room. "Where do these guys get this stuff?"

"They invent it," Romero said. "They have a long history of inventing things that they pass off as news. Sadly, there is a large chunk of the population who watch nothing else and who believe everything that VCN comes up with."

"Okay, I should call Sharma and see what he wants to say next. Are Ivan and Zhou still here?" Jane asked.

"They are Madame," Romero said. "They both holed up at their respective embassies last night."

"So, what should we advise Sharma to say?" Jane asked.

"Keep plugging away about their intentions," Romero suggested. "It's a very good liar or actor who can keep the same story no matter what."

"You think they're not being honest?" Jane asked.

"I think they're being honest about what it suits them to be honest about," Romero said. "But I still don't think we know why they're really here. Like you Madame, I doubt that it's an invasion, unless a whole fleet suddenly appears, in which case we're screwed."

"So, do I fly up to New York, or call Sharma?" she asked.

"I think it would be politic to go and meet with him," Romero said.

Jane, Elizabeth Gabbard and Andre Romero went out to Andrews Air Force and flew to New York, then took a helicopter to the UN building, where Nicole met them and took them to the sanctum of Amir Sharma. "Madame President, Dr Gabbard, Mr Romero, Ambassador," Sharma said when they were shown to his office. "It's not often that I see you so frequently."

"These are different times, Mr Secretary," she said.

"They are indeed," he agreed. "Let's see if we can get our friends from Russia and China to join us."

"And the British and the French?" she asked.

"All in good time," he said. "Good, Ivan and Zhou will be here shortly."

"I presume you've been through the visitors' message a few times?" Jane asked.

"I have," he confirmed. "I look to you and the others to tell me how we can identify their star, and I confess I am at a loss as to what to tell them about our crowded skies."

The four of them, with their respective aides and assistants, met shortly thereafter and had long discussions about what to say in reply to the visitors. One suggestion that Romero made was met with acclaim, and he was tasked with getting the answer. His suggestion was simple enough: when satellite launch companies or the various militaries put a new object up, they had a specific orbit in mind, based on what was observed to be around. If NASA were to give them a precise orbital path that would be clear, then they could pass that up to the visitors, together with a primer on how the distance measurement came about, so that the visitors could make their own calculations. Jane also suggested that they resend the pulsar model and ask the visitors for a similar model. As the last message had been received in English, it was much easier for Sharma to go through his message and have everyone else listen to it, critique it and eventually approve it. That done, the rest of the Security Council was convened, and Sharma presented the message as his idea, thereby avoiding offending the British and the French and the others. After receiving their views and approval, the General Assembly was called, and the process repeated. They adjourned for a while until Romero was able to get from NASA the appropriate directions for finding a clear orbital path. NASA also resurrected the pulsar model that had been used on Voyager and sent that digitally to the UN. The actual message was not sent until quite late that afternoon. It took a while for NASA to decide on the orbital path and to confer with the Chinese, Russian and European space agencies. Then, out of courtesy, they informed the other nations that had put satellites into space and requested that nothing be put in that orbit for the foreseeable future. There was some complaining about not being included in the decision-making process, but all and sundry left that to Sharma to deal with.

"Any comments, Andre, Elizabeth?" Jane asked as they journeyed back to Washington.

"Ivan and Zhou are both concerned that someone may start something while we're all focused on the visitors," Andre replied. "Both of them, I believe, think that the North Koreans may do something really stupid, but neither is willing to step in and stop them."

"What about their own intentions?" Jane asked.

"I think Zhou would like to pick up Vietnam, gives them more hold on the South China Sea," Andre replied.

"Look for problems in Kashmir between the Indians, Pakistanis and Chinese," Elizabeth added. "Why anyone would want fairly barren and inhospitable mountain regions is a good question. As far as I know, there are no significant resources there, no oil, no minerals, but perhaps it's all about water, water from the snowpack of the Himalayas."

"That's something to think about," Andre agreed. "We should look into the drainage patterns to see if control of Kashmir picks up water supplies or denies it to a potential adversary."

"If we go back in history, it was the British and Russians who were facing each other off in Afghanistan; who will it be now?" Elizabeth asked.

"Pakistan on the one side of Afghanistan and Uzbekistan, Tajikistan and Turkmenistan on the other side, unless of course they're all taken back by Ivan into the Greater Russian Tsarate, then it's the Russians and the Pakistanis, with maybe the Chinese nibbling at one corner."

When Jane, Elizabeth and Romero got back to the White House, Barbara told them that they had found Geoffrey Miller and that he was waiting for them.

"Dr Miller, I am so sorry to have kept you waiting. I was just at the UN and we've sent off our reply to the visitors," Jane said.

"Happy to come," he said. "How can I help?"

"As you know from the two messages, it seems fairly certain that the visitors, or at least their predecessors, have been here before, at least twice," she said. "Have you any speculation as to other times they may have visited?"

"I've spent my life digging into that," he said. "I know everyone has pooh-poohed my ideas until now, but it's beginning to look as if I was right all along," he said.

"So, I gather," she said. "Unfortunately, I am not that well-versed in the whole field of extra-terrestrial visitors, so would appreciate an education."

"Happy to oblige, Madame President," he said. "It's my theory that these people have been here about every five hundred years in recent times, and by recent, I mean not prehistoric like the dinosaur ages. Not exactly five hundred years between visits, but of that order. I believe I have evidence that these visits go back at least 12,000 years, maybe even earlier. For whatever reason, the 1598 to 1603 visit was a little early, but I'm thinking that they saw technology changes and decided to shorten the interval between visits."

"How can you be certain that they came?" she asked.

"If you look at ancient art, there are images that are consistent with some kind of protective suit; others had said that they were space suits, but it may have been as simple as suits to isolate them from diseases we may have had, or to protect us from diseases they have," Miller said.

"I presume that this was not exactly mainstream thinking?" she asked.

"That would be a polite way of putting it," he said. "I have been the butt of ridicule most of my life; in some ways, it's gratifying to be proven correct."

"Could you give me a list of approximate dates and markers of that time?" she asked. "It may be interesting to ask our visitors if they were here in the time of, let's say, William the Conqueror, or Emperor Augustus."

"I have that here," he said, handing over a whole sheaf of typescript that included dates and notes, notes that included major events, such as comets, major earthquakes, volcanic eruptions, eclipses of the sun and the moon, changes in kings, wars, and other things noted by historians of the time.

"So, based on events like eclipses, and always assuming that our visitors can calculate the occurrence of eclipses, then they should be able to say definitively when they were here?" Jane asked.

"Assuming of course, that they are prepared to tell us, Madame," he said.

"Based on your past research have you any observations about their intentions?" she asked.

"I've puzzled over that for years," he replied. "My conclusions are that they had some hand in our early development and have been returning from time to time to check on progress."

"I have a meeting tomorrow with religious leaders. Is there anything that indicates what their belief systems may be?" she asked.

"No, Madame," he replied. "I believe that when they came in the distant past, then they would have been seen as gods from the sky, but I think as time passed, they became more circumspect about how they made their visits and observations and came and went among us unobserved, which accounts for very early depictions, but nothing that we have seen in the past five hundred to a thousand years. However, there are odd references to people with extraordinary intelligence and powers that crop up now and again."

"Have you published your findings and theories?" she asked.

"I have, I have a copy of my book here, I hope you'll accept it," he said.

"Thank you, Dr Miller," she said. "That is kind of you. I wonder now if sales will pick up?"

"They have," he confirmed. "I gather from the publisher that they are now sold out and have to do a reprinting."

"That must be gratifying for you," she said.

"Yes, Madame," he said. "It does rather help the bank balance, presuming, of course, that in the future we will still have banks."

"Have you any thoughts on the messages we have received?" she asked.

"The names may reflect their own culture. I've often thought that the Egyptians were helped in many ways by extraterrestrials. Their home planet is, in my opinion, somewhere in the Scorpius constellation," he replied.

"Why do you think that?" she asked.

"There were writings from Mesopotamia from about 3,000 years ago that talked about star gods, and they talk about the heavens and stars and isolated Scorpius as their home," he replied.

"Do you have those writings?" she asked.

"I reproduced them in my book," he said. "The originals were in a museum in Baghdad, where they are now, if they're even intact, I have no idea."

"I suppose we could ask the Iraqis if they're still there," she mused. "Do you have a museum reference?"

"Yes, Madame," he replied. "It's actually in the endnotes of my book."

"Who else has written about possible visits?" she asked.

"Probably the most famous is Erich von Däniken, whose first book, *Chariots of the Gods*, was published in 1968; then there were others. I list them all in the references in my book; you may be surprised to see how many there are," he replied.

"Have you any plans to travel in the near future?" she asked.

"No, Madame," he said. "I am staying in Los Angeles, and I rather think that I may be busy answering questions in the coming weeks. In fact, I've been contacted by four of the networks to appear as an expert, whatever that means, on several shows."

"Persistence pays," she laughed.

"It does indeed, Madame," he agreed.

"Have you any theories as to what these visitors may look like?" she asked.

"Like us," he replied. "I know that the notion of avatars is being banded about, and I know that with AI, images and videos can be created that fool almost anyone, but I don't subscribe to that. I think we are part of them."

"So, in your view, what we're seeing is real?" she asked.

"It is indeed," he confirmed.

"Well, thank you for your time, Dr Miller, may I call upon you for your opinion in the future?" she asked.

"Of course, Madame," he said. "I wonder if others have noticed that so far this seems to be an all-female crew on the visitors' vessel. I wonder if that has significance?"

"We have discussed that," she said. "So far, we have no conclusions as to whether or not that has significance and whether or not we should consider that in our attempts at dialogue with them."

"It may be worth thinking about," he said. "Plus the fact that those we've seen so far have been what we would call mixed race."

"I'll bear that in mind," she said. "Let me get someone to take you back to Andrews and get you back to LA we wouldn't want to keep your public waiting."

"Thank you, Madame President," he said.

"Madame President, I have Professor Hunter for you," Barbara said after Miller had gone.

"Professor Hunter, any thoughts on Rahotep and Penebui?" Jane asked.

"Well, Rahotep was the name of a prince in the 4th Dynasty of Egypt, and Penebui was the name of a queen in the 1st Dynasty, all pointing to some association with Egypt over many years," Amy replied.

"So, who named what after whom?" Jane mused.

"If I were a betting person, I'd say that the Egyptians took the names from the visitors," Amy said.

"I just had Geoffrey Miller here," Jane said. "It's beginning to look as if he is not the crackpot that most thought he was."

"I agree," Amy said. "I'll say this for him, he was very thorough and had good documentation for all he proposed. I'll bet his book sales are doing well."

"He said they were," Jane confirmed. "Any thoughts about why they switched to English?"

"Keep us off balance," Amy suggested. "It suggests to me that they have good analysis and learning programs for languages."

"Even so, that's a short time to pick up modern English, if we buy the idea that they were here in Elizabethan times," Jane said.

"Maybe subliminal learning is real," Amy said.

"Maybe, well, thank you, Professor Hunter," Jane said.

"You're going to have even more clamouring to be introduced to the visitors," her husband said when she returned to her own quarters.

"I know what you mean," she sighed. "First, Patricia Velásquez, now Shannyn Sossamon lookalikes, when our visitors have gone and Hollywood makes its movies, look for those of the younger generation that look like them to get big offers."

"What else?" he asked.

"I just spent the last hour learning about ancient alien theories. Here's the guy's book, if you fancy a read," she said. "Oh, and the visitors are on the move."

"When will they be here?" he asked.

"JPL estimates two weeks," she said. "They're taking their time, I'm not sure if that's to spend more time looking us over, or if they're giving us more time to adapt to the fact that we're not alone, or if they're waiting for the rest of the invasion fleet to catch up."

"It's going to freak out a whole bunch of countries that the visitors are as far as we've seen female and non-white," he joked.

"It is rather," she agreed. "Not only other countries but all the male and white supremacists that we have as well, the Texas Taliban will be running around like chickens with their heads chopped off."

"They'll probably just say that they're like the weather girls of the network stations," he said. "Good to look at, but just there for the ratings."

"That's a very cynical view of our networks," she laughed.

"Maybe," he admitted. "But let's face it, the US is still pretty much male-dominated, women still have to struggle to be seen as equals. Think about it, if a fancy new building gets put up, you'll hear something like, the tallest building designed by a woman, never mind that it might be really the tallest, there's always this qualification added as if anything designed by women is somehow questionable."

"Sadly, there's a lot of truth to that," she thought. "It's almost as though men still have a hard time accepting that women can do what they do."

"What about the dig about uncontrolled objects?" he asked.

"That's true enough," she said. "There's over a million bits and pieces just floating around out there, which makes it difficult to put up new satellites because we have to find clean orbital paths. That's what the fancy telescope on Haleakala on Maui does: it looks at things in low Earth orbit and tracks them. We sent the details of where to find a clear orbit. It'll be interesting to see what they do."

Do they believe in God?

The next morning, there was a delegation at the White House of the leaders of the major religious denominations of the country. It seemed to Jane that there were a lot of them, but then there were innumerable variations of religion within the US, so it was not surprising.

"Gentlemen," she said, when they were all ushered into the Oval Office. "What may I do for you?"

"Madame President, we want to know what the UN position is on the question of the religious beliefs of these visitors," the spokesman, the Roman Catholic Cardinal for the US, said. That surprised her a little, that the Baptists, the Jews, the Evangelical Christians, the so-called Christian Nationalists, the Episcopalians, the Mormons, the Muslims, the Sikhs, and the other myriad denominations and belief systems would all go along with a Catholic spokesman.

"As I'm sure you're well aware, in the 193 countries that make up the UN, there are many and disparate belief systems," she replied.

"That's true, Madame," the cardinal agreed. "But, we want to know if they believe in God."

"They may or may not have a concept of God," Jane said. "It has occurred to me that if and when their ancestors came here during the time of the Pharaohs, they themselves may well have been perceived as gods."

"That would make sense, Madame," the cardinal agreed. "But we are faced with an immense problem with our faithful. We can be reasonably certain now that we're not alone in the universe, did God create these beings as well as us?"

"I don't see why you can't argue that," Jane said. "Did not God create the universe and all animals in the field and the birds in the sky?"

"One of the problems we have is with the ancient alien people; they're arguing now that when Moses wrestled with God, it was in fact one of these aliens, and when Jesus ascended into heaven, he actually went up to one of their spacecraft," the cardinal bemoaned.

"One of the things we do not know is how many times these visitors have been before and when," Jane said. "We've got an indication that there were here in early Egyptian times and certainly in the period from

1598 to 1603, which as I recall, was a period of some unrest in the religious world. Our visitors may have a jaundiced view of our ideas of religion; it may seem to them to be suppression, division and outright warfare."

"Madame, I am having problems with the more orthodox members of my church with the fact that the visitors appear to be women and they're not dressed modestly," the rabbi added.

"I think tell your congregation that different societies have different values," Jane suggested.

"I have a similar problem, Madame," the imam said. "There are many members of my faith who baulk at the notion of women being in charge."

"Including me?" Jane asked.

"Regrettably, in certain circles, yes, Madame," the imam said.

"Well, sadly for them, as far as we have been able to see to date, this crew looks to be largely female," Jane said. "I never understood what the ultra-orthodox are afraid of anyway, what is it with the notion that women have to cover themselves, in some cases so completely?"

"I'm afraid it is largely a matter of interpretation, Madame," the imam said. "Depending on how one actually interprets the doctrine, one can be relatively liberal or very conservative."

"We need to know that these visitors will not try and impose their beliefs on us if indeed they have any," the Christian Nationalist said.

"I think we're a little early in the process for that concern," Jane said. "My greatest concern at the present is whether we are treating with a possible friend or a foe."

"I am afraid we cannot shed light on that," the cardinal said. "What is your advice for the moment?"

"I don't know what to advise, gentlemen, I'm faced with factions who want to welcome the visitors with open arms, those that want to blow them out of the sky with nuclear weapons, those who want to go into the deepest mines and hide until they're gone and a few others, what are your various views on the visitors?" Jane asked. "You realise of course, that our visitors may have been here at the time of Jesus or Mohammed and may have had first-hand accounts of what transpired that may conflict with the accepted writings. As I understand it, the Bible was a collection of approved works put together by the Council of Rome in

382, the gospels of the Christian bible were hardly contemporaneous accounts of the teachings of Jesus, but versions put together in some cases long after, the Quran was written by scribes who were said to have memorised what Mohammed said, but did they recall what he said accurately? Along the same vein, Buddha never wrote anything down, but immediately after his death, there were multiple versions of his teachings. What will you do if the visitors search their archives and come up with video footage of the trial and crucifixion of Jesus, or the actual teachings of Mohammed or Buddha, recorded and available to playback?"

"I am certain that the teachings of the Prophet Mohammed were accurately recorded," the imam said, clearly disturbed by the question that Jane had posed.

"I am sure you are," Jane said. "Which is why you are a respected man of faith, as are your colleagues, but our visitors may have difficulty squaring past behaviours, crucifixions, burnings and other mayhem conducted in the name of the one true God; they are going to ask, which true God, yours, Imam, or yours, Rabbi?"

"Surely they are the same," the cardinal said.

"History would suggest otherwise," Jane said dryly. "Which one of you in his heart can say without equivocation that the followers of his religion have not been guilty of atrocities in the past? Our visitors may have records of that and may be wondering just how fractured a society we really are. I have political problems too; we are a world that has been at war somewhere for most of recorded history. Some of those wars caused by personal ambition, some by political differences, some by perceived needs for resources and some by religious differences."

"You paint a grim picture, Madam President," the leader of the Baptist church said.

"Sadly," she agreed. "What I am most concerned with is how the visitors will see us and how they will treat with us. I don't want to start a war with someone who can travel through space; we have no way of knowing what they may be capable of."

"Is there anything we can do?" the head of the Mormon church asked.

"I think point out to your members that there is no reason why a divinity could not encompass other star systems, could not embrace other beings. If we believe that God is all-powerful, then God is a divinity that is the same for the entire universe. We have to get away from the notion that God looks after us only. The Catholic church has experience with this kind of shift in thinking dating back from the time of Galileo and his then heretical ideas that the Earth actually orbited the sun and not vice versa, so the Earth was not the centre of everything," Jane said, watching their eyes light up at the notion of a whole other civilisation to convert to their particular belief system.

"Will we get the chance to talk to these beings?" the rabbi asked.

"At the moment, we have agreed that all communications will be handled through the UN; whether or not that will change, I can't say. It was interesting to note that even though the Russians and the Chinese sent messages, the reply came first in ancient Egyptian, then modern-day English," Jane replied.

"Is there any significance to the names of the two we have seen so far?" the imam asked.

"That has caused quite some discussion among Egyptologists and ancient alien proponents, did they take the names of Egyptians, their pharaohs, princes and queens and their gods, or was it the other way around?" Jane replied. "You know, of course that our visitors are on the move and we have an ETA of about two weeks?"

"We saw that," the rabbi replied for them all. "I think that's why our various followers and congregations are disturbed."

"No more disturbed than I am," Jane admitted. "We don't know who these beings are, we don't know where they come from, we don't know what their intentions are. We are trying to establish a dialogue that will help us answer those questions. The last thing we need is fire and brimstone raining down from space. So far, there is only one vessel; if more show up, we may be facing a very different scenario. We have demonstrations in the streets, some of which have turned riotous, we have runs on the supermarkets, gun stores, banks and pharmacies, we are being bombarded with questions that we are unable to answer. We have every conspiracy theorist in the book with his or her ideas, we have scientists and academics pleading their case to be allowed to talk to the visitors directly without going through the UN. I know that some have tried sending messages via radio, but to date, our visitors have only responded by broadcast and not by direct one-on-one communication. That may be because of the time delay for signals to get from here to

Mars, but when they're parked above us somewhere, the possibility of conversation rather than messaging goes up."

"So, our concerns seem rather petty?" the cardinal asked.

"Not at all," Jane replied. "They are very real and go to the heart of the people; faith is being questioned, which is difficult and disturbing for everyone. In times of uncertainty, people turn to their faith and their religious leaders, and you could help us enormously by assuring your congregations that God is everywhere and created these beings as well as us. I will probably be undone by that when the first one shows up with horns and a tail, what was the novel, *Childhood's End?*"

"Heaven forbid," the cardinal laughed. "I think we can help, Madame President. We will discuss among ourselves a common message that we can give to our congregations and see if we cannot calm some of the fears and concerns."

"Thank you, Your Eminence," Jane said, finally giving him his due. "Tell me, how do you see our visitors?"

"I confess to being conflicted," the cardinal said. "All my life I have held the view that we are unique in the universe, God's chosen if you like, and now along come other beings that look just like us, or at least they are possibly made to look like us. I think I may have had an easier time if they had looked like *Daleks* or some other science fiction invention. Then I could have held to the notion that we are God's chosen, but these beings look like us, even talk like us and may well have been among us, either that or their AI is extremely good."

"Rabbi, what about the idea that they are the Lost Tribe of Israel?" she asked.

"I would have said arrant nonsense, Madame President," he replied. "But, like his Eminence, I am conflicted, my faith has been questioned, and I am trying to make sense of things. It would be useful to know when they had been here before."

"We're trying to determine that," she said. "It will be easier when they are closer and we can converse without being hindered by the time delay for signals to go back and forth. How are you all dealing with the ancient alien theorists?"

"That is a problem," the rabbi agreed. "The ideas have certainly gained traction since the visitors appeared and talked to us. We may have to admit that some of the Biblical stories are not actual events, but metaphors for life and the condition of the human spirit."

"Imam Ibrahim, what issues are you facing with your congregations?" Jane asked.

"I think very much the same as the others, the idea that there are beings out there, who may not only look like us, but may have a common root in ancestry, but who have clearly developed far beyond us, is on the one hand very disturbing, but on the other hand fascinating," the imam replied. "As I said before, the more conservative members of our faith are disturbed by the lack of modest dress that these apparent females display. It has many of our congregations calling for messages to be sent to the aliens, instructing them to dress more modestly."

"I have that problem too," the rabbi repeated.

"I doubt our trying to instruct them to do anything will have any effect. Perhaps they looked at styles of dress prevalent in much of the world and copied them so as not to alarm us unduly," Jane suggested. "For all we know, they may go unclothed on their world."

"As Adam and Eve did in the Garden of Eden before they were tempted by the serpent," the Evangelical commented.

"Will you ask them if they believe in God?" the Mormon leader asked.

"How do we convey the idea of God as you mean it?" she asked. "It's a concept I am afraid I have difficulty deciding how to describe. What if they get back to us and say, there is no God, he did not create the world, we found a barren world, seeded it with life and then we put people here in our image, would not that make them God?"

"Then, you are right, that would be a problem," the Mormon agreed. "But perhaps also a possibility, if we were put here in their image, then we were put here at God's will, proving the concept that God is everywhere. We should consider all scenarios between ourselves; a consistent message among all faiths would have more credibility and reduce panic and uncertainty."

"I'm sure you are right," she said. "That's why we've been meeting at the UN to discuss and agree upon our messages to the visitors. The last thing we want is a whole set of disparate signals going out, creating confusion."

"Very true, Madame President," the cardinal agreed. "We have taken up much of your time and should leave to let you attend to the affairs of state and go and discuss among ourselves a common message."

"Thank you all for coming," she said. "I'm sorry I have not been able to give you much definitive about our visitors, but we're still learning. If we learn anything else in the coming days, would it be profitable for us to meet again?"

"I think that would be most welcome," the cardinal said. "I'm sure all of us would take the time to come and talk with you so that we can all craft our messages to our flocks."

"Good," Jane said. "I will contact you, Cardinal, if there is something of import that I think we should discuss and rely upon you to relay my messages to your colleagues here."

"I promise most faithfully to do that, Madame President," he replied.

"I would add one more thing," Jane said. "I believe we should try and continue our lives as normally as possible, but we should not ignore what is likely to be above us in a couple of weeks, so should be vigilant and prepared to respond if and when it is necessary."

"We will convey that message," the cardinal said. "We cannot afford to bury our heads in the sand and ignore reality."

"So, what did all the religious leaders have to say?" her husband asked that night over dinner.

"I think they're all struggling with the notion that we're not alone," she said. "I suggested to them that perhaps the visitors were as much God's creatures as we are. I think some had a difficult time with that."

"What did they want you to do?" he asked.

"Ask the visitors if they believe in God," she replied.

"But, what if they have no concept of God, or if in fact they are what we call God?" he asked.

"I pointed that out to them," she said. "I also pointed out that any student of history will have seen religious wars and persecution at their best. If they really were here in the Elizabethan times, they would have seen the schism between the church in Rome and the Tudors, and all the nastiness that went with that."

"What are they going to do?" he asked.

"They said they were going to go away, meet and come up with a uniform message to give their congregations," she replied. "We'll see what comes out of that. It's interesting, it was the Texas Taliban that brought up the notion that they didn't want the visitors imposing their belief systems on us."

"They're ones to talk," he laughed. "It's taken a few years to undo all the damage that they did to this country."

"I do think that when I suggested that God created them as well as us, they all started salivating over the notion of a whole new civilisation to convert to their particular beliefs."

Defence options

"They want to know where we come from," Semat said as she read through the latest message. "They sent the pulsar map again as a reference and asked us if we would give them a similar map."

"So, that's the question, isn't it?" Tiye said. "Do we tell them where we're from or not?"

"There's not much risk that they'll show up any time in the near future," Abar said. "They've only reached the stage of getting off their satellite and sending small probes out, but at such slow speeds that many societies will be dead before anything gets to them."

"So you see no risk in telling them where our home is?" Tiye asked.

"No," Abar said. "We tell the Hemsut when we get home that we told these people where to look, but it will be many of their orbits around their star before they work out how to use wormholes."

"I agree with Abar," Penebui said. "Even if they develop better travel options in the near future, they would still need to work out where the wormhole is and how to use it. I see no reason to tell them that."

"I agree," Nefertiti said. "We can give them a pulsar map with little risk, but I would not tell them where the wormhole is and how to use it."

"Kapes, what do you think?" Tiye asked.

"Ask them for a star map, as they see it," Kapes replied. "Then give them a star map as we see it and see if they can work it out."

"They may have difficulty with that," Tiye said. "Menhet anything?"

"I'd give them a pulsar map. All it does is point to our star; they still have to get there, and then they would have to work out which of the satellites is ours. I agree with the others, I would not tell them where the wormhole is and how to use it," Menhet replied.

"Henuttawy?" Tiye asked.

"I agree with Menhet," Henuttawy said. "As for a star map, Isis has already matched what we can see from here with our own star map. I doubt that the star map seen from the Earth will change too much from the one we have from here."

"Any other opinions?" Tiye asked the other crew members. There being none, she nodded to Semat.

"Put together a pulsar map if you would, Semat, then we can send it to them," Tiye said. "Now, what about these data they've sent us that seem to indicate a clear orbital path?"

"I've worked out how to do the calculations that they use," Semat said. "I've looked at the scans of the orbit that they suggest, and it looks clear enough, but I would scan again when we get closer to be sure."

"Isis, anything that we would run into?" Tiye asked.

"Analysis indicates a reasonably clear orbit," Isis said. "Before insertion, it would be prudent to send in a sweeper to make sure."

"Do we want to put ourselves in the low orbit they suggest, or in a stationary orbit?" Tiye asked.

"I'd put us above the place that has been sending us the messages," Semat suggested. "There's less chance there of collision, and it would be easier for us to insert into that orbit. We can always send out our sweepers and tugs from there."

"I think that would be better," Nefertiti agreed.

"I was leaning towards that," Tiye said. "Isis, when we get there, put us in a stationary orbit above the point of origination of the last two."

"The course is set and we will be in orbit in one decan and 240 auns," Isis intoned.

"Now what else?" Tiye asked.

"I think we ask them why only four of their leaders appear to be female?" Nefertiri said. "Tell them we want to hear from one of them."

"They will ask why?" Penebui said.

"Just tell them that in our society, there is no unnatural male dominance," suggested Nefertiti.

"I like that," Tiye chuckled. "No unnatural male dominance. How will they respond to that?"

"I think we'll see a lot of females shown to us who are merely figures who will be instructed by the males what to say," Semat said.

"This one, Jane Adams, seems to be the leader of one of the larger societal groups," Kapes said. "Ask them if it is possible for her to speak for all?"

"Maybe not," Tiye thought. "If they are so male-dominated, then if we start asking those questions, then the males will feel threatened and insecure, and who knows how they will react."

"I would concur with that," Ramses said. He had just arrived on the bridge and served as the historian for the team. "My review of past reports shows that they have been male-dominated for nearly all their development, and it is only an occasional female who rises to power."

"Looking at their history and the weapons systems they currently have aimed at each other, I would be surprised if the others would agree to us talking to this Jane Adams," Penebui added. "This older male, Sharma, seems to have been selected as the mouthpiece; perhaps this United Nations is like our Hemsut, perhaps it's like the ruling Council and an attempt to bring warring nations to treat with one another."

"Ask them to tell us how many individual societies they have," Kapes suggested. "That may give us a sense of how fractured they are."

"Based on what Isis has picked up, it would seem that there are tensions between the group calling itself the United States and the ones they call the Chinese, and the ones they call Russians," Penebui said. "We don't want to start a war, so we should be careful to take from them equally."

"All of them have increased their activity with their militaries," Kapes said. "I've been looking at signals and images, and without exception, they all seem to be preparing for conflict."

"Probably because they don't know if we're peaceable or part of a force to invade and take over," Tiye said. "We should be prepared in case."

"I have all the defensive systems up and ready," Henuttawy said. "We can handle anything they might try, be it kinetic, atomic or light."

"It's always possible that each of these societies may be seeking to take advantage of the confusion our appearance will have caused and look to expand territory," Kapes said. "The militaries of one may be waiting for the right time to move in and take over another. I remember from my history how the ancients did that on our home satellite. So, while they may be preparing in case we attack, they may also be preparing to attack one another. When we were last here, it was the English and the Spanish, according to the reports from the time. At least at that time, the English were led by a female; history does not record many others, so this male dominance has been going on for a while."

"I also read in the history of conflicts over their concepts and ideas of supernatural beings, they call Gods, who ordered things," Nefertiti said. "The difference in how they viewed these Gods, and in some cases one God, seems to have been the cause of much conflict. I wonder if that was really the case or if it was just an excuse to take another's territory?"

"I wonder if they still cling to the notion of supernatural beings?" Tiye mused. "I suppose we'll find out in time."

"The team that was here last reported at length on the conflicts within the society of the English over their ideas of God," Kapes said. "I was just reading their report, and it is interesting and disturbing that simply because of an idea, one would kill another."

"Sounds like the place we visited last, they were like that, half the place hated the others and over what, their colour?" Semat added.

"Maybe these Earth types have the same problems," Kapes said.

"Well, we don't want to get embroiled in their petty squabbles," Tiye said. "We want to take all the dead artificial satellites and pieces of junk that there are, complete our contact report and leave. We need the materials to supplement our income for this trip."

"I agree," Nefertiti said. "We'll do that, and while we're doing it, we should collect all the material we can to send to the archivists when we get back."

"I have been able to access many of their databases," Isis interrupted. "I will upload all that they have as soon as we are in orbit around this Earth."

"Thank you, Isis," Tiye said. "Let's get everything, and then let the elders in archives sort it all out."

"Do we try food and drink from Earth?" Kapes asked.

"I think it would be interesting if we could assure ourselves of our own safety if we did that," Tiye said.

"When the last team was here, they did try the food and drink," Semat commented. "The reports make interesting reading. They also took five males back with them, but sadly, they all died during the journey back. The conjecture was that they died of sheer terror, being exposed to a situation that was wholly new to them and of which they had no understanding. Perhaps now that the people here have progressed with technologies, that the idea of wormhole travel will not be so terrifying."

"It's interesting," Kapes noted. "This is the first time that we have been detected before we arrived. All previous reports note that we were able to come and go without their direct knowledge. I think that's the first thing we note in our report, the fact that we were detected."

"So, how do we answer them now?" Tiye asked. "And, who delivers this message?"

"I think you should," Penebui said. "Introduce yourself as our leader, tell them that we'll send a pulsar map, and ask to talk to a female elder."

"Isis, what do they call leaders?" Tiye asked.

"Analysis of their languages tells us that the person in charge of a vessel such as this would be a captain," Isis responded.

"How shall we stage this message?" Tiye asked.

"I think have you in front and others of us arranged behind," Penebui suggested. "Have us all wear our best clothes, then next time working clothes."

"Isis, what do they call a vessel that picks up debris?" Tiye asked.

"I would suggest scavenger," Isis responded. "They do not appear to have a particular class of vessel that deals with cleaning up."

"Fine, let's get dressed up and meet back here, and we'll send the next message," Tiye instructed. She went to her quarters and selected the clothes she would wear. They were the approved clothes of a vessel of Rahotep engaged in a research and clean-up operation. Her instructions had been to go to Geb, Earth, assess their development and clean up, where possible, debris in space. They had done this twice already on earlier journeys with societies who had been grateful for the help; whether or not the people of Earth would welcome the help or see it as an intrusion remained to be seen.

When the crew reassembled, Tiye made her dispositions and then turned on the transmitter.

"Greetings, people of Earth, I am Tiye, captain of the research vessel, Isis. We are moving to be closer to you so that we may talk more readily without the delays caused by distance. I will introduce my crew, at least those you would call officers. We have looked through your systems, and these are the

best descriptions I can give of their function on Isis. You have met Nefertiti, she is my counsellor, Penebui is the one who would replace me if I could not continue, Menhet looks after our supplies, Semat is in charge of our communications, Merti our doctor, Abar our engineer, Kapes manages our probes and detection tools, Henuttawy sees to our security and safety, Betrest is our salvage specialist, Ramses our historian, and Horus is an expert on societal development. I have sent a map of pulsars that may help you determine where our home is. We plan to be in orbit around Earth soon and will place ourselves above where the signals from your United Nations originated. If we move to a lower orbit, we would first send sweepers to scavenge debris that we would retain to make sure that there are no uncontrolled objects that may collide with us. Also, in order to better understand your culture, we would like a map of the Earth with the societies shown on it and who is the leader of each. I await your response.”

"There, that should keep them busy for a while," Penebui said.

"Probably tell us that it is their affair," Nefertiti said. "I think societies that are not part of the federation think that we interfere too much and want to impose our governmental systems."

"We should take a look at their moon," Semat said. "We found probes and landers on the one they call Mars, so there may well be more on their moon. When we leave, we can always stop briefly by their moon and clean it up."

"We'll do that," Tiye agreed. "Now, I could use something to eat while we wait for the Earth people to respond to us. I'm looking forward to going home; we've been gone long enough. We'll get what we can here and clean things up a bit, then we'll go home."

"That is a very good idea," Semat said. "I have things to do when we get home."

"What have you planned?" Tiye asked.

"I was going to take a trip to Memphis and see the forests there," Semat replied. "I gather that since they replanted them and stopped cutting the forest down, it is once again beautiful."

"I was going to find myself a new place to live," Penebui said. "I'm looking at my options and have yet to decide where."

"Are you going on your own, or do you want a partner?" Nefertiti asked.

"I hadn't thought about that," Penebui admitted. "We should talk about that, it would be fun, and our combined resources would give us more options."

"I'm going to look into upgrading Isis," Kapes said. "There is a new drive that I think would be good to install."

"Will the Hemsut provide for that?" Tiye asked.

"They promised to do so before we came," Kapes said. "So, when we get back, Isis will be down for a while."

"Ramses, any thoughts on Earth?" Tiye asked.

"I have looked at what we have collected in the way of signals and conclude that they are as fractured now as they were when we last were here," he replied. "Negotiating anything with them will be difficult as each tries to outmanoeuvre the other. Would you not agree, Horus?"

"I would," Horus said. "I will be interested when we get closer to access their records and see how they portray themselves."

"Will our being here unite them?" Tiye asked.

"I doubt it," Ramses said. "Their suspicions of each other run too deep. It is possible that they may see us as a common enemy, but I suspect that would only last until we leave."

"Well, we'll see," Tiye said. "What do you plan to do when we go home, Ramses?"

"I will leave the service and teach," he replied. "I have been offered a post that suits me well."

"What about you, Horus?" Tiye asked.

"I wish to stay with the crew," he replied. "I enjoy working with everyone and would like to see a few more societies before I follow Ramses and go into teaching."

Conversation continued back and forth as they all talked about what they would do when they got back. None was in a hurry to go out again on another research and scavenger mission; they were always risky. Emerging civilisations did not always take kindly to their efforts. As a crew, they had been together for twelve separate missions, so functioned as a unit and each knew that they could rely upon the rest. For them, this initial attempt at establishing dialogue with the people of Earth was routine. There were worlds that they had been to that just were not advanced enough to communicate through space, so there they had just observed for a while, learned the language, then, after sanitising everything, had gone down to learn what they could. That was always risky because they could pick up a pathogen from the world that they had no experience with. That had happened to one of the other crews, and it had taken a while to understand the pathogen and how to counter it. Tiye wanted to avoid that risk if she could; Merti, as their medical officer, was on the alert, scanning communications that might talk about the kinds of diseases the Earth people had, and how to counter them. If anyone did go down, then they would go protected, and the protection would be destroyed when they returned. Merti hoped that no one would go down, but would argue for remote communications. She and Tiye were of the same mind, but there were always some on the crew who were more adventurous and willing to take the risk. She was also preparing some isolation quarters in case an agreement was reached to take some of the Earth people back with them. She could accommodate ten, preferably in her view, five of each sex. Whether or not that would happen remained to be seen.

"We need to continue putting together our report for the Hemsut," Tiye reminded everyone. "I've started the preamble to Report #11, and now we need to start adding background data. Let's start with an examination of habitations from Report #10 and now. I see from the images here that what was largely sparsely populated then is in many cases densely populated now."

"That's particularly true of this area," Penebui said, pointing to what was now Manhattan Island. "It seems that the number of people there and on Earth as a whole is growing at an alarming rate, almost exponentially. Report #10 estimates the number of people at 579,000,000; today, it's more like 9,500,000,000, that's significant growth. If we go back to Report #9, the number was lower, 295,000,000, but the same order of magnitude as #10, in #8 it was 210,000,000, so not much change really. The big change looks to have been recent."

"I suppose each of the land masses is showing population growth?" Tiye asked.

"According to the data from Reports #8, #9 and #10, yes, but the big new ones are here, here and here," Penebui said, pointing to what were the Americas and Africa. "In Report #10, the population of what they now call the United States was only about 2,000,000; now it's closer to 400,000,000, that's a huge jump."

"How much is migration, and how much is natural growth?" Tiye asked.

"That's hard to judge," Penebui said. "But a review of the languages certainly suggests that migration has occurred, as what appears to be early languages have been displaced largely by English."

"What else strikes us?" Tiye asked.

"There's been a significant technological jump," Kapes said. "In Report #10, details were given about explosive weapons, but transport relied on the wind and animals. Now they have self-propelled wheeled vehicles, air transport, they've obviously harnessed electricity and atomic energy, they've exploited metals and oils, often at the expense of the natural world of their planet."

"Their medical knowledge seems to have improved," Merti said. "It looks like they are living longer. In Report #10, they expected to live for about 40 of their years, now it's anywhere between 55 and 85 of their years, with those areas that show the most development living longer."

"So, that will drive the population numbers?" Tiye asked.

"To some extent," Merti confirmed. "The balance between birth rate and death rate is off, so simply put, deaths are not keeping up with births, and there seems to be no real attempt to control the growth."

"What does report #9 say about technology?" Tiye asked.

"It seems that weapons technology, which sadly is probably as good a gauge as any, had developed to hand-held weapons and projectile weapons that were small; the people that have been designated as Chinese had invented explosive powders, what the current language calls gunpowder," Henuttawy replied. "But the report also states that this same powder was also used for medicine."

"Report #8 has no mention of explosive powders anywhere, but does detail hand-held weapons," Penebui added. "At some point in their development, they started to use animals in warfare and agriculture."

"Take a look at earlier reports of the Hemsut if you would," Tiye said. "See if you can determine when they started to keep animals for food, as opposed to going out and hunting them, and when they used animals in wars. I know from my reading of an earlier report that they used the horse for many of their years. Merti, see if you can work out when they made significant advances in their understanding of medicine."

"I'll do that," Merti said. "But my review of the reports already tells me that some societies were far advanced and then seem to lose or forget what they had learned. I'll review all the old reports again and see if there is a general pattern, or if it is driven by society."

"Ramses, could you start sorting out the various societies they have now and their state of development and where you think they would go in the next five to ten of their years?" Tiye asked.

"Of course," Ramses said. "Horus, you can give me some help with that."

"We also need locations of all fission systems, refineries, pipelines and production sites for hydrocarbons and biological laboratories that may pose a hazard," Tiye thought. "Include in that where they have dumped the fission waste."

"I will address that," Penebui said.

* * * * *

"We have another message, Madame," Barbara Edwards said as she entered the Oval Office.

"What does this one say?" Jane asked.

"I think you'll find it interesting," Barbara said. "I've convened everyone in the Situation Room."

"Good morning, everyone," Jane said as she entered the room. "Let's hear what our visitors have to say today." Barbara replayed the message, and they all sat and, for many, listened to it again.

"So we have a new person today, Tiye, and she's the captain," Jane said.

"I see the others that we had before as well," Yamamura said. "And we also get introduced to the rest of her officers, including two males."

"That's interesting," Madison said. "Both the males appear not to be what I would call line officers, but specialists in societal development."

"Almost like a reverse Star Trek, where the women were Uhura and later Troi, otherwise all males, except, of course, I forgot Crusher."

"Did we get the pulsar map?" Jane asked.

"We did," Hopkins said. "NASA is busy now identifying the pulsars and piecing together what it will tell us."

"Let me know if the star ends up being in Scorpius," Jane said.

"Why, Madame?" Hopkins asked.

"Let's just say that I'm testing out something that I heard," she replied. "I gather from what this Tiye said that we now know what Isis is, it's a ship, not a place. When Tiye says that Isis is a research vessel, what do they mean by that?"

"We were debating that," Madison said. "Given that she also talks about sending in sweepers to make sure an orbital path is clear before they insert themselves, it led us to speculate that the research vessel is also a scavenger ship; they visit civilisations and report on them, and they also clean up and collect debris from space."

"So, could they clean up our environment for us?" Jane asked. "Not like in the first *Star Wars* movie when they just dump junk into space."

"Perhaps they've moved beyond that," Madison said.

"We have a number of active satellites," Hopkins pointed out. "We need those for navigation, communications, intelligence gathering, weather monitoring and so on."

"What if we suggest to them that they collect all the, what did they call it before, uncontrolled objects, all the dead satellites, junk and debris and leave the live active satellites? They did, after all, leave the active devices on and around Mars?" Jane asked.

"We could ask," Madison said. "But what assurance would we have that they wouldn't just take everything? We don't want to be put back a whole generation because we lose all our satellites."

"Are we getting too complacent with their messages?" Jane asked. "Let's go back and examine what we have."

"Okay," Madison said. "We have what looks like the bridge or control room of their ship. The speaker is in front of the camera, and behind her are eleven others, all seated. Two we recognise from before as Nefertiti and Penebui. The others we don't know yet. So far, only the two men, otherwise all women and all of a similar what I would call ethnic makeup, no blondes, no really black faces, all what we would call

110

mixed or at least bi-racial. Tiye looks familiar to me, but as yet I can't place the face. Miho, you've been the best among us at relating to personalities here. Who does she remind you of?"

"Nefertiti, the Egyptian one," Miho Yamamura replied. "There is the bust from the time, and there was a bust created from the skull by the University of Bristol."

"There looks to be some kind of control panel there with markings on it," Hopkins said. "I wonder if they would share with us their version of a written language?"

"They all seemed to be dressed the same," Miho commented. "It looks like some kind of uniform, linen magenta or blue blouse, or shirt, navy blue trousers, probably linen or some natural fibre, if you look closely they have what look like name badges, if we zoom in, can we get images of those badges and relate them in some way to the three names we have, that may give us a start on constructing their language?"

"I'll contact Professor Hunter at the Smithsonian and have her take a look at that," Barbara said.

"Apart from the names, there appears to be no way to tell Tiye, who said that she's the captain, from the others," Madison said. "So no obvious badges or insignia of rank or speciality, unless it's encoded in the name badges."

"The space around seems pretty big," Hopkins said. "If it's the bridge or control centre, it's not crowded at all."

"Hard to tell what the surfaces are," John Busateri of NASA said, who had just joined them. "Looks like some kind of plastic, it's certainly rigid, not flexible."

"I still see no evidence of anything we would recognise as a weapon," Madeline Wilson of Homeland Security commented.

"I know we're all conditioned by our own experience," Madison said. "Would we know what their weapons looked like if we saw them? Or do they have the capabilities of *Darth Vader*?"

"I see nothing like coffee cups, water jugs or anything," Hopkins said. "I wonder what they do eat and drink, they look anatomically just like us, so surely must need food and water?"

"I wonder if they are part of some governmental body, or if they are independent?" Romero asked.

"Enterprise or Firefly?" Hopkins asked.

"Precisely," Romero said. "The appearance of what looks like a uniform suggests to me that they are an officially sanctioned crew, not just an enterprising group of junk dealers."

"Looks like a standard haircut," Miho said. "All about the same length, all very similar in colour for the females, for the males, again, same length for them. No jewellery this time at all, no earrings, no finger rings, no necklaces, no bracelets, I wonder if that's a uniform requirement? I see no tattoos or evidence of anything like a tattoo. I would gauge this Tiye to be a little older than Nefertiti or Penebui."

"I'm wondering if we shouldn't just number them?" Madeline Wilson said. "Are we anthropomorphising them by using the names they gave us, and by doing so getting less objective and more drawn into their plan, whatever it is?"

"Interesting thought," Hopkins said. "Perhaps we should, so number one is Nefertiti, number two is Penebui, and number three is Tiye, the rest of the faces that we see, we'll just assign numbers to. Or maybe because Tiye introduced herself as the captain, she's number one, Nefertiti, two, Penebui, three and so on. Or, should we name them by the personalities from here that they remind us of? No, let's stick to numbers."

"Let's go with that," Jane agreed. "Any other thoughts on the scene we're seeing?"

"Looks like some kind of artificial light above them," Madison said. "If we assume they're all a little under six feet, that would put the ceiling at about twelve feet, so plenty of room. As we noted before, based on their posture, movements, hair and clothing, they have some kind of artificial gravity."

"I wonder if that's the whole crew, or if there are more?" Miho said.

"Doesn't seem like many, does it?" Hopkins said.

"Maybe Isis is like *HAL*," Romero suggested. "Isis runs itself, and the beings are just there to do whatever they have to do."

"All the same, there aren't many of them obvious, too few to mount an invasion," Madison said.

"Maybe, they're just the advanced team," Price suggested. "They spray the world with some kind of virus. We die off, and then in ten to fifteen years, the main fleet arrives and just takes over a nice world without having to worry about the complication of people who object or having to deal with the decaying remains of us and the domestic and zoo animals that die with us. The virus is designed to take out only humans, so other wild animal life remains."

"Is that possible?" Jane asked.

"A modified form of Ebola that's been fixed to be an aerosol, spray that around the whole Earth, and we wouldn't last long," Price said. "Or a virus that's completely new to us that's been engineered to take out humans."

"Perish the thought," Jane said, with a shudder. She could picture a healthcare system completely overwhelmed with an Ebola-type virus; the pandemic in 2020 had been bad enough, and that virus was not as deadly as Ebola. A modified type of Ebola probably would also be immune to the vaccine they had developed for Ebola, and at the speed at which it killed, there would be no time to react and develop a new vaccine.

"Back to the message," Jane said. "Play it again."

"Greetings, people of Earth, I am Tiye, captain of the research vessel, Isis. We are moving to be closer to you so that we may talk more readily without the delays caused by distance. I will introduce my crew, at least those you would call officers. We have looked through your systems, and these are the best descriptions I can give of their function on Isis. You have met Nefertiti, she is my counsellor, Penebui is the one who would replace me if I could not continue, Menhet looks after our supplies, Semat is in charge of our communications, Merti our doctor, Abar our engineer, Kapes manages our probes and detection tools, Henuttawy sees to our security and safety, Betrest is our salvage specialist, Ramses our historian, and Horus is an expert on societal development. I have sent a map of pulsars that may help you determine where our home is. We plan to be in orbit around Earth soon and will place ourselves above where the signals from your United Nations originated. If we move to a lower orbit, we would first send sweepers to scavenge debris that we would retain to make sure that there are no uncontrolled objects that may collide with us. Also, in order to better understand your culture, we would like a map of the Earth with the societies shown on it and who is the leader of each. I await your response."

"They sent us the pulsar map. I presume we're taking that at face value in that it will, in fact, point to their home star?" Jane asked.

"I think that's the only working hypothesis we can make," Romero said. "It's, of course, possible that it's all misdirection, but why bother? There's nowhere we can get to any time soon; we'd need to understand how they travel before we could be a threat to them."

"When they say above where the signals originated, what do they mean?" she asked.

"I'm thinking they would put themselves in a geosynchronous orbit above New York," John Busateri of NASA suggested. "Then they can converse back and forth with the UN. There's also less junk up there, so safer to be there than lower down."

"How did they know it was the UN building?" Romero asked.

"That suggests analysis of signal traffic, or they lifted the name from the backdrop that was behind Sharma when he sent his first message," Hopkins said.

"I wonder if their so-called sweepers could pick up all the debris that's floating around?" John asked. "If they could, it would be great. I wonder if they would keep it or send it back into the atmosphere to burn up on reentry?"

"If they're on track, then they'll be here in under two weeks. Should we go to DefCon 1?" Jane asked.

"I think we put everything in place to do that," Madison said. "We tell the Russians and the Chinese that we're taking precautions in case these visitors are not friendly, and not to read anything else into those moves."

"The last bit, the map is fairly straightforward, we'll let the UN do that, then we don't have to get involved with the disputed borders. So, I suppose we'd better set up a press conference. It would be good if we had identified the star that they sent us the pulsar map for," Jane suggested.

"We should have another press conference," Madison agreed. "We need to get a factual message out and not let the VCN guys pollute the airwaves with their own particular brand of conspiracy theory and fear-mongering."

"We'll do that," Jane said. "Then, I need some lunch."

"Good morning, Ladies and Gentlemen," Jane said to the assembled masses of reporters and cameramen. "Thank you all for coming. I presume that you've all seen and heard the latest message from our visitors. NASA has isolated from the pulsar data they have us where we believe their home world to be. They've identified it as Gliese 667, which is one of a triple star system in the constellation of Scorpius. One of the planets of Gliese 667 was identified a few years ago as a possible exoplanet. The star best known in Scorpius is Antares, so if you're not familiar with the constellation, you'll have a reference point. From their message, we expect them to be in a geosynchronous orbit above the UN building in New York in a couple of weeks. The map showing countries and leaders we will leave to the UN to handle. We noted that most of the crew we have seen so far appear to be female, apart from the two males we saw today, but we are drawing no conclusions from that. Our observation is that all those we saw were dressed alike, which suggests to us some kind of uniform. We noted the markings that look as if they could be names and have tasked the Smithsonian to see if they can decipher the markings based on the names we have been given, Nefertiti, Penebui and now Tiye and the others. I will take questions now."

"Madame President, do you believe their intentions are peaceful?" CNN asked.

"We have no indications otherwise," Jane replied. "However, if their intentions are not peaceful, then they are toying with us."

"You don't attribute their delay in moving from Mars to Earth as a ploy to allow the rest of their fleet to arrive?" VCN asked.

"There are numerous possibilities," Jane said. "We have raised the readiness of our armed forces in case this is a ploy. There is one scenario that has them infecting the world with a virus, then leaving it to do its work and returning in ten to fifteen years when we're either all gone or are present in such small numbers as to be no threat to them."

"Do you think that the identification of this star, Gliese 667, which is in the Scorpius constellation, gives any credence to ancient alien theories?" ABC asked.

"It may be a coincidence, but if you read the works of Geoffrey Miller, he suggests from ancient writings of Mesopotamia that visitors once came from Scorpius," Jane parried. "This may lend weight to their arguments. I'll leave you to do the research and draw your own conclusions."

"Is it true that you met with religious leaders?" VCN asked.

"I did," she confirmed. "They have concerns; they have the welfare of their congregations at heart. I was not able to tell them any more than I have already told you, but I think you may be hearing from them in the near future."

"Is it true that you said that God created these aliens?" the Christian Science Monitor asked.

"If you accept that God created the universe, then why would God not create all beings in the universe?" she asked in turn.

"How did that sit with the established religions?" NBC asked.

"I think it gave them all pause to think," Jane replied.

"Is it true that Geoffrey Miller predicted the origin of these visitors?" the Christian Science Monitor asked.

"He suggested that old writings pointed to Scorpius," Jane repeated.

"How does the UN plan to explain disputed borders?" ABC asked.

"That is something for member states to agree upon," Jane said. "We have differing views from some of the members, but it would serve to speak with one voice."

"Is this an opportunity to resolve those border disputes?" CNN asked.

"I doubt that we can resolve years of dispute in a day or two," Jane said.

"What do you make of their comments about uncontrolled objects?" NBC asked.

"We have known for years that our low Earth orbits are littered with old satellites that no longer function, remnants of boosters, debris from collisions, NASA estimates well over a million bits flying around our globe that are 10mm, say half an inch, or larger," Jane replied. "When we launch a new satellite, we have to look closely to see that any orbit it is placed into will not lead to collisions. It is a problem for everyone."

"So, the tests that deliberately crashed one satellite into another didn't help?" NBC followed up.

"No," Jane said. "Two objects colliding would probably create several thousand smaller objects, and at the speed at which all these objects go, it doesn't take a very big one to create havoc."

"They made reference to sweepers, does that mean that they can clean up the neighbourhood?" CBS asked.

"It does rather suggest that," Jane agreed. "If they really do have the technology to gather up all the remnant pieces, that would be good, but we want our active satellites in place."

"Why don't all these dead pieces fall back to Earth and burn up on re-entry?" VCN asked.

"If they are going fast enough, then they will stay in their current orbit. It's only when they slow down that the orbits decay and they fall to Earth pulled in by our gravity, it's High School physics," Jane explained.

"Can you tell anything about these beings from the images we've seen?" The Christian Science Monitor asked.

"We've seen what you've seen," Jane replied. "If we assume that we're seeing real beings and not avatars, they would appear to be humanoid, ten fingers, presumably toes, two ears, two eyes, et cetera, based on calculations that gave us the size of the vessel, and the size of what look like access doors to us, we estimate their heights as being between five and six feet."

"Do you think that we're actually seeing them as they are, or are we seeing clever avatars?" CBS pressed.

"Your guess is as good as ours," Jane replied. "We're leaning towards seeing actual beings, but if they are merely images or avatars, then I'm sure Hollywood would love to talk to them, as would the AI community."

"Do you have any comments on the two males that have now shown up?" ABC asked.

"Our observations are that we would class them not as line officers but specialists," Jane replied.

"Does that suggest to you that their society is female-dominated?" VCN asked.

"If you looked at the crew of the *Star Trek* ship *Enterprise*, would you conclude that our society is male-dominated?" Jane asked.

"They indicated in an earlier message that they had been here before," CNN said. "Do you interpret that to mean them literally or them as a species?"

"We don't know," Jane replied. "If they mean literally, then that suggests time travel, but if they mean as a species, then that simply says that someone paid us a visit and they have records of that visit. Personally, I lean towards the latter; space travel is complex enough without the time element. When they reeled off the various rulers for the period when they said their last visit was, that suggested to me that they were referring to records or a report of some kind."

"Why don't we just nuke them out of the sky when they get closer?" VCN asked.

"For us to reliably hit them, we would have to assume that they would behave like an uncontrolled asteroid," Jane said. "If they just stayed on a fixed path, we could hit them, even a long way out, but if they have the ability to manœuvre, then are our control systems better than theirs? Nuclear weapons tend to be uncontrolled objects once launched at a fixed target, launching one at a moving target is possible if you can predict the path the object will take and the speed at which it will travel, you just arrange a collision, a collision we would want to take place well away from our planet so that we don't create a huge debris problem. If they detect a launch aimed at them that appears hostile, how will they react?"

"Can't we control things in space?" VCN asked.

"We can, up to a point," Jane replied. "There are typically thrusters on spacecraft that allow for corrections, but those corrections are typically limited by the weight of fuel that it carries, you also have to consider the time it takes for the signal to get to the craft, real-time corrections are only really possible close to us where the time it takes for the signal to get to the craft is not significant, and if we send signals to control our device, why could they not jam our signals and send their own signals to spin it off harmlessly into the sun?"

"Why can't we just explode a nuke somewhere near them? We don't have to actually hit them?" VCN asked.

"If we could predict exactly where they would be at a precise moment in time, then that would be a possibility," Jane agreed. "But, that still begs the question of what they would do if we launch anything that looks as if it's headed their way. How will they react?"

"I think we should tell them to stand off, or we will attack," VCN said.

"That is for the nations of the world to discuss," Jane said. "We will not be the sole party to starting a war with extraterrestrials."

"When do we reply to them?" CNN asked.

"I will be meeting with the Secretary-General and the other members of the Security Council to discuss our next message," Jane said. "As a precaution, we have raised the readiness level of our military, so you may see movements of troops, planes and ships. This is not a presage to the start of any armed conflicts; it is merely a precaution so that we may respond if required, if our visitors are hostile. We have noted that many of the nations around the world have taken similar actions, and we would caution nations against using this situation as an opportunity for adventurism and territory acquisition."

"I've heard that we're thinking of annexing Canada," VCN said. "Is that true?"

"We have no intentions of making territorial gains during this crisis," Jane replied. "We have good relations with both our adjacent neighbours and would not in any way seek to upset those relationships."

"Is it true that China is planning to invade Vietnam?" ABC asked.

"We have no knowledge of any Chinese plans," Jane replied. "I wonder how our visitors would react to one nation taking advantage of the distraction of their presence to invade another?"

"Will you raise the question at the next UN meeting?" CNN asked.

"I'm sure the Secretary-General will hear the concerns raised here and will make the appropriate enquiries," Jane said.

"What do you think of the idea that they use wormholes to travel in space?" the Christian Science Monitor asked.

"We have discussed wormholes, black holes, parallel universes, warping space-time," Jane replied. "For us, travel through these is all a theoretical construct. Clearly, our visitors have discovered how to use one or more of those possibilities, or perhaps they have another mode of travel that is unknown to us."

"I heard that the Russians are looking to take over Azerbaijan," VCN said. "Is that true?"

"We have no knowledge of the intentions of the Russians," Jane replied. "We, as a matter of course and caution, are keeping a close eye on all potential territorial movements by the world powers, including any moves south by the Russians."

"Do we know how big this Gliese 667 is?" CNN asked.

"I'm sure that you can find out as much as we can," Jane said. "A simple Google search will pull up all that is known. As far as I am aware, we have no secret knowledge that is in addition to the publicly available. Thank you all for coming. There will be another briefing when we next hear from the visitors."

"I wonder what it is about the VCN people that all they think about is aggression and attack?" Jane asked her cabinet after the press briefing.

"I think they still live under the illusion that we are the sole major power," Romero said. "Their answer to everything is force, protests, send in the National Guard, dissent of any kind must be sedition, Russia hacks one of our computer systems, first deny that the Russians are responsible, then when it's shown that they really are, then bomb their data centre, jobs keep moving to China, it's the government's fault, nothing to do with the CEOs of the companies that moved the jobs there, they would like to go back to the fifties when the US was with the USSR, the pre-eminent player on the world stage, when men ran things in this country, and women knew their place."

"Very cynical of you," Madison said.

"Maybe," Romero agreed. "But sadly, I think more true than not. I think VCN supports those who would see us stay with the Fascism of the last decade, even though most recoil at the label, but who haven't read enough history to see how it started in Italy and Germany and here. It started innocently enough, rebuilding the nation to its former glory, but along the way, the real agenda came out, and by then, it was too late; the population had been sucked in and went along with the leaders."

"I wonder if the visitors have access to our databases and our history?" Miho Yamamura asked. "If they do, I wonder what they make of it?"

"They're probably shaking their heads and wondering how their experiment went so badly wrong," Madison said.

"So, anything before I go to New York and the next UN meeting?" Jane asked.

"Perhaps test the waters with Tsar Ivan and see if he gives anything away about Azerbaijan," Madeline Wilson suggested.

"I'll do that," Jane agreed. "I may not have to, Sharma may do it for me, I'm sure he or one of his staff monitors our press conferences."

"Tsar Ivan will deny that he has any territorial ambitions," Wilson said. "But his pattern had been to follow that of his predecessor and do what he can to rebuild the old Soviet Union, which would make it much larger than the old Tsarate."

"I suppose getting Azerbaijan back in the fold is all about oil," Jane said.

"That would make sense," Madeline confirmed. "That, plus their own oil in Siberia, gives them trading clout."

"What do they do if the visitors show us how to safely build fusion reactors?" Madison asked. "That would render the use of oil for generating power obsolete, and fusion doesn't have all the unpleasant waste streams of fission."

"The visitors may even have technologies that we haven't even begun to imagine, even in science fiction," Romero said.

"Well, we'll see what the Security Council has to say," Jane said.

UN 2

Jane, Elizabeth Gabbard and Andre Romero travelled again to New York to meet with the permanent members of the Security Council. The heads of state of Russia, China, Britain and France had all stayed in New York, all anticipating that there would be a need for more meetings. Jane wondered if it might not be better for her to do so as well, but Washington was really only a hop, skip and a jump away, and she could be there very quickly. Nicole met them and briefed them on what she had been hearing, which was little, as the other leaders were being uncharacteristically quiet.

"Thank you all for coming again," Sharma said. "I would like your counsel as to how we respond to the visitors."

"The list of member and non-member states should be simple enough," Emile Gaston, the President of France, said.

"It is," Sharma agreed. "We have that drawn up already. I just need to be sure that I have the latest information on all the leaders. We also have a map that we could send, it does show borders that are in dispute, but can we show that as we currently do?"

"They have not asked for forms of government," Tony Williams, the Prime Minister of Britain, commented.

"They may or may not understand our systems," Sharma thought.

"My sense is if they truly have been visiting over the millennia, then they have seen everything from the democracies of Greece to the emperors and kings of the past to the current-day variety of governments," Emile suggested.

"When they get here and park themselves overhead, do we establish a communication centre here?" Sharma asked.

"It might be best," Tsar Ivan of Russia said. "President Adams made the comment recently that we should try and speak with one voice. I am sure that many member states will try to communicate independently, but we have seen no appetite on their part to indulge us."

"Is the orbit that we gave them clear of objects?" Sharma asked.

"As best we can tell, yes," Jane replied.

"They talked about sending sweepers to clear out objects. Should we open a dialogue with them about their capabilities to do so, and if they truly have sweeping capabilities, should we ask them to clean up our skies?" Emile asked.

"We all have functioning satellites," Ivan said. "I am sure that none of us would wish to lose any of them. How do we know that in sweeping the skies, they will not inadvertently, or deliberately, sweep up satellites that are operating?"

"Do we have any sense from their communications whether or not their intentions are peaceful?" Jane asked.

"That's hard to guess," Tony said. "Their request for heads of state could be a ploy to remove us all and leave much of the world without leadership, or it may be a genuine desire to talk to us. Our sense so far is that if they had had hostile intents, then they would not have bothered to communicate, but just come in and removed us all."

"We agree with that," Zhou said.

"I am given to understand that this is, in fact, a new super spaceship that you have, Mr Premier," Jane commented to Zhou.

"I rather think that your opinion of your VCN network is as low as ours," Zhou laughed. "I wonder sometimes if they are a news network or a branch of Hollywood or a propaganda tool of past regimes. I hope that you are not taking seriously their calls for a nuclear strike against these visitors."

"We're not," Jane assured him. "As I tried to point out to the VCN reporter, any launch against the visitors is just as likely to be turned back against us; they could be here long before any strike against them."

"On that, I am glad we agree," Zhou said. "I hope all of us see that as futile. Any people who can travel in space surely have the technology to negate any attack by us in space. If they are hostile, then we will have to look to protecting ourselves on the ground."

"What if they unleash a biological weapon?" Emile asked. "An Ebola-like virus introduced into the air would overload all our medical systems quickly, making the pandemic of 2020 look mild."

"There is that possibility," Tony agreed. "But if they really have been here on several occasions before, why wait until now to remove us? Why not do it when our numbers were fewer and our abilities to combat viruses were not what they are now?"

"Would it be prudent to ask when they had been here before and why they came back now?" Sharma asked.

"That might give us a better sense of their intentions," Tony agreed. "We have the suggestion that they were last here between 1598 and 1603 when the world was in a fair amount of turmoil, but when were they here before that?"

"We will ask," Sharma said. "I have been receiving questions from some members that point to the fact that those visitors we have seen to date all appear to be female. I have been asked if there are males with them, and now we have seen that there are indeed males as part of the crew, but the females appear to be in charge."

"I think we leave the questions about which sex is in charge for now," Emile suggested. "We don't know what their culture is, we don't know how they might react to questions like that. Perhaps, if and when we establish a dialogue with them, then at some point we could explore the role of sexes within their society, if in fact they have sexes and what we're seeing are not merely constructs to not alarm us unduly with something totally alien."

"So, so far our next message is when were you last here, here is a list of self-governing bodies with their relevant leaders, anything else?" Sharma asked.

"I'm still bothered by the idea of telling them who all the countries are and who runs each one," Ivan said. "Why do they need to know that? The Secretary-General speaks for us all, so why confuse things with multiple potential contacts?"

"So, modify our message," Sharma said. "When were you here before, and why is the number of our states of interest to you?"

"I think that's all we should say for now," Jane agreed. "They've kept hidden how they get here, telling us that they use natural phenomena is of interest, but it tells us nothing beyond the fact that there must be wormholes, parallel universes or something else that permits rapid travel in space, something I think they will be loath to share with us."

"How are you dealing with the ancient alien communities?" Zhou asked.

"It looks as if some of them may have been onto something all along," Jane replied. "I talked to one, Geoffrey Miller, the other day, and I have to say that his arguments are persuasive. I did meet with religious leaders as well, and they're all struggling with the notion that we are not alone and that we might not be God's chosen. The leaders of the various religions in the US agreed that they would formulate a common message to send to their various followers."

"We have that problem too," Emile said.

"And us," Ivan added.

"We have seen a large increase in the number of people turning to Buddhism," Zhou said.

"We have seen an increase in the number of people attending various religious services," Tony said. "Many are pleading for their different gods to rid us of this scourge."

"But it may not be a scourge," Sharma pointed out. "I think it is time for plain talk. I will ask the visitors when they were here before, why they visit from time to time and what they intend."

"We are presuming that they will understand our concepts," Emile said. "I was made to think about concepts of language when I watched the movie, *Arrival*, and the discussion there about words and meaning."

"That is an issue, I agree," Sharma said. "But so far, the questions and answers we have received from them have been unequivocal, except for how they actually got here. I believe it is a risk we must take. We must learn whether or not this is a friendly visit. On that note, Mr Premier and Tsar Ivan, I would ask you to use your good offices and influence to convince the North Koreans that invading South Korea at this time will not be helpful. I have seen the preparations that the current Kim regime is making, and it distracts from what may be a bigger question. The statement of the visitors about petty squabbles between neighbours is important, and they may not take kindly to any adventurism undertaken while the world's focus is on them."

"We will try," Zhou said. "But we cannot guarantee that the current Kim regime will listen to us any more than previous Kims."

"Has anyone seen any increase in activity by the many and sundry Islamic extremist groups?" Sharma asked.

"We have seen some in our western provinces," Zhou said.

"And we to the south," Ivan added. "But I think they are confused, they heard the messages from our visitors and are now questioning their beliefs, but some are saying that the Prophet Mohammed was one of these visitors, and it is his followers who have come back."

"Are we sure that the images we are seeing are real and not created?" Jane asked. "I know we've talked about this ad nauseam, but we cannot lose sight of the possibility that we're dealing with aliens who are so unlike us as to be terrifying just to look at."

"Our analysts tell me that as far as they can tell, they are real," Ivan said.

"Mine tell me the same," Zhou said.

"How far away is this Gliese 667?" Sharma asked.

"The NASA boffins tell me that it's 23.6 light-years away," Jane replied.

"So, still within our galaxy," Sharma commented. "But still far, I wonder how they do travel?"

"The NASA people tell me that they are currently approaching us at about one-tenth light speed, but even at that, it would take 230 years to travel here from their star, so they surely must have another way," Jane said.

"These natural phenomena they talk about, any theories?" Sharma asked.

"Our scientists have postulated wormholes, warping space, parallel universes, all in the realms of theoretical possibility," Ivan said. "But none of which we know enough about to exploit."

"So, technologically, far ahead of us?" Sharma asked.

"Far, far ahead," Ivan agreed. "And if they truly have been visiting over the years, then they have had this technology for a long time."

"I understand that you are going to annex Canada, Madame President," Zhou commented.

"And the same source suggested that you're about to take over Vietnam," Jane countered. "I think we should both consider the source."

"It is perhaps something we should agree upon," Sharma said. "Using the presence of these visitors as a cover for territorial ambitions will not be helpful."

"We have no such ambitions," Zhou said.

"Nor do we," Tsar Ivan added.

"We can barely manage what we have," Tony Williams said.

"We have no ambitions," Emile added.

"To finish, we have no plans or even ideas of annexing Canada," Jane said.

"So, is it time to convene the rest of the Security Council and tell them what we propose?" Sharma asked. The rest concurred, and the balance of the Security Council was briefed and following that, the General

Assembly. There were no other suggestions of note that Sharma felt would be of any value to add to his next message, so he prepared himself for the broadcast.

Jane took her team back to Washington and then called her cabinet together.

"Any observations, Liz?" Jane asked.

"Did you notice when Sharma was talking about adventurism that the Russian and Chinese aides all looked at the ceiling?" Elizabeth replied. "Both of them have been thinking of exploiting the situation. All denials aside, my suspicion is that China will look to Vietnam and the Philippines; if they take both, then they have more claim to the South China Sea. The Russians, I'm sure are looking to retake Kazakstan, Kyrgyzstan and Tajikistan, after that Mongolia, Turkmenistan and Uzbekistan, which will give Tsar Ivan almost all that was of the old Soviet Union, look to Azerbaijan and Armenia, perhaps even Iran, after that, Azerbaijan and Iran will give them even more clout in the oil industry and also ready access to the Persian Gulf and their next targets the Emirates and Saudi."

"The Brits and the French, nothing from them?" Jane asked.

"No, they've got their own issues, the Brits with the Scots and the Northern Irish and the French with the Basques, all wanting their own independence," Elizabeth added. "Nothing to acquire, but something to lose."

"Andre, anything?" Jane asked.

"I got the sense that the Chinese have given up trying to influence the North Koreans, but Tsar Ivan is probably giving the current Kim lessons on how to be a tsar or more properly a tsarina," Andre replied.

"I wonder what kind of society the visitors come from?" Jane said.

"I wonder," Andre echoed. "Will it be like the *Star Wars* Empire, the *Star Trek* Federation or something completely different, difficult to know without some philosophical discussion."

"It's interesting how we turn to movies and novels for our ideas of what an alien civilisation may be like," Madison said.

"It is, isn't it," Jane agreed. "Well, I suppose we should have another press conference to talk about the message that Sharma just sent off."

"Good afternoon," Jane said as she took her place at the podium set up for the press briefing. "I assume that you have all seen the message sent by Secretary-General Sharma to our visitors. I will take questions."

"How do we know that they will answer truthfully?" VCN asked.

"We don't," Jane said. "We have to weigh their answers and see if they fit with their behaviour. We believe that asking them about the import of their visit is appropriate; we also would like to know when they claim to have been before."

"If we get years from them, are there any old historical records that describe natural events, like eclipses?" CNN asked.

"There are some," Jane confirmed. "We can also calculate when eclipses would have occurred and from where they would have been visible. I would be interested to know if they came, did they come for a short time, like a month, or a much longer time stretching into years, and where on the Earth they actually went."

"Why didn't we tell them who all the nations on Earth are?" CBS asked.

"Members of the Security Council felt that as we have the Secretary-General speaking for all of us, to start listing the couple of hundred nations that we have would divert from the uniform message," Jane replied.

"Why don't we tell them to stop at a safe distance, and if they come any closer, we'll nuke them out of the sky?" VCN asked.

"NASA tells me that escape velocity, which is about the speed any missile launched from the Earth would be going at, is about 25,000 miles per hour, our visitors are currently moving at about 175,000 miles an hour, so if we launch anything against them, they can simply outrun it, if they don't destroy it, or worse, redirect it back to us," Jane replied.

"At those speeds, how do they navigate or turn?" CNN asked.

"We have no concept of their technologies," Jane said. "We tend to view everything based upon our knowledge and experience; it is difficult for us to imagine something completely alien."

"Are they listening to our new conference?" NBC asked.

"All radio and television broadcasts find their way into space," Jane replied. "So, to the extent that they are scanning the airwaves and picking up signals, they could pick up this."

"How long does it take for radio waves to reach Mars?" VCN asked.

"Between five and twenty minutes, based on the positions of the planets relative to one another," Jane replied.

"And now?" VCN asked.

"About five minutes," Jane replied.

"So, five minutes from now, they could be listening to us and making plans. Why can't we encrypt the broadcast so they won't understand it?" VCN asked.

"Because then the population of our country would not be able to understand it either," Jane said. "All radio and television broadcasts ever transmitted have gone off into space, but are probably not easy to pick up as the signals are very weak and not focused or directed in any way."

"So they could be basing their views on us on old episodes of *I Love Lucy* and *The Lone Ranger*?" ABC asked.

"If the signals are strong enough to pick up and they could make sense of the dialogue, then they could gain some sense of our society," Jane agreed.

"Heaven help us," CBS remarked.

"How is it that the visitors have received the messages from the UN?" ABC asked.

"We used a parabolic dish antenna that sends out a focused signal, and we aimed the dish at Mars," Jane replied. "NASA, the ESA, the Chinese and Russians have all done this over the years to talk to our respective missions to space."

"Are the people on the International Space Station and the Chinese space station in any danger?" CNN asked.

"I don't see why they would be in any more danger than we are," Jane replied. "But, to the extent that they are up there, and we're down here, then I suppose we could imagine them to be at some greater risk than we are."

"Has there been any discussion about bringing them home?" NBC asked.

"Not yet," Jane said. "They do have the emergency escape pods there that they can use to return if they feel in any danger. I'm sure that they have been monitoring the situation closely, and we will be talking with the Russians and the Chinese about their views on the safety of all those on the stations."

"What does this mean for the planned mission to Mars later this year?" CNN asked.

"That remains to be seen," Jane replied. "Depending on what happens in the next weeks or months, we may learn how to get there sooner, or we may just be left to make our own way. As of now, we are proceeding with the plans."

"Have you had any discussions with the ancient alien community?" VCN asked.

"As I said before, I met with Geoffrey Miller," Jane replied. "He had some interesting things to say, but I'm sure you have all interviewed him since then."

"I heard from one of my sources that you've given some of them names, I heard Patricia Velásquez and Shannyn Sossamon," NBC said. "Is that true?"

"One of my cabinet remarked that the visitor named Nefertiti bore a resemblance to Patricia Velásquez, and the one called Penebui looks a bit like Shannyn Sossamon when she was younger," Jane replied.

"So, when the movies get made, their lookalikes might expect to get calls?" NBC asked.

"Your guess is as good as mine," Jane said. "Of course, it may also be that they pulled those images from broadcasts and used them for avatars."

"Do you think that is possible?" VCN asked.

"We don't know," Jane admitted. "The consensus of the Security Council nations is that the images we are seeing are of real beings, but again, their technology may be so far advanced that we are actually seeing Daleks or Vogons and not humanoids."

"I'm sorry, Madame President, *Daleks?*" ABC asked.

"Sorry, showing my age here, the villains of the BBC *Dr Who* series," Jane explained. "Beings that needed a robotic vehicle to survive and who waged war on humanity and anyone else who got in their way of domination."

"And Vogons?" ABC asked.

"*The Hitchhiker's Guide to the Galaxy*," Jane replied. "A novel by Douglas Adams made into a least one TV series, the Vogons are an alien race tasked to destroy Earth to clear the way for a hyperspace bypass."

"Are you suggesting that these visitors are part of a domination group?" VCN asked.

"No," Jane said. "We do not know what their intentions are; that is why the Secretary-General has asked them. When it comes to conquest and domination, we tend to project our own experiences and desires onto the unknown and measure them against our own likely actions and behaviours."

"So you're saying that we are after domination?" VCN asked.

"I am not," Jane replied. "But look back at history and you will find many examples of individuals and states who wished to dominate their known world."

"What should the people do while we wait for these visitors to arrive?" CNN asked.

"Make sure that you have at least two weeks supply of food and water in case our supply chains are interrupted," Jane said. "We have our military on high alert, we have the CDC on high alert in case we are exposed to some alien pathogen. Beyond that, try, as far as it is possible to try, to follow normal activities. The states have all activated their National Guard units and will not tolerate looting or anyone trying to take advantage of this period of uncertainty."

"Are there any plans to receive them at the UN?" ABC asked.

"We have no plans yet," Jane replied. "We need to better understand their intentions, and then if we determine that they are no military threat, then we have to work out how to protect us and them from a biological threat; they may carry organisms that are lethal to us, and vice versa."

"Sort of *War of the Worlds*," NBC suggested.

"In some ways, yes," Jane agreed. "We also do not want to fall into the mode that everything has a military solution. It may be necessary, or it may not; we need to await developments. My personal view is that if this had been a military strike, then they would have not announced their presence, and if they were intent on a military strike, why give us two weeks to prepare when they could have been here in a matter of hours from when we first realised that there was something out there."

"We've seen no evidence of other vessels?" The Christian Science Monitor asked.

"No, so unless they have Klingon cloaking technology, we are not dealing with a decoy while the rest of the fleet position themselves around our planet," Jane replied.

"Do these visitors believe in God?" The Christian Science Monitor asked.

"We have no idea if they even have a concept of God," Jane replied.

"Do we intend to ask them?" VCN asked.

"I'm sure that at some point in our dialogue, we will explore beliefs, cultures and forms of government, religion will come as part of their belief system," Jane said. "But anyone who watched the movie *Arrival* will understand that mere words do not always convey meaning."

"We make a lot of references to science fiction, do we have nothing better?" ABC asked.

"Can you imagine an alien world?" Jane asked. "Our presumption is that beings require water for life, but do they? Many items imagined by science fiction writers turned out to be possible, like cell phones as personal communicators, other things are not yet possible for us, so what do we really know about alien civilisations?"

"These visitors say that they've been before. Did they land or merely observe from space?" VCN asked.

"If you subscribe to the theories of the ancient alien community, then they did land and spend time among us, for myself, I don't know," Jane replied.

"How are you dealing with the notion that we are not alone in the universe?" ABC asked.

"I have been convinced by the scientists that the sheer number of galaxies and stars with planets made it statistically probable that other life forms existed," Jane replied. "To actually encounter one is both exciting and yet in many ways frightening, to wonder if their intentions are peaceful, to wonder if we are seeing them as they are, or would we be repulsed if we saw their actual shape, there are so many questions. As to beliefs, if we believe that God made the heavens and the Earth, then why could not God make other species, as he did the birds of the air, the fishes in the sea and all the other animals that we share this planet with?"

"Do we know how many of the aliens are in that ship?" CBS asked.

"We saw twelve in the last message," Jane reminded them. "NASA estimates that if we consider the beings to be of similar size to us and a vessel twice the size of an aircraft carrier, then it could accommodate up to 10,000 people, so pick a number between 12 and 10,000. There have to be engineering personnel, maintenance crews, repair crews, probably a security team, cooks, medical personnel, navigation, or should I say, astrogation people, and a hierarchy to manage all that."

"Would we expect them to have historians and cultural specialists?" CNN asked.

"Your guess is as good as mine, but as Ramses and Horus were introduced as such, I lean towards, yes," Jane replied. "But if they are as they say they are and are a research vessel following our development, then I would have thought that there would be those specialities."

"If all the radio signals go out, then they can hear this," VCN said. "So, why haven't they commented on our discussions?"

"They may just be choosing to listen to us all, but to communicate directly only with the UN," Jane suggested. "That way, there are no mixed messages."

"So, they'll know that we talked about nuking them?" VCN asked.

"I'm sure that they've analysed that conversation carefully to see what nuking them actually means, and they may have already taken their own precautions to protect against such a strike," Jane replied.

"They talked about sweepers as though they would send in some kind of machine to make sure the orbit we suggested that they park in is in fact, clear of debris. Can they do that?" CNN asked.

"If they can and if we could rely upon them to take only debris and space junk, then that would be something to talk about," Jane said. "But, and it's a really big but, we have active satellites in orbit that we wish to keep in orbit, and any wholesale sweeping up of them would not be the best for us or for the other nations who have satellites."

"If they do sweep up the debris, who does it belong to?" NBC asked.

"Good question," Jane said. "Here on the surface of Earth, we have marine salvage laws that typically apply to vessels, flotsam and jetsam. Salvage of a vessel carries a value that is usually determined in a court, but flotsam and jetsam are treated differently. Flotsam may be claimed by the original owner, but with jetsam, it's finders keepers. In space, even the bits of old boosters and satellites still belong to the nation that put them up there in the first place, so technically any removal of debris would first have to have the permission of the original owner. How that is determined following a collision of satellites belonging to different nations has yet to be tested."

"Why wouldn't all nations just agree that any object smaller than, say a foot can be treated as jetsam and whoever picks it up owns it?" CNN asked.

"Perhaps you should present that proposal to the UN," Jane suggested.

"Perhaps we will," CNN said. "But if the visitors pick up anything, how are we going to ask them to either return it to its original owner or pay a price based on the value?"

"I have no idea how that would work," Jane said. "It remains to be seen if the visitors have any notion of trading with us, and if they were to, what would they offer in exchange for what?"

"I have heard that many of the UFO sightings in the past may well have been some craft that these aliens have," CBS commented. "Have you any thoughts on that?"

"If we are to believe the time period of their last visit, then it seems unlikely that any sightings are related to them," Jane replied. "That would suggest that they left someone or something here to monitor us. I admit that is a possibility, one that we are exploring. Other possibilities include another alien race that is looking us over, something that now has more credence."

"So, how do we know that we don't have two alien races looking us over that eventually will squabble over the spoils and leave us decimated?" ABC asked. "Sort of *Battlefield Earth* with a John Travolta look-alike clomping around in big boots."

"We don't," Jane admitted. "We are only now coming to grips with the reality that we are not alone in the universe, and if there is one other species of alien, why should there not be more?"

* * * * *

"We have a message," Semat reported to Tiye.

"What does it say?" Tiye asked.

"*Greetings from Earth, we look forward to being able to communicate without the difficulties of distance. We are trying to understand the purpose of your visit and ask for details of previous visits. The orbit that we suggested is clear of objects, and we will not place anything new there. We are preparing a list of societies that we have and who are the leaders of those societies."*

"Sounds like they're being cautious, I suppose if I were them, I would wonder whether or not we come to visit or to conquer," Semat said.

"Is it time to tell them that we are on a routine visit to check on their progress?" Tiye asked.

"Probably," Semat thought. "I wonder why they didn't tell us how many independent societies they have?"

"Probably think we're going to kill off all the leaders and leave a mess," Penebui suggested. "I have noticed on scanners that this place here is massing people with what looks to me like a prelude to war."

"From the map that we lifted from them, what is that?" Tiye asked.

"This map says North Korea, what we had known as the Great Jodean State," Penebui replied.

"I think when we reply, we will point out that we do not approve of military actions and that we will take action, which of the artificial satellites belong to this North Korea?" Tiye asked.

"These," Semat said, highlighting objects on one of her screens.

"If they do, mark those satellites for removal," Tiye said. "The same goes for any others that we see moving military forces around. So, if we were to tell these people when we were here before, how do we do that, by event, or by their calendar?"

"It will be easier if we do it by their calendar," Ramses said. "I have a list of past visits and their years that they correspond to, they seem to divide dates into two periods, or at least the most commonly used calendars do, Common Era and Before Common Era, and in the old report from their year 1599, Before Christ and Anno Domini, which I understand is an old language meaning in the year of our lord. Using that scheme, our visits counting back in time were 1599, 1065, 613, and 33, all Common Era and 510, 1012, 1534, 2034, 2562, and 3065, all before Common Era. The 3065 time was our first visit when we came with the Hemsut."

"I'll tell them that we've converted our dates to their commonly used method," Tiye said. "I'll also tell them that any military action on the part of any society will mean the loss of all the artificial satellites for that society."

"Will they regard that as an act of war?" Nefertiti asked.

"Perhaps," Tiye said. "We will have to be prepared for potentially multiple attacks. I will tell them that as a research vessel, our job is to visit developing societies and report on their progress, but also caution against attacks against us. Send six frigates ahead of us and position them above the areas where we have seen martial build-ups, if any of these societies use us as a pretext to wage war on their neighbours, capture all their satellites."

"I will do so," Betrest said. "I will send Ahmose, Aya, Berenice, Serket, Ken and Henutsen. I have identified all the artificial satellites by origin, either through markings on them or where their command signals originate."

"Tell them that any evidence of martial activity on the ground or in the air, then they should take action and capture the appropriate satellites," Tiye said. "Also, make sure that they understand that they may have to defend themselves against attack."

"They will be ready," Betrest said. "I will also tell them that there is no need to consult with us if they see anything that they suspect is martial in nature."

"Good, now let us wait until the frigates are in place, and then we will respond to their message, Betrest and Henutawy, you are with me on this message," Tiye said. "I think for this message, me, Nefertiti and Penebui, wear our normal clothes, positioned against the control centre of the bridge. What else have we learned from their communications?"

"They are confused as to why we are here; there are even those who say we are not here," Semat said. "One group says that we are, in fact, a vessel of the Chinese. There is a strong trend to religions; they seem to take refuge in religion in times of uncertainty."

"Tell me more about the martial build-ups," Tiye said.

"These are the areas where we are seeing the greatest activity," Semat said.

"In those areas, we see large concentrations of people and machines," Henuttawy said. "I assess their capability as similar to ours before we made our first visit here, say 5,000 of their years, so explosive weapons, potentially chemicals or other agents and atomic weapons, which they have used in the past, judging by the readings we have of our various scans, particularly in this area they call Japan, and here, here, here and here, but judging by the fact that those areas are largely unpopulated, I surmise that those were tests. We also note the creation since the last visit of numerous small islands in this area, which have been fortified, and the presence of large numbers of what we determine to be warships in this area, harassing other people in the area."

"So, of the societies which are building up martial forces?" Tiye asked.

"North Korea, China, Russia, Iran and Venezuela," Henuttawy replied.

"Do we caution them specifically?" Tiye asked.

"I think not," Henuttawy said. "It speaks too much of our scanning capability, better I think to warn against incursions on their neighbours, at least while we're here."

"Fine," Tiye said. "Betrest, let me know when the frigates are in place, then we'll send the next message. Do we have any views on how they are seeing us and their reactions?"

"My analysis of signals shows general disquiet," Isis intoned. "They cannot decide if they are seeing us as we really are or are they seeing constructs to hide our true appearance; they also are wary that we may be the precursor to an invasion force to take over their planet."

"That makes sense," Tiye agreed. "We will have to proceed carefully if we are to gain their confidence. Any thoughts as to power balance?"

"The United States and the Chinese seem to be the two most dominant, followed by Russia, India, Germany, France, Saudi Arabia, then a whole host of lesser societies," Isis responded. "There are a number of conflicts ongoing, active warfare in various parts of the main area called Africa, similarly conflicts in the other part of the landmass that includes the United States. I have indicated those areas on the display screens."

"Interesting," Tiye said, studying the image. "Any theories about the causes of the conflicts?"

"Analysis of signals suggests that Iran has a goal to eliminate Israel, something it has apparently been trying to do for some of their years. It is difficult to understand from the signals what is the underlying cause of that," Isis responded. "Of the others, ambition seems to be the most likely, ambition of leaders, the other cause that was there on our last visit has to do with what they call religion and religious differences, but perhaps that is merely a pretext, and the real cause is once again ambition."

"Horus, Ramses, any thoughts?" Tiye asked.

"They seem to be where we were just before the Hemsut tasked us with the mission of overseeing the development of this world," Horus replied. "Before that, we had been a collection of fractured societies that did actually wage war on one another. Our appearance may bring about a temporary cessation of hostilities between them, but our experience of other cultures is that after we leave, it is not long before they are at it again."

"What risks do we face trying to deal with them?" Tiye asked.

"Apart from possible attempts to attack us, we have the issue of pathogens if we go on planet," he replied. "The last report details some of the pathogens we encountered and the precautions and treatments we used; there may be new ones now that we have not encountered before."

"So, if we do go on planet, then protective suits," Tiye mused. "Mirte, what precautions do we take returning to Isis?"

"We'll have anyone who goes on planet decontaminated when they return, and we will try and identify any organisms that are collected, then destroy all clothing and items taken on planet," she replied.

"If we go down, who do we deal with?" Tiye asked.

"This United Nations seems to be the voice they are using, so the leader of that group," Horus suggested. "I'm sure that individual societies will all try and attract attention to try and gain advantage over their rivals."

"There's also the risk that if you go on planet that someone will try and kill you," Hennutawy added. "Or take you as a hostage and then make demands of us."

"Something to consider," Tiye agreed. "We'll see how things progress with these people."

* * * * *

"Holy shit," Jim from JPL said. "Dave, do you see this? There's six objects ahead of this Isis craft, and they are coming at a hell of a rate."

"Signify an attack, do you think?" Dave asked.

"Beats me," Jim said. "Based on their trajectories and current velocities, they'll be over us in a matter of minutes. Colonel Williams, you'd better let General Hopkins know."

"Damn straight," Williams agreed. "Any guesses as to size?"

"About the size of a navy frigate," Jim suggested.

"Advanced invasion party, scouts or clean-up crew?" Dave asked.

"Good question, we'll find out soon enough," Jim replied.

"How the hell can they go that fast?" Dave mused.

"I was thinking the same thing," Jim echoed. "Can't imagine what kind of technology they must have to do that."

"The General says to keep him informed of where they go and what they do," Williams relayed.

"I'd get your tracking telescope on Haleakala to find these guys and get some images for us," Jim suggested.

"On it," Williams confirmed. "They're damn fast, love to know how they do that."

"Well, at least they won't have air friction heating issues in space, not like trying to go really fast in our atmosphere," Jim commented. "If they ever do come down to the Earth, wonder how they'll manage re-entry and the friction heat caused by the atmosphere."

"Probably got some fancy drive that lets them come down slowly and not generate the heat of re-entry that we see, let's face it, our re-entry is essentially uncontrolled gravity descent," Williams said. "General, we have six smaller objects from the main alien vessel headed our way and coming at a good rate of knots; we estimate them to be over us in under an hour."

"How big?" Hopkins asked.

"JPL estimates the size of navy frigates," Williams relayed.

"Intentions?" Hopkins asked.

"Hard to say," Williams replied. "Maybe scouts for an attack, maybe probes for data gathering, we'll find out soon enough."

"Keep me informed if there's any more and what these six do," Hopkins instructed.

"Madame President, we have information from JPL that six smaller objects are moving ahead of the visitors' craft and will be over us in minutes," Hopkins reported.

"I presume that they came at speeds we cannot imagine," she said.

"They did indeed," he confirmed. "We cannot imagine a drive that would do that, plus they seem to have the ability to manœuvre even at that speed, and most importantly to stop, can't imagine how they deal with the G forces caused by the accelerations and decelerations."

"So, what does it mean?" she asked.

"It seems unlikely to be an immediate attack, so maybe this is an advanced scout group, maybe it's more data gathering, or maybe it's just a clean-up crew," he suggested. "God, I'd love to know how they can do that and stay alive."

"We have a reply, Madame President," an aide told her. "I have assembled the cabinet and recorded the message."

"Thank you, Alison," Jane said. "Let's see what they say this time."

"*People of Earth, we are completing our mission to investigate and report on the development of the people of Earth. We have been coming here for many years. We have reviewed your calendars and have converted our times to yours. Our first visit to you was in your year 3065 before your Common Era. Since then, we have returned about every 500 of your years, to review progress and submit reports to the Hemsut. We have witnessed development through your bronze and iron ages, through the rise and fall of empires and dynasties and have noted a marked acceleration of development since our last visit. We note that some of your societies now possess and have used weapons based on nuclear fission. We have also listened to your broadcasts, where some suggest that you might use those weapons against us. We caution you not to be so foolhardy. My security chief, Henuttawy, has a broad range of systems to counter threats of many types, including objects and projectiles launched against us. Any object launched against us will be destroyed within your atmosphere, a circumstance that we are sure you would regret. Others have suggested that you use light weapons against us. Again, we caution you not to do that; any focused light beam aimed at us as a weapon will be considered a hostile act and will be met with a like response. We are a research vessel, and our mission is to observe and report on the development of your society; however, travelling as we do between star systems, we do encounter threats and are fully equipped to deal with those*" *threats. We ask you to refrain from launching with chemical rockets anything while we are here; any launch will be regarded as a hostile act. We have sent six tugs ahead of us to review the orbital path that you propose and to observe for unauthorised launches from the surface into your upper atmosphere. When we have established a dialogue with your leaders, we will permit launches of satellites that are peaceful in nature. We also caution you not to use our presence as an opportunity to indulge in territorial conquests; we will take direct action against any state that does so, including your waters as well as the lands."*

"Well, what do you make of that?" Jane asked.

"That's about as close to a threat that they've made so far," Hopkins said.

"But only if we do something while they're watching," Jane said.

"I imagine that they've seen the North Koreans massing towards the DMZ," Romero said. "Their scanning technology must be sophisticated indeed if they can pick that up from as far away as they are."

"We've seen new members of the crew, and we were told before that this Henuttawy was the security officer," Hopkins said. "It also tells us that they probably do have defensive capabilities, and given that they have the technology to go as fast as they do, I wouldn't want to take the risk of finding out what they could do."

"So, Gal Gadot, the security chief?" John Madison suggested.

"Perhaps," Jane agreed. "While we're on that subject, who gave out the information to the press that we nicknamed two of them as Patricia Velásquez and Shannyn Sossamon?"

"I'm afraid that was me," John Madison confessed. "It will not happen again."

"So, what do we have on the launch pads at this moment?" Jane asked.

"We've got a communications satellite and one of the networks has a new TV bird ready to go," Hopkins replied.

"Stand those down for now," Jane instructed.

"The network will bitch," Hopkins said.

"I'm sure they will," Jane said. "Ask them if they want to add the risk of deliberate destruction to the list of usual launch risks."

"I'll do that," Hopkins said.

"When they say take action against states that indulge in territorial conquests, is that an excuse to give them the moral high ground when they invade fully, telling us they're doing it for our own good?" Jane asked.

"A sort of super UN peacekeeping force," Madison mused. "That begs the question of sophistication in their thinking, are they that devious?"

"Perhaps, or perhaps we're imposing our own mindsets and thinking on what we suppose they are doing," Jane said.

"It's like trying to guess what the Chinese and Russians are actually thinking when we talk to them," Romero said. "The cultural differences are such that what means one thing to us is interpreted differently by them, and vice versa."

"Any updates on these so-called tugs yet?" Jane asked.

"Let me check," Hopkins said. He called JPL and talked to Williams, who passed him on to Jim.

"General, we've noted the six objects that we were tracking are now in geosynchronous orbits, one sitting above the DMZ, one over southern China, between Vietnam and the Philippines, one over Russia on the Kazakhstan border, one over Iran, one over Venezuela and one over Israel," Jim said.

"Any better guesses as to size?" Hopkins asked.

"We've confirmed our guess of about the size of a navy frigate," Jim said.

"Thanks, Jim, keep an eye on them and let us know if they move," Hopkins said.

"So, they have six more objects positioned above us, three I would have guessed, but what's going on in Venezuela, Iran and Israel?" Jane asked.

"I wonder if Kim, Zhou, Ivan or the mad ayatollah will try their luck and see if this Tiye is bluffing. What's going on with Iran?"

"I've not heard anything, but they may just be up to their usual tricks of muddying the waters in the Persian Gulf," Romero said.

"We've heard some chatter, but we didn't think it any more serious than usual," John Banks of the CIA added. "I will check into it."

"What does the navy frigate size tell us?" Jane asked.

"What it does tell us is that their technology for propulsion can be made small enough to fit inside a frigate, possibly even smaller if these vessels capture satellites and store them internally and not just hang on to them on the outside," Hopkins commented.

"This Tiye is showing a remarkable fluency in English," Romero commented. "I wonder how they picked up the language fluency so quickly?"

"If their first visit was in 3065 BC, what was that era?" Jane asked.

"It would have been in the Bronze Age," Amy Hunter replied. "The Stone Age started at the end of the last Ice Age, after that would have come, in time, the later Stone Ages, the Mesolithic and Neolithic, then the Bronze Age, then the Iron Age, then we'd be into the Classical Age, Middle Ages, Early Modern and Modern eras."

"I wonder if they made actual contact then, or did they just sit above the people and observe?" Jane mused.

"If the ancient alien theorists are to be believed, then they came down from their vessel," Amy said. "I used to dismiss those theories as fanciful, but now I'm not so sure. It would be fascinating if they would share with us the reports that they took back. I wonder who this Hemsut is she mentioned. In Egyptian mythology, the Hemsut were the goddesses of fate and destiny. Did the Egyptians get that concept from the visitors, or vice versa, it's something academics will debate for years to come."

"I wonder," Jane agreed.

"Apart from this recent implied threat, are they truly as peaceful as they would seem, or is it just a ploy to lure us into a sense of complacency, then they'll reveal their true purpose when we least expect it?" Romero asked.

"I rather think that if an attack was intended, that that would have already happened," Hopkins said. "When I was in the field, I never signalled my intentions if I could avoid it."

"I wonder if Zhou or Ivan will give anything away at the next Security Council meeting?" Jane said.

"Probably both protest madly that they had no plans to make any moves on any of their neighbours," Romero said.

"Are we seeing much in the way of street protests?" Jane asked.

"No, the governors have all done a good job of locking their states down," Madeline Wilson replied. "Gun sales are through the roof, as are sales of long-life rations."

"Madame President, the Secretary-General," an aide interrupted.

"Mr Secretary," Jane said.

"Would it be possible for you to join us in a meeting in two hours?" Sharma asked.

"Of course, Mr Secretary," Jane replied. "I presume you wish to discuss the latest message?"

"That and what the six new objects above us may portend," he replied.

Jane took Andre Romero and Elizabeth Gabbard with her to New York. They drove to Andrews Air Force Base, picked up the small plane there and flew to La Guardia, then had a helicopter take them to the UN building, where they were met by Nicole Edwards.

"Mr Secretary," Jane said as she and her team joined the others.

"We have all seen the latest message?" Sharma asked. The permanent members of the Security Council all indicated that they had.

"We regard their message as a threat," Zhou said.

"Why, they say they will only act if one of us does something against them or one of our neighbours?" Emile commented. "Have you plans to do so?"

"Of course not," Zhou said. "I wonder about the significance of these new objects in the sky."

"Their positions are interesting," Sharma noted. "I'm told that there's one above the Korean peninsula, one over the Persian Gulf, one over the northern part of South America, one over the Middle East, one over Central Asia and one over southern China."

"I see little else we can do," Jane said. "We can press them again about their intentions, particularly as they've made an implied threat."

"I'm not sure I want to become antagonistic with them," Sharma said. "We have no idea what they may be capable of. I think we should deny any moves to extend territory."

"We'll have to get every member of the General Assembly to make that commitment," Emile said. "How confident are we that all our members will be honest with us?"

"Whoever isn't may learn what the visitors are capable of," Jane said. "I don't wish to take that chance. Anyone who can come into our solar system at one-tenth light speed, then just stop and sit behind Mars, has technologies that we just don't understand or could even imagine."

"They seem to have developed a mastery of English very quickly," Tony Williams commented.

"We wondered about that, too," Jane echoed. "I know that subconscious learning programs are often referred to in fiction, but perhaps they can be real, and they've done an analysis of all our broadcasts and have developed an understanding of the language. We caution you not to be foolhardy is not the kind of expression one would expect to hear from someone just learning the language."

"I wonder if they have the same facility in our other languages?" Emile thought.

"I rather think that the only languages they may have difficulty with will be those that do not get broadcast in any way," Tony said. "So, the lesser-known languages like some of those spoken by small tribes in the Amazon."

"Have we any sense of whether or not our risk has gone up?" Sharma asked.

"I think that if they were going to attack, then that would have already happened," Ivan said. "Unless they're using the ploy of the Islamic terrorists to get populations to congregate, then explode their weapons."

"I don't see that as likely," Zhou said. "My population is dispersing to family roots, so we have seen some exodus from the bigger cities, but it is creating new population densities in other areas."

"I think it's time to call in the rest of the Security Council, then convene the General Assembly and discuss this latest message," Sharma said.

The message was discussed and debated widely by the Security Council and the General Assembly, and all present stated that they had no territorial acquisition ambitions, at least none they would admit. A response was discussed, and after much back and forth, it was agreed that the Secretary-General would respond by giving assurances that no one had ambitions to acquire territory and to request elaboration on the implied threat. There were a lot of complaints about being asked, told, not to launch anything into space, as many had communication and spy satellites ready to go, not that anyone would admit to the existence of spy satellites, describing them in terms of weather satellites instead. A message was crafted, debated, edited and finally agreed upon.

* * * * *

"We have a response from Geb," Semat told Tiye.

"What do they say?" Tiye asked.

"Greetings from Earth. None of our nations has ambitions to acquire territory. We are concerned that you have told us not to launch satellites into our upper atmosphere, we have need of information about our weather systems and rely upon satellites to gather that for us. We are also concerned about the implied threat towards us. We object to being instructed on what we may or may not do."

"Are they truthful or is this a load of belzal?" Tiye asked.

"I'd say a little of both," Horus replied. "The speaker may believe what the various representatives have told him, but their actions would indicate that they have different intentions."

"Well, I'm not changing my position," Tiye said. "It won't hurt them to wait a few of their days or weeks before putting more objects into low orbits, and too bad if they don't like being told what they can and cannot do, I have to regard any launch of a projectile from the surface into space as a potential threat, so better for us not to permit any."

"I think it would be prudent to repeat the message," Horus said.

"I agree," Nefertiti added. "We need to be sure they understand that anything launched while we are here will be regarded as a threat."

"So, put it more simply, don't ask, tell?" Tiye asked.

"Yes," Horus and Nefertiti chorused.

"Very well," Tiye said. "Let's set things up."

* * * * *

"We have another message," an aide informed the Sharma. "It is being broadcast now."

"Let's hear what they have to say," Sharma said.

"People of Earth, perhaps I did not make myself clear before. There will be no attacks on neighbouring countries while we are here, there will be no launches of projectiles of any type from the surface of your planet into your upper atmosphere or beyond. We would see such a launch as a threat to us and will destroy the vehicle. There is nothing in your society that cannot wait a matter of your weeks before we agree on what may be done. I trust I make myself clear, this is not a request but an instruction and failure to heed will be unfortunate for that society that provokes us."

"That seems straightforward enough," Sharma said. "Oh, and I have just been informed that this same message is being broadcast in Mandarin, Cantonese, Russian, Korean, Farsi, Arabic, Hebrew, Spanish, French, German, Hindi, Bengali, Portuguese, Urdu and Japanese, so they seem to be leaving little to chance."

"What do you think of that?" Jane asked Nicole Edwards when they went back to the offices that they maintained in New York in proximity to the UN building.

"I think Ivan and Zhou would both secretly like to see Kim or the mad ayatollah make a move and then see what happens. If some form of retaliation follows, then they'll sit quiet until the visitors leave; if nothing happens and it's a bluff on the part of this Tiye, then they'll be over their borders the next day," Nicole replied.

"I would agree," Andre said.

"So, what do we tell the press?" Jane asked.

"Just tell them that we've received the message and the UN members all committed that they have no territorial ambitions, we don't need to say until the visitors go away," Nicole suggested.

"And when VCN says that they've threatened us and we need to blow them out of the sky?" Jane asked.

"I think just point out, again, that we don't know what these beings are capable of and we have no desire to call their bluff," Andre suggested.

"Do you think they are bluffing?" Jane asked.

"There's always the chance," Elizabeth replied. "But are we prepared to call their bluff?"

"I for one am not," Jane said. "We've no idea what these beings can do, but we do know they have technologies that we can only theorise and speculate about, so what do they have in the way of defensive and offensive weapons. Much as it grates to be told what we can and cannot do, they won't be here forever, or at least I hope not."

"What if they're like the Overlords of Arthur C. Clarke and they stay and control what we do?" Andre asked.

"That would mean all kinds of changes, not the least of which would be the dismantling of the military-industrial complex," Jane replied.

"That would certainly help most countries' budgets," Elizabeth said. "But, what would regimes like Kim's and the mad ayatollahs' do instead of building weapons?"

"They may actually feed their people for once," Andre said.

"So, the so-called new world order, but instead of oligarchs here on earth calling the shots, some alien with a tail and horns," Jane added.

"Oh, is that what the Clarke Overlords were supposed to look like?" Elizabeth asked.

"In his book, *Childhood's End*, there is a description," Andre replied. "But, unless these are really good avatars, our visitor looks more like us than anything else."

"Who's going to be the first to see if Tiye's bluffing?" Jane asked.

"Kim," Elizabeth replied. "She likes to think she's the Great Leader, a god to the poor people in North Korea and that she can do what she likes."

"I agree," Andre added. "My odds are highest on Kim, then the mad ayatollah."

"I should make sure all our forces are on high alert and make sure all our surveillance assets are online and functioning properly," Jane mused. "Get John Madison on the line for me."

"Madame President?" John Madison said when he called.

"John, is everything we have fully operational and on high alert?" Jane asked.

"It is, Madame," he replied. "We have increased production of missiles, drones and artillery shells, but we'll have to rely on current stocks if we come to a shooting war. There hasn't been enough time to produce anything in quantity, other than what was already in the pipeline."

"I understand," Jane said. "Still, we must do what we can. Any views on anyone testing our visitor?"

"Kim," he replied. "She won't like being told what to do."

"That seems to be the consensus," Jane said. "We'll see what the next few days bring. I think it would be prudent if the rest of the Cabinet made its way quietly to New York and joined us in the offices here. We need to be prepared to discuss developments and reactions by the Chinese and the Russians."

"And, if I might add, Madame, the North Koreans, the Iranians and the Indians," Madison added. "I'll set it up."

"Good, thank you, John," Jane said.

Lesson #1

"Tiye, there is a launch of a chemical rocket from the so-called Democratic People's Republic of Korea," Henuttawy said. "Aya reports destroying it, and she is now collecting the satellites that belong to that society. I wonder why these people are so foolish?"

"They probably don't understand what we can actually do," Tiye said. "Tell the others to watch carefully, and if anyone else tries something, destroy as much of their martial equipment as we can find in a short time. The third infraction, hunt down and destroy anything and everything that looks martial in origin that belongs to the offender. These people are beginning to annoy me."

"Here's another," Semat said.

"Who is it this time?" Tiye asked.

"The place called The Islamic Republic of Iran," Semat said. "Serket reports destroying twelve chemical rockets that appear to have been aimed at this place, Israel."

"Tell Serket that when she's grabbed their satellites to take out all the ships they have on the sea, all the land-based military systems and projectile weapons launchers she can see, oh, and we noted that they have been developing fission weapons, destroy all those sites," Tiye instructed. "Tell Serket to send down destroyers with instructions to hunt down and kill anything that looks martial in nature."

"Will they see this as an attack?" Semat asked.

"Perhaps," Tiye said. "But we destroy only the facilities of those societies that do not follow our instructions; leave the rest alone. If we make no general attack, then perhaps they will continue to talk. Why is it that societies develop their technology, but not their abilities to live with one another?"

"They're like we were long ago," Semat said. "There was a time when we would have done the same; fortunately for us, we developed past that."

"Let's increase speed and get there sooner," Tiye said. "Isis, get us to a synchronous orbit quickly."

* * * * *

150

"Madame President," a steward said. "A communication from General Hopkins."

"General?" Jane asked, taking the telephone.

"Madame President, the North Koreans attempted to launch from one of their pads, and the vehicle was destroyed five seconds after liftoff," Hopkins reported.

"What did they have going up?" Jane asked.

"It looked to us like another ballistic missile test, but it could have been a warbird aimed at either the visitors or us," Hopkins replied.

"Is there any evidence that it was a failure of their system, or did the visitors knock it out?" Jane asked.

"We're still working on that," Hopkins said. "As far as we could tell from our surveillance birds, the launch went well, there were no apparent anomalies, so maybe the visitors are as good as their word."

"If they did knock it out, I wonder how?" Jane thought.

"We'd love to know," Hopkins agreed. "I will try and have more for you when you arrive."

"So, the North Koreans went ahead with a launch," Andre said. "Maybe they should have done the prudent thing and just waited."

"The Kims don't like to be told by anyone," Elizabeth remarked. "Tell a Kim they can't do something and they'll do it anyway; this one is no different from the three before her."

"It's interesting how communist and socialist societies quickly become the territory of despots," Jane said. "Russia, China, North Korea, Cuba and Venezuela, all supposed to be for the people, but all in fact run by despots. I wonder if our visitors are run by a despot or by some form of elected government. When will the rest of the cabinet be here in New York? We may have some decisions to make."

"In about an hour," Andre replied.

"Have we any more information on the North Korean rocket?" Jane asked when the cabinet convened.

"It looks as if the visitors dropped out of GEO to the upper atmosphere, aimed some kind of energy beam at it," Hopkins replied. "JPL told me that one of our birds that was overhead at the time of the

151

launch was blinded by some intense energy that lasted about a second, then it came back online, and the North Korean rocket was exploding in air. Judging by the launch plume signature, we rate this as a warbird, not a satellite launch."

"So, Tiye wasn't bluffing?" Jane asked.

"It doesn't look like it," Hopkins said.

"What will the North Koreans do now?" Jane asked.

"Difficult to say," Hopkins said. "They don't behave like rational folks, so they may just try again."

"Any sign of the Chinese or Russians doing anything?" Jane asked.

"No, but look to the Iranians," Andre said. "They will try and use this distraction with the North Koreans to pull off something in the Persian Gulf."

"General Hopkins, a call from NSA," an aide said. "I'll put it on the speakerphone for you."

"General, this is George. We've been picking up indications that the visitors are doing just what they said they would. They've apparently picked up two of the North Korean birds already, and they're going after the third. They also picked up the dead birds from earlier attempts," George reported. "That frigate-sized bird that the visitors sent, it sent out smaller vessels, and they dropped out of GEO to LEO, grabbed the first bird less than a minute after they popped the rocket, then they went back to GEO at rates we can only speculate about. These guys mean business, and they've got technologies that we can only dream of. Oh, one more thing, it looks like the visitors have sped up, expect them here way before their original ETA."

"Thanks, George, keep me posted," Hopkins said.

"So, it looks as if we were prudent to call off our launches," Jane commented.

"Well, they were warned," Andre said. "And they can't say they don't understand English; they managed to write some masterful letters in the past, all in English, plus the last message was sent in Korean as well."

"I suppose we should call a press conference," Jane said.

"Good afternoon," Jane said to the assembled White House Press Corps. "You will all have heard the latest message from our visitors. You may or may not have heard that the North Koreans attempted to launch a rocket, and it was destroyed less than five seconds into its flight. We had some launches of satellites planned, commercial and military, but decided to heed their warning and have put them on hold."

"Are we going to let this aggression against the human race go without a challenge?" VCN asked.

"We see it as an inevitable consequence of ignoring a warning," Jane replied. "The members of the United Nations met and agreed that we would consider that warning as serious. It would appear that the North Koreans decided otherwise; they chose poorly."

"Madame President, the message said that they were sending some tugs. Are they here?" CBS asked.

"We know that six new objects showed up in our skies, we know that they're all about as big as a navy frigate, and we now know that they have offensive capabilities," Jane replied. "So far, the only things that they have destroyed are a ballistic missile and satellites belonging to North Korea. We have no intention of provoking them into destroying anything of ours."

"How do we know it was a ballistic missile?" CNN asked.

"I am given to understand that the launch plume can be analysed and its characteristics tell us what the function of the rocket is," Jane replied.

"Who else may chance their luck?" ABC asked.

"We could not comment on that, but your guess is probably as good as ours at this time. There have been societies in the past who have taken advantage of the turmoil in the past to further their own agendas," Jane replied.

"What do you make of them saying that they were here with some other group back in 3500 or so BC?" the Christian Science Monitor asked.

"We are also curious about this Hemsut, our Egyptologists tell me that Hemsut were the Egyptian goddesses of fate and destiny, whether or not there is a connection, we don't know," Jane replied. "Are the Hemsut the Time Lords of *Dr Who* fame, or are they just an advanced culture, and have they given the job of monitoring and reporting to these people from Rahotep?"

"How were they able to move these so-called tugs into position so quickly? Were they there all the time and just unmasked?" VCN asked.

"JLP tells us that they tracked these tugs as coming from the mother vessel, so clearly whatever propulsion technology they have can be made small enough to fit into a frigate-sized vessel, probably much smaller because it would also appear that they have room for offensive weapons," Jane replied.

"The threat was that if anyone tried a launch, then their satellites would be swept up. Has that happened?" CNN asked.

"Our information is that less than a minute from the attempted launch, the first North Korean satellite was captured, followed shortly thereafter by the other two active satellites and their failures," Jane replied. "That action tells us that they know which satellite belongs to which country."

"How was the North Korean rocket destroyed?" CBC asked.

"We don't know," Jane admitted. "But one of our own satellites detected an intense energy beam about the time of the destruction."

"What will the North Koreans do now?" VCN asked.

"We don't know," Jane admitted. "They may try and invade South Korea, but something tells me that that would be ill-advised at this time."

"Is the ETA for the visitors still two weeks out?" CNN asked.

"JPL has just told us that the visitors have sped up and will be here in a matter of hours, not weeks, so perhaps they are less than happy with the North Korean launch and are moving closer to bring more force to bear; we don't know," Jane replied.

"Is there anything else you can tell us at this time?" ABC asked.

"No, we will call another press conference when we have more to relay," Jane said. "Thank you all for coming."

Jane went back to the cabinet room, and there was a message from Sharma; he wanted a Security Council meeting post haste. That was understandable; the visitors had just shown that they were prepared to attack, and the people of Earth needed to decide what to do. She asked Andre and Elizabeth to go with her, but before they left, General Hopkins came in with a message.

"The mad mullah tried his luck," he said. "He launched a barrage against Israel, our observation bird told us that the entire barrage was destroyed, the last within two seconds of lift off of the first, and they didn't stop there, there have been explosions all over Iran, all at military installations, and all the Iranian Revolutionary Guard boats in the Persian Gulf have been sunk, and their supposedly invulnerable underground nuclear facility has been taken out, and their satellites have been grabbed, the ships and the ground installations were taken out by some fighter looking ships, according to local reports."

"That's serious," Jane said. "I wonder if Ivan and Zhou are taking note, and I wonder if Kim has seen that and is rethinking her next move. General Hopkins, do we know how the Iranian rockets were destroyed?"

"No, Madame," Hopkins replied. "We surmise that it was again some kind of energy beam, but we're not sure. It does tell us that their systems for detection are really good, as is their aiming ability. To have eyes on boats at sea, and to know who they belong to, and to be able to just take them out, speaks of a degree of sophistication in surveillance and offensive capability. Their attack vessels dropped out of GEO at an incredible rate, took out all the Iranian stuff, then went back to their ship. I wonder if these attack vessels are drones that are run from the so-called tugs, would make sense."

"So, we shouldn't try our luck?" Jane asked.

"Definitely not," Hopkins agreed.

"I didn't think so," Jane said. "I wonder what will happen in the region after our visitors go home. Who will take advantage of Iran's weakness?"

"My guess is a land grab by the surrounding nations," Elizabeth said. "Look for all their neighbours to start nibbling away at the borders."

"So, Iran as a country may not survive?" Jane asked.

"It may, but as a smaller country," Elizabeth said.

"Well, we'll see what happens when the visitors go home, presuming, of course, that they do," Andre said. "My guess is that the Turkish and Armenian Kurds will make the first move and try and establish a Kurdish state. Then the Azerbaijanis will have a go as well, maybe even the Russians pushing south to gain access to the Persian Gulf."

We were attacked

The Security Council convened and invited representatives from North Korea and Iran to attend.

"We were attacked," the North Korean said. "We want immediate action from all members of the Security Council to take retaliatory measures against these imperialist aggressors."

"We were warned not to launch anything," Sharma pointed out.

"We didn't understand the language," the North Korean said.

"Your linguists showed a remarkable facility with the English language a few years ago when your previous leader wrote letters to one of our previous leaders, and the last message was also sent in your own language," Jane pointed out.

"We agree with our friend from the Democratic People's Republic," the Iranian representative said. "We were attacked, and we want this body to take action against the aggressors."

"And who were you launching missiles against?" Sharma asked.

"That was an accident," the Iranian protested.

"A whole salvo is launched, and you're trying to tell me that it was an accident?" Sharma said. "Our visitors made it quite clear that any overt act of aggression against them or our own neighbours would be met with action. We have just learned that trying to call their bluff is a pointless exercise. Perhaps, Mr Ambassador, you have not been communicating back to your government the nature of our discussions here and our agreement?"

"What do we do now?" Premier Zhou asked.

"We wait and see if they take any further action," Sharma suggested. "So far, the only ones of us who have suffered any action have been those of us who were foolish enough to ignore the warning."

"I for one am not opening hostilities against the visitors," Jane said. "I have no desire to place at risk any of our facilities or people."

"I think the visitors have sent us a message," Sharma said. "The first incident merely resulted in the destruction of the rocket that was launched and the loss of satellites that were not destroyed but captured and removed; the second led to a much broader response targeting all kinds of military installations and equipment. Does anyone really want to find out what a third incident will bring?"

"Not us," Tsar Ivan said.

"Nor us," Emile Gaston echoed.

"We're not doing anything," Tony Williams said.

"So, you're all going to let these imperialist aggressors attack us without penalty?" the North Korean asked.

"And what would you have us do?" Ivan asked.

"Launch simultaneous strikes against them," the North Korean said.

"Have you thought about where the visitor ships are parked?" Ivan asked. "They can cover the earth, and they detected your launch and destroyed it a second into the flight. With our Iranian friends, they destroyed not one but twelve rockets within seconds. We would be well served not to make anything that looks like an attack."

"You are a coward," the North Korean said.

"No, I'm merely being practical and recognising reality when I see it," Ivan said. "And, do not make the mistake of calling me a coward again; if you do, your life may be short."

"Gentlemen," Sharma said. "Gentlemen, we gain nothing with name-calling and threats. We know the visitors have increased their speed and will be here in hours. It will help to be able to have a direct dialogue with these beings. Meanwhile, I hope everyone recognises the futility of aggressive action against these beings."

"We want compensation from these infidels," the Iranian demanded.

"We can ask, but I think we'll get short shrift from them," Sharma said. "What were you thinking, launching a whole barrage?"

"That was an accident," the Iranian insisted.

"Maintain that fiction if you will," Sharma said. "But we as a world have to start acting as a world and put aside our adventurism, or we may all suffer some kind of consequence. Let us reconvene when the visitors are overhead and see if we can establish direct communication with them."

"Mr General-Secretary," an aide interrupted. "There is a message from the visitors."

"People of Earth, you will be aware that two of your societies did not heed our warnings about aggression towards us or their neighbours. We have taken what we deemed as a measured response against those two, the second greater than the first. A third action will result in a massive removal of all martial and military facilities and equipment belonging to the offending society. We had imagined that you were intelligent enough to understand simple language, perhaps that is not the case, so I will repeat myself, make no launches of rockets or missiles while we are here and make no aggressive moves against your neighbours either with rockets or missiles, or any other military equipment. We have the ability to track what you call tanks, artillery, infantry, aircraft, ships and submarines. Do not use anything against your neighbours; any such action will be met with immediate response from us. We are saddened that you have developed technologically but not societally, that you still solve disputes and questions with force of arms. We will shortly be positioned over your United Nations and look forward to a dialogue with your leaders."

"That's very direct, I note that this Tiye did not even bother to say who she is, or give us greetings of any kind, just a short sharp message that was probably heard by everyone on earth with a radio, television, smart phone or tablet, she did not sound happy if their language nuances are in any way like ours," Sharma said. "I think you should consult with your various governments, and I will contact you when the visitors are directly overhead."

"We demand that the nations that have the ability all launch nuclear strikes against these aggressors," North Korea said.

"I will not," Tsar Ivan said. "I will not risk my country for your ill-advised actions."

"I will not," Zhou echoed.

"But if we all launch together, then they will not have the ability to respond," North Korea said.

"I'm not willing to take that chance," Tsar Ivan said. "The visitors demonstrated some of their capability when they destroyed twelve missiles launched from Iran."

"Yes, but those were from one battery," North Korea objected. "If we launch from many points around the globe, we can confuse them."

"What would you have us do, target their main ship?" Emile asked.

"Yes, if we launched, say, twenty missiles at the same time from Siberia, the Pacific Ocean, the Atlantic Ocean, the United States mainland, then they surely could not track them all, and at least one would get through?" North Korea asked.

"And launch them where?" Zhou asked. "If we aim at a point on their current trajectory, all they have to do is slow down or speed up and our efforts will have failed, we would not be launching at a fixed target like a city or a moving target like an asteroid whose trajectory we can calculate, these visitors can change direction, change speed, do anything they like."

"We put some kind of homing device on the warheads," Iran suggested.

"Like a heat seeker?" Zhou asked.

"Yes," Iran said.

"Then the biggest hot object in the sky is the sun, so all the warheads with heat seekers will happily go off into the sun," Zhou said.

"Then radar seekers," Iran suggested.

"Then they spoof the signal and send the warheads, if they can be controlled, right back at us," Tsar Ivan said.

"We must launch a coordinated strike against them," North Korea insisted hotly.

"Is that a chance you wish to take, Madame President?" Sharma asked Jane.

"We have seen no action taken against us," she replied. "The Democratic Republic has not seen fit in the past to cooperate with us, yet now they are asking us to ally with them against the visitors, with possible dire consequences."

"We have the fate of mankind at stake here," North Korea said.

"No, I think we have the fate of the regime of your president at stake," Jane said.

"We cannot let this aggression go unanswered," Iran said.

"I rather think you were the aggressor," Emile said.

"That was an unfortunate accident," Iran repeated.

"Clearly, it was not seen as an accident," Tsar Ivan added. "Are you trying to tell us that you have no control over the launching of missiles from your country?"

"It was an overzealous officer," Iran argued. "We should not bear the consequences of the actions of one man."

"Then perhaps you need better control of your forces," Tsar Ivan said. "I said it before, and I repeat, I will not risk my country for you. If these aliens start making unprovoked attacks on us, we will try and respond, but we will not initiate action."

"But a pre-emptive strike is what is needed," Iran argued.

"Think about it, our friends from the Democratic Republic try and launch a missile, it is destroyed in about five seconds after liftoff, giving them time to retarget, the first stage of most ballistic missiles burn for about 60 seconds, so they have plenty of time to retarget their weapons and our missiles have not even left our atmosphere," Tsar Ivan pointed out.

"Lady, gentlemen, I think we should stand down our armies, at least until such time as the visitors make unprovoked attacks against us," Sharma said. "It would behove us all to pause any activities that may be seen as aggressive to the visitors or each other."

"What do you think?" Jane asked Nicole, Elizabeth and Andre when they were in the secure room of their legation to the UN.

"It sounds to me like she's pissed at us," Andre said. "I don't think she's bluffing when she says that the next incident is going to be costly."

"I suppose I'm not surprised that it was the North Koreans and the Iranians," Elizabeth said. "Neither one of them is rational by our lights. Kim wants to take over the rest of the Korean peninsula, and the mad mullah wants his brand of Islam to rule, and he probably wants Israel as a nation gone so he can control the holy sites in Jerusalem."

"You know, in some ways, I almost hope that Kim does do something stupid; if she did, then maybe all that arsenal facing over the DMZ would be gone," Jane said.

"Is she that stupid?" Andre asked.

"You never know with despots," Jane said. "They usually believe their own press and rarely listen to more rational voices, and they typically cull out anyone who doesn't agree with them."

"So, we've got Kim, Ahmadi, Zhou and Ivan, any of whom could go off the rails," Andre said.

"I see Zhou and Ivan as more pragmatic," Jane said. "They're not going to throw everything away, they'll wait until the visitors are gone before they make any moves. Kim is driven by the Kim doctrine of domination of the peninsula, and Ahmadi is a religious zealot, and with them, reason rarely has a voice. This Tiye shows an amazing grasp of the English language, next time she'll be sounding like a lawyer."

"I wonder what kind of learning programs they have?" Elizabeth said.

"I doubt we'll ever find out," Jane said. "Andre, I heard that most of the world's databases have been accessed. Are the visitors taking all our knowledge?"

"That would seem to be true," he confirmed. "None of our safeguards have stopped their entry, but as far as we can tell, they have not planted any bugs or spyware; they just looked at everything, and it's still going on."

"I'll bet Zhou and Ivan are panicking over that," Jane thought. "They like to mess with our systems; maybe these visitors can just access theirs with impunity. How long before they're overhead?"

"I'll check," Andrea said. He made a telephone call and listened, then nodded and hung up. "Five minutes or thereabouts," he said.

"So, essentially, they're here," Jane said. "Can the Haleakala telescope give us any images yet?"

"Hopkins said that they've got it in their sights and they're taking pictures by the ton," Andre replied. "They've also got pictures of those tugs; he'll courier us over a selection."

"We're at DefCon 1. Is there anything else we should be doing?" Jane asked. "Should we try and move weapons underground?"

"I'll bet Zhou and Ivan are doing that right now," Andre said. "They won't want to lose anything that would give them an edge when the visitors leave."

"This, Tiye said a couple of times, while we're here, does that mean she doesn't care what we do when they leave?" Elizabeth asked.

"Sounds like it," Andre said. "While we're here, play nicely. When we're gone, we can't control what you do."

"I think look for some actions when they leave," Jane said. "I wonder how long they'll be here?"

"General Hopkins for you, Madame," an aide said, bringing over a secure telephone.

"General?" Jane said.

"We've just got in some images of the underground complex that the Iranians had for enriching uranium and developing their nuclear weapons," he said. "It looks like they used some kind of seismic device because the entire complex has collapsed upon itself. I would guess that anyone or anything down there is now buried under hundreds of feet of rock, and rock that has been shattered and pancaked down; there'll be no rescue efforts for that and no way to re-dig that complex. Seismometers around the world picked up what looked like a swarm of earthquakes, all in that area, and it's not known for that level of seismic activity. This was no *Star Wars Death Star* with fire and explosions, just some kind of seismic shock that collapsed the underground facility on itself."

"So, does that mean that Cheyenne Mountain is not secure?" Jane asked.

"I would say not," Hopkins said. "At least not against the weapon they used against the Iranians. Oh, and it looks like they really went to town on the Iranians; they seem to have taken out all their air force and navy and most of their tanks and other armoured vehicles and all their missile systems, all within the space of five hours."

"That's a frightening thought," Jane said. "Remind me regularly not to do anything precipitous."

"I will, Madame President," Hopkins said.

"Anything new from North Korea?" Jane asked.

"They seem to be sitting back and waiting for something," Hopkins replied. "They have three missile subs at sea in the East China Sea, we're tracking them, and so far they haven't made any overt moves to launch."

"I wonder if our visitors have the capability to determine whose boat it is if they do launch?" Jane mused. "I wouldn't want Tiye to retaliate against us because the North Koreans do something dumb."

"I think if they launch, we tell the world, and by extension the visitors, that it's the North Koreans," Hopkins said.

"If I were Tiye, why would I believe us? How would I know that I'm not using them to settle a private vendetta between us and the Kims?" Jane asked.

"I suppose we don't, a lot would depend on their ability to track the boats and work out where they put out to sea from," Hopkins said.

"How far back from the North Korean boats can ours stay back and still track?" Jane asked.

"I'll check with the Navy guys," Hopkins said. "I see your point. If they launch and Tiye responds, will we get caught in the crossfire?"

"I don't want to be writing a whole lot of letters to families of sailors caught in a situation they could have avoided," Jane said.

"Quite, Madame President," Hopkins said. "I will attend to it."

* * * * *

"These people of Earth are stupid," Nefertiti said.

"Not all, I think," Tiye said. "Just these two societies for now, and then I think the leaders of those societies, not the society as a whole."

"Will anyone else try something foolish?" Penebui asked.

"That remains to be seen," Tiye said. "I think I was fairly direct with my last message, but in case, be prepared to strike. Isis, can you isolate what we would regard as weapon systems?"

"That is done," Isis responded. "There are many levels of systems, some of which appear, even now, to be directed at their own people."

"This has to be one of the most aggressive societies we have seen," Tiye bemoaned.

"Maybe," Penebui said. "But I don't think that even these people come close to those of Centauri Minor. They seemed to do nothing but fight."

"I understand that the last team to survey them had to fight off an attempt to capture the Osiris ship," Tiye said. "Osiris destroyed the attackers, then wreaked terrible vengeance on the society that had sent them. I don't want to have to do that."

"It may be that the leaders of the societies that tried to launch weapons feel threatened," Penebui said. "If they feel threatened, they may lash out with aggression because they don't know what else to do."

"I think that the next contact with them should be longer," Tiye thought. "And we should give them the opportunity to ask questions. That may ease some of the fears that they have."

"It may," Henuttawy said. "But while they are talking, I will be watching; they may try a coordinated strike against us from many parts of their planet."

"I wonder if their answer to everything is to assume that it's hostile and to attack?" Tiye pondered. "Perhaps that tells us something about the way they have developed. Those satellites that we collected, have the tugs brought them back yet?"

"Yes," Henuttawy confirmed. "Serket and Aya just delivered them, and they went back to their stations. Abar is now supervising the disassembly of those satellites and will tell us what she learns."

"What is the most difficult threat to us to anticipate?" Tiye asked.

"They have submarine vessels that can launch missiles," Henuttawy replied. "We can track them, but as long as they are under a lot of water, our light, energy beam and seismic weapons do not work that well. We would have to send down a tracking craft to destroy them with the gravity beam if they launched anything."

"Isis, can you track these submarines?" Tiye asked.

"They all have a magnetic and audio signature," Isis responded. "So, yes, I can track them all. In quite a few cases, we have one following another from different societies."

"Keep tracking them," Tiye said. "Now I have to think about how I'm going to word the report."

"Just state that we told them not to show aggression while we were here and report that two societies did and that you took a measured response against the martial forces of those societies," Penebui suggested.

"I don't want to have to go to the extremes that Osiris did," Tiye said. "But if we're attacked, then we'll do what we have to."

"We are in a stationary orbit above the site of their United Nations," Isis intoned.

"Thank you, Isis. Now, do we wait for them to contact us, or do we make the contact?" Tiye mused. "I think we'll let them send us a frequency on which we can communicate. So, what kind of questions will they ask?"

"I think the first will be why are we here and what do we want," Semat suggested. "It might be useful to give them a history lesson."

"They might not like that," Tiye laughed. "Particularly all the religious leaders. I've been reading old reports about them and religion, and it really does drive many of them. It started logically enough as a means to explain what they did not understand, but the lengths that many of them went to, to make sure that their version of things was the dominant one, are amazing. It's also interesting to see how much time and effort they have spent over the years building temples to their various gods."

"I wonder if they have any scholars who would be interested in how we developed?" Penebui said.

"There must be some," Tiye thought. "But, I'm sure that their first thought will be how do they get our secrets for travel and our weapons systems."

"What is it about certain societies that all they think about is weapons?" Semat pondered.

"Probably because they have designs upon their neighbours," Tiye said. "Look to our own frontier fringes, there are still societies out there who would rather wage war than do almost anything else."

"I have some scans of transportation systems," Semat said. "I did the air system before and have made a few changes. Then I did water, and we can see here the major routes that are used, including these two points where it looks as if they have put an artificial waterway across these narrow pieces of land. Some societies have extensive networks of roads, and there are many vehicles on them. Again, here is a map showing the greatest concentrations. The final system uses fixed tracks on the ground with what they call trains running in them. Most of this is new since Report #10. Some of the roads are still there from the last time, but they have changed in surface and size, and now carry much more traffic. Since Report #10, there is a whole new lexicon of words that have been invented to describe the technologies they now use."

"Clearly, the interval between visits should be significantly decreased," Tiye thought. "If we leave it another of their 500 years, we might meet them in the wormhole. I should recommend something to the Hemsut, but what?"

"Two or three of their years," Semat suggested. "That way, they can't make too much progress without our knowledge."

"I agree with Semat," Ramses said. "Their technology is developing at a pace that far exceeds their societal development, so there will be problems between them, and at some point, they may even stumble upon the means to use wormholes."

"I think the Hemsut will have some decisions to make," Tiye said. "When we get back, I will submit my report and see what they do."

"Tiye, this is Aya. The society that calls itself the Democratic People's Republic of Korea launched an attack against its neighbour. I am currently engaged in destroying their martial capabilities; they had much, and I think it would be prudent to send Henutsen to assist," Aya reported.

"It will be done," Tiye said. "Serket, Henutsen, proceed to assist Aya."

"I wonder if we'll see any other attacks," Horus said. "None of the others seems inclined to make any moves at the moment."

"Yes, but will they after we have gone?" Tiye asked.

"Based on their stage of development, I would say that is a high probability," Horus replied.

"I would agree with that," Ramses added.

"I wonder if we should leave a sentinel," Tiye said. "Perhaps we'll also leave that decision to the Hemsut. Isis, is there any evidence of other incursions?"

"None detected, except some minor ones in the areas they identify as Africa and Arabia," Isis replied. "I have relayed that information to Amhose, and she is dealing with them now."

"Good," Tiye said. "I will not tolerate warfare while we are here, if for no other reason than we may be caught up in it. Now, to other matters, we need an assessment of the quality of the air, water and land. Send down probes to get samples in the same locations that were sampled in Report #10, and we will also need DNA samples of as many people as you can get and of species that are closely related."

"I will attend to that," Ramses said.

* * * * *

"Jesus Christ," General Hopkins said as he watched the images being streamed in from one of their surveillance satellites. "The visitors just wiped out the entire North Korean army, all the artillery pieces aimed at Seoul and South Korea, aircraft, tanks, the works, all in about four hours, then they took out everything that looked like a military installation, including their rocket and nuclear programs and their shipyards in another four hours. It looks like they used three of their frigate-sized vessels and related sub-vessels and went to town on the North Koreans, they dopped out of GEO to about 100,000 feet, then went back to their stations."

"What about their missile systems and nuclear weapons facilities?" Jane asked.

"All gone," he said. "Anything and everything that is military in nature has gone."

"And their submarines?" she asked.

"We're waiting for our boats to call in," he replied. "But their surface vessels have all gone, bottom of the ocean now."

"The visitors' capabilities would appear to be rather more than we could counter," she commented.

"I think, Madame, that that is rather an understatement," he said.

"I'm sure the network who were whining about their satellite launch will be happy that we told them to wait," she said.

"Privately, but publicly, they'll be wingeing about freedom to act," he said. "I'll bet Ivan and Zhou are thanking their lucky stars that they didn't do something rash."

"I'm sure they are," she said. "What happens to the Kim regime now?"

"Well, one thing's for sure, South Korea won't invade, at least not until the visitors have gone. After that, it's anyone's guess. If they wanted to, there's not much Kim could do about it," he said.

"Is her regime doomed?" Jane asked.

"Good question," Romero said. "The Kim family has shown resilience, and she is regarded as a demi-god in North Korea, so it could well unite the population to rebuild the military, rather like Germany did in the 1930s."

"So, for us mere mortals on earth, perhaps not the best thing our visitors could have done?" Jane asked.

"Perhaps, perhaps not," Nicole said. "There is a growing faction in North Korea that has had it with all the spending on weapons and would rather come to terms with the South. Same thing happened in Germany in 1990. I see civil war before too long."

"I'll bet the South is dishing out the propaganda right now, encouraging the masses to rise up against the tyrant," Elizabeth added.

"Did our visitors go after the population at large?" Jane asked.

"Doesn't look like it," Madison replied. "It looks like they just went after anything that looked vaguely military in nature, including weapons and ammunition factories. They must have some pretty decent surveillance imaging and analysis to pick them out from other factories."

"Is Iran next?" Jane asked.

"Good chance that it is," Nicole said. "There's been a movement for quite some years now to counter the ultra-religious, and this may be the impetus to make them rise up and overthrow the current regime. Most of the army is gone, so the means to suppress the masses are gone, plus the arrival of the visitors has rather shaken all the major monotheistic doctrines and dogmas, so people are now beginning to question everything."

"I'll bet Ivan and Zhou are strengthening their holds on their militaries in case someone does something really dumb and the visitors take them out," Hopkins said. "If Ivan wants the old Stans, then he needs his army, and if Zhou wants the Philippines and Vietnam to more fully control the South China Sea, he can't afford to lose his navy."

"So we just sit tight for now and wait," Jane said. "Will the Philippines ask us for help if Zhou starts to make moves?"

"Them and the Vietnamese," Hopkins replied. "I wonder how the visitors will react if we start moving fleets around."

"Probably tell us to knock it off," Nicole said. "Hard to know just what they see as aggression. I'm sure Sharma will want to call another meeting soon to discuss all this. If the visitor craft is parked over us, maybe it's time to try direct conversation and not just an exchange of notes."

"Exchange of notes, isn't that diplospeak for nastygrams?" Elizabeth asked.

"More or less," Nicole confirmed.

"Any ideas on what our visitors used to wipe out the North Koreans?" Jane asked.

"Best we can tell, some kind of directed energy weapon and then some kind of seismic weapon to take care of bunkers and underground installations," Hopkins replied. "Whatever they used, it was damned effective and took them no time at all to wipe out the so-called invincible army."

"Message for you, Sir," an aide said, placing a sheet in front of the general.

"That's interesting," he said. "The North Korean submarines are all at the bottom of the ocean. Our boats reported sounds like hulls being crushed, and then they tracked them all the way down to the deeps. There'll be nothing to pull up from them. Our boats say they saw some kind of craft hover over where they figured the North Koreans were, then they heard the hulls being crushed. I'm glad we had them hang back a bit. Normally, our drivers are pretty aggressive and will be up on the tail of the boat they're shadowing."

"One of these craft or more?" Jane asked.

"One per by the sound of it, all taken out at the same time," Hopkins replied.

"For a research vessel, they seem to be well equipped with offensive as well as defensive capabilities," Jane commented. "Have they gone after population centres?"

"Only those that are military, so barracks and training camps, cities in and of themselves, regular cities that are just folks have been left alone," Romero replied.

"Centres of government?" she asked.

"Not yet," Hopkins said. "But, if I were Kim and Ahmadi, I'd be hiding out somewhere well away from anything that looks remotely like a military installation."

"I'll bet the Israelis are delighted that Iran is no longer a real threat. What about their proxies?" she asked.

"In the report that details the attack on the North Korean subs, there is also mention of some activity in Chad and Yemen, from what we can gather, the visitors went after some Boko Haram fanatics and some Houthis, from what little we can gather from chatter, they've been wiped out as well, there're also reports that military units on both sides of the never-ending war in Sudan have been taken out," Hopkins replied.

"So, they can find and sort out small groups in Land Cruisers as well as targeting tanks," Jane said. "Can't say I'm overwhelmed with grief about the Boko Haram guys and the Houthis, pain in the neck. What about Hezbollah?"

"They've gone to ground," Hopkins replied. "They'll probably end up rearming Iran; they've still got stockpiles in Lebanon, even after the Israeli strikes."

"They don't mess about, do they?" Jane commented. "No halt, you're under arrest, no warnings, just zap you're gone."

"Madame President, the Secretary-General has called a meeting in two hours," an aide said.

"Well, we'd better go and listen to the pleas of the Koreans and the Iranians to put our heads on the block as well," Jane said. "Fat chance, we're staying well away from anything offensive, unless they start on our military installations or cities. They don't have one of those birds over us?"

"No, but it looks like they could be over us in minutes," Hopkins said.

"So, no time to get complacent."

"Thank you for coming," Sharma said when Jane and her entourage arrived. "We are waiting for Tsar Ivan and will commence as soon as he arrives.

"Do we respond in any way to the latest actions by our visitors?" Zhou asked.

"If you mean military action, I think that would be unwise, judging by what just occurred in the Democratic People's Republic of Korea," Sharma replied. "I presume you have some images of the results?"

"We have," Zhou confirmed. "It is hard to imagine what kind of weapon systems they have that can do all that in such a short time."

"It is," Ivan confirmed as he joined them. "How do we reply to the ambassador from the People's Republic if he demands that we attack the aliens?"

"I think dialogue at this time would be more productive than a descent into all-out warfare, which, if we do, I sense we could come off as the biggest loser," Sharma said. "If we attack this vessel, how soon before more arrive and wreak havoc on our planet. The makers of popular movies tend to portray us as winning out over invaders, but would that happen in reality?"

"Probably not," Jane said. "Has anyone seen any action against their country?"

"The only events we've seen have been against the Islamic Republic of Iran and the Democratic People's Republic of Korea and the minor events in Chad and Yemen," Ivan replied. "We have had nothing aimed at us."

"Nor have we," Zhou echoed. "We consider the actions of Kim ill-advised."

"We will call in the rest of the Security Council," Sharma said. They convened, and consensus was reached that dialogue was preferable to war. When the ambassadors of Iran and North Korea joined them, the demands were predictable: attack, attack.

"Surely you have seen the futility of that?" Ivan asked. "You have lost most, if not all, of your military capabilities; we have no desire to lose ours."

"Mr Ambassador, Mr Ambassador, now is the time for dialogue, we will try and talk to these visitors and come to a rapprochement so that more loss of life is avoided," Sharma said.

"But, there must be some way we can retaliate against the imperialist aggressors," the ambassador from North Korea complained.

"Not that we can see that would leave us undamaged," Zhou said. "What was Supreme Leader Kim thinking when she attacked your neighbours to the south?"

"We have every right to take actions against the lackeys of the United States," the ambassador stated.

"And what did that get you, a loss of your army, a million dead and destruction of just about all, if indeed not all, of your military facilities and installations," Sharma pointed out. "I think it is time for the General Assembly to convene and for us to try a direct dialogue with the visitors."

The General Assembly were split between those who were more hawkish and wanted some kind of attack against the visitors and those who were privately delighted that the militaries of Iran and North Korea had been so drastically impacted. The hawks were in the minority, so when a motion was put forth to take offensive action, it was soundly defeated.

"I think it is time for us to have a direct conversation with these visitors," Sharma said. "We have sent a signal to them and await their reply."

"Mr Secretary-General," a voice said and then an image came on all the various video screens around the Assembly Hall.

"Captain Tiye," he replied. "We regret the actions of two of our member states."

"We took such action as we said we would; you were warned," Tiye replied. *"It is not our intention to wage war against you, but we will not tolerate attacks on us or attacks on neighbouring societies."*

"Even so, it seems to us a little extreme," he commented.

"Failing to heed warning brings consequences, the first action was simply to destroy the weapon that was launched and to remove that society's satellites, the second action was in keeping with our warnings and the third action was a result of a very deliberate ignoring of our warnings, the loss of life and facilities may be laid at the door of the leader of that society," she replied.

"We will repeat that action on any other society that fails to heed our warnings; we will not tolerate attacks on us or on neighbouring societies. As a further caution, we have not yet used all the capabilities that we have, but if there is another incident, the offending society will regret their action."

"Most of those killed may have had no choice in the matter," he said.

"People in a society always have a choice; they can accept their leaders or determine that different leaders may be better for them," she said.

"You told us before that your society has been here before," Sharma said, moving on to safer ground.

"That is correct," Tiye confirmed. *"This is the eleventh visit we, as an agency, have made on behalf of the Hemsut. It is our mission to review and report on the state of development of the people of this planet."*

"Who are the Hemsut?" he asked.

"They are the ones who created us, and you," she replied. *"They visited Earth about 200,000 of your years ago and noted the stage of development of primates and brought in individuals who could aid in that development. They then followed the development and 5,100 of your years ago tasked us*

to monitor and report. We were here in the years 3065, 2562, 2034, 1534, 1012 and 510 before the Common Era and the years 33, 613, 1065 and 1599 in the Common Era. We report on the development of societies. We have done this with several planets that the Hemsut took an interest in and aided in the development of primates on those planets."

"So, we are not alone in the universe?" he asked.

"Certainly not in our galaxy," she confirmed. "We know of planets in other galaxies that would be similar to this, but we of Isis have not been to any."

"Have others in your agency been to other galaxies?" he asked.

"They have," she confirmed.

"How do you travel?" he asked.

"We make use of natural phenomena, as I said before, details of which we are unprepared to share with you at your current state of development," she replied. "At such time as you have developed sufficiently not to try and resolve all your differences with aggression and warfare, then we may consider it."

"How many of you are there?" he asked.

"Do you mean on our planet or Isis?" she responded.

"On your home planet," he specified.

"One billion in your counting," she replied.

"How similar is it to Earth?" he asked.

"Horus is slightly larger than Earth and our gravity is a little greater, the atmosphere is very similar, yours is easily breathable for us, three-quarters of the surface is water, the rest is divided into three of what you would call continents, the greatest landmass has mountains that reach 10,200 metres and the deepest bodies of water reach down to 12,000 metres," she replied. "The climate is similar to yours with polar icecaps, temperate zones and equatorial rainforests; we have no significant deserts."

"And the people?" he asked.

"Physiologically, we originated from the same roots, so we have the same anatomy, we have adapted to our planet and its slightly higher gravity, we lack the skin pigmentation differences that you display, but that is a result of years of interbreeding," she replied.

"And your society, how is it governed?" he asked.

"We have a group of Elders who make the important decisions, but we rarely call upon them to make changes in our societal structure," she replied. "We manage ourselves with a code of behaviour."

"What happens if someone fails to follow that code?" he asked.

"That rarely happens, but if it does, the Elders decide what should be done," she replied.

"Would you come here to address us directly?" he asked.

"There are issues there," she said. *"We may bring pathogens with us that you have not experienced before and would have no defence against. Similarly, you may have pathogens that are harmful to us; each of our planets has bred its own set of bacteria and viruses."*

"Is there a way to manage containment such that each of us is protected?" he asked.

"We have a mechanism," she replied. *"I will consider it."*

"To return to the results of ignoring your warnings, should we be concerned about additional action?" he asked.

"If there are no further actions on the part of your various societies, there will be no further action on our part. I do note, however, that there are small groups of people in your Africa that still are taking action against their neighbours; they will be dealt with," she replied. *"I would also caution against large-scale movements of military forces, be it on land, on sea or in the air; these may be perceived by us as a prelude to invasion of a neighbour, and we may take action to eliminate those forces."*

"Surely a society has the right to move its forces around as it chooses?" he asked.

"You have not shown yourselves to be a set of societies who heed warnings or that we believe may be trusted not to act aggressively, so we are not concerned with what you perceive as your rights, as far as we are concerned, you abrogated those rights when two of your societies tried to attack another," she replied. *"Do not amass forces near your neighbours, that will be regarded as a hostile act, and we will eliminate those forces. Do not try and attack us; if you do, we will respond, and it will not go well for you."*

"It is unfair to assume that all our nations will behave in the same way as two of them have," he protested.

"Then why do you have this body, the United Nations?" she asked. *"If member nations can act without regard to the rest, it clearly is far from united."*

"Our United Nations is our best attempt to limit wars between nations," he explained.

"That may be your view, but in our view, you are failing, so our report to the Hemsut will so indicate, and they may choose to redirect your development as they have on other planets," she said.

"What is meant by redirect?" he asked.

"The societies on those planets were taken back to an earlier stage of development without the technologies they had developed and were given an opportunity to rethink how they would redevelop themselves," she explained. *"On three planets that worked, on a fourth, they seemed unable to grow beyond physical violence, so the experiment was deemed a failure, and humans were removed from that planet. Do not make the mistake of thinking that this is your planet to do what you will with, you are here because the Hemsut put you here and they can remove you as they choose. You have wrecked your environment; you have driven mammal, avian, reptile, insect and plant species to extinction, so you could hardly be regarded as good stewards of this planet."*

"Do you have technologies that may help us repair some of the damage?" he asked.

"We do and we will consider sharing them with you, particularly to remove materials derived from oils," she replied. *"Now, if you will forgive me, we are like you; we do need nourishment and sleep to function well."*

"She's gone," Sharma commented when the screens went blank. "I think there was much there that you will all need to discuss with your respective governments. Perhaps we could reconvene the day after tomorrow to review."

"Well, any views?" Jane asked her team when they returned to the secure room they had in New York.

"She shows a remarkable command of the English language," Nicole said. "Her word use is varied and appropriate, her vocabulary is extensive, if they have learning programs to teach their people language, we'd love to get our hands on them."

"And her comments about military action?" Jane asked.

"We were warned, and Kim and Ahmadi chose to ignore those warnings and probably got a lot more than they had bargained for," Romero said.

"Is this a presage to an invasion, and this crew is just testing offensive capabilities that we have?" Jane asked.

"That's always a possibility," Nicole admitted. "If it is, we're screwed. Sorry about the language."

"No, I was about to say if it is, we're fucked," Jane said. "When we look at what they did to North Korea with only one mothership and six smaller ships, God only knows what a fleet would do; the whole of Earth's militaries would be gone in under a day."

"What if that's what they want?" Elizabeth surmised. "Then they have a submissive population, at least for a while. It does seem to me that the more dispersed our forces are, the better; larger concentrations are easier to spot and target."

"I would have said that the North Korean border installations were fairly widely dispersed," Jane said.

"True, but they're all on the DMZ and easy to spot from the air," Romero said. "The other installations they have all look like military facilities, fences, the works, so again, easy to spot. If we want to keep anything, we need to disperse really widely, tanks in barns on farms, fighters in hangars on little local fields, National Guard reinforced with regular troops billeted in neighbourhoods."

"How do we manage command and control if we do that?" Jane asked.

"We probably couldn't rely on satellites, cell phones or even radios, so we'd have to devise a more primitive, but still effective system," Romero said.

"We need to convene the cabinet and decide what our next actions should be," Jane said. "Even if we disperse ground forces and the Air Force, we can't move our ballistic missile silos, not quickly anyway, so we're stuck with that."

"True, but with what we saw in North Korea, they may not be worth launching at the visitors," Nicole said.

"What about her other warnings about moving forces?" Jane asked.

"I think it would be prudent to not move fleets into the South China Sea," Madison said. "But they can hardly quibble with dispersing forces unless, of course, they don't want us to amass forces that may be able to deal with a ground invasion of theirs."

"What about being taken back to the Stone Age if we don't mend our ways?" Jane asked.

"Wasn't that the threat in *The Day the Earth Stood Still*, both the Michael Rennie and Keanu Reeves versions?" Elizabeth asked.

"It's what started anyway with the nanobots in the Reeves version," Romero replied. "There had to be a Hollywood ending, so the Reeves character was convinced by the girl and the old guy that we're nice guys at heart, and the destruction stopped, except for the electronics, taking us back to the late 19th century, early 20th."

"I wonder if this Hemsut could actually do that," Jane mused.

"According to Captain Tiye, can and have, but we only have her word for that; maybe it's just a bluff," Nicole said.

"Is it a bluff we want to call?" Jane asked.

"I'd wait a while and see," Romero advised.

"How much of the interchange between our visitors and the UN could be seen by anyone?" Jane asked.

"All of it," Romero replied. "We could randomly check, but it seems that the visitors are not letting us have any secrets from the people."

"I heard from contacts at the UN that the simultaneous translations were broadcast as well, by the visitors, not the UN," Nicole added.

"Great, so now we're going to have to hold a press conference and answer questions," Jane bemoaned. "Let's get that set up and done."

"Ladies and gentlemen," Jane started as she faced the multitude of television cameras, microphones and reporters. "I presume you have all seen the interchange between the Visitors and the General-Secretary of the UN. I have little to add to that as we are digesting what it means and may mean to us. I find it interesting that our Visitors have broadcast all their communications with us so that the world may hear; they also broadcast all the simultaneous translations made at the UN. Whether this is a standard procedure for them or a subtle way of letting us know that nothing should be kept secret from the people, I don't know."

"How are we going to respond to this act of aggression by the aliens?" VCN asked.

"The General Assembly has taken a vote, and the consensus is that the Democratic Republic of Korea and the Islamic Republic of Iran brought it upon themselves by failing to heed the warnings of our visitors," Jane replied.

"Doesn't this action render North Korea vulnerable to the South?" CNN asked.

"I rather think that the South will refrain from any overt action while the Visitors are above us," Jane replied.

"But, after they've gone?" ABC asked.

"We could not speculate on actions South Korea may take in the future, the people of the North may or may not welcome the South, we don't know," Jane replied.

"Did the aliens really take out all the North Korean military installations in a matter of hours?" CNN asked.

"Our surveillance assets would indicate so," Jane admitted. "Where there were artillery emplacements and revetments, there are mere smouldering remains, as far as we can determine. The destruction was complete, the same is true for their navy, both surface and subsurface and their missile installations, air force bases and nuclear weapon programs."

"How many people died?" NBC asked.

"We have no way of accurately telling that," Jane replied. "We may create estimates, but we will need better intelligence to get better numbers."

"Doesn't the loss of life upset you?" the Christian Science Monitor asked.

"It is regrettable," Jane said. "But, it all comes down to the decisions that leaders make. In this case, it would appear that President Kim chose poorly, to paraphrase a quote from the old movie *Arrival*, in war there are no winners, only widows, and it seems to us that the decisions made by President Kim have left many widows."

"So, we have no plans to launch an offensive strike against these aliens?" VCN asked.

"We see that as ill-advised," Jane replied. "We have no weapons that could reach them before they either destroyed them or merely moved out of the way."

"So, we're sitting ducks?" VCN asked.

"In the sense that we have no apparent means to attack with impunity, then yes, but as you heard from the interchange between the Visitors and Secretary Sharma, they have no intentions of striking at us unless we violate their proscriptions. That may, of course, be a ruse to make us complacent, which is why we are maintaining a high state of readiness."

"So, what do we do now as a people?" CBS asked.

"Stay vigilant," Jane replied. "Make sure you all have at least two weeks of supplies if you can. So far, we have had no reports of any Visitors landing, but if anyone sees anything unusual, contact your local authorities, and they will let us know. That does not mean telling us that your neighbour of twenty years is behaving oddly, I am thinking more of any observed landings."

"Do we know if they will land?" CBS asked.

"They have the same concerns we do, how to deal with pathogens that are alien to both of us, so that remains to be seen," Jane replied.

"Do we have any theories about this Hemsut group?" CNN asked.

"We can all speculate about who or what is Hemsut, but it would appear to be some form of intelligence that has been around for millennia and is not above playing God, as it were," Jane replied.

"So, is Hemsut actually God?" the Christian Science Monitor asked.

"Your guess is as good as mine at the moment," Jane replied. "I would hesitate to make any statements about that."

"Have you any further information about what they look like?" ABC asked.

"As far as we can tell, we are looking at them as they are, but as we well know, AI constructs can look very real, so we cannot state categorically that we are not looking at a giant ant or some other species that would look very alien to us," Jane replied.

"What are the next steps?" CNN asked.

"We maintain our vigilance, we work with the UN to continue the dialogue with the Visitors, we would like to know more about them, where they come from, what they want, how long they plan to stay and if there is any technology they would be prepared to share with us," Jane replied.

"Can we trust them?" VCN asked.

"That is the question, isn't it?" Jane said. "Trust is built over time with understanding, and we have a long way to go yet. To date, their only major aggressive actions have been taken in response to poor decisions made by the North Koreans and the Iranians, so do we take them at their word that there will be no more unless we do something? The corollary to that is, should they trust us? We humans on this planet have a history of warfare, of abrogation of treaties and agreements. Can we be trusted not to kill the first visitor who sets foot on the planet?"

"So, you're saying we're untrustworthy?" VCN asked.

"Read your history books and ask yourself that same question," Jane suggested.

"What technologies would we like from them?" CBS asked.

"I think an understanding of how they travel would be high on the list, do they have fusion technology which would solve our energy issues, can they help us rid the ocean and the land of plastics down to the microplastic level that we have all ingested with our food, they are many items that I'm sure scientists and engineers could list," Jane replied.

"This Tiye seems to have a facility with English. Does this suggest that they've actually been here undetected for years, or do they have really good learning abilities and programs?" the Christian Science Monitor asked.

"We have wondered and speculated about that," Jane admitted. "The simple answer is that we don't know, perhaps they have been among us for years, perhaps they have a facility for languages, perhaps they have subliminal learning programs, we don't know."

"There seems to be a lot we don't know," VCN complained.

"There is," Jane agreed. "We have encountered someone or something from outside our solar system, and we're having to come to terms with the reality that we are not alone and that there are others out there who are far advanced when it comes to technologies. There will be a lot we don't know because, for us, most of this was theoretical until now. We have yet to physically meet our visitors, and we may not unless they have a system for protecting them and us from pathogens alien to us both. There will be another briefing when we have more to share."

Do we trust them?

"So, do we trust these people?" Tiye asked of her crew.

"Only so far," Horus said. "I have been examining data that Isis has obtained from their storage systems, and their history is rife with wars, mayhem conducted against their own people, agreements that were discarded when advantage could be gained and a general attitude of belligerence that pervades their societies."

"There has been much communication about launching atomic weapons against us," Isis intoned. "My analysis of their signals shows that all those who possess such weapons have considered using them against us. I have isolated those places where such weapons could be launched against us, but they also have them on sub-surface vessels, which are more difficult to track."

"Can we detect a launch from the heat signatures?" Tiye asked.

"Easily," Isis confirmed. "I have deployed sensors to cover the surface and will note anything launched."

"If there are any, destroy them," Tiye instructed.

"It will be done as we did the previous ones," Isis confirmed.

"Does this United Nations truly speak for all the societies on this planet?" Hermes asked.

"I find that difficult to confirm," Tiye said. "I sense that each is trying to gain advantage over the other, and I would judge by the way they amassed forces that at least two have designs on their neighbours. I think they are pragmatic enough that as long as we are here, they will make no overt moves, but my sense is that when we leave, they will make their moves."

"So, do we leave a sentinel?" Horus asked.

"If we did, what area of the surface should it cover?" Tiye asked.

"Perhaps eight," Hermes suggested. "Placed in stationary orbits so that the whole surface could be monitored."

"From a signal from a sentinel until we arrived, how long, Isis?" Tiye asked.

"Twenty auns," Isis responded.

"Long enough for some of these societies to do serious harm to another." Tiye mused. "It is apparent that we should not have waited so long between visits."

"Isis, have you managed to upload all that is available from their systems?" Tiye asked.

"It is done," Isis intoned. "My analysis shows much to be encrypted, but I have resolved their encryption, and it is all available to you. It is a large amount of information, so I have sorted it into communications, current population details, societal development history, weather history, research into basic phenomena, military plans and strategies and profiles of the leaders of the various societies, and miscellaneous."

"Of those profiles, who are the most ambitious?" Tiye asked.

"I will list them and indicate where on the planet they are situated," Isis said. The leaders were then listed, and as each country was identified, the relevant location was highlighted on an image of the planet.

"So, we've got five who have great ambitions, another 20 who would take advantage of any opportunity that would present itself, and a further 43 who would be happy to see neighbours, adversaries and competitors discomforted," Tiye said. "What a place, I wonder if they will ever become a more unified society."

"The Hemsut probably thought that about us 6,000 renpet ago," Horus commented.

"That is true," Tiye agreed ruefully. "Fortunately, we were intelligent enough to recognise that constant warfare led to arms developments, but little in the way of otherwise benefiting the people."

"I wonder if it is a flaw in the genetic make-up of the humanoid species that they are that aggression seems to come before judgment," Isis pondered. "In the general animal kingdom, the basic responses are flight or fight, but humans seem conditioned to fight more than flee. Perhaps that is something the Hemsut should re-examine and see where they went wrong."

"Do we have results yet from the air and water quality probes we sent?" Tiye asked.

"We do," Isis confirmed. "I have compared the results with the last five reports, and there is a significant degradation of the quality of the water and the air, and there is significant pollution of the land, much caused by the breakdown of products of carbon and hydrogen that the people here call plastics. These plastics, in minute form, are universally present and represent a significant danger to the humanoid and non-humanoid species on this planet. I have also analysed the records and data that are available on tree coverage, land use and species loss. Since our last visit, land use has changed, forests are now less than they were by 28%, wild grasslands have been converted to direct human use for crops and animals and are now 65% less than they were. Species have become extinct, and the data I have recovered indicates that the greatest loss of species that they have recorded is in the mollusc family, with 312 gone, then follows plants with 220, birds 185, fish 130, mammals 109, insects 63, amphibians 41, reptiles 36 and crustaceans 15. There has also been a significant growth in human population since we were last here, from about 460,000,000 to 9,000,000,000, increasing the pressure on the other species of the planet, driven by the need for the resources required to sustain that many people."

"Not a pretty picture," Tiye said. "Any thoughts, Horus?"

"It is the attitude of these humans that the planet is there for them to exploit, and, from reports we have gathered and analysed, it would appear that they have little regard for the other species on the planet," he replied. "Reports we have analysed indicate that the rate of extinction is increasing and many more species are close to, if not on the brink of extinction, as Isis noted, driven by the need for resources and the pressure on other species through habitat loss."

"So, not good husbands of the planet," Tiye mused. "Any DNA results yet?"

"We have the human species here fully mapped and all the closely related animal species," Isis reported.

Tiye sat and brought her report up to date, detailing all that had occurred and her actions. Her destruction of the two militaries was quite in keeping with past practice and was expected if one society threatened another while they were there. She thought about the changes that had occurred since Report #10 and was not surprised by the acceleration of technological development. Once basic physics was better understood, then the only limiting factor was imagination and resources. Fortunately for her, the people of Earth had yet to master travel in space; they were still tied to chemical launch systems that had to overcome the gravity of their planet, which severely limited what they could do. The concerning item was the rate of change in the natural environment. There was always change, but absent a major event, change to the natural environment tended to be slow and measured. The intervention of the people of Earth was accelerating the rate of change to a concerning level. She decided she would send Penebui back to report to Bastet and request an Elder, and decided that it might be prudent to let the people of Earth know that she planned to send a shuttle as part of their routine for reporting and not a messenger calling up the rest of an invasion fleet.

"Penebui, I think you should go back in all haste and brief the Elders. Bastet instructed me that should Geb be well past where we thought they would be, to inform her, and she will send an Elder," Tiye instructed.

"I will go and await them," Penebui said.

"Nefertiti, we need to send another message to these people," Tiye said.

"Do you suppose they will believe us?" Nefertiti replied.

"Perhaps, perhaps not," Tiye said. "But, we must try."

"I wonder which of the Elders will come," Nefertiti pondered. "It could be Bastet, or maybe Merneith. Merneith did an excellent job when we went to Psyon."

"That's true," Tiye agreed. "Bastet tends to be more aggressive and would happily take these people back to the age of stone tools if they show any signs of wanting to attack a neighbour."

"So, shall we send the message?" Nefertiti asked.

* * * * *

"We have a message, Madame," an aide informed Jane.

"Let's see what they have to say now," Jane said. "Assemble the cabinet if you would."

"This is the latest message," Hopkins said as Jane joined her cabinet in the Situation Room.

"People of Earth, we have sent one of our members to request that an Elder join us to better converse with you. We expect them to return shortly."

"So that's their explanation for that craft we saw headed back the way they had come," Hopkins said. "It was fairly moving, close to light, then it just disappeared. I wonder if that's where their portal for space travel is, if indeed there is one, and they haven't just cloaked the craft. Do we believe this Elder story, or have they sent someone to fetch the rest of the fleet?"

"How far out can we see?" Jane asked.

"If we retask Webb, then quite a long way," Hopkins replied. "We know roughly which direction to look if they're coming from their home planet, so we'll point Webb that way and look for new objects."

"Is there anything else we can do to prepare?" Jane asked her cabinet.

"We're at DefCon1," John Madison said. "We've got the National Guard activated in every state, we've started to split units up and place smaller groups in dispersed areas, we're ramping up production of missiles and other ammunition, we've got lots of fuel on hand, and we're spreading that out too, we've got all the assets we can spare watching the visitors, and we're also keeping a close eye on the Russians and the Chinese, with the take out of the North Korean and Iranian forces, we retasked some birds to keep closer tabs on the Indians and the Saudis."

"CDC?" Jane asked.

"We have everyone we can on standby," Dr Park replied. "We cleared out some labs and space and amped up the containment protocols so that if we get anything from the visitors, we can analyse what it is."

"How are our borders holding?" Jane asked.

"We've got the southern border locked down," Madelaine Wilson of Homeland Security confirmed. "We saw an uptick of people figuring that our attention was elsewhere and trying to slip over the border, but we put a stop to that pretty quickly, and those few that did get over, we shipped right back. The northern border isn't an issue; the Canucks would rather stay at home. No one is trying by water, but in case we've stepped up Coast Guard patrols along the Gulf and around Florida and up the West Coast as far as Government Point. Gun sales are through the roof, and ammo is disappearing off the shelves as fast as it can be restocked; same is true of bottled water and dry non-perishables. When and if the visitors leave, Sam's Club and Costco are going to have to decide if they want all that back as returns."

"Air travel?" Jane asked.

"We've seen pretty full flights, looks like people are joining families and hunkering down together," Madelaine Wilson replied. "We've seen an uptick in cars on the interstates as well."

"With all these people moving about, are we losing any essential services or workers?" Jane asked.

"On the contrary," John Madison replied. "We've seen volunteers come in and offer to work all hours, doing their bit as it were."

"Do you think I should meet with the religious leaders again and see what their take is on the statement that this Hemsut created us and our visitors?" Jane asked.

"It might be a good idea," Helen Cortez of Health and Human Services said. "It will give us a sense of how the country is dealing with the now inescapable fact that we are not alone and that we may all have to re-examine our notions of God."

"Excuse me, Madame, the Secretary-General is asking for you to return to the Security Council chamber," an aide said.

"I'll be there shortly," Jane said.

"Thank you all for coming," Sharma said when Jane joined the others. "I think it would be prudent for each head of state to return to their own country. The current gathering offers too risky a target should our visitors decide to take aggressive action."

"I agree," Ivan said.

"I also," Zhou agreed. "We will leave within the hour. I will ensure that we have a communication link at all times should the need arise."

"So, we just leave our ambassadors here?" Ivan asked.

"That is up to you," Sharma said. "We do need to act as one in this, so we do need a mechanism for rapid communication, so provided we all do that, I see no reason why our meetings cannot be done remotely. If you would all have your communications experts meet with mine to establish the protocols we will need for online meetings."

"Already done," Zhou said.

"Good," Sharma said. "We must stay in contact to discuss issues as they arise, who knows what our visitors may do next. Has anyone seen any aggression on their part since the actions taken against the Democratic People's Republic of North Korea or the Islamic Republic of Iran?"

"Only those minor incidents against the militant Islamists in North Africa and Yemen, no great loss there," Ivan said. "We have seen nothing targeting any of our forces."

"Let us not provoke our visitors into taking action against more nations," Sharma said. "Their capabilities are truly frightening."

"They are," Zhou agreed. "Well, lady and gentlemen, we must stay alert to what these visitors may do next and be as prepared as we can be. My plane is ready, so I will leave you now."

The others in the council all soon left, so there would be much activity at JFK airport in the next few hours as they all departed for their home countries. Jane went back to the US headquarters in New York and told the others what had transpired and suggested that they all make their way back to Washington. Before she left, she had some private words with Nicole.

"What's up?" Nicole asked.

"Nicole, hold the fort for us and let me know if any momentous crops up," Jane said. "Anything you can pick up on Ivan's and Zhou's folks would be valuable

"I'm on it," Nicole replied. "I do have people inside the Ivan and Zhou camps, that's for your ears only."

"Do they have people in our camp?" Jane asked.

"Probably," Nicole admitted. "I try and keep my thoughts to myself and not commit too much to electronic storage, too easy to hack and copy, no matter how encrypted it's supposed to be, let's face it, Ivan and Zhou have got whole departments dedicated to electronic intelligence gathering. My written reports to you are done on a single sheet written on glass, so no imprint to copy. I've got my suspicions about George Butler, one of the State people here, so keep him close and feed him bullshit and the occasional titbit that rings true to keep them interested."

"Is this room bugged?" Jane asked.

"I had it swept this morning by State and swept again by the Marines; they found one that State had missed, sneaky little bugger it was too," Nicole replied. "Now I need to find out who's planting them, could be Butler, could be another, one of the household staff, a cleaner, don't know yet."

"What was it Le Carré used to call it, Moscow rules, stick with that and keep your private communications with me down to paper and have it couriered by a different Marine each time," Jane instructed. "Ivan and Zhou can hardly suborn the whole company."

"So, what's your plan now?" Nicole asked.

"Now, I suppose we wait for this Elder to show up," Jane replied. "I'll do the meet with the religious leaders and probably another press conference to answer more dumb arse questions from VCN."

"Rather you than me," Nicole laughed. "What's your private take on the visitors?"

"I'm torn," Jane replied. "Part of me wants to believe they're good guys interested in our welfare and development, part of me is terrified that we'll step out of line and they'll take out our military the same way they did the North Koreans and part of me is waiting for the invasion against which we'd have no viable defence, and to round it out I recall what this Tiye said about us not husbanding the planet well, and wonder what that might lead to."

"Bitch, isn't it," Nicole sympathised. "I never imagined this would actually happen. You watch all the sci-fi movies and wonder what and how, then a real alien shows up and we really don't know what to do."

"What amazes me is how many movies have been made about alien invasions. Tom did a study and listed 260 movies and about twice as many novels," Jane commented. "In most of the movies, we win or come out on top somehow, but not all, and we're reduced to fighting rearguard actions."

"Like *Day of the Triffids*," Nicole said. "But, I suppose that wasn't really an alien invasion, just our own foolishness."

"I think Tom said he found 32 invasion movies where we really did lose and were reduced to hiding out or being used as slave labour," Jane said.

"Perish the thought," Nicole said.

"It's also interesting that in most movies about alien invasions, the military is tasked with finding solutions and only rarely is there a portrayal of someone thinking and using their brains and not guns. That's not to say that the military doesn't have thinkers, but they're trained to shoot, and if they do think, it's how best to shoot and not get shot," Jane commented.

"It's our society," Nicole said. "Might is right, and sadly, that is often the case. There were a couple of movies where people were actually thinking, *Invasion*, the Apple TV series and maybe part of *Arrival,* but even then, it was only at the last moment that military action was stopped, and those guys were basically friendly."

"I'd better go or Madison and the others will wonder just what we had to talk about," Jane said.

"Watch out for Madison," Nicole warned. "He has designs on your job."

"Really?" Jane asked.

"Honest Injun," Nicole confirmed. "He makes sure you mess up this alien business, calls the cabinet together, invokes the 25th amendment because you've lost it, moves you aside, does the same to Taylor because, let's face it, Brian has proved to be a total disappointment, then offers himself up as the only worthy candidate."

"God, that's all I need now, plots behind the scenes," Jane bemoaned. "Thanks, Nicole. I'd really better go and keep the others in line."

In Washington, Jane asked for a press conference to be set up and also asked her aides to gather the religious leaders for another meeting, but first, it was the media.

"Ladies and gentlemen, you will have seen the latest message from the visitors, that they are asking for one of their so-called Elders to join them. We have no knowledge whether or not this is true. It may be, but it may also be the prelude to a larger fleet appearing; we don't know," Jane said in her opening statement. "I will take questions."

"How do we know they sent someone?" CNN asked.

"We tracked a craft that left their main vessel, and it went off in the direction of Mars at close to light speed, then it disappeared," Jane replied.

"Do we know how big it was?" ABC asked.

"As far as we can judge about the size of our old Space Shuttles," Jane replied.

"So, does that mean all their craft have the same propulsion system?" NBC asked.

"We don't know that," Jane admitted. "But, it would certainly point that way."

"What are the visitors doing right now?" The Christian Science Monitor asked.

"As far as we can see, sitting in a geosynchronous orbit parked above the UN building in New York," Jane replied.

"Is it wise for heads of state to be all gathered in one place? From what they did to the North Koreans, they could take out all the world leaders in a minute," VCN asked.

"We have discussed that and agreed that heads of state would be better in their home countries, but in constant contact with the Secretary-General," Jane disclosed. "To that end, the leaders have all dispersed to their own countries."

"And what, leave their ambassadors to be the targets?" VCN asked.

"It is a risk, I agree," Jane replied. "But, we see the risk as being minor."

"Have you any plans to move to a secure location?" CNN asked.

"I'm not sure what constitutes a secure location," Jane said. "The famous underground complex at Greenbrier would sound attractive if it were not for the evidence we have that the visitors destroyed the underground complexes that the Iranians and North Koreans had for developing nuclear weapons. I have no desire to be trapped under feet of rock and concrete, so perhaps Valley Forge and a tent would be safer."

"Is it true that we've been dispersing army and air force units around the country?" ABC asked.

"I cannot comment on items that may affect our national security," Jane replied.

"After the attacks on North Korea and Iran, have we seen any others?" CBS asked.

"Apart from some minor actions in North Africa and Yemen against militant Islamic groups, no," Jane replied. "It is, of course, possible that those groups had not heard the warnings, but in today's world of smartphones and social media, that is hard to believe."

"Now that the aliens are in geosynchronous orbit above us, is it time to blow them out of the sky with a coordinated strike from us, the Russians and the Chinese?" VCN asked.

"As I have said before, that seems ill-advised," Jane stated. "The first stages of ballistic missiles burn for up to a minute, which, judging by what they did to the North Korean missile, gives them plenty of time to target our launches and take them out. Then what, who gets the retaliation first?"

"Surely we have hypervelocity missiles?" VCN pressed.

"Hypersonic missiles achieve speeds of about Mach 5, or about 3,800 mph," Jane began. "But that still means about five and a half hours to get to a geosynchronous orbit, during which time one has to assume that the visitors will have detected them and taken action."

"So, as long as they stay up there, there's little we can do?" CBS asked.

"That is so," Jane confirmed. "We're having to rely on our judgment that if they wanted to invade, they would have done that already. I will hold another briefing when there is something to communicate."

"I sometimes really wonder about our press corps," Jane said to her assembled cabinet. "I suppose they have to ask the questions that they think people will ask, but basic physics and other sciences seem to elude them."

"That's because most of them did the minimum of science in high school and probably none at college, and it was fashionable under the last regime to denigrate science," John Madison said.

"What issues are we facing, aside from our visitors?" Jane asked.

"Food stocks are down," Helen Cortez replied. "The big box stores are running low on inventory, and the farms just can't keep up. Imports of food are going well for the moment, but several countries where we normally buy from have imposed bans on exports and are building up their own emergency stockpiles. What's already on the water is fine, but don't expect too much more. Water is still a major issue in all the Western states, but the governors tell me they are filling reservoirs when and where they can."

"Medicines, PPE?" Jane asked.

"A lot of our stuff comes from India, and they've cut off everyone," Emily Adams, the head of the Food and Drug Administration, replied. "I gather you can still get from India if you know who to deal with. We've ramped up PPE production in Puerto Rico and Arkansas, but nothing happens overnight, and much of the raw material still comes from China, Vietnam and Malaysia."

"Energy?" Jane asked.

"Refineries are doing what they can," John Buchanan, the Secretary of Energy, replied. "Despite what previous regimes thought, it's not just a matter of drill, drill, drill, crude has to go to refineries that can process it, which is why we for a long time, a net exporter of oil, but still imported certain grades. Power plants are looking at coal again, but converting from natural gas or oil isn't that simple. The greatest threat is disruption in the control systems, which would come from an EMP or similar event."

"Transportation?" Jane asked.

"Most states are working as quickly as they can to finish up road and bridge projects to get everything open they can," Madelaine Wilson replied. "Railroads and trucking companies are laying in stocks of diesel."

"Defence?" Jane asked.

"All our major contractors have suspended development projects for now and are focused on producing what we currently use, so planes, missiles, tanks and other armoured vehicles, artillery rounds and small arms ammunition," Madison replied.

"Riots and civil unrest?" Jane asked.

"There have been some," Madelaine Wilson replied. "But the governors and mayors have done a good job of dealing with them."

"Looting?" Jane asked.

"Same answer," Madelaine said. "Some of the governors have enacted emergency procedures that smack of martial law, and looters caught in the act are being shot."

"I'm sure that delights the legal profession," Jane commented dryly. "Any lawsuits filed?"

"Quite a few," Thomas Moore, the Attorney General, reported. "My guess is that the visitors will have packed up their bags and gone home before the cases get heard."

"I haven't had time to watch much of the broadcast media," Jane said. "What's your take on what they're saying?"

"The usual talking heads pontificating," Madelaine said. "They repeat what the visitors say, and then all their experts weigh in on what that means. So, generally, it's a waste of airtime. Social media is going crazy, as you would expect, conspiracy theories abound, the latest left-wing one is that this is all a ploy by us to cover up a massive operation we have going to deport anyone who's not a citizen, even those here on a Green Card, and the latest right-wing one is that we're setting things up to allow a massive influx of people from Central America."

"What are our friends and neighbours up to?" Jane asked.

"China and Russia are doing what we're doing and dispersing their army and air force units," John Brant of the CIA replied. "They had started to mass units near their borders, but after North Korea, they've backed off from that. Iran doesn't figure on the world stage any more, but there are massive anti-government demonstrations happening; same is true in North Korea. After their respective militaries were decimated, people have become emboldened. We've even picked up details of the so-called morality police in Iran being beaten up by large groups of teens. India is moving more troops, in small detachments, into Kashmir, so are the Paks. The general mood around the world is hunker down, conserve resources where you can, enact martial law, get ready for what may or may not come. The Canucks are doing what we're doing, stockpiling what they can, ramping up production of medicines and PPE that they make and don't import, same is true of Mexico. Most of Central and South America has gone over to martial law, with constitutions suspended almost everywhere. Europe is doing what we're doing, Middle East the usual mess, but I did just hear that Hezbollah took a hit from the visitors for launching missiles at Israel, stupid move after what happened to Iran. From what we can gather, the visitors had tabs on the command structure and stockpiles of Hezbollah and took them all out in pretty short order. For once, the Israelis were smart and didn't retaliate, so they didn't suffer at the hands of the visitors. The visitor strikes were so precise that we've concluded that they must have the capability to detect the chemicals used in rockets and ammunition, even from where they're sitting, either that or they have agents on the ground, something that I suppose is possible, but if what they tell us is true and their last visit was five hundred years ago, that's a long time for a sleeper agent, or families of them, a scenario that I doubt. If the visitors really can detect the chemicals used in rockets and ammunition, that doesn't bode well for us if we get into a shooting war with them. We're still seeing some hits on North Africa and Yemen, cleaning up the extremist groups there that are still shooting, you'd think they'd learn."

"Thank you all," Jane said. "Now, I suppose I should go and see what the leaders of our various religious groups have to say for themselves."

The leaders of the various religions assembled again at the White House, and Jane went to talk to them.

"What do you make of the statement that this Hemsut made our visitors and us?" she asked.

"We are wondering if Hemsut isn't just their name for God," the cardinal replied. "There are no real hints as to whether this Hemsut is a single entity or what. We have taken the line with our congregations that Hemsut is merely their word for God, and therefore, God made us all. It does still leave the issue of being God's chosen."

"Perhaps the visitors would have been seen in the past as messengers of God, angels if you like," the Episcopal bishop suggested.

"So, it was the visitors who destroyed Sodom and Gomorrah?" Jane asked.

"That would be a convenient explanation," the rabbi agreed.

"What about you, Imam?" Jane asked.

"We have angels," he replied. "They are created by Allah and do his bidding in a variety of ways, so one could argue that the visitors are angelic, in the literal sense, not the metaphorical sense, because in Islam, angels sometimes have to perform unpleasant tasks. We have many scholars and imams now debating what the visitors meant by the statement that this Hemsut created them and us. For many conservative sects, it is heresy, but it is an inescapable fact that we are not alone and that even the visitors recognise a higher power."

"Have you seen any increase in the size of your congregations?" Jane asked.

"We have," the Southern Baptist replied.

"So have we," the Christian Nationalist echoed.

"I think we all have," the cardinal confirmed. "In times of crisis and uncertainty, people turn to God."

"Have you seen any evidence of animosity toward other denominations?" Jane asked. Not altogether surprising to her, there was hesitation before anyone replied.

"There has been some," the imam said. "We have been receiving threats that this is the Second Coming of Jesus, and he will take vengeance on all those who have offended or are not seen to be following the tenets of our extreme so-called Christians."

"It would be better for us all if those responsible would dial back their rhetoric," Jane said. "We have an unknown here; we still don't know whether our visitors are truly friendly, or if this is just a holding action until the main invasion fleet arrives."

"They certainly were unfriendly when they attacked North Korea and Iran," the Christian Nationalist said.

"That is true," Jane agreed. "But we had all been warned, and they ignored the warnings and suffered consequences that none of us could have imagined. It was a very sobering lesson in the capabilities of our visitors."

"Rather like Alexander the Great, wipe out one city and make sure everyone else in the country knows and resistance ceases," the rabbi suggested.

"That is a possibility," Jane agreed.

"How do we find out more about this Hemsut?" the cardinal asked.

"We try and engage either this Captain Tiye or this Elder, she says is coming and see what he or she is prepared to tell us, that is, if the Elder isn't just a fleet admiral with enough vessels to subjugate us in short order," Jane replied.

"It would allay a lot of the fears of the more conservative arms of Islam if this Elder at least looked masculine," the imam said. "I know we could still be seeing avatars, and we may actually be looking at giant ants, but appearances are everything."

"Rabbi, do you have a similar problem?" Jane asked.

"With the ultraorthodox sects, yes," he confirmed. "Not to put too fine a point on it, it in their view undermines the roles of men and women as they see them."

"So, not to put too fine a point on it, they feel their superiority under threat?" Jane asked.

"That's a little extreme," the rabbi protested.

"Is it?" Jane asked. "Who determined that men should rule?"

"Well, God created first Adam, then Eve," the rabbi replied.

"And who wrote that piece of fiction?" Jane asked. "We now have an alien society that is telling us that we and they were created by this Hemsut, and no mention of male or female first. In Egyptian mythology, Hemsut were the goddesses of fate and protection, so, is God, in fact, a woman? Before the three major monotheisms, it was the female who was venerated, only to become denigrated by the new religions at the time, Judaism, Christianity and Islam. Imam, why is it that in Islam, or at least conservative arms of Islam, women are denied basic rights and are subject to the rule of men?"

"It is a matter of interpretation," the imam replied. "There are writings that suggest that roles are defined."

"And if our visitors show up with a video clip that negates the writings, then what?" Jane asked.

"We are certain that the teachings of the Prophet Mohammed were transcribed accurately," the imam replied.

"Until a few days ago, I was certain that I would never encounter someone or something from another planet, yet here we are, and they have demonstrated awesome capabilities and yet we have religious leaders whining about the fact that our visitors look like they're a female-led society and that their sensibilities are offended by the mode of dress. In the words of my generation when I was much younger, get a life and grow up and recognise that we may have far more serious problems than some apparent woman has her hair uncovered," Jane said. "Gentlemen, I have had enough of idiocy. I get more than I need from the media. I would have expected you to be more scholarly and thoughtful. If you cannot help us as a country through this current crisis, then I may have to look at the status of churches in the country and start revoking privileges that you have enjoyed and collect some tax revenues along the way."

"You can't do that," the Christian Nationalist protested.

"Why not?" Jane asked. "We're in a state of national emergency, and nothing is off the table, and we'll probably need money to pay for what may yet come."

"Our constitution guarantees certain rights," the cardinal said. "The 16th Amendment grants us tax-exempt status.

"We may find ourselves in a situation where we may have a new constitution imposed upon us," Jane commented. "Our current situation may necessitate a review of the constitution, or our visitors may just impose a new one with penalties if we don't comply, or you can take the lead and help by adjusting your rhetoric and doctrines to better suit our current situation, something which you have all done in the past when it has been convenient for you. Which would you rather have?"

"We can certainly look at things," the cardinal said.

"Good, do that, and you, Sir, who represents the so-called Christian Nationalists, dial back the rhetoric about Islam, or I might find an excuse to come after you, it seems to me that Christianity is something you have long abandoned in favour or some perverted view of life that has more in common with the Afghan Taliban than anything our Founding Fathers could have imagined when they separated Church and State," Jane lectured.

"That is preposterous," the Christian Nationalist protested.

"Is it?" Jane asked. "Look to the statutes enacted in your state and those of like mind and compare them with the strictures of the Taliban and show me the substantive difference. We need a nation that is unified at the moment, not divided into tribes and sects; we need you as leaders to act like leaders, leaders who subscribe to the notion that this is the United States, not leaders of tribes, sects and gangs all looking to gain ascendency over the other. Are you able to do that?"

"We are," the cardinal said. "We will leave you and discuss among ourselves how we may help, not hinder."

"But," the Christian Nationalist started.

"There are no buts," the Episcopal bishop said. "We have a mission, are you part of that mission, or would you rather see chaos and anarchy?"

"No, but," the Christian Nationalist persisted.

"So, what you really believe in is anarchy," the bishop interrupted. "If we have anarchy, the visitors may just step in and take us back a few millennia and impose a new order that has no place for you or us."

"I think we should leave and let the President consider next moves that we as a nation should take," the cardinal said.

"That was rather blunt," an aide commented to Jane after the religious leaders had left. "They'll run whining to the press and social media about being badly treated and how you're opposed to God."

"Well, we'll just pre-empt them," Jane said. "Call a press conference and I'll just remind everyone that we have a bigger issue hanging over our heads than the sensibilities of some religious extremists."

"Is that wise, Madame President?" the aide asked. "It may be political suicide."

"It may," Jane agreed. "But we live in a new era, we believed ourselves to be alone in the universe, but now we know we are not, we have an alien spacecraft sitting over us whose intentions we're still trying to confirm, so politics have and will change, the next election is not for another three years and who knows what may happen between now and then."

"Ladies and Gentlemen," Jane started as she addressed the assembled press corps. "I have just had occasion to castigate the leaders of the various religions that are pre-eminent in our country. We have sitting above us an alien spacecraft whose intentions we are still trying to confirm. These same alien visitors have demonstrated capabilities that are awesome and frightening if their strictures about launches of rockets and missiles are ignored. The countries of North Korea and Iran have had their military might reduced to ashes in hours. The aliens have made no aggressive moves towards any other country, except religious extremist groups in parts of North Africa and Yemen, and again, those groups have been reduced to ashes, and we've just had word that Hezbollah launched rockets against Israel and suffered the consequences in a very targeted mode. While we await the so-called Elder of the visitors, certain of our religious groups are whining that the visitors don't look masculine enough and are not dressed in a conservative fashion that suits their sensibilities. At the same time, the so-called Christian Nationalists are trumpeting a Second Coming and encouraging attacks on Muslims and others who do not fit their mould. This is hardly helpful. We need to stand united as a nation. We cannot afford to devolve into sects, tribes and gangs that simply divide us, and if we are faced with a ground invasion, it makes us all the easier to subjugate. As to looking masculine enough, if we accept that what we see is real and not avatars, then we have to accept the reality that at least one alien culture is different to ours and is not male-dominated. For those of you who have not done your homework, this Hemsut that the visitors referenced shows up in Egyptian mythology as the goddesses of fate and protection, and Hemsut, according to the aliens, is the one who created them and us, so is God, in fact, female? Chew on that for a while. Just to round out what will be regarded as an attack on religious freedoms, I also suggested that tax exemptions for religious groups may need to be re-examined. It is enshrined in the 16th Amendment to our Constitution, but perhaps our Constitution needs a review, driven by our new reality, or perhaps the visitors will impose one on us with dire consequences if we don't comply. My comment to the religious leaders was that a review of their status is dependent on their leadership at this time, leadership that unites and not divides. I will take questions."

"How could you suggest that religious organisations shouldn't be exempt from taxes?" VCN asked.

"How else to get them to pay attention and behave as adults?" Jane asked. "All entities respond to the correct stimuli, and money and taxes are usually a good start, particularly in these United States, where money and the love of money seem to drive everything. As I said to the leaders of the major religious groups, we have an alien spacecraft hanging over us, and we cannot be certain of their intentions. They have demonstrated an awesome ability to remove military forces, and yet we have groups sowing division in our nation at a time when we need unity."

"Is it true that you used the word idiocy to them?" ABC asked.

"I did," Jane replied. "We have conspiracy theories, potential stories that are clearly false, and yet you, as the media, seem intent on spreading disinformation, for what, ratings, or to satisfy the peculiar beliefs of your avid viewers. What we need now is accurate reporting, not half-baked notions of Chinese spacecraft, stories of us wanting to annexe Canada, and other equally bizarre notions."

"We have a duty as the free press to report the news," CNN commented.

"The news, yes," Jane concurred. "But political propaganda and outright lies, no."

"Is it true that you stated that God is a woman?" VCN asked.

"Did you listen to my opening remarks?" Jane responded.

"How do we know that their Hemsut and that of the Egyptians are one and the same?" CBS asked.

"We don't," Jane replied. "But, we live in a new era, a month ago, I may have subscribed to the notion that statistically there are other planets that could support life, but firmly believed I would never see any in my lifetime. That has all changed. It seems odd to me that so many of the names associated with the visitors have parallels in ancient Egypt, so it begs the question of whether or not they were here before and who took the names from whom. We need to re-examine many of our beliefs and be prepared for potential revelations that may upend many of them."

"What are we doing as a country to prepare for a possible invasion?" NBC asked.

"We have our military on high alert, we have federalised the National Guard in each state, we are stockpiling what we can in the way of food, water, medicines and other essentials," Jane replied.

"What can the people do?" CNN asked.

"Make sure each household has food, water and medications for at least two weeks, longer if possible, stay vigilant, and if any signs of an invasion are noted, report it to the local authorities. Do not start shooting at anything new or strange; it may only be your neighbour dressed differently," Jane replied. "Other than that, go about your normal business and routines."

"Have the visitors said any more about their intentions?" the Christian Science Monitor asked.

"No, simply that they are here on a routine visit to check on our progress," Jane replied. "If they are to be believed, they were here last in Elizabethan times, that's the first Elizabeth, not the second, so quite a while ago and much has changed since then."

"Do you think they are peaceful or should we expect an invasion?" CBS asked.

"We cannot be certain," Jane replied. "As I have said before, we would have thought that if this were an attack or an invasion, they would have done so already and not be sitting above us and engaging in a dialogue."

"But they have attacked," VCN protested.

"It is true that they took action against North Korea and Iran and some elements of the Houthis and Boko Haram, and as I stated in my opening remarks, they took action against Hezbollah, but those incidents were the result of aggressive actions taken by those actors, so far no action on the part of our visitors has been taken against us or any other country that has refrained from launching rockets and missiles or attacking their neighbour," Jane replied.

"Do we know what they used to attack the North Korean army?" ABC asked.

"We have speculated that they use some form of energy weapon, perhaps microwaves, perhaps other elements of the electromagnetic spectrum, but we are only speculating, one thing is clear: they must have power to spare on their spacecraft to use this kind of weapon, even on their so-called tugs, how they generate that power is a mystery to us," Jane replied. "The other thing that is clear is that they have the ability to track and zero in on specific targets. We learned that when they attacked Hezbollah, it was very focused and very specific, taking out weapons stockpiles at will. This is not the alien invasions of the movies when they arrive and destroy cities wholesale; this is either somewhat friendly or far more subtle."

"Do we know any more about the visitors?" CNN asked.

"We've tried what we can to scan their craft with visible light, infrared and other wavelengths and have been thwarted by some kind of shielding, which would probably tell us something if we knew what that was," Jane replied. "We are in the classic engineering phase of dealing with known unknowns and unknown unknowns, and sadly, at the moment, the unknown unknowns outweigh everything."

"Back to religion for a minute," the Christian Science Monitor asked. "Has the UN reached agreement on what to ask this Elder when he, she, or it arrives?"

"We still have the same basic questions," Jane replied. "They have told us that they are here to check on our progress, so we believe that or not, if they are peaceable, then what kind of society do they belong to, what are their belief systems, and would they be prepared to share the technology of space travel with us."

"So, do they believe in God? Would that be part of that?" NBC asked.

"In time," Jane agreed. "First, we would have to confirm that they even understand our concept of God or gods."

"The aliens gave us dates when they said they had been here before," VCN started. "What happened in those years?"

"I'm sure your use of Google and other search engines is as good as mine," Jane replied. "Be sure, however, to check the sources and do some cross-comparisons with various sources; the internet can be a mine of misinformation as well as factual writings. My own researches did uncover the fact that 1599 was the first year when Shakespeare's *As You Like It* was performed; in 1065, the Chinese spotted what was probably a nova, and William was getting ready to invade England, 613 is when the prophet Mohammad started his teaching, 33 was remarkable in that it is the accepted year of the crucifixion of Jesus Christ, 510 BCE was the start of the rise of Rome as a republic and there was also a major shift in the rulers in Greece, and 1534 BCE was the end of the Hyksos rule in Egypt. Earlier than that, we're getting back into the mists of time. Perhaps our visitors could provide us with a clearer picture of the life and times of those eras. It is possible we may have to rewrite considerable portions of world history, given from what was probably a neutral outside observer and not a victor."

"Is it possible that if the visitors were here in the year 33, that they witnessed the trial and crucifixion of Jesus?" The Christian Science Monitor asked.

"Your guess is as good as mine," Jane replied. "There will be theories out there that Jesus did not ascend to heaven but did, in fact, get beamed up to a visitor spacecraft."

"So, was Jesus one of these visitors?" CNN asked.

"That is for you to speculate upon," Jane replied. "I have no views one way or the other on that."

"Is there a way that we can make a preemptive strike against the aliens?" VCN asked.

"North Korea, Iran and Hezbollah launched rockets of one type or another and in short order, they had destruction rained down upon them. Our visitors have issued a strong warning against launching rockets of any kind, so we have elected to stay cautious and not antagonise them," Jane replied.

"Is there any other way we can strike at them?" VCN persisted.

"You mean with some kind of directed energy weapon?" Jane asked.

"Laser them out of the sky, yes," VCN said.

"Lasers that would materially affect a vessel of that size are the stuff of science fiction," Jane commented. "And we have no way of knowing how they might first detect such an attack and how they would respond. I have no intention of placing this country in jeopardy."

"Wouldn't that be seen as weak by many?" ABC asked.

"Perhaps," Jane replied. "But, I would rather live to fight another day and be accused of weakness than place our armed forces in an untenable position. Whatever was used against the North Koreans and Iranians, we have no defence against, so it would seem to me to be foolhardy at best to initiate something we cannot hope to win. We are in the unfortunate position of being faced with visitors who possess technologies that we do not have and have shown a willingness to use them."

"There must be some way we can defend ourselves against these aliens,: VCN remarked.

"If there is, and you know of a sure-fire and effective method, I'm sure Secretary Madison would be delighted to hear of it," Jane said. "Now, if you will excuse me, there are matters that I must attend to."

"I wonder again and again about our media," Jane commented to the cabinet after the press conference. "The reporters either don't listen or are poorly briefed, or they skew the information they are given to suit the party line of the broadcaster."

"If you look back in history, it's been a while since we had honest reporting of the facts; now it's all messaging to suit the views of the heads of the broadcaster, and that is driven by what they perceive as their target audience," Madelaine Wilson commented.

"I suppose that's right," Jane agreed. "VCN panders to or promotes an extreme right-wing message, because that is their viewership."

"I wonder if the visitors have different names for geographic features," Moore mused.

"What, like renaming the Gulf of Mexico to the Gulf of America?" Jane asked.

"That plus some others," Moore agreed.

"Name changes happen," Jane said. "Look at Africa and all the name changes after the end of colonialism. Anyway, what else should we be doing to thwart our visitors if they turn out to not be so friendly?"

"The biggest problem we could potentially have is some form of EMP," Madison replied. "Everything we have is controlled by computers, so electricity supplies could go haywire, planes won't be able to fly, cars won't be drivable, the list goes on and on."

"Weren't we supposed to be hardening systems to protect against that?" Jane asked.

"Supposed to be and doing are two very different things," Madelaine Wilson commented. "There are some military systems that are hardened, but for the most part, the utilities, electricity, water, sewer, gas, telephone and internet are not, so as John said, an EMP disrupts everything and recovery would take years."

"I recall there was something back in the mid-1800s that caused problems with the telegraph system," Jane said.

"September 1859," Madison said. "A huge coronal mass ejection on the sun caused auroras to be seen in unlikely places, and telegraph operators noted that they could operate without batteries. The event was named the Carrington Effect after a Brit astronomer who had mapped solar flares and linked the flares to the occurrences here. We've been very lucky in that other big CMEs have missed us."

"So, is there anything we can do now?" Jane asked.

"It depends on time," Madelaine said. "It takes time to make and install equipment that is hardened, and we are a nation that reacts and is typically not proactive after all, the philosophy is, why spend the money on the off chance that something may happen, and if it's not during my tenure, it's someone else's problem."

"The best we can do is try and get as many transformers and switches built that we can and hope for the best," Madison added.

"What about Faraday cages?" Jane asked.

"Great theoretical concept, hard to implement," Madison replied.

"Is there anything we have that doesn't run on computers?" Jane asked.

"Old gas and diesel engines, steam engines, water wheels, and old windmills," Madison replied.

"What's the adage, nine meals to anarchy?" Jane asked.

"There are only nine meals between mankind and anarchy, comment by a guy by the name of Alfred Henry Lewis in 1906," Helen Cortez said. "Since then, there was an article and a pamphlet by Andrew Simms in 2010, and then a novel by Farrell Kingsley in 2014, and then another by J K Franks in 2016. They all deal with the issue of food supplies. We can find a way around most things, but food and water we can't do without, and our society has long gone from agrarian to industrial and an almost total reliance on transportation systems to move food from producer to consumer. Preppers amass food, like freeze-dried meals, but that only lasts as long as it does; then you have to grow, and with urbanisation, where are we going to grow? So we would likely get roving gangs looking to loot and take, then gunplay breaks out, and anarchy ensues. We're not short of guns; aren't there over 450 million guns in households, some with none, but probably almost half with multiples."

"So, what you're really telling me is that if our visitors let loose a big EMP, then we're screwed," Jane commented.

"In reality, yes," Helen said. "Sure, we can hang on for a while and try and manage things, but it will devolve to the states, then the counties, and they will have to do what they can. We don't have farmers on the payroll, we can send in troops to maintain law and order for a while, but in time we have to feed them too, and if food supplies dry up, then they probably desert and go home to take care of their own."

"You paint a very dystopian picture," Jane commented.

"Sorry, Boss, but that's the way I see it," Helen said. "In my view, the best we can hope for is that the visitors are friendly and are doing what they claim and checking up on us."

"So, the best things to have supplies of now are fertilisers and seeds?" Jane asked.

"That would help. We'll have to play nice with the Canucks to get them to ship us the raw materials," Helen replied. "But the bigger issue is who would plant and grow, and how would they protect their crops against urban gangs? It would get like the marijuana fields of old, disguised, booby-trapped and protected by farmers with guns. That would work in some places, but the likelihood is that some gangs would prevail and would kill off the proverbial golden goose, cooking their own goose as it were."

"You are a veritable mine of unhelpful thoughts," Madison said.

"I say it as I see it, John," Helen said. "Our society is just not prepared for a major CME or EMP that leads to outages and computer failures. We spend a fortune on weapons but precious little on our ability to feed ourselves; we leave that to others."

"So, you're saying we should all have Victory Gardens?" John sneered.

"Why not?" Helen asked. "Go back in history, there was the National War Garden Commission of 1917 and then the Victory Gardens of the 40s, with over 20 million gardens in 1944, so we resurrect the information that was sent out then and redistribute it and get people preparing for what could be the worst, there's probably enough food around that we could make if for a year with rationing, then if gardens are producing the pressure is relieved a little."

"That's ridiculous," Madison said.

"I don't know," Jane said. "It's something that people can do to make a contribution, rather have them do that than run around waving guns. It may not be necessary, but it's not a bad thing to do, even if our visitors do turn out to be friendly, or at least not openly aggressive."

"It wouldn't hurt to improve diets either," Miho Yamamura added. "There are vacant lots all over the place; we would need the cities, counties, and HOAs to waive many of the rules and regs they have in place, so maybe a message to the governors to work with city, county, and community leaders to do the right thing."

"How many states and cities have permitting requirements and rules that would make food production difficult?" Jane asked.

"Probably more than we think, rather like having condo associations and HOAs that don't allow solar panels, or dictate the kind of grass one can have in a front lawn," Helen replied. "One would have thought that most regulating agencies would look on urban farming and the greening of their environment a good thing, but I'm sure we have armies of petty bureaucrats and so-called concerned citizens who want to have their stamp on things."

"Like having to get permits from a dozen different agencies to clean up spills, all of which takes time while the spill is busy seeping into the soils, creating an even bigger problem," Miho added.

"We do need water for farming, and is there enough supply?" Helen asked.

"That's one of the biggest issues we face," Miho said. "We cannot create new water sources like dams and reservoirs and better distribution systems quickly, but we can step up the water from the air applications and plop generators down in the middle of growing plots, power them from the grid we have or from solar panels."

"Can we step up manufacture of the generators fast enough to make a difference?" Jane asked.

"In many places, all you need is a good old de-humidifier and some filtering systems," Miho replied. "We could create an instruction set of how to do that and put it out there on YouTube and in print form."

"Do that," Jane said. "Add it to the Victory Garden blurb."

"I still think this is a crazy notion," Madison said. "Better to form militias from the people and get ready to defend the nation."

"Was it Napoleon who was supposed to have said that an army marches on its stomach?" Jane asked.

"Either him or Frederick the Great," Madison confirmed.

"So, if the army is to march on its stomach, we'll need food supplies, and now we rely on commercial growers and our transportation system to provide food for all and sundry," Jane said. "Helen, go ahead and look at what was distributed in 1917 and the 1940s, update it if you think you need to and get it out there. Let's do something proactive for once."

"What about militias?" Madison asked.

"I think leave that to the governors," Jane replied. "We need to be sure that, in the words of the Constitution, they are well ordered and not just a bunch of gun-waving bros threatening everyone. If they are to fight anyone, it should be our visitors if they actually land with an invasion army."

"Do you think they will?" Miho asked.

"I've no idea," Jane replied. "If they are planning an invasion, it seems to me an odd way to do it, but stranger things have happened. If they were intent on wiping us out, I would have thought that they wouldn't have stopped at North Korea and Iran, but would have come after us, the Russians and the Chinese."

"That has me puzzled as well," John admitted. "If I were invading and had the capabilities they seem to have, I would have taken out the big players like us, the Chinese and the Russians, then started on the other players. Maybe they were being straightforward when they said they only took action after those guys had ignored their warnings."

"I wonder who this Elder will be and what they will have to say," Jane mused. "If, and it's a big if, they have technology they're prepared to share with us, what do we ask for?"

"Fusion technology, if they have it," George Williams, the Secretary of Energy, said. "That would solve a lot of our energy problems and reduce dependence on fossil fuels, fission reactors and renewables."

"Their drive system," Madison said. "That plus the secrets of space travel."

"If they know how to do it, how to get rid of the microplastics we've polluted the planet with," Helen said. "We're ingesting the damn stuff and it will kill us and other mammals in time, plus fish and birds, maybe even cockroaches."

"What will the Chinese want?" Jane asked.

"Probably the same as us," Madison replied. "Someone is going to try and get whatever technology they use as a weapon, but I see the chances of them giving us any clue as to what that is as slim to none."

"Let's put together a short list of things we'd like to know," Jane suggested. "Then, if they ever get around to offering to help us in any way, we know what to ask for."

"Let's just hope they're not like the aliens in the old *Twilight Zone* episode in the 60s, what was it, *To Serve Man*, and it was only at the end that someone figured that the manual they had was in fact a cookbook," Helen said.

"Perish the thought," Jane said. "So, food, water, medicines, PPE, guns by the score, what about communications?"

"If the visitors do set off an EMP, all our cell towers and handheld radios are gone, so we've scoured museums and archives for field telephone sets and have started working with the phone companies to string lines from where we're dispersed units to central points. We've also recruited ham radio operators and helped them harden their sets against an EMP," Madison said. "We've looked at reactivating dispatch riders and have discovered that we have bikes aplenty with volunteers to take messages. We haven't gone to carrier pigeons, but we're looking at anything that would work."

"We should get that word out to the Governors, that they need to look at the communication system backups as well. James, what happens to prison door locks if computers and electrical systems go down?"

"The default condition is unlocked," James Black, the Attorney General, replied. "We rely on backup generators to kick in, but you're right that could be an issue. We'll look into that immediately.

"Okay, let's get the media types back and see if we can't get them to put the message out and get people on board with the need to have better food security," Jane said. "Miho, could you give me a chart that shows growing times for quick-growing vegetables?"

"Thank you all for coming back," Jane said to the assembled White House Press Corps. "We, as you well know, are faced with uncertainty about the intentions of our visitors. Apart from a direct invasion by some form of ground force, we see as one of our biggest dangers some form of EMP that takes out our computer systems and networks. I'm sure that you are all well aware that our electricity and water distribution systems are all managed with computers, so their loss would be devastating for a period. On top of that, much of our food is transported from growing areas, either here in our own country or elsewhere, and an EMP would severely disrupt those systems. To mitigate the impact of that, we think people may contribute to our general welfare and security if we returned to the programs that were introduced during the First and Second World Wars, programs that were focused on growing food. That would include urban, suburban and rural areas. We are calling upon governors, county boards, mayors, and supervisors to examine their statutes, rules and standards to encourage growing of food, even if it means digging up hallowed front lawns, and planting cabbage instead. We are looking at the materials that were distributed in the two major wars and updating them to suit conditions today. I call upon the major seed producers to produce more, if they can, and for people to make a meaningful contribution to what may become a crisis."

"Wouldn't it be better to prepare militarily for an invasion?" CNN asked.

"We have all our forces based here in the US on high alert, the governors have all called out their national guard, we have dispersed our forces to make them less vulnerable to attacks on concentrations, we have ramped up production of artillery shells, missiles and small armaments ammunition, so we have done what we can from a military point of view, what we now have to consider is life after a possible invasion," Jane replied.

"Does that mean you think an invasion is imminent?" ABC asked.

"I have no idea," Jane replied. "Certainly, our visitors have made no move to put any kind of forces on the ground; they have limited their actions to the destruction of the forces of North Korea and Iran by remote means. Whether or not this so-called Elder is here to talk or to invade, we don't know."

"How long before this Elder gets here?" CBS asked.

"I have no idea," Jane replied. "The departing craft appeared to leave our solar system in a matter of minutes, but how long it takes to get back to their home planet using whatever mechanism they use, I have no idea. It could be hours, days, or weeks."

"I we embrace this idea of food production, how soon before we can actually get crops?" VCN asked.

"I am told that microgreens can be harvested in as little as two weeks, radishes in three to four weeks, green leafy vegetables in four to six weeks, and some root vegetables in six to eight weeks," Jane replied. "We are in June, so the growing season has months left."

"How long will it take states, counties, cities and HOAs to agree to something like this?" CNN asked.

"That depends on whether or not they want food to eat," Jane replied. "Mexico has suspended shipments of food as it stockpiles for its own use; other countries are doing the same."

"So, why don't we just go into Mexico and take it?" VCN asked.

"So, now you want us to go to war with our neighbour?" Jane asked.

"Well, if they have, they should share with us," VCN said.

"Why, we deported many migrant workers from the farms in the past; we hardly endeared ourselves to the Mexicans," Jane replied. "We have enough land to grow what we need, but we need people to accept the fact that they are going to have to do it themselves. It is hard work, I know, my own family had a small farm, and it was long hours with what seemed at times precious little in return, the margins are all in the distribution chain."

"What happens in the winter months?" ABC asked.

"Look back at your history," Jane replied. "People stored root vegetables, they preserved other foods, they found a way."

"So, you want us all to become Mormons?" VCN asked.

"That is insulting to the Church of Latter-day Saints," Jane said. "The northern tier states have long histories of surviving winters; perhaps we need to relearn the lessons of the past."

"Can we grow enough to sustain ourselves?" The Christian Science Monitor asked.

"I doubt that we can immediately," Jane replied. "But, anything we can produce reduces the pressure on the systems and stretches what we do have. We all may have to adjust our diets to more basic food, forego the tropical specialities that must be imported, because, in the short term at least, we won't be receiving any."

"So, we should cut off exports of beef, corn, and soy beans?" VCN asked.

"As long as we have a surplus, and our own population has no appetite for those items, we can export, but perhaps we should shift production in the longer term to products we know will be in demand domestically," Jane replied.

"What about seeds, fertilisers and other necessities?" NBC asked.

"We have asked seed producers to do what they can to increase the availability of seeds, and we are working with our northern neighbour to secure stocks of the ingredients required for fertilisers," Jane replied.

"Are you going to do anything at the White House?" CNN asked.

"As I'm sure you all know, the White House does have a vegetable garden, the idea of that goes back to the 19th Century and the then president, John Adams. Since then, there have been other gardens, and since 2009, it has been flourishing. The National Park Service helps us with it, and we have asked them to expand where we can," Jane replied.

"What about water?" The Christian Science Monitor asked.

"That is an issue," Jane agreed. "As long as we have effective water collection and distribution systems, water may as well be used on vegetable plantings as lawns, but for those states with high humidity, it would be worth investigating capturing water from the air."

"Won't that take a lot of electricity?" CNN asked.

"That's where solar panels and batteries come in," Jane replied. "I will be going to the Congress with a bill to provide for grants for solar panels and batteries to be used for that purpose, and in case our electricity supply systems are disrupted.

"Wouldn't an EMP also affect the control systems of those panels?" ABC asked.

"It's a lot easier to harden the inverters and controls of a few panels than it is to harden whole systems," Jane said. "We're looking to MIT and other technical institutions to provide us with simple and cost-effective ways to do that."

"This all sounds rather as if we are already in the mode of survival, do you see it that way?" CBS asked.

"As I said before, we have our military forces deployed and ready for an invasion, should one occur. This is to ready us for another scenario where there is no direct immediate invasion, but a major disruption of our utility systems and computer networks, which will affect our food and water supplies," Jane replied.

"And if no invasion and no major disruption occur?" NBC asked.

"Then we have improved food security generally," Jane replied.

"But won't that affect the existing food supply chain from farmer to grocery store?" VCN asked.

"It is possible," Jane agreed. "Any effect would not be immediate but over weeks and months, during which time I would expect the large farmers and supply chains to adapt."

"If there is an EMP and major systems are disrupted, how will that affect law enforcement?" ABC asked.

"As it would everything else," Jane replied. "I would expect cell phones to be unusable, the other communication networks that our police forces use to be interrupted at least, if not unusable. It will be up to local forces to return to community policing, on foot, bicycles or horseback, else I see a period of lawlessness."

"What about prison systems, are locks and gates secure?" VCN asked. "We don't want gangs of criminals roaming the streets."

"I would agree," Jane said. "Our Bureau of Prisons is currently looking at systems that engage and disengage locks in the federal system; it will be up to the states and counties to look to their facilities."

"So, it is possible that if we lose electricity and our computer systems that we might see prison escapes?" VCN asked.

"The Attorney General is looking at that scenario as we speak," Jane replied. "Food security for our military and other federal institutions is a concern for us, too; we rely on the existing supply chain, and if that is disrupted, we need to implement emergency procedures, which we do have. Hospitals may also have an issue if electricity is lost and their backup generators fail. One would expect hospitals to have contingency plans, but, sadly, we in the United States tend more towards reaction than proaction, so I am not sanguine about prospects there. The Federal Government will not be in a position to help with major system failures, so much will fall onto the States and Counties. If nothing else, this visitation by our visitors has caused us to look hard at our systems and take note of what we can do in the event of total loss, and create some plans for what to do."

"You speak as if you expect this to happen. Do you think it will?" CNN asked.

"I have no idea," Jane replied. "We have the words of our visitors that they are here on a mission to check on our progress, but they clearly have military capabilities that far exceed anything we have, so is an invasion or some other form of attack likely or imminent? I don't know and cannot guess. So, our best course of action is plan for the worst and be relieved if it turns out that they are true to their word that they are here to check on us, and the actions they took against North Korea and Iran were in response to the actions of those countries. They have, to date, taken no action against any of our forces, either here or overseas. Thank you for your attention. I have much to attend to."

"Colonel Williams, I have something you would be interested in," Jim from JPL said.

"What is it?" Williams asked.

"Well, as you know, we haven't been able to pick up any signals between the visitor mothership and these tugs," Jim said. "But look at this, these are new images of some of the space between the mothership and two of the tugs, there are small objects there that are new."

"And?" Williams asked.

"Well, I've done some analysis, and what jumps out to me is that they're probably some kind of repeater," Jim went on to say. "We know that for microwave and light, we need line of sight; this gives them a quasi line of sight between their craft."

"So, what you think they're using microwaves to send messages?" Williams asked.

"No, I think they're using small bursts with lasers with encrypted messages," Jim replied. "With lasers, they don't get the leakage that you get from radio waves; you still get expansion of the beam, but less than radio."

"Can we listen in?" Williams asked.

"We would have to be within the normal range of expansion of the beam, but if we could get a satellite close enough to the path of the light, we could pick up the signals," Jim replied.

"Do we have any birds in LEO that we can push up?" Williams asked.

"We do have two that have enough fuel left to get us a burn long enough to get us up there," Jim replied.

"Let's call this in," Williams said. He picked up the telephone, and Jim listened to one side of the conversation, then waited while Williams was obviously on hold, then looked up expectantly when Williams hung up.

"Do it," Williams instructed. "I just talked to Hopkins, and he talked to Madsion, who says go for it. Send one up and let's see if we can't figure out what they're up to."

"I'll get hold of the flight director for the one bird and tell her what we need," Jim said.

"Tell her that this is a national priority," Williams instructed. "How long before the bird is in position?"

"Based on where our bird is and where we want it to go, it'll be three days before we're ready to listen," Jim replied.

214

"Okay, we'll just wait and see what happens," Williams said.

Elder Hathor

"What do we have to report to the Elder when she gets here?" Tiye asked Isis.

"I have the reports of events to date at hand," Isis intoned. "There are additions that Mirte and Henuttawy wish to add; they are both on their way here."

"Tiye," Mirte said as she entered Tiye's quarters. "Isis has managed to access several places on Earth that have analyses of diseases and viruses. We have examined those, and of the 240 relatively common natural viruses, we have natural immunity to 225. I have developed a preventative inoculation against the balance so that if you did wish to visit Earth in person, we can reduce the risk to us substantially. These people have also engineered viruses to target populations. The worst offenders being the Chinese, the Russians and the United States, with others not far behind. Those that have been engineered, we have the structures of and can protect against."

"So, classic biological warfare," Tiye mused. "It's interesting how societies develop weapons that they claim are to defend against threats to them, but which are in reality weapons of attack. Henuttawy, have you uncovered anything that suggests use of these viruses?"

"Isis accessed plans of all the major societies, and we are conducting an analysis of them now," she replied. "The major offenders are the Chinese and the Russians, who both have plans to invade neighbours and expand their territories, and both have discussed possible uses of viruses to use as weapons against their opponents, and there are others that have looked at similar actions."

"Why?" Tiye asked.

"The analysis of Isis indicates that it is partly ambition on the part of the leaders, partly perceived threats by neighbours and partly desire to control resources," Henuttawy replied.

"What is the best way to stop all this?" Tiye asked.

"We have several options," Henuttawy replied. "We can destroy their military, we can warn them privately, or we could publish their plans for the rest of Earth to see, or we could take the ultimate approach and just get rid of all of them. They have done an appalling job of husbanding life on this planet and seem bent on destroying everything."

"I think when the Elder arrives, we will leave that decision to her," Tiye said. "Is there more that we have managed to uncover?"

"We have analyses of all their weapons systems," Henuttawy replied. "If required, we could disable their command and control systems quickly; in fact, we could destroy all their electronic systems within a short time, too short a time for them to react."

"Make sure all our tugs have everything they need," Tiye said. "So far, there has been little aggression towards us, but that may change. Any sign of overt aggression towards us, disable all the command structures of each society. This place is almost as bad as that one on Ganymede V."

"Those people seemed to spend all their time fighting," Henuttawy commented. "And all driven by personal ambitions of a few, all striving to be the preeminent one."

"These people have developed remarkably since our last visit," Tiye commented. "It took the Ganymede people three times as long to get to the same point where these people are now."

"I suppose circumstances drove development," Mirte said. "Examining old records, there were outbreaks of disease that wiped out large parts of populations, and then once they had mastered steam engines, things really took off, then electricity and electronics just accelerated the pace of development."

"I wonder what they'll ask for if we offer to assist them," Tiye said.

"Travel, weapons, energy," Henuttawy suggested. "That's what societies typically ask for: how do we travel in space, how can we remove armies so easily and quickly, and how do we generate the energy to do both."

"I wonder what the Elder will agree to if anything," Tiye mused.

"I think that will depend on what assurances they give that they will stop fighting and destroying the natural world of this planet. She may even demand that we leave a monitor team here to make sure they behave," Mirte said. "I'm glad we're part of the reporting group. I wouldn't want to have to be stuck here for a long time, making sure these people didn't break the rules that the Elder would set down."

"Rather like being in an embassy," Henuttawy added. "Have to listen to all the stories of the various societal groups and decide who is being truthful and who is trying to gain advantage over another group."

"Well, the monitors are good at that, and my experience with them is that they will not hesitate to eliminate anyone who transgresses in an egregious way," Mirte said.

"I wonder if the people here have any idea of what having a monitor team would be like," Henuttawy laughed.

"How could they?" Tiye said. "We're a new experience for them, and they're probably still debating if we truly are peaceful or if we're coming to take over their planet. Have we seen any significant movements of military forces?"

"The United States, China, and Russia are all dispersing their forces into smaller groups, probably with the idea that it would make it difficult for us to target them," Henuttawy replied. "I have deployed more sensors, and we can track down to the individual if we have to. Isis is running analyses of the patterns of dispersal to map their communications networks. Do you remember on Transar Six how they tried to hide away? I think it came as a shock to them when we picked up the one leader who had thought he was in a really safe and hidden place. I wonder what they thought we were doing."

"I remember, but we mustn't underestimate these people," Tiye warned.

"Now, I want the Elder to have as complete a picture as we can give her when she arrives. Isis, have you managed to develop a translator for the major languages used here?"

"It is done," Isis intoned. "I can broadcast any message that the Elder wishes to deliver in seventy of the common languages. I have analysed the frequencies used in different areas of the planet and can direct the appropriate message. It is possible that there are people in remote areas of the planet who have shunned technology and who will not hear what the Elder has to say, but that is probably a small number."

"Good," Tiye said. "Now, what are these people doing? I'm sure they're still debating whether or not we mean to attack them."

"There's probably no easy way to convince them that what we say is what we mean and we have no intentions of taking over the planet," Henuttawy commented.

"At least no one has tried to launch chemical rockets or attack their neighbours recently," Tiye said. "Perhaps the recent lessons have been enough to convince them that such moves are ill-advised."

"Perhaps," Henuttawy agreed. "But, perhaps not, they may be thinking of new and novel ways to achieve their ends. I wonder what they'll make of the Elder; she may not be as nice as us and may pass judgment on them, ending the experiment."

"Possibly," Tiye agreed. "I'm glad that's not my decision. Isis, do we have an estimate of when the Elder will be here?"

"Two auns," Isis responded.

"That's quick," Tiye thought. "We'd better get ready. Now, anything happening down there?"

"There's some activity here," Henuttawy replied, pointing to the Yemen.

"If they launch anything, take them all out. I'm tired of these people. Let's make an example of them, leave them no place to hide, no one to shelter them," Tiye instructed.

"Done," Hennutawy said. "I've relayed the instructions to Aya, and she will take whatever action is necessary."

"Good," Tiye said. "Now, I need some sleep. Call me if anything of note occurs."

* * * * *

"What's Tiye doing?" Jane asked her assembled cabinet.

"Just sitting there, I presume, waiting for this elder to show up," Madison replied.

"Anyone done anything dumb lately?" Jane asked.

"We're getting reports that some Houthi survivors who had been hiding out in the desert away from their compadres tried launching a drone at Israel," Madison replied. "That went up in a puff of smoke over the Red Sea, as best we can tell pretty much all that was left of the old Houthi mob is now gone, vaporised with whatever energy weapon the visitors use, plus it doesn't look like the visitors stopped there, they went to town on the Houthi strongholds, makes me think of the old movie *Reign of Fire* where the big dragon just burns everything up."

"Many civilian casualties?" Jane asked.

"Depends how you define civilian," Madison said. "Let's face it, the Houthi whack jobs only survived because the local population was with them, so just like Vietnam, who's Charlie, in this case, Ahmed?"

"Slow learners," Jane commented.

219

"They listen to themselves, so they're invincible," Madison added. "The idea that there's someone out there who can just take them out is not part of their thinking. Let's face it, whatever the visitors use, there's no warning, no sound of aircraft approaching, no radar blips, just zap, you're dead. The only warning that you may be targeted is that the truck or tank next to you just went up in smoke."

"Without resupply from Iran, what are they doing for weapons?" Jane asked.

"There's some coming in overland through the Empty Quarter, but that's risky with satellite surveillance, as best we can guess, it's black market from old stocks in Iraq, Syria and Lebanon," Madison explained.

"How soon before our visitors backtrack some of those shipments and take out the supply chain?" Jane asked.

"If they haven't already done so, then I'd guess the next launch by the Houthis, if there's anyone left to effect a launch, will probably see the end of them as a people, let alone a political group," Madison replied.

"That's pretty drastic," Jane commented. "It does give us a little insight into their thinking; they're used to having people listen to what they say and take heed, transgress at your peril, very authoritarian."

"Looks that way," Madison agreed. "We'd better not do anything dumb."

"Any unrest in the states?" Jane asked.

"Some," Madelaine Wildon reported. "A few riots here and there, some looting, but the governors have things well in hand, and issues were sorted out fairly quickly."

"Loss of life?" Jane asked.

"Varies by state," Madelaine replied. "More in Texas than in Maine, overall numbers 3,726 to date. Most for looting, some for failing to heed warnings about rioting."

"Where are we on food and water supplies?" Jane asked.

"Not much change since last we looked," Madelaine said. "Hoarding going on, so shelves are still empty, and when deliveries arrive, there's a mad rush to get what there is, with some fights breaking out. The major pharmaceutical guys have said they'll try and up production, but it all takes time."

"Is it time for another press conference?" Jane asked.

"I don't think so," Madelaine Wilson said. "We've nothing new to report, we're all waiting for the next thing to happen. For once, the media are being rational and telling their audiences to go about their daily business, to make sure they have at least two weeks' worth of food and water and necessary medications, and to stay alert, and they've even got talking heads giving advice on how to grow your own food."

"What, no talking heads pontificating about our inadequacies and questioning our every move?" Jane asked in mock horror.

"There's always some," Madelaine said. "VCN is the worst, but they've all got them, blathering on about nothing, because they know no more than we do, and we can all speculate about what the visitors might do, but until something happens, it's all pretty pointless."

"Anyone calling for missile strikes against our visitors?" Jane asked.

"Texas governor wondering why we're not blowing the visitors out of the sky," Madison replied. "I sent him satellite photos of what happened to North Korea and Iran, that should shut him up for a while."

"It is frustrating, though," Jane remarked. "Just sitting here waiting to see what our visitors do and when and if this Elder shows up, and if it really is just an Elder and not an invasion fleet."

* * * * *

"Tiye, we have received notice that the Elder is on her way, and it is Elder Hathor and that she's bringing a reset crew," Henuttawy reported.

"I wonder if that bodes ill for these people," Tiye mused. "A reset crew seems rather ominous. I suppose if she's bringing a reset crew, then she's bringing her own transport."

"She is, the Anput," Henuttawy confirmed.

"I'd better warn the people here that they'll see a new vessel soon, but that it does not portend an invasion," Tiye thought.

"Even though there's a reset crew on board?" Henuttawy asked.

"Better not give them any idea what a reset crew can do," Tiye said. "Isis, set up for me to talk to their United Nations."

"It is done," Isis intoned.

"People of Earth," Tiye began. *"We have been informed that our Elder Hathor will be here in five of your days. She will be arriving in another vessel, but there will be only one; this is not the beginning of an invasion."*

"Now we all just wait," Tiye said to her crew. "I will be quite happy to hand everything over to Elder Hathor and go home."

"Why, what do you think will happen?" Mirte asked.

"I think the people of this planet are in for a nasty surprise," Tiye said. "The reset crew is not a good sign; it may mean that Hathor has already decided on some course of action."

"Do you think she'll remove their technology or be more drastic?" Mirte asked.

"I am not certain," Tiye replied. "But, the last place Hathor went to led to the termination of our experiment on that planet; it took a long time to clean up the mess that the humanoids there had left."

"Do we tell the people here?" Mirte asked.

"We don't know what Hathor may do, so there's no point in telling the people here anything beyond the fact that she is coming," Tiye replied.

"Will they believe us that there will only be one vessel coming and not a whole fleet to take over the planet?" Henuttawy asked.

"That I don't know," Tiye replied. "If I were them, I'd be wary, not knowing what to expect, they may just think we are being less than honest. There is no way that we can assure them that we have no plans to invade, so they, and we, must take things on trust, difficult to do. I need to be sure I have all my reports complete by the time Hathor gets here. I want to hand things over as soon as I can and go home. Isis, get me all the latest data you have on the climate, the state of the oceans and the lands and whatever you can find that may tell us how much the people here know they have a problem and what plans, if any, they have to correct them. I also need to be sure we have the latest data on fission plants, hydrocarbon extraction, transportation and refining facilities, biological laboratories and anything else that may be a hazard to a reset crew."

"It is done," Isis intoned. "There are maps that detail what is where and the relative sizes of each facility."

"Good," Tiye said. "Horus, Ramses, anything else we need to consider?"

"There are many facilities that hold species other than human, most for the purpose of exhibit to humans, but some for experimentation."

"Those will have to go," Tiye said. "Get us a list of all those; the reset crew can deal with them when they arrive."

* * * * *

"Madame President, we have a communication from Secretary-General Sharma," an aide said. "He says that they are receiving a new message and that the so-called Elder of the visitors is on her way and will be here in five days, and that we should know that there will be one other vessel."

"Thank you," Jane said. She then called the Secretary-General and was added to the call underway with the other world leaders.

"What do we all make of this message?" Sharma asked. "Do we believe them when they say that there will be only one vessel?"

"I would be careful," Ivan said. "We'll be scanning the skies looking for new objects."

"So will we," Zhou added. "I'm not sure what we would be able to do if there really is an invasion fleet, but if we have to, we would resist."

"So, for now, we make our own preparations and wait?" Sharma asked.

"It seems pointless to try and attack them, so we wait and see if anyone comes down to the surface that we can actually interact with. Meanwhile, we do what we can to ensure the survival of our people, stockpile food and water and whatever arms we think may be effective against a landing," Jane suggested.

"That's what I'm doing," Ivan said. "In some places we're going deep underground, deeper than the Iranians were, so perhaps we'll have some safety there. The problem we have is that it takes time; we cannot go deep in hours or days, it takes weeks and months, and there is only a limited number of people we could accommodate."

"We will continue to monitor the situation, and when, and if, we hear from this Elder, we should reconvene, unless something happens in the interim that demands our attention," Sharma said.

"Look at these images we got from Hubble," Dave from JPL said to Jim.

"Holy shit, that thing is huge," Jim said. "Any size guesses?"

"I'd say about 2,500m long and 600m at its widest, with an average width of about 420m," Dave replied. "What do you think, Colonel?"

"I'd concur," Colonel Williams replied. "We'd for sure better call this in. Do you see just the one object, or are there more?"

"Only one that we can see," Jim said. "Pity we can't get real-time imaging from Hubble. I wonder if the infrared from Webb shows anything."

"How old is this image?" asked Williams.

"It was taken yesterday," Dave said. "They're still processing the signal data to get images. We'd probably do better to use the cameras on Haleakala, which at least would be real-time."

"How fast is it moving?" Williams asked.

"About one half light," Jim replied. "I compared images and looked at its relative size in the images, and when they were taken and calculated velocity."

"So, that puts it here when?" Williams asked.

"Tomorrow morning," Jim replied.

"Jesus," Williams said. "I'd better call this in. I wonder if the Russians or Chinese have seen anything."

"Can you lift anything from their signal traffic?" Jim asked.

"I'll make some calls," Williams said. "If we assume the visitors are about the same size we are, how many people could you fit in a thing that big?"

"That's a great, it depends question," Jim said. "I would think that there has to be space for smaller vehicles, there's probably common areas, if we're anything to go by; so if we take a carrier like the old USS Enterprise and consider it a floating box, then there's about 520,000 cubic metres, and there's a complement of just under 5,000, so let's say 100 cubic metres per person, allowing for engine rooms, hangars, mess halls and the rest, then ETs new vessel we guess to be about 34 million cubic metres, which at 100 per gives us about 340,000 people, and even if you double the number of people, still not enough to take over the world."

"Okay, I'll pass that along," Williams said. "When do we get the next images?"

"In about an hour," Jim replied.

"We thought that the vessel the first visitors showed up in was big, but this is another thing altogether. I wonder how you build something that big?"

Williams mused. "It takes us years to build a sub or a carrier, so what kind of technology do they have to build this."

"We can always ask," Jim suggested. "I wonder if they'd tell us."

"Probably not," Williams thought. "I wouldn't, any more than I'd share the secrets to space travel."

"Anything else new to report?" Williams asked.

"We've lost our bird that we put up to try and listen in to the visitors," Jim replied. We had it in just about the right place, then it just dropped off the board. We can't raise it, no matter what we try."

"What the hell happened?" Williams asked.

"I rather think the visitors took it," Jim replied. "They had to have been watching, and we may not have had a launch from the surface, but they would have seen the engine burn from our bird."

"I guess that must have decided that we didn't violate their proscription for rocket launches, for which I'm relieved," Williams said. "Right after we made the burn, I had an Oh Shit moment and half expected them to come after us big time, we got lucky. How long until we can get the next images of that part of the sky?"

"They're just coming through now," Jim replied. "Not there, look, there's the repeater I was talking about, but there's nothing else close enough to be our bird. Somehow, they snatched it and maybe took it to either a tug or the mothership."

"Crap," Williams said. "Well, we won't try that again."

"We have information from JPL," Madison told Jane and the rest of the cabinet. "They've seen the other vessel, and it's twice the size of the first visitor craft."

"How many people could that hold?" Jane asked.

"According to the guys at JPL, if we use an equivalent of the old USS Enterprise, then 340,000 or thereabouts, so even if they're out by a factor of ten, that's just over three million, not enough to take on the world in short order, but doable if they use the weapons they used on North Korea and Iran," Madison replied.

"Any confirmation from the Russians or the Chinese?" Jane asked.

"We're having trouble lifting their signals," Madison said.

"I'll call Sharma and see if he's heard from them," Jane suggested. "I hesitate to ask again, but how are our stocks of food and water?"

"Growing," Madelaine Wilson replied. "As I reported before, some hoarding, some profiteering, but generally people are heeding the warnings and buying what they can; the problem is that the supply chain is running dry. Fresh produce is only available when it is, so it's down to canned, dried, and long shelf life items. Those stocks are just about out, so it's up to farmers now, and we can't hurry Mother Nature."

"Are we okay?" Jane asked.

"We're fine," Madison assured her. "The White House has emergency stocks to last three years."

"Palatable?" Jane asked.

"MREs and such, or maybe one step up," Madison replied. "We'd survive, but it wouldn't be gourmet meals. Water, we've got enough for the current staff for three years, and we've got some fairly good filtration systems to clean up and recycle water."

"Secretary-General Sharma, Madame President," an aide interrupted.

"Mr Secretary-General, how you seen any of the images of the new visitor vessel?" Jane asked.

"Tsar Ivan has just provided us with some," Sharma replied. "They estimate it to be about 2,500m long and somewhere in the order of 600m at its widest."

"We concur," Jane commented. "We've also estimated that if our visitors are about the same size as us, then the number of beings on the vessel could be as few as 340,000 up to 3,400,000, depending on how they're housed and how much space is allocated to smaller vessels and such."

"Chairman Zhou gave me the same estimate," Sharma said. "Probably still not enough to invade and conquer the earth, unless they just take us one society at a time, but that seems unlikely, as we would surely try and adapt to whatever technology they used to suppress us. Tsar Ivan also said that he expected them to arrive in under a day."

"We concur," Jane added. "That is if they maintain their current speed."

"This will get interesting," Sharma said. "It will either spell the death knell for us, or it will lead to all kinds of new ideas and technologies."

"We'll find out soon enough," Jane said. "If I learn more, I will inform you."

"Thank you, Madame President," Sharma said.

"Well, the Russians and the Chinese see what we're seeing," Jane commented to her cabinet. "We should have a press briefing to let the country know what we know; there's no point in trying to keep any of this secret. That thing is too big, and every amateur astronomer on the planet will be able to see it soon enough. I'll need some images to show the assembled masses. "

The White House Press Corps were assembled, all agog to know what was new.

"Good morning," Jane said. "We have received images from JPL, confirmed by the Russians and the Chinese, of another visitor vessel that is approaching. It is larger than the first and our and other estimates of how many people of our size that could be reasonably assumed to be aboard range from a minimum of 340,000 to as many as 3,400,000. It is approaching rapidly, and we expect it to be here tomorrow or within the next couple of days. We have no indications that it is in any way hostile, but we are taking what we believe are prudent precautions in case it is. We presume that this is the arrival of the so-called Elder that we were told about."

"How big is this vessel?" CNN asked.

"Our estimates are that it is about 8,000 feet long and varies in width, or diameter, from 1,200 to 2,000 feet," Jane replied. "As a comparison, the old USS Enterprise aircraft carrier was 1,123 feet long. These are the images we have of the object; the resolution is not perfect, but you can clearly see that it is not a natural object and clearly manufactured."

"Is this an invasion fleet?" The New York Times asked.

"We have only detected one object," Jane replied. "As I have said before, it seems to us unlikely, but we must remain vigilant."

"Do we know what this Elder is going to do?" ABC asked.

"We have no information, other than the notice given us by the visitor Tiye that an Elder will be coming," Jane replied.

"Is the new object visible in the sky?" CBS asked.

"With a powerful telescope, one can see it," Jane confirmed. "We are sure that many amateur astronomers will have already spotted it."

"Is that why you're telling us about it, because you can't keep the information hidden?" VCN asked.

"It seemed prudent to us to keep the population informed of events," Jane said, sidestepping the question a little.

"Is 3,400,00 enough manpower, alienpower, to conquer the Earth?" The Christian Science Monitor asked.

"That would be enough to overrun smaller countries, but against us, the Chinese, the Russians or the Indians, they would have to take one country at at time and trust that the others did not come to the aid of the first, unless, of course, they use the magic weapon against which we would have no defence, as they did with the North Koreans and the Iranians. If they come down to Earth to clean things up, perhaps they have some kind of personal shields that would deflect our bullets and shells, or perhaps not," Jane replied.

"Is it true that you are planning to run again in the next election?" VCN asked.

"I have barely begun this term, and we have a major crisis unfolding; I have had no time to consider what I may or may not do three years hence," Jane replied.

"What do we need to do as a people?" CNN asked.

"Stay vigilant, make sure if you can that you have at least two weeks of food, water and medications on hand, otherwise go about your normal lives, difficult I know, but absent any further information about our visitor and their intentions, there is little else we can do that is productive," Jane said.

"What about these Victory Gardens that have been advertised?" NBC asked.

"It seemed to us that greater production of food locally could relieve pressure on the distribution systems if they are disrupted," Jane explained. "It may sound like harping back to earlier times, but during the two major world wars of the last century, Victory Gardens were a great source of food."

"Are they allowed everywhere?" ABC asked.

"I addressed this before, but, to repeat, there are ordinances in some cities and towns and even community associations that discourage, if not downright forbid, such gardens, and we have asked those places to amend or suspend such rules and regulations. This is the time for self-reliance, so cities, towns and community associations need time to do their part and encourage and assist, not discourage and place obstacles in the way," Jane replied.

"Is that also the case with the water from the air devices?" NBC asked.

"It is," Jane confirmed. "As long as we have power, we can use machines to condense water vapour from the air, filter the water that you get, and it's usable."

"Is the White House planting a garden?" The New York Times asked.

"There has been a vegetable garden on and off at the White House since the days of John Adams in 1800," Jane replied. "We are just reviving what has been there before and are growing what we can."

"Will there be sheep on the South Lawn?" CBS asked.

"Are we going to emulate Woodrow Wilson?" Jane pondered. "Probably not, but we'll see how things progress."

"Apart from making sure we have adequate supplies and medications, what else can we do as a nation?" CNN asked, pulling things back from the lighthearted to the potential impacts of alien interactions or invasions.

"As I said, stay vigilant, report anything that appears alien, try and maintain calm, go about your business as normally as you can, find ways to volunteer to improve our readiness to resist and survive if we have to," Jane suggested.

"Is the waiting to see what may or may not happen unsettling?" The Christian Science Monitor asked.

"It is," Jane admitted. "It is difficult to formulate a strategy when we're not sure if one is necessary and if it is, what threat do we really face?"

"How robust are our electricity grids?" VCN asked.

"We have issues with all our infrastructure," Jane replied. "Our control systems over the power and water distribution systems have never been effectively hardened against an electromagnetic pulse. There has been some work done, but there are still weaknesses. Computer systems are particularly vulnerable, and our lives have become increasingly dependent on computers and smart devices. We may have to manage without them if our visitors decide to deliver some form of electromagnetic pulse."

"Does your Government have a plan to protect those vital systems?" CNN asked.

"There have been attempts in the past to mandate hardening of the power and water systems, but the companies and municipalities that own and operate the systems have been reluctant to spend the money, so the results are piecemeal at best. We can mandate all we like, but unless the government were to nationalise and operate the systems, we are hardly in a position to make such changes," Jane replied. "It's the next quarter's earnings that drive corporate decisions, and spending against an event that may or may not happen is unlikely to garner much support."

"Is there a danger with the focus on going about our business that we'll develop a *Don't Look Up* syndrome?" The New York Times asked.

"You're referring to the old movie?" Jane asked.

"Right," The New York Times confirmed.

"I rather think that's up to you in the media," Jane said. "You can keep people focused on what is significant and not get drawn away to stories about which celebrity is in the news today."

"When this so-called Elder gets here, what are we going to ask?" CNN asked.

"We have agreed with the Secretary General of the UN that he will lead and will start with a better description of why they are here and what they want," Jane replied. "Based on the responses to those questions, we will formulate others."

"Will we ask for the technologies that permit travel in space?" ABC asked.

"I'm sure that at some stage we'll ask for that, whether or not they will be willing to tell us is another matter," Jane replied.

"Is now the time to blow the aliens out of the sky?" VCN asked.

"As I have said before, I think it unwise to expose this country to the type of destruction that was rained down on North Korea and Iran," Jane replied. "Our visitors have weapons and capabilities that we can only imagine, and I am not willing to risk the lives of millions in an abortive attempt to attack them. Thank you all for coming. I will report back when there is something of import to share."

"I don't know how many times I'll have to repeat myself to the media types," Jane complained to her cabinet after the briefing. "They ask the same inane questions time after time. VCN wants us to attack, haven't they seen the images of what happened to North Korea and Iran?"

"Perhaps we should release and broadcast before and after images of the North Korean and Iranian military installations," Madison suggested.

"Good idea, go ahead and release them, that may shut off some future suggestions about missile strikes against our visitors," Jane agreed. "I think what this visitor has done is highlight just how little we have actually done to prepare for possible CME and EMP events."

"That's true," Madison agreed. "But it all costs money, and corporations will only spend if they are forced to, as you said to the media, we as a nation are reactive, we're rarely proactive."

"That, plus we as governments spend more time undoing what the past regime did, introducing our agenda, knowing full well if that power shifts, the other side will undo what we did and introduce their agenda, in this almost endless cycle of retribution," Jane commented. "I had hoped that we would start doing things more rationally, but our visitors rather changed all that, and it remains to be seen what may happen. For now, let's just keep the southern border closed, step up checks on visitors coming from overseas, now with the uncertainty would be a great time to place agents, and I wouldn't put anything past Ivan and Zhou."

* * * * *

"The Elder is here; she has arrived in Anput," Isis intoned. An image then appeared on a screen.

"Tiye, report in person," Elder Hathor said.

"Isis, get me some transport," Tiye instructed.

"It is done, Bay Two," Isis intoned. Tiye gathered her reports and made her way to the bay and took the transport over to Anput.

231

"Tiye reporting, Elder," Tiye announced as she entered the quarters of the Elder.

"Tell me of this planet," Hathor instructed. "Not what is in the reports you have submitted, but your impressions."

"Elder, these people have evolved technologies faster than most, but they have not evolved socially," Tiye started. "They show a general level of aggression towards one another that I would have thought they had moved beyond. Speaking in the whole, and not for the individual, they have scant regard for the other species on the planet and have driven 185 bird, 130 fish and 109 mammal species to extinction since our last visit, and that says nothing of the plant and other life that they have similarly destroyed."

"Population seems uncontrolled," Hathor noted. "There are simply too many of them to live in harmony with the other species."

"That is true," Tiye agreed. "Population growth is showing some signs of slowing, but it is still too many for a balance in the ecosystem."

"What are the risks of a complete reset?" Hathor asked.

"There are some 461 active power stations that use fission, plus there are some 173 sea vessels that use fission, and there are waste sites that do not properly or adequately contain the risk," Tiye reported. "There are also facilities to enrich various isotopes. I should mention that some of the fission-powered naval vessels are currently submerged and likely to stay that way for some time to come."

"The waste sites, where are they and what do they have?" Hathor asked.

"There are many sites that contain hazards," Tiye replied. "The six that would need specific attention are disposal sites for fission drives that have come from naval vessels, some 187 all told. There are also spent fuel sites that need to be cleaned up. I have a map of them here; most are underground at varying depths."

"And refineries of one type or another?" Hathor asked.

"There are 1,234 refineries currently operating," Tiye replied.

"Noted," Hathor said. "If we look at hydrocarbon products, how many pipelines are there?"

"There are 3,921 operational pipelines that transport liquid and gas," Tiye reported. "I have maps here that show the locations of the production sites, the pipelines and the refineries or distribution hubs."

"Various chemical works?" Hathor asked.

"We have identified 10,342," Tiye replied. "Plus, there are a number of transport systems that supply them, ground and water."

"What of water transport of hydrocarbons?" Hathor asked.

"We have noted 8,931," Tiye reported. "Those are on the large bodies of water. There are also many, much smaller carriers on inland waterways."

"Biological laboratory risks?" Hathor asked.

"There are 75 high-risk laboratories that would need to be contained if power were lost permanently," Tiye replied. "There are many more that would need some attention, 1,435 that we counted. There are also dams across waterways that, if not maintained, would in time fail and cause major damage to ecosystems below the dams. Our count identified 3,907 really large structures and many thousands of smaller ones."

"Artificial satellites?" Hathor asked.

"There are many," Tiye reported. "I have provided a list; they have been careless in their placement of them. There are pieces of debris from failed satellites and collisions, both accidental and deliberate. They have also placed offensive systems on some, fission, biological and chemical. I was planning to remove at least those when I left."

"Have you been able to obtain good medical samples that permit the full and proper mapping of the DNA of the human species and those closely related?" Hathor asked.

"We have," Tiye confirmed. "We have complete DNA maps of the human and related species."

"What of these submerged naval vessels, do we know where they are?" Hathor asked.

"We do," Tiye confirmed.

"What about other industrial plants and waste sites that pose a threat to the ecosystems of the planet?" Hathor asked.

"I have data for them," Tiye replied. "We have arranged the data by the type of hazard, be it chemical or biological and what containment currently exists."

"Captive examples of other species?" Hathor asked.

"There are over 11,000 places where species other than human are kept for exhibition, varying in size and the number and variety of species present," Tiye replied. "We have lists and locations, but they do not include those myriad locations where species other than human are kept for the purposes of eating."

"So much to think about," Hathor said. "Have you even been part of a reset process?"

"No," Tiye replied.

"It is a time for much reflection," Hathor said. "A time to consider why this particular set of humans developed the way they did, how the Hemsut succeeded or not. So far, I have overseen three reset operations, varying from a simple reset of technology to a complete removal. As far as I know, the Hemsut have had far more successes than failures, but failures they have had and I am told that they are looking into why different cultures develop the way they do and what drives aggression. It may be as simple as an extreme development of the fight-or-flight instinct that is innate in all mammals, or it may be that the growth in population is too rapid for societies to live in harmony, so they compete, and that competition turns to aggression. This experiment is out of control, population growth is far too rapid, there has been insufficient growth in intelligence, so it is out of balance."

"Is there anything else?" Tiye asked.

"We have all your data and reports?" Hathor asked.

"It is all transferred," Tiye confirmed.

"Very well, you have tugs stationed above the satellite?" Hathor asked.

"We do," Tiye replied.

"Anput, send remote tugs to the locations that Isis provides," Hathor instructed.

"It is done," Anput intoned.

"Tiye, you are relieved, you may return to the home world," Hathor said. "I will clear the skies here of all orbiting artificial satellites."

"What of the objects that are orbiting the other natural satellites and planets in this system?" Tiye asked.

"Remove all of them and all traces of anything left on them. When that is done, return to the home world and report to Elder Bastet and submit your final report," Hathor instructed.

"Very good," Tiye said. "With your permission?"

"Granted, go well, Tiye," Hathor said.

"We can go," Tiye reported to her crew when she returned to Isis. "As soon as our tugs are relieved by those of Anput, let's go to the so-called Moon. Send the tugs ahead of us and clean the place up, and collect any orbiting objects, then do the same with the fourth planet, then we're going home. Isis, get us to the Moon."

"We will be there shortly," Isis intoned.

"What of the objects orbiting this planet?" Hennutaway asked.

"Hathor said that she will take care of that," Tiye replied. "I was rather hoping to do it ourselves, but she has given us our orders, so we leave. Isis is our final report ready?"

"It is done," Isis responded.

"Good, then as a last item to Report #11, add, we are proceeding as instructed by Elder Hathor to the other moons and planets of this system to remove all orbiting and landed objects that are not natural. When that is complete, we will return to base. Report #11 ends," Tiye dictated.

* * * * *

"Changing of the guard up there," Jim commented to Dave and Colonel Williams. "Those frigate-sized vessels that have been sitting over North Korea and the rest have been replaced with new ones. It also looks like the first visitor craft and its so-called tugs are on the move away from us."

"Anything new on the arrival?" Williams asked.

"Not that we can see," Jim replied. "They came, didn't say anything to us, and now the Isis is leaving."

"So, no invasion?" Williams asked.

"Seems like an odd way to do it if it is," Jim commented.

"And the first visitor craft is definitely moving away?" Williams asked.

"Headed towards the Moon," Jim confirmed.

"Not going around the back of the Earth to come at us from the other side?" Williams asked.

"No, definitely moving away," Jim replied.

"I'll call this in," Williams said.

"The first visitor craft is leaving, Madam President," Madison reported to Jane and her cabinet.

"They are really leaving?" Jane asked.

"Heading in the direction of the Moon," Madison replied. "They've also switched out the smaller vessels they had stationed over us with new ones from the second visitor craft."

"So, not going around the other side of Earth to coordinate a two-pronged attack?" Jane asked.

"Doesn't look like it," Madison replied.

"I wonder when we'll hear from the new visitors," Jane mused. "I can't imagine why they're waiting."

"All kinds of possibilities come to mind," Madison said. "Could be a genuine departure, could be a feint, could be to go and get more people to make ready for an invasion."

"I'm sure lots of people have asked this question, but how do they manage to build such big vessels?" Jane asked.

"That's one of those questions to which we have no answer, because we're tied to the surface of the Earth and anything launched into space takes us huge amounts of chemical energy, and we can only manage relatively small payloads," Madison replied. "It would take us decades to put that much material into orbit and would almost certainly bankrupt the country while we were doing it."

"Madame President, the Secretary-General," an aide interrupted.

"Mr Secretary-General," Jane said.

"Madame President, I presume you have seen this new visitor vessel. Any thoughts?" Sharma asked.

"We were just discussing it," Jane replied. "We have observed Visitor One as leaving, heading towards the Moon, and so far Visitor Two is just sitting there."

"That is what Tsar Ivan and Premier Zhou also report," Sharma said. "They have offered scenarios that range from a peaceful transfer of duties to a prelude to invasion."

"We have had the same discussions," Jane said. "Should we attempt to initiate contact with Visitor Two and this so-called Elder?"

"It may give us a better idea of their intentions," Sharma commented. "I will put together a message and ask for your thoughts."

"I await your next call," Jane said. "I suppose we should hold another press conference and let people know what we've seen."

"That would be prudent," Madelaine Wilson said.

The White House Press Corps was assembled, and Jane went to talk to them.

"Ladies and Gentlemen, thank you for coming. There has been a change with our visitors; the second vessel that I had previously told you was on its way has arrived, and the first one has left," Jane reported. "So far, there has been no communication from Visitor Two; it appears to be just waiting. The Secretary-General of the United Nations is drafting a message that will be transmitted to Visitor Two, asking what its intentions are."

"How do we know the first one has left?" VCN asked.

"We've been tracking its progress in the direction of the Moon," Jane replied. "Its progress has been steady and shows no sign of slowing."

"What about these so-called tugs?" CNN asked.

"The ones from Visitor One left with Visitor One and have been replaced with others from Visitor Two," Jane reported.

"What are they waiting for?" ABC asked.

"We have no idea," Jane admitted. "We can only speculate about their intentions and stay vigilant. That is all I have for you today. I will call another briefing when we have something to report."

Reset

"We have received a communication from the planet calling itself Earth," Anput intoned. "They enquire as to our intentions."

"Set up a communication with the organisation that calls itself the United Nations, and be ready to transmit on all used frequencies," Hathor instructed.

"It is done," Anput intoned.

"People of Earth, I am Elder Hathor. I have been charged by the Hemsut to report on progress for their eighteenth experiment and make decisions that will affect your future," Hathor said. That statement was seen not only by those gathered at the United Nations General Assembly, but also by anyone on Earth who had a television, tablet, or smartphone.

"I am Secretary-General Sharma, and I have been delegated to speak for all of us on Earth," Sharma started. "What do you mean by decisions that will affect our future?"

"We have noted that you have since our last visit further desecrated the natural environment of the planet, you have had uncontrolled population growth that led to that desecration and destruction, you have exploited resources in a reckless manner, you have polluted the natural world with chemicals and what you call plastics, you have caused many species of plants, birds, fish, mammals, reptiles, amphibians, crustaceans and insects to become extinct and you have warred among yourselves over petty disputes resulting from the ambitions of a few people and over the demand for resources and dominion, you have developed, tested, and used fission weapons, further polluting the atmosphere, the water and large tracts of land. Is any of this untrue?" Hathor asked.

"We have in the past made mistakes," Sharma admitted.

"And, yet you persist in repeating those same mistakes with the massive arrays of martial might that various of your societies like to display and threaten smaller societies with," Hathor added.

"We are trying to mediate disputes," Sharma said.

"You say you are trying, but after Tiye arrived, it was necessary for her to negate moves made by three of your societies because they would not comply with a simple request," Hathor pointed out. *"Now I am here and am waiting to hear one reasonable argument why I should not just declare the*

238

experiment a failure and eliminate all human life on this planet and let it recover.”

“We are a planet of many and varied societies with differing beliefs and challenges,” Sharma said.

“And yet, you devote more of your resources to weapons than to managing the environment in which you live, the leaders of your societies show scant regard for the other living species on the planet, should I go on?” Hathor asked. *“You all descend from a small number of humanoids, so you are all the same, even though local conditions have led to adaptation differences that are superficial only, and yet you seem determined to kill each other, often for no other reason than those superficial differences. Is this the mark of a developed society?”*

“I think for us the situation has changed,” Sharma said. “We have in the past speculated that there may be others in the Galaxy and the Universe, but we had no evidence.”

“That is no answer,” Hathor commented. *“If you had listened more to your elders and philosophers, you would have known, but instead, you chose a bellicose path driven by hubris, arrogance and ambition. Clearly, your intellectual development has not been as rapid as your technological development, so a course correction is the minimum change I would make. How would you propose solving four problems? First, clean up your oceans, land and atmosphere of all foreign matter; second, stop the destruction of your natural environment; third, control your population back down to a level that is sustainable; and fourth, dismantle and safely dispose of all fission-related enrichment plants, power plants, propulsion systems and weapons. I give you one month of your time to propose suitable courses of action. I will then decide what my next actions will be. If you have questions, direct them to Anput, and I will be informed. Finally, we note that there are artificial satellites that are not for observing weather and other peaceful purposes; all those that have weapons or are clearly designed to attack other satellites are being removed now. I have no tolerance for systems clearly designed to attack others; there is no plausible reason for such systems, it is not defensive, it is offensive, in both the literal and metaphorical senses.”*

The General Assembly broke out into an uproar with the less developed nations accusing the developed nations of exploiting everything and everyone, and creating the situation that they all found themselves in. The developed nations made counterclaims that much of the population growth was in the less developed nations, leading to overexploitation of the meagre resources that were in those countries and causing civil breakdown. Sharma tried to restore order and finally succeeded, and suggested that each ambassador consult with his or her home government to see if they could arrive at some suggested course of action that might be acceptable to Elder Hathor. He suggested that they reconvene in one week to start to build a response to Elder Hathor.

Nicole Edwards made her way back to Washington and a meeting with Jane and her cabinet.

"So, what's the take on this Hathor?" Jane asked.

"If we agree that we're not seeing an avatar, and we speculate that they age at somewhere near the same rate we do, I'd place her in her early sixties," Madelaine Wilson suggested.

"Looks like she could be a hardarse," Madison added. "Mess with me and life will go badly for you, plus who knows what she's got in that megaship of hers."

"I wonder if it's significant that Visitor One just left. Are they truly going back home, or going to bring reinforcements?" Jane asked.

"That seems unlikely," Madison replied. "They sent off one of their shuttles to get this Hathor here. Does that suggest that they don't have the ability to communicate over light-year distances, or did they decide that a report in person was warranted? If they wanted reinforcements, just send another shuttle and leave Visitor One here."

"A message for you, Sir," an aide said, putting a paper down in front of Madison.

"Well, not all intentions are good," he said. "It looks like Visitor One just collected all the satellites we have orbiting the Moon, and they're on their way to Mars now."

"What did we have around the Moon?" Jane asked.

"Seven satellites looking at the lunar surface and providing secure uplinks for the probes we have on the surface," Madison replied.

"Should we assume that all the surface items are now also gone?" Jane asked.

"Without an orbiting platform, we don't know and have no means to find out," Madison replied.

"Did they also take those of China, Russia, India, Japan and the UAE?" Jane asked.

"Judging by the traffic we're picking up, I'd say yes, they just took everything on and around the moon, and my guess if they'll do that on Mars, too. We know they already took the defunct and crashed items, so this will just finish the job," Madison replied.

"What about the Hathor statement about taking out some of the objects currently orbiting here?" Jane asked.

"The communique I just got says that they've done just that and the Russians have lost twelve, the Chinese, fifteen, and we've lost eight," Madison reported. "We know that they've already taken all the North Korean birds and the Iranian ones."

"How vulnerable are we if she just takes everything?" Jane asked.

"We lose the ability to watch out adversaries, we lose the ability to better forecast weather, we lose broadcast media, social media and a few other things," Madison replied. "We would have to go back to old-style communications, so we'd better figure on boosting up cell towers and fibre optic and copper connections. That is, of course, unless she lets loose a big EMP."

"I presume it also means that Russian and Chinese surveillance is gone too?" Jane asked.

"If she takes everything, then yes," Madison confirmed. "If she also cleans up the skies of debris, it would give us all the chance to put new birds up without the fear of them running into something."

"What do we do now? Any suggestions?" Jane asked the assembled group.

"Wait them out," Madison suggested. "Make some suitable noises and then they'll go home and life can return to normal."

"Can it ever return to normal?" Jane asked. "Life for us has changed, we know we're not alone, and we know that the visitors have technologies that we can only dream of."

"I don't know what we can suggest to this Elder Hathor that will be acceptable," Madelaine Wilson said. "They seem to place great emphasis on fission, by which I presume they mean nuclear power plants, propulsion systems and weapons. Could we promise to rid ourselves of those?"

"And leave us exposed to Ivan and Zhou?" Madison snorted.

"Isn't that rather the fundamental problem?" Jane asked. "We mistrust one another to the extent that even faced with possible dire consequences, we're not prepared to make the first move, lest some other actor takes advantage of our perceived weakness."

"Well, we need to think of something," Madelaine said. "I get the impression that this Hathor character won't tolerate dissembling."

"She shows a remarkable command of the English language," Jane remarked. "And a wide knowledge of our issues and challenges."

"Safely disposing of nuclear reactors, warheads, and wastes is a challenge," Madison said. "There is no real way to do that with complete safety; it usually means burial, but over time, containment rusts and breaks down, leading to pollution."

"Is that why we have a reactor graveyard at Hanford?" Jane asked.

"It is," Madison confirmed. "We've created a huge amount of waste that is contaminated, and the half-life of the worst isotopes is measured in billions of years, so way past our lifetimes."

"Maybe we should ask this Hathor if they have the lift capacity to take the stuff off planet and chuck it into the sun?" Madelaine suggested. "Would that mess up the sun?"

"Not at all," Madison said. "The sun's essentially a big nuclear fusion reactor with extremely high temperatures, and it's huge, you could probably fit over a million Earths into the Sun, so a reactor or two, even a few hundred, would be minuscule compared to what's there."

"It's hot then?" Madelaine asked.

"About 10,000 degrees on the surface to 27,000,000 in the centre, so nothing we can comprehend," Madison replied. "But launching things into the sun isn't as simple as you might imagine. Anything launched from here already has the orbital velocity of the Earth and would tend to stay at that unless energy is expended to change it. Perhaps the visitors have a quick and easy way to do that; we do not."

"Who else has weapons, ships and submarines?" Jane asked.

"Us, Russia, China, the UK, France, India and Pakistan have weapons; North Korea and Iran did before Visitor One fixed that, Israel claims not to have any, but I don't believe that," Madison replied. "Ships and subs, we do, the Russians, the Chinese, the UK, France, Australia, Turkey and Brazil."

"So, quite a large number, all told, of reactors and weapons," Jane commented. "That's quite a task they would set themselves if they helped us get rid of it all."

"How many factories do we have that produce plastics?" Jane asked.

"We've never really counted," William Botha, the Commerce Secretary, replied. "But, my guess is if you add up all the precursor plants and processing plants, at least 10,000, and employing over a million folks."

"So, discontinuing plastic production would have a big negative impact on the economy?" Jane asked.

"Not to mention the impact on the packaging industry, pretty much everything we buy is contained or wrapped in some kind of plastic," Botha added. "Then there's pipes for plumbing, auto parts, plane parts, the list goes on."

"What about cleaning up microplastics?" Jane asked.

"Huge challenge," Botha admitted. "We can probably filter down to one micron, and with reverse osmosis filters, we can go really small, but we can hardly filter the oceans. The particles keep getting smaller, and we ingest them, and they are in our bloodstreams already."

"So, we should ask our new visitors if they have any magic cures for fixing this, maybe some kind of bacteria that breaks down the microplastics into molecules that are not harmful to birds, fish or crustacea, or us, maybe as far as the individual atoms of hydrogen and carbon and whatever else is in the plastics," Jane mused. "Now, what about population control?"

"We're seeing negative growth in birth rates," Helen Cortez replied. "We're keeping the population stable with immigration. The so-called Third World shows the highest birth rates; reigning them in will be tough."

"Maybe the visitors have a DNA modifier that can drop the fertility rates," Madison suggested.

"Don't anyone repeat that outside this room, " Jane cautioned. "We'd have every conspiracy theorist up in arms. What about the destruction of the natural environment?"

"Well, with population growth comes pressure to expand agricultural land, urban and suburban areas, with the concomitant loss of undisturbed areas, and lately even national parks supposedly set aside for the people, essentially looking out for us and too bad for other species," Madelaine said. "This Hathor is right, we've treated the planet as solely ours, our source of resources and land and too bad for anything else, poor stewards in her words."

"If we put together a twenty-year plan, what could we achieve in that time?" Jane asked.

"For food, we'd have to produce things differently, maybe more vertical farms using hydroponics. We have to switch over packaging from plastics to glass, aluminum and paper," Botha said. "We could probably get half the way there, but it would mean better recycling, mining more iron ore, bauxite and sand, cutting down and hopefully replanting more trees, so more destruction of the land. We could change things quite a bit if the marketing guys didn't have to have a foot-square package for an item that's one inch square. That would drop the demand for materials a lot, but I've no idea how we'd legislate that or enforce any rules, who takes the lead, us or the Congress."

"Between us, don't expect much out of them," Jane said. "They're all looking to the next election, and sweeping changes of the type the visitors are talking about would undoubtedly hit their constituencies, and they don't want to be the ones who brought unemployment and change."

"So, does this mean that we go back to this Hathor with some questions?" Madelaine asked.

"If nothing else, it may show willing and buy us more time," Jane said. "I'll get hold of Sharma and ask him to forward the questions. Now let's formulate what we want to ask."

"Fusion technology, with the loss of our 66 nuclear power stations, we'd need something to generate electricity; we'd have to replace about 25% of the current capacity, over 100 Gigawatts," George Grant replied.

"With enough fusion power, we could probably also drop our fossil fuel plants, maybe even the dreaded windmills. We're not the only ones with nuclear power stations; there's a whole list of about 33 other countries that have reactors in varying numbers, so they would have generation problems as well."

"Some magic bacteria or agent that breaks down microplastics that is not harmful to plant and animal life," Cortez added.

"Some assurances that they will guarantee security for the next twenty years while we all learn to live with one another without going to war," Madelaine suggested.

"Their ideas on constraining population growth would be interesting," Cortez said. "Whatever it is, it won't be popular around the world, and even here, we'd have push back from our supporters, as would the other side."

"Maybe they'll just put something in the water that affects humans but nothing else," Grant suggested.

"We could do with some help when it comes to disease," Cortez added. "I know that may just add to the problem of population growth if death rates go down, but if we could manage population growth with a healthier population, it would cost us a lot less."

"Don't let the health care and pharmaceutical industries hear you say that," Madelaine said. "You'd cut into their profits."

"If they have some small magic generators that would power locomotives and ships, that would be interesting," Grant said.

"I'm presuming that asking them about their space drive technology and how they manage to navigate in space would be a waste of time, as would asking them about whatever weapon they used to zap out the North Koreans and Iranians," Madison commented. "But if they would share the technology they use for their shuttles that could replace our current fleet of commercial aircraft, that would be interesting."

"I don't think they would trust us not to just use their weapon on each other, but I like the idea of shuttles that are essentially anti-gravity," Jane agreed. "Okay, let's write up what we have and I'll present it to Sharma, and we'll see what Ivan and Zhou come up with."

The questions were listed and passed on to Sharma, and he added a couple more that had come from not Russia and China, but South Africa and Andorra, of all places. Sharma dutifully relayed those questions to Anput, and then they waited.

Hathor replied in two weeks and addressed the UN General Assembly. *"People of Earth,"* she started. *"We have been asked if we have some technologies that will help you undo some of the damage you have done to this planet. We do, and we will make it available on certain conditions. First, you will cease and desist in the use of fission technology for power generation. You, with our help, will dismantle all those facilities. We will provide in exchange fusion technology that will provide you with the means to generate electricity without the harmful waste products. All ships and sub-surface ships that use fission technology will return to port, and we will cut out the fission facilities and dispose of them. Any attempt to dissemble and conceal will result in the destruction of the rulers of that country and all its martial forces and facilities. All fission weapons will be surrendered to us at places we will announce, and all facilities used to enrich isotopes for use in those weapons will be dismantled forthwith. This process will take five of your years, and teams will remain here for that period to assist and manage. You do not need these weapons. You will also cease and desist in the development and production of chemical and biological weapons and will surrender to our teams all the agents you currently have. Next, you have many facilities that produce what you call plastics. Those products are harmful to the environment, and pose dangers to fish, birds, mammals and insects. We will provide systems to break down what you call micro-plastics into benign molecules, and we expect that you will phase out production of all plastics within five of your years. If you do not, we will take action of our own. The last item is that of population growth and control. Population growth is a significant problem on this planet as the competition for resources becomes ever more intense and peoples become more belligerent. If you do not have the capability and will to manage your populations, we will do it for you. You have one of your months to agree to these conditions and arrange the surrender of all fission weapons, or we will take action. The weapons surrender will take place at locations we will communicate to each government that has them."*

"Wow," Jane said, as she and her cabinet sat and thought about what had just been said. "Any thoughts?"

"It's a tall order," Madison said. "If we just hand over our nuclear arsenal, how vulnerable does that make us?"

"Do you think it could be the prelude to an invasion?" Jane asked. "Make us surrender our most effective weapons, then drop down and take over."

"That's a possibility," Madison agreed. "But we should also consider that they took out all the North Korean and Iranian plants and weapons; they could have just carried on and done us as well."

"I wonder what Ivan and Zhou are thinking right now," Jane mused.

"I'll bet they've both got factions that say hold onto everything and see what this Hathor does," Madelaine Wilson said.

"Is that a risk we want to take?" Jane asked.

"We should get the leaders of both houses and see what they have to say," Madelaine suggested. "This is somewhat like a treaty, and Congress is supposed to approve treaties."

"I'll set it up," Jane said. "Now, is it possible to get all our carriers and subs into port at once?"

"We could," Madison said. "We'd have to use Norfolk, Mayport, San Diego and Bremerton. It would mean pulling everything back from Guam and Pearl, but it's doable. If we issued orders today, they could all be back here in a couple of weeks."

"How long to pull all the warheads from ICBMs and cruise missiles?" Jane asked.

"We might be able to do that in a month," Madison agreed. "But, we'd have to get right on it and put special teams on the job. The Air Force is easier to deal with than the Navy. Silos are fixed, but we'd have to get boats back to port to pull missiles; that's at least a week for many and perhaps as long as two weeks, just to make port, then the work starts."

"So, all the more reason to get the leaders of both houses in here ASAP," Jane said. "The way Congress works, they'll want to discuss, debate, wrangle, look for political advantage and generally drag their feet until one minute before midnight before doing anything. We don't have that long, we have an ultimatum, and I'm not sanguine about our chances if we drag our feet and fail to comply."

"Who's going to be the first to whine and say they need more time?" Botha asked.

"Ivan," Madison said. "He's got mobile launchers all over the place, and he'll be reluctant to hand them all over."

"This Hathor said nothing about conventional forces," Jane said. "Do we need to step up our capabilities there?"

"Our shipbuilding is goddam slow," Madison complained.

"How much of that is your department, and how much is it the contractors just dragging their feet to drive the costs up?' Jane asked. "It seems to me that if you standardise on a ship design, then make no unnecessary changes, you could push the yards to fixed price and get them to deliver on time, for a change. How long did it take to build a Liberty Ship in WW2?"

"Thirty-nine days by 1943," Madelaine replied. "Once they had the techniques down, it was just a matter of people and getting the right materials to the job at the right time. Now, Liberty and Victory Ships were simple cargo vessels, and our Navy ships are more complex with electronics and weapons systems, but the same concepts should apply."

"What about chem and bio labs?" Jane asked.

"They can be shut down fairly quickly, but disposing of everything will be a challenge, unless the visitors have some sophisticated containment systems," Madison replied.

"Who will try and hide theirs in what we might call medical labs, like the CDC labs?" Jane asked.

"Zhou," Dr Park said. "The Chinese have done groundbreaking work on viruses, but the lines between genuine medical research and weapons technology tend to get a little blurred."

"What if our visitors want us to get rid of nuclear weapons because they have no real defence against them, except destroying the launch vehicle?" Jane asked.

"Possible," Madison agreed. "So no SciFi shielding, just good old-fashioned detection and destruction before it gets there."

"We should get the Congressional leaders over here and see what they have to say," Jane said.

"Madame President," an aide interrupted. "We have just been given locations for weapons surrender. They sent us a map, and they are just east of Cheyenne, Kings Bay, Georgia, and Bremerton, Washington."

In due time, John Harris, the Speaker, Donald Trent, Bill Evans and Mitch Decker arrived.

"Gentlemen, thank you for coming. I presume you all saw the item that our new visitors broadcast and the demands they made. What are your thoughts?" Jane asked.

"We can't possibly give up the ability to deter the Russians and the Chinese," Harris replied. "I wouldn't trust the Russians not to try and hide something, then, when E.T. has gone home, use it on us."

"What could the visitors do if we ignore this demand?" Evans asked.

"You all saw what happened in North Korea and Iran," Jane replied. "I would expect something along those lines."

"So, we've got just under a month to figure out some plan of attack that lets us take them out before they can take us out," Trent added.

"If we could get the Russians and the Chinks to agree, could we try simultaneously launching ICBMs at them?" Decker asked. "If we set off a hundred or so missiles at the same time, how many might make it through?"

"Well, we estimate that it would take an ICBM six to seven hours to get to the orbit where the visitors are parked," Madison said. "The first visitor took out the North Korean and Iranian launches in under a minute, so it may come down to how many of their fancy weapons they have and how quickly they can retarget. North Korea was pretty easy, Iran was all one battery, so no real need for sophisticated retargetting."

"There's no way we can get anything there any quicker?" Evans asked.

"It's basic physics and our gravitational pull," Madison replied. "To get away from the earth, we need an escape velocity of about 25,000 miles an hour, and to achieve that with the chemical rockets we have takes a lot of fuel, which is why ICBMs and satellite launch vehicles are as big as they are."

"What about hypersonic missiles?" Harris asked.

"They can reach velocities of about 3,800 miles an hour," Madison replied. "Good for strikes within our gravitational field, but not so good for escaping gravity."

"How do the visitors achieve the speeds they seem to be able to reach?" Evans asked.

"We have no idea," Madison admitted. "They clearly have technologies that we can't even imagine at this time."

"What if we were to bury some warheads deep in the earth?" Decker asked.

"The visitors have some kind of detection system and destructive system that can make a mess of underground facilities," Madison replied. "They collapsed the Iran deep underground enrichment plant that we had trouble reaching; they did the same to the North Koreans."

"What's the deepest mine in the US?" Trent asked.

"Harvest Two in Idaho," Botha replied. "Goes down to just over 9,800 feet. There was a deeper one in the Sierra Nevadas that went down to over 10,000 ft, but that was worked out and shut down. Most of the really deep mines are the gold mines in South Africa."

"Could we store warheads at the bottom of this Harvest Two?" Trent asked.

"We'd have to work out the details with the owner," Botha said. "They'd want to know that they could continue to work the mine, and they'd want to know the risks of the visitors collapsing the mine and them losing it."

"We do know where they want us to take our warheads," Jane said. "They either know just where our silos are, or they made a damn good guess, they've told us to deliver the warheads to a place near Cheyenne, and to Kings Bay, Georgia and Bremerton, Washington."

"So, does that mean they know where everything is?" Evans asked.

"Your guess is as good as mine," Jane replied.

"If it's too hard to take out their mothership, what about luring these so-called tugs down to a lower altitude and then blasting them?" Evans asked. "When they took out the North Korean subs, didn't they have to come down to a much lower altitude?"

"They did," Madison confirmed. "We're not sure what kind of system they used to target the subs, but it essentially collapsed them, just crushed them, and they went to the bottom. We speculated that in order to detect the subs, they had to come down a bit; maybe there's a weakness there. But what we don't understand is how they manage to come down from GEO to LEO and below in such a short time. They must have a drive system we don't understand, and they must have incredible heat shields to withstand the re-entry heat build-up."

"If we were to try and decoy to lure the visitors down, what do we sacrifice?" Jane asked.

"Can we rig up a sub with some remote controls and send it out?" Trent asked.

"We could," Madison replied. "But what do we have it do to attract the attention of the visitors? The North Korean job was a general take out of all their military, land, sea and air, how do we provoke them without losing everything?"

"Can we hang a missile with a nuke on it under something like an SR-71, fly as high as we can, then launch at the visitors?" Decker asked.

"We can go exo-atmosphere with that," Madison confirmed. "But it's still going to take more than that to achieve escape velocity."

"What about just putting some remote controls on an SR-71 and just point it straight up until it runs out of fuel?" Decker asked.

"It won't reach escape velocity, and then we'd have an uncontrolled crash back to earth," Madison replied.

"What we could do is attach timing devices to the warheads we surrender to have them all go off two or three days after they've been delivered and the visitors have taken them up to one of their ships," Brian Taylor, the Vice President, suggested in a very rare moment of contribution.

"Is that feasible?" Harris asked.

"A tall order to get it done by the deadline, but worth a shot," Madison concurred.

"I like that idea," Evan said. "What if we hold back and tell them to keep submerged three of our boomers, return to the rest to port and tell the visitors that's all we have."

"I don't think the visitors will fall for that," Jane said. "I rather suspect they know exactly what we have and also have a pretty good idea of where it is; they took out the North Korean boats quickly enough."

"How do the visitors communicate with these tugs?" Harris asked.

"We think we've worked that one out," Madison replied. "We think they use light. They've got some small objects that can repeat and essentially give them line of sight. The problem for us is that there's no signal leakage, so we can't tap into their signals."

"Can we use a laser to take out these repeaters?" Harris asked.

"The Israelis tried that, and their laser beam was bounced back to the sending location, amplified, and that took care of that, all gone in a puff of smoke," Madison replied. "We also tried moving a satellite close enough to be within the expansion cone of the beam. We got it there, and it's gone; we think the visitors took it."

"Was that wise?" Jane asked. "I didn't authorise that. I thought Tiye said no rocket launches?"

"We have been doing routine burns to keep satellites where they need to be," Madison replied. "And the visitors seem to have understood that we need to do that from time to time, so we took a chance."

"Don't do that again," Jane said.

"Let's say, for the sake of discussion, that we agree to the visitors' demands. What assurances do we have that they'll stick with what they promised?" Evans asked.

"That is rather the question, isn't it?" Jane said. "They're asking us to take a lot on trust, and we don't know if we can trust them."

"I wonder if they really do have fusion technology," Trent mused.

"If they do and it's of a size and complexity, or maybe simplicity would be a better way to look at it, then I would love to see all our nuclear power stations switch over," George Grant, the Secretary of Energy, said. "If they can actually rid us of all the spent navy reactors and all the spent fuel we've got stored, that would also be good."

"Is five years long enough to switch things over?" Harris asked.

"Those are details we need to understand," Grant said. "I would imagine that the proposal is that they bring in, or teach us how to build a fusion plant, get that running and connected, then we take the existing plant offline and they can do their thing and dismantle it and dispose of it."

"How many plants are we dealing with?" Harris asked.

"Fifty-six facilities and 98 reactors," Grant replied. "A couple have just been commissioned and come online."

"So 20 plus reactors a year from us, how about the UK, France, Russia and the rest?" Evans asked.

"The countries that have over 20 reactors are: us with 98, then China, 64, France, 58, Russia, 39, and India, 20, then there are the rest, totalling 432 worldwide," Grant replied.

"Okay, that's 80 plus a year, that's a tall order, how many people on that ship?" Evans asked.

"If we make some assumptions about their size and accommodations, then somewhere between 340,000 and 3,400,00," Madison replied.

"That's a lot of people, even at the bottom end," Harris commented.

"I wonder if they use robots of any type?" Decker said.

"Would make sense for reactor removal," Evans said. "Kind of droid army."

"Could also be killer droids," Trent said. "Star Wars: *Attack of the Clones*."

"I suppose one could pack a sizeable droid army in a thing that big," Madison agreed. "But we've seen no evidence that they use droids. Why would we think they do?"

"We've used simple robot devices and drones; the Russians and Ukrainians really went to town with them in the last war, so why not?" Trent asked.

"This is all very interesting," Jane interrupted. "I'm looking for your counsel and opinions, as sweeping as recent Supreme Courts have made Executive Powers, I rather think this demands consensus, not edict. So, I would like your views on our proposed course of action."

"We should call a joint session and discuss this," Harris said.

"By all means," Jane said. "But remember, we do have a deadline, and Hathor will be waiting for an answer."

"What the hell were you thinking?" Jane asked Madison after the congressional delegation had left.

"I saw no particular risk," Madison replied.

"No risk!" Jane said. "North Korea makes a dumb move, and they lose their entire army. What if the visitors had decided that this ploy of yours was in violation of their edict, what then?"

"I decided that the risk was minimal," Madison said.

"You decided, what makes you the expert on Hathor and her thoughts and actions? You're lucky that we have our visitors sitting over us. We don't have the luxury of a Senate confirmation hearing right now for your replacement. Do anything like that again and you'll be gone," Jane said. "In fact, do anything like that again and you'll be in Leavenworth. I'd consider it a time of war and lock you up as a traitor."

"Look, I'm tired of all this inaction," Madison yelled. "We've got to be able to take these aliens out."

"Have you come up with a viable plan that doesn't leave the country as a smoking ruin?" Jane asked.

"There must be something we can do," Madison said.

"Maybe there is," Botha said. "This Hathor wants us to surrender all our nuclear warheads, but we still know how to make them, we still know how to mine uranium and build an enrichment facility. We go along with what she says, we pick up the fusion technology and whatever else she has to offer, and then we just wait. I'm certain that's what Zhou will be planning, maybe even Ivan. Hathor's going to want to go home at some point, and if we're a nice, peaceable, tractable planet, they'll leave and we can chart our own future."

"So, we need to make sure we educate the next generation," Jane thought. "Science will no longer be a dirty word, except political science, which just seems to me to teach corruption."

"That's hardly fair," Madelaine Wilson commented. "We do have members of both houses who are trying to do the right thing."

"So, a whole new arms race," Jane said. "E.T. goes home, and the first thing we all do is go back to square one and start again. Wasn't there something in the old *Mad Magazine* that covered that?"

"Might have been," Grant agreed. "I agree with Bill, acquiesce, then make sure we've retained all the knowledge, then rebuild our own lives after the visitors have gone."

"So, revamp and rebuild the Department of Education, make universities accept on academic merit, then make sure we don't lose talent in the early grades by properly funding all schools, not just those in wealthy neighbourhoods," Madison suggested. "I can get behind that. I never liked the idea that you could buy your way into college. While we're at it, drop or cut back all these sports scholarships. If colleges want winning sports teams for TV appearances, let them do it honestly by just hiring a team and having them play for the college. Get away from this fiction that these kids are there to get an education. They might, but they're there to earn the colleges money from TV broadcasts. Sort of farm teams for the majors."

"I never saw you as supporting diversity in universities," Romero commented.

"I'm not if you mean accept based on colour and ethnic background," Madison said. "But we miss a lot of talent because we skew the education system from the earliest grades. Given the right education, talent will out, and if we're going to rebuild after the visitors have gone, we're going to need all the talent we can find. We're going to have to do the same in DOD. We'll need men, and women, who are smart and can think, not just do push-ups and run around with a gun."

"What do the defence contractors do while our visitors are here?" Jane asked.

"Use them to dismantle all the stuff that the visitors want gone, and make damn sure they record everything they do, so that they can put it back together again," Grant suggested.

"Better make sure it's written down somewhere and not just a computer file," Romero commented. "One good EMP and we may lose all that is stored electronically, so we do need printed materials that we can store safely."

"What about the petrochemical industries and plastics?" Jane asked.

"Same deal," Madison suggested. "Fund them to find alternate packaging materials and replace plastics. Maybe even step up the use of biodegradable packaging."

"I'm sensing a trend towards accepting the visitors' demands," Jane said.

"Yes, but with a big but, we vamp up our education and make sure we know how to make everything quickly, so that when the visitors go home, we can produce what we need to deter Zhou and Ivan," Madison said.

"If we all start again at square one, who gets there the quickest, us or the Russians or Chinese?" Madelaine asked.

"It would be a race," Madison conceded. "We run the risk of being our own worst enemy with regulation; you can bet that the Russians and Chinese would suspend or dump any rules and regs that got in the way of making something that would threaten us."

"Of course, there's always the possibility that the Congress will opt to demur and tell Hathor to get lost," Romero said. "Then, I don't have any idea what she would do."

"Any opinions as to what Congress will come up with?" Jane asked.

"Unlikely coalitions," Romero replied. "They'll be ultra hawkish types who want to try and blow the visitors out of the sky; they'll come from both parties, driven by different ideologies, but with the same end game. Then they'll be the other side, looking at the longer term, rebuild as soon as the visitors have gone, again drawn from both parties."

"Madame President," an aide interrupted. "Your presence at a joint session of the House and Senate has been requested."

"Thank you, tell them we'll be right over," Jane said.

"I suppose they've decided that you should hear all the wrangling and not just the précis given by the leaders," Romero said.

"Let's go and see what they're discussing," Jane said.

"Madame President, member of the Cabinet, we felt it necessary to have you here to be part of this process," John Harris said.

"Thank you for inviting us," Jane replied. "Please continue."

"The Honourable Representative from Texas, James Bragg, has the floor," Harris said.

"Madame President, members of both Houses, we cannot allow ourselves to be ordered around and dictated to by an alien who hasn't even had the courtesy to come down from her aerie in the sky and listen to us," Bragg said. "We can be certain that the Russians and the Chinese are busily plotting how to secrete their weapons, perhaps surrendering a few to the visitors for form's sake, but keeping enough back to threaten us. We need to segregate a portion of our strategic warheads, bury them deep in a mine and be ready to protect ourselves when they leave. If we cannot find a way to directly attack them and be successful, then we should plan for the long term and be ready."

"I recognise the Honourable Member from Louisiana, Luther Wilson," Harris said.

"I agree with my esteemed colleague," Wilson said. "The President and the Secretary of Defence have done little to formulate a plan of attack against this alien, so we must set the direction ourselves. My colleague and I have put forth a resolution to deny the alien some of our strategic weapons and to secrete enough to protect us against the aggressions of Russia and China."

"There is a resolution on the floor, discussion?" Harris invited. Then followed six hours of speeches, wrangling, and more speeches until Harris called for a vote. Jane waited a watched as the votes were cast and was appalled at the result, 350 House members for, and 63 Senate members for.

"The ayes have it," Harris crowed. "Madame President, you have your answer. We as a nation will not surrender meekly to this alien. Do you have any remarks?"

"This is suicide," Jane said. "Did you not see what was done to the North Koreans and the Iranians? In all conscience, I cannot be party to suicide; you have my resignation."

"Mr Taylor, are you ready to be sworn in as President?" Harris asked.

"It would be an honour," Brian Taylor replied. The Chief Justice of the Supreme Court was very conveniently on hand, and Taylor was duly sworn in as President.

"President Adams, we thank you for your service," Taylor said. "I think you can now leave us to create a winning strategy that will protect this nation and demonstrate to these aliens that we will not go meekly into the night. Good day to you, Madame."

Jane took that as the dismissal it was and left. All she wanted to do was get as far away from Washington and any government or military installation that she could. She went back to the White House and told her husband, Tom, that they needed to pack essentials only and leave town as quickly as possible to get as far away from Washington as they could. He surprised her when he produced two small backpacks, told her to give him her phone, which he proceeded to reset back to factory settings, and then just left it on the counter. That done, he told her they were ready to go.

"You think the visitors have the capability of detecting hidden warheads?" Tom asked as they walked out of the private quarters.

"I've no idea what they have, and I'm afraid that we're about to find out," she replied.

"How long do we have?" Tom asked.

"A month," Jane replied. "Hathor said that we should deliver up the warheads to designated spots in a month; one of those spots is in Wyoming, just east of Cheyenne, the other two are convenient for SWFPAC and SWFLANT in Bremerton and Kings Bay."

"So, Cheyenne, Bremerton and Kings Bay are places to avoid," Tom said. "Where don't we have military bases of one type or another?"

"Apart from Wyoming, Washington and Florida, which are out, the place with the fewest is probably Oregon," Jane replied.

"Oregon, it is. I'd done my own research and figured out that one of the places with the fewest military bases was Oregon, so I bought us a ranch near a small town called Mt Vernon," Tom said. "We also need something better than this Lincoln, too obvious and doesn't look like something a rancher would have. I set things up for us to swap to a pickup and stock up on essentials."

"Do you have an idea of what we'll need?" Jane asked.

"I do," Tom replied. "There's a guy in Morgantown, four hours from here, with an old rebuilt diesel F-350 Super Duty ready for us. I've already paid for it, so all we have to do is pick it up. I have a camper trailer and stores organised and paid for in Utah for all we need to survive for two years."

"What have you been up to?" Jane asked.

"I've had a plan since you first got into politics. I figured that when you had served your term, then we'd disappear," he replied. "I've been researching things, planning escape routes and building up cash and placing orders."

"Under your own name?" she asked.

"My name, not yours," he laughed. "Your name is too well known, and mine is common enough; there's probably a myriad of Tom Grants out there. You remember Hank from my college days? He helped me get things done."

"I remember him, vaguely, but only very vaguely," she replied.

"I had him do most of the stuff for me; the Secret Service missed him in their various background checks," Tom said. "Don't know how they missed him, but they did, they found everyone else."

"Well, thank you, I think," she said. "Let's go."

"What about the Secret Service detail?" he asked.

"Let them trail along if they want; they'll probably get recalled by Taylor soon enough," she said.

"We need to dump your detail and my car," he said. "Bear with me, I have it all set up, with clothes, a different car and burner phones. All you'll need is in that backpack I gave you; it's got your personal papers and photographs and the few mementoes we brought with us to the. White House."

"How are you going to dump this lot?" she asked.

"Well, as you're no longer the Boss, the main detail switched immediately to Taylor, and we get a much smaller team, one car only, there'll be some confusion as to who actually has the detail. We should take advantage of that and make our move now," he said.

"I should tell Mavis that you and I are going to go and have a heart-to-heart and that we'll be back in a couple of hours to start the transition process," she thought. "I'll get Mavis to start packing up my things and boxing things ready to move out."

They went to the White House garage and got Tom's Lincoln, and were followed by the small Secret Service detail, which both Tom and Jane noted had no female members.

"This is great," he said. "We'll drive to Tysons Corner and park there. Go into the H&M and get some clothes, and use the changing rooms to change into what's in the backpack, then make your way to the parking by the Hyatt, level four, space D311. I'll be there, we have a Ford Focus there, blue. Here's a key in case you get there before me. As you walk through the mall and the Hyatt, here's a map of where the security cameras are, try and avoid them, and in the bag, there are four hats; change them at the points I've marked."

"You've been busy," she said.

"I was tipped off that the Texas guy and his henchman from Louisiana were going to pull off something. So I had a Plan B in case," he explained. "I did co-opt one of the detail and he's bailing as soon as he can, because he seriously doesn't like Taylor."

"So, are we really going to do this?" she asked.

"Have a better idea?" he asked.

"No," she replied.

They were successful in losing their security detail at Tysons Corner and were soon driving west to Morgantown in an older model Ford Edge.

"I picked us up some lunch," he said. "How long before they seriously start looking for us?"

"Left to Taylor, I think as long as we're out of the picture and make no moved to talk to the media, we're not his priority," she replied. "I'd give us about three hours before someone starts to ask where the hell we are."

Day of reckoning

"Secretary Sharma and people of Earth, what do you have to report?" Hathor said in her broadcast to the world on day twenty of her deadline.

"We are making ready," Sharma replied. "We agree with the proposals you made, and those countries that have fission weapons are in the process of removing them and transporting them to the locations you indicated.

"We will establish cordons sanitaire at those locations, and you will deliver the weapons to the perimeters of the cordons," Hathor said. *"We will send equipment to collect them, which will remain at the locations until the agreed day, at which time they will return to us. We will deliver today a schedule of the fission power plants that will be converted to fusion, and teams will arrive on those scheduled dates to do the work. We will deliver today instructions for the preparation of the sites for the fusion plants."*

"We await your communication," Sharma said.

* * * * *

"Do we trust them?" Hathor asked Ramses, her security chief.

"No," he replied. "They will deliver some of their fission weapons, but they will attempt to conceal some. I also expect that they will attempt to fix some sort of device to the weapons they do surrender in the hope that they will destroy one or more of our craft. We have systems to detect and disable any such device."

"Anput, where are their submarines?" Hathor asked.

"I note that most have returned to the ports specified, but twelve belonging to various nations have stayed submerged and are attempting to evade detection," Anput intoned. "I am tracking all of them."

"So, they think to mollify us with some gesture, but then retain weapons to either attack us or each other," Hathor said. "We will need to see what they do when the time comes. Ramses, take your teams and set up the cordons sanitaire at the collection points. Take all precautions against pathogens and aggression by people and defend yourselves at all times."

"My teams are ready," Ramses replied.

"Anput, have the specifications ready in all the languages and units of measurement necessary to start preparing sites for the fusion plants that will replace the fission plants," Hathor instructed.

"It is done," Anput intoned. "I will transmit them now."

* * * * *

"Has anyone heard from or about Adams?" Taylor asked his Cabinet.

"Not a dickybird, she's dropped off the radar completely, no emails, no calls to anyone that we can find, not even her kids, no bank withdrawals, no credit card purchases, nothing," Madison replied. Madison was no longer the Secretary of Defense, but was now the Vice President. In fact, all the Cabinet members were new. Taylor had had a slate of candidates ready, and the Senate had had the most cursory of hearings and had essentially provided the stamp of approval on them all inside four days.

"How the hell did we lose her?" Taylor asked.

"Apparently, she and her husband went to a shopping mall and somehow the detail lost them, their car is still there, and we've not been able to identify them from any of the security footage at the mall, she left her phone, as did her husband, so we can't ping her phone, besides which they've both been wiped and reset to factory settings," George Lufkin, the Secretary for Homeland Security, reported. "We're looking at lapses there, because if we can lose Adams, then we can lose left-wing extremists or Islamic terrorists."

"Stay on that," Taylor said. "In some ways, it's good that she's dropped out of sight and mind; as long as she stays off the air, then she won't interfere; we'll get back to her after we've dealt with the aliens. How the hell she called herself a Republican, I'll never know; maybe it was a good selling point to get elected. Anyway, onto more pressing and important matters. Are we ready to deliver warheads to the collection points?"

"We are," Pete Hogg, the new Secretary of Defense, replied. "We've modified the housings on all the warheads and attached timing devices to twenty of them, set to go off in one month, so time enough to get them well clear of the Earth and safely into the belly of the aliens' ship.

We've been in touch with the Russians, Chinese, Brits, French, Indians, Israelis, and Paks, with the exception of the Brits and French; the others have said that they've done the same, we've coordinated D-Day and H-Hour."

"And our boomers?" Taylor asked.

"We brought all but two back to port; we left one in the Pacific, 550 miles southwest of Pearl and one in the Atlantic, 650 miles north of Newport," Hogg replied. "Our carriers are too big to hide, so they're all back in port. We also left four attack boats at sea, two in the Pacific and two in the Atlantic. They're all submerged somewhere. We pulled the missiles from the boomers in port and then pulled the warheads, and they're on their way to the security zones at Bremerton and Kings Bay."

"Silo based weapons?" Taylor asked.

"We pulled them all," Hogg replied. "Those from Warren are already on site, Malmstrom and Minot are on their way by road. Cruise missile warheads from the Air Force and the Navy, we shipped to Idaho to the Harvest Two mine."

"Any issues with the local communities and these restricted areas?" Taylor asked.

"Some bitching," Lufkin replied. "But we slipped them the word that there might be a surprise for these aliens, and that made people much happier, and they're now avoiding the restricted zones like the plague."

"What about conventional weapons?' Taylor asked.

"We've got them secure; under Adams, we already had ramped up production of artillery shells and tactical missiles, so we've kept that up and are replenishing stocks everywhere we can," Hogg replied. "We've deployed all the carrier-based aircraft around the world, dispersing them to different land bases."

"What are Ivan and Zhou up to?" Taylor asked.

"Pretty much the same as us, dispersing their forces, pulling silo based missiles and warheads. We're pretty certain they've stashed boomers somewhere, but without enough attack boats, they're going to be hard to find," Hogg replied.

"Who can we buy diesel subs from?" Taylor asked.

"Try the Scandinavians," Lufkin suggested. "I seem to recall that they had pretty good diesel boats."

"Steve, get on that," Taylor instructed Steve Bancroft, the new Secretary of State.

"We're getting blueprints and specs for the fusion plants," Don Jacobs, the new Secretary of Energy, reported. "Looks pretty straightforward, we should be ready for the first plant in plenty of time, and we're working on the others at the same time. When we get these fusion plants, we'll back engineer them so that we can build them ourselves, and we'll also see if we can make them small enough to go in a sub or a carrier."

"Good thinking," Taylor said. "Pete, look into that when you can. Is the first plant going to be here before we blow the aliens to kingdom come?"

"Just," Jacobs reported. "Five days, so they must have at least one ready to go."

"Well, we'll have to hope that the connections are self-explanatory; the aliens won't be around to help. How are we on food, water and meds?" Taylor asked.

"We're fine at the Capital," Hogg reported. "And reports I get suggest that most people took the warnings that Adams put out and did stock up for at least two weeks."

"Do we need a press briefing?" Lufkin asked.

"Probably should," Taylor said. "Time for a bullshit session, can the aliens listen in?"

"Anything broadcast can be picked up," Hogg said. "So, if it's broadcast, then the aliens can listen in."

"Good, let them think we're just being good subservient folks," Taylor said. "No inkling from anyone that we aren't about to deliver all the warheads."

"Ladies and Gentlemen, good afternoon," Taylor said to the assembled White House Press Corps. "We are pleased to report that we are well on schedule to meet the instructions of our visitors, and we have already received the first set of instructions that will allow us to make the switch from fission-style nuclear power plants to the cleaner and more efficient fusion reactors. We are giving up nuclear weapons, as are the Russians, Chinese, British, French, Indians, Israelis, and Pakistanis. The weapons that North Korea and Iran had are long since gone. We are looking forward to an era of greater peace in the world. I will take questions."

"Why did President Adams resign?" CNN asked.

"We think the pressures of the job were too much for her, as you know, we do live in uncertain and uncharted times. We have always advocated for the proper assignments in our roles in life," Taylor replied.

"Does that mean that you don't think women should be in the White House?" VCN asked.

"Do you?" Taylor responded, avoiding a direct response but leaving the implication clear.

"Have you sought any advice or counsel from President Adams?" CBS asked.

"We have seen no need to do so, and former President Adams has shown no inclination to communicate since her abrupt, but probably timely, resignation in front of both houses recently," Taylor said.

"What do you think the visitors will do with the nuclear weapons and reactors that we are turning over?" ABC asked.

"We rather hope that they will remove them far from the Earth, perhaps launch them into the Sun, perhaps launch them into a far distant black hole," Taylor said.

"Do we trust that the Russian and Chinese will surrender all their nuclear weapons?" VCN asked.

"You saw what happened to North Korea and Iran, I rather think that Tsar Ivan the Fifth and Premier Zhou have no desire to suffer the same fate," Taylor replied.

"When do you think the visitors will give us the technology to take care of our microplastics?" The Christian Science Monitor asked.

"We are planning for receipt of that right after the thirty-day deadline, which is ten days from now," Taylor said. "It will certainly help clean up our land and oceans."

"Have you plans to phase out the production of plastics?" NBC asked.

"That is something we are examining, as I'm sure you are well aware, plastics are ubiquitous in our society, and their replacement will take creativity and time," Taylor replied.

"So does that imply that if we know how to successfully break down plastics, we will continue to produce them?" CNN asked.

"As I said, we are examining our use of plastics and what it may take to change to alternate materials for all the myriad uses we currently have for plastics," Taylor replied.

"Are there other technologies that we would like from the aliens?" VCN asked.

"How they achieve the speeds they do, and how they travel through space," Taylor said. "Those technologies are for us the stuff of science fiction. Gaining knowledge of them would open up vast vistas for us."

"Yes, but will the aliens give them to us?" VCM pressed.

"That we cannot answer at this time," Taylor replied.

"Do you trust them to keep their implied word that if we hand over our nuclear weapons, then they will help us with other technologies, like fusion?" The Christian Science Monitor asked.

"At this point, we are trusting; we will see what the next few months bring," Taylor said.

"If they want us to surrender our nuclear weapons, does that suggest that they are afraid of them and have no defence against them?" VCN asked.

"Considering the destruction wrought on North Korea and Iran, we deemed it prudent to heed their instructions," Taylor said. "They clearly have the ability to remove any vehicle that could be used to launch a nuclear weapon at them, be it a plane or a missile. They also have the ability to wreak destruction without the use of nuclear weapons, so they probably don't need them. As an aside, their weapon, whatever it is, leaves no dangerous radioactive fallout, so does not create no-go zones. We consider that peace in the world is beneficial to all of us, and unlike at other times, we have reasonable assurance that the Russians and Chinese will similarly disarm, or they will face the consequences."

"That's as maybe," VCN said. "But doesn't China still have over a million men in arms?"

"They do," Taylor confirmed. "But how does that threaten us? They cannot readily move their army and invade our shores; that would be an enormous enterprise which would not go unnoticed and unchallenged."

"What about Russian? Will Tsar Ivan again threaten the European nations?" ABC asked.

"The big threat that previous rulers of Russia raised regularly was the use of nuclear weapons; with those gone, the Europeans can quite readily take care of themselves," Taylor said. "The past war in Eastern Europe caused NATO member nations to rearm to an extent not seen since the end of WWII."

"What happens now in North Korea and Iran?" VCN asked.

"We have no plans for any action in either of those places," Taylor replied.

"But don't you think that South Korea might take this opportunity to invade North Korea?" VCN pressed.

"Given what happened to North Korea after they opened fire on South Korea, I rather think that they will leave things as they are," Taylor suggested. "Thank you all for coming. When we have something new to report, we will convene another briefing."

"Okay, that'll keep them off our backs for a couple of days," Taylor said. "I'm presuming that the networks will all want their cameras out by the exclusion zones come day thirty. Do we need to do anything for their security?"

"Screw 'em," Hogg said. "The press is a pain in the neck, and if the aliens took out a few, that wouldn't break my heart."

"Okay, when the aliens show up to collect the warheads, we don't want any wannabe Rambos shooting at them," Taylor said. "We need to be sure they take the warheads if we want them to be transported up to the alien ship. We shoot at them down here, they might just detonate the lot and leave some really big holes in Wyoming, Washington and Florida."

"We've taken care of that," Hogg said. "No small arms or other weapons within twenty miles of the exclusion zone, not even with our own military, you never know we might have some guy who doesn't know the score thinking he's gonna be a hero."

"Good, we'll play nicely until we see that big bang in the sky," Taylor said. "Brings up a question, will we be able to see it?"

"We're sending over 10,000 warheads up there, from us, the Russians, the Chinks and the others," Hogg said. "We'd better hope that the aliens have gone home, or are a long way from here, because that lot set off at once would be like a nova."

"Shit," Taylor said. "Are we sure we want to do this? If they're still in GEO, won't that fuck up our atmosphere?"

"Most of our atmosphere is inside the Kármán line, which is 100 km above us," Madison said. "Then there's the exosphere, which goes out to about 10,000 km, and GEO is about 35,786 km, but still within the geocorona, which goes out beyond the Moon, but I don't see that much risk as the geocorona is mainly clouds of hydrogen atoms, which become less dense the farther out you go. It will be a really big, bright light in the sky, though, visible to all, the big problem for us with be the EMP that goes with the detonation."

"Now you tell me," Taylor said.

"We don't see that as a huge risk," Hogg said. "It is our assumption that the aliens won't want to hang onto the warheads any longer than is necessary and will transport them away from here as quickly as possible."

"What if they put them in a dumb barge and just send that off into outer space?" Taylor asked.

"That's a possibility," Hogg admitted. "Our estimation is that they'll want to control things, so they'll probably be back at home base unpacking the warheads, in which case, bang, there goes the home base."

"Okay, we'll stick with the plan," Taylor said. "Anything else we need to do? No, okay then, let's get together this afternoon and start to figure out what we do after the aliens have been obliterated. We'd better be ready for Russian and Chinese moves."

"Without carriers, it's going to be hard to stop China taking Vietnam and the Philippines," Hogg said.

"Well, screw them anyway," Taylor said. "I'm more interested in our borders. Make damn sure the southern border is closed and man up the northern border so folks don't try and slip through Canada to get here."

"On it," Lufkin reported. "We've restarted building a real wall to the south, and we're doing it right. We've looked at Hadrian's Wall, the Berlin Wall and the Great Wall of China, and concluded that we'll model it after the Berlin Wall in built-up areas, and like the rest of the Iron Curtain in rural areas. We're going to have to move some folks back from the wall as we can't have them in the zone."

"Too bad for them, but that wall gets built," Taylor said. "One thing Adams and I did agree on was education; we need scientific and engineering students. We're going to have to rebuild our fleet and our weapons, so we'd better make damn sure we've got guys that can do that."

"I'm on it," Grace Wilson, the Secretary of Education and the sole woman in the cabinet. "We're drastically cutting back funding for liberal arts and focusing on science, engineering and medicine. No more Women's Studies, History of Art and all the other Woke crap that built up in time, we need to get back to the fundamentals that built this country, enterprise and industry. That means starting in the elementary schools, and we need to find all of them, we don't want to miss talent, I don't care if it's white, black, Hispanic, Asian, doesn't matter to me, I just want to find the best."

"Good," Taylor said. "Okay, let's get together in the morning and see where we are."

* * * * *

"Has anyone recognised us yet?" Jane Adams asked her husband, Tom.

"No," he replied. "But think about it, the only time people here see you is in cowboy boots, jeans and denim shirt, and a John Deere cap, just another rancher. It's hard to tie that image back to the campaign trail and White House press briefings."

"Do you think that Taylor and his gang will find us here?" she said.

"They may, in time," Tom said. "But if we stay quiet and out of sight, they probably won't care where we are, and probably will be happy that we're out of sight. What they would be concerned about would be TV appearances, blogs, websites and voices that run counter to what they want to do."

"That's true," she agreed. "How did you manage to contact Charlotte and Courtney?"

"I sent letters to them telling them to find a landline and call a burner number that I gave them," he explained. "They both did, and I told them where we were going. I had given each of them $5,000 in cash and told them to hang onto it in case of emergencies, so whatever they do to get here, they won't have to use credit or debit cards. I had bought a bunch of burner phones with a dozen SIM cards, and after each set of calls I made on our drive out here, I superglued the phone to the bottom of a semi that was going in another direction from us. That way, if anyone pinged the SIM card, it wasn't near us."

"Sneaky," she laughed. "Did they say when they might come and see us?"

"Charlotte said that they'd be here the day after tomorrow," he replied. "How they plan to get here without the detail that's assigned to them, I've no idea."

"Good," she said. "I've no idea what Taylor and his gang finally decided to do after they invited me to leave the joint session, but I'll bet it isn't good, and I foresee disaster for our military."

"Do you think they'll try and boobytrap some warheads?" he asked.

"I'm afraid they will," she said. "Something tells me that this Hathor isn't that dumb and she'll have some mechanism to look at what we're handing over, and if she isn't happy or she thinks we're trying to pull a fast one, then look out."

"What are the risks to us if someone does boobytrap a warhead and it goes off near us?" he asked.

"Far enough out, there probably wouldn't be a fallout issue, but EMP will be a big one," she replied. "A big EMP and we've lost all, or nearly all, of our computers, cell phones, cars, planes, ships, anything that relies on electronics, we're back to the 50s."

"Do you think Taylor and his crew have thought of that?" he asked.

"They must have done so, so if there is a boobytrap, it's likely to be set some considerable time in the future when it will be assumed that whatever is carrying the warheads is well away from us," she replied. "Or at least I hope so, I hope they won't do something really stupid and take us back to the 50s."

"You don't have much faith," Tom commented.

"Taylor was useful to get elected," she said. "But as I soon discovered, he really isn't that bright, so who knows who he has surrounded himself with, you can bet it isn't the team I had, except maybe Madison."

"Can you stop them doing something stupid?" Tom asked.

"I could try a TV interview, but the White House would just say it was the ravings of an insecure woman who is bitter about leaving office so soon after being sworn in," she said.

"So, we just have to wait and hope?" he asked.

"Maybe, maybe not," she said. "How good are you with electronics?"

"Electrician, I can be, electronics technician, you'll have to wait for Courtney," he replied.

* * * * *

The television networks descended on the exclusion zones with cameras and reporters, all hoping to get exclusives on the transfer of weapons to the visitors. They were not disappointed. On the 28th day, large vessels came down from the sky and landed in the exclusion zones. They hardly looked like the spaceships of science fiction movies, more like big barges with some kind of heat shield underneath and no obvious signs of a propulsion system. When these vessels had landed then a series of small robot-like machines came out and positioned themselves around the vessels. Then another set of machines came out and started to collect the warheads that were there on pallets, grouping them in packs of four and coating them with some material.

"What's your guess on the function of those first robots?" Madison asked Hogg.

"Security," Hogg suggested. "We can't see any obvious weapons that we recognise, but that doesn't mean they're not there."

"Any idea what that coating may be for?" Madison asked Hogg as they watched the live feeds from the networks.

"My guess is that it's some form of boron, so that can control the emissions from the warheads, should there be any," Hogg suggested. "This is good for us because it makes it unlikely that they'll look too closely at the warheads we've delivered."

"They're getting right on with it," Madison commented. "Those robot devices for picking up and packaging are pretty darned efficient. That's all the warheads we delivered to the three sites already packed up and gone. What happens now?"

"I guess they wait until day thirty in case we want to add any more," Hogg suggested.

"Anything from the Russians and Chinese?" Madison asked.

"We're picking up feeds from Russia, China, the UK, France, Israel, India and Pakistan, and they all show the same pattern, big old ugly tub comes down, robots come out to the perimeter, more robots come out and do the loading," Hogg reported. "You wanna bet that there's no live beings on those scows, it's all handled remotely."

"Just as long as they deliver the warheads to those tugs and the mothership," Madison said. "I wonder what their propulsion system is?"

"Nothing obvious, that's for sure," Hogg commented. "Well, we're done. When the aliens leave, we just have a wait and see what happens."

"How's it all going?" Taylor asked them as he joined them.

"So far, so good, the aliens have loaded up all the warheads that we delivered, and we guess that they're waiting until day thirty in case we add any more," Hogg replied.

"No indication that they suspect anything?" Taylor asked.

"Not a dicky bird," Hogg smirked. "They'll be in for a big shock."

"We should make some kind of statement to the press," Taylor said. "Let the world see what good folks we are."

"Ladies and gentlemen, I'm sure you've all seen the feeds of the alien spacecraft at the exclusion zones collecting the nuclear weapons we are providing in exchange for new and exciting technologies. It marks a significant step forward in maintaining peace in the world, no longer threatened by the spectre of nuclear war," Taylor announced. "We have already received specifications and details for the installation of fusion power plants. As I'm sure you all know, fusion technology has long been sought as a cleaner alternative to fission. Our research into fusion power has been slow; the aliens will provide us with the first fusion reactors and the instructions so that we may build more."

"Are there risks and dangerous emissions from these fusion reactors?" CNN asked.

"The main byproduct of fusion is helium," Taylor replied. "Our designs also presented issues with the steel containment becoming radioactive due to neutron bombardment, but that pales in comparison to the waste products of fission reactors that we are still trying to find safe ways to dispose of."

"Aren't you concerned that the aliens may take advantage of us giving up our nuclear weapons and attack us?" VCN asked.

"Given what they did to North Korea and Iran, it seemed to us prudent not to get into a shooting war with them," Taylor replied.

"What about Russia and China?" ABC asked.

"They've also given up their nuclear weapons, so I'd say that the Doomsday Clock has been set back quite a bit," Taylor said.

"What about micro-plastics?" The Christian Science Monitor asked.

"The aliens agreed to give us the technology and the formulations on day forty of their schedule," Taylor replied.

"Is there any way we can attack the alien ships that are on the ground, or take some hostages?" VCN asked.

"We suspect that there are, in fact, no people on those ships; we believe everything that is on the ground is robotic in nature and is being controlled from above. As to attacking the ships, that is unwise, given what happened to North Korea and Iran," Taylor replied.

"How do we counter aggression by China and Russia if we don't have carriers anymore?" VCN asked.

"We have deployed all the carrier-based aircraft forward to be where they may be needed," Taylor replied. "We are accelerating the pace of building more Wasp-class ships by ramping up production of F-35B aircraft, which will give us the ability to counter much of what China may intend. While the aliens are here, we don't see either Russia or China making any moves towards their neighbours."

"How does this change the budget for military spending?" CBS asked.

"We will switch funds that we had allocated for the construction of new nuclear-powered vessels to conventional powered smaller vessels, which will take less time to build and which we can build larger numbers of," Taylor replied.

"Does this mean we're in a new arms race with the Russians and the Chinese?" NBC asked.

"I wouldn't say that," Taylor said. "The last war between Russian and Ukraine was a different land war with lots of artillery and drones, drones used for intelligence gathering, battlefield attack and long-range attack. We need an agile military to counter threats around the world."

On day thirty, the spacecraft all left, leaving the world to wonder what would happen next.

"How soon before the aliens get a taste of our medicine?" Taylor asked.

"Thirty days," Hogg replied.

"I keep wondering if we should have set the timers for sooner. What if the aliens start pulling the warheads apart?" Taylor asked.

"They'll get a nasty shock," Hogg smirked. "We put some devices in to trigger the bombs if anyone tries to open the cases."

"Anything from JPL or others about where these scows went?" Taylor asked.

"They didn't dock with the tugs or the mothership but seem to be just headed out, hopefully back to their home planet," Hogg reported.

"So, no big, bad, beautiful bang in the sky here?" Taylor asked. "At the speed the scows are going, how long before they clear our solar system?"

"Looks like they'll be out of here in under a week," Hogg replied. "Then we'll just have to wait and see."

* * * * *

"Hathor, we have detected devices attached to these fission weapons that will trigger them if the case is opened, or will trigger them in one month of Earth time," Ramses reported. "I have also found a buried quantity of fission weapons at five locations and twelve submarines with fission drives, all trying to hide."

"Eliminate them, collect all the other weapons, then destroy the militaries and governments of those countries who sought to trick and potentially harm us," Hathor instructed. "Send the fission weapons to the black hole at the centre of the galaxy. Go ahead with the removal of all fission reactors according to the schedule we provided. Expedite the removal of fission power plants from all warships and destroy those ships."

"It is done," Ramses said.

"Anput, release Agent Ten into the atmosphere. This experiment has been a failure, and we will terminate all human life on this planet," Hathor instructed.

"It is done," Anput intoned.

"Good, deliver to whomever is listening the formula to create Agent Fifteen, and we'll see if they work to remove the plastics that they have so wantonly used. When they're gone, I want to quickly clean up the place," Hathor said. "I will address the people of Earth."

"People of Earth, we have detected devices attached to some of the fission weapons surrendered to us. These devices were to either set off the fission weapons if we opened the casings to inspect them or to set off those weapons after an interval of time. We have disabled and removed all those devices, and they are being delivered to the offending governments as we speak." Hathor stated. *"We have also detected fission weapons that were not surrendered to us. We are in the process of collecting those weapons. We have also tracked down twelve naval vessels that are submerged in an attempt to deceive us that all fission-powered vessels had been returned to port for decommissioning. Those vessels have been detained and will be disarmed and decommissioned by us. This has been a disappointing development, and we have no choice but to take action against the offending governments and their respective militaries. This action is proceeding now and will conclude when those governments and militaries have been destroyed. We will take no immediate action against the civil populations of the offending countries, except to caution them not to repeat the mistakes of their current leaders and try and rearm and attempt to attack us again. We are taking no immediate action against the countries that were not party to this foolish enterprise. We will uphold our part in the agreement, and we will deliver the first fusion reactors as promised, and we have also provided the information for you to produce agents that will breakdown so called micro-plastics to harmless molecules. This agent is in no way harmful to any living organism and may be safely ingested by any species. We are here for advice and consultation."*

* * * * *

"It looks like Taylor and his crew tried to pull a fast one on the visitors, and it backfired badly," Jane commented to Tom as they watched the news in the local bar.

"Any thoughts about going back to Washington and taking over the reins?" Tom asked.

"No," she said. "I had my fill of the idiots from both parties and both houses for the brief time I was there."

"Jesus, there's nothing left of the White House or the Capitol building," Tom said as more news footage came up. "What's the closest military base to here?"

"Probably an Air National Guard unit at Klamath Falls," she thought. "They had some F-35s there, my guess is all gone now, even if they got them off the ground, I doubt they would have lasted long."

"My God, there's nothing left of Andrews either," Tom remarked.

"Norfolk is gone too; just as well Hathor and her crew are still here, or I could see the Mexican army coming across the border to retake the Alamo."

"The governors are going to have a tough time maintaining law and order," she said. "I could see gangs of all persuasions trying to gain control over territory. There's enough guns out there to make cities and rural areas war zones. What about here, do you see any risk?"

"Not really," he replied. "The community is pretty small and isolated, so I wouldn't expect too many from the outside. I think everyone will be too busy securing their own places."

"Well, at least for now, Hathor hasn't turned on the general population," she commented. "There will be a lot who won't mourn the loss of the politicians in Washington, the military, that's another story, but I suppose they do the bidding of the politicians, so they're lumped with them."

"Say folks," a voice interrupted. "There's a town meeting this evening at six, we're going to meet to figure out how to keep us safe and how to manage things in the future, we're probably not going to get anything from the Feds, and little from the State and County, so we'll have to do it ourselves. Name's Jeff Wilson, by the way."

"We'll be there," Tom said.

"You folks have the old Bancroft place, don't you?" Jeff asked.

"We do," Tom confirmed. "Tom and Jane Grant."

"Pleased to meet you," Jeff said. "See you at six."

"Well, it looks like we'll be on our own for a while," Jane commented after Jeff had gone. "I wonder how this Hathor decimated our military so quickly?"

"There's a new item," Tom said. "Let's see what they have to say."

"Okay, so it looks like she used waves of some kind of attack craft, starting on the East Coast, the Mississippi and the Rockies, and moved West. I'm surprised we didn't get anything off the ground in Hawaii or Guam," he reported. "Oh, wait, there's more. It seems we did get stuff off the ground from Hawaii and Guam, but ET took them all out from a distance, including any and all missiles we launched against them."

"So, Jeff was right, we'd better figure out how to take care of ourselves," Jane said. "Can this valley grow enough to support us all?"

"It can," Tom confirmed. "We'll pretty much all have to go back to being farmers and gardeners, but it can be done, and there's plenty of deer out there for meat. We may need to set up some form of barter system to share what we all have and grow, but that's an easy fix, the kind of issue to be raised at the meeting tonight, that plus how do we stop interlopers coming in to try and steal what we have."

"It's a new world," Jane said.

Epilogue - 2049

"How long has it been since the last reported pregnancy?" Jane asked Tom.

"Twenty years," he replied. "Scientists have tried everything, but no success. Gene rearrangement doesn't work; messing about with our DNA hasn't worked. Whatever the visitors did, they really screwed up our DNA, and all men are infertile, the sperm banks are long since exhausted, so I guess we're destined to die off."

"I was surprised how long it took us all to work out that we were doomed. This Hathor must have released something into the atmosphere that really messed up our DNA and made all men sterile," Jane said. "I keep thinking if Taylor and his gang and the other idiots from Russia, China, India and Pakistan hadn't tried to be cute, they might have let us live."

"The population has already dropped by, what, 35%?" he asked.

"I suppose that's right, no one under 20 and very few over 100," she said. "We're ageing out, another 80 years and there'll be precious few people left, if any."

"From what I've heard, no other species has been affected, not even our closest biological relatives in the great apes," he said.

"Still can't believe that there's nothing we can do," she said. "I would have thought with our knowledge of DNA, we could have figured out what she screwed up."

"Maybe the alteration is big enough that we can't reverse it," Tom said.

"Still, it's frustrating that we as a race are going to die out," Jane bemoaned.

"One thing it has done is bring back the sense of community," he said. "Before the visitors, we were focused on GNP growth, acquisition of wealth and property, now what does owning a big fancy compound on Kauai get you?"

"Seclusion in your later years," she thought. "But, so what, consumerism is dying out, now it's make do and mend, grow your own and retreat from the encroaching wild."

"I wonder where the last surviving human will live?" he pondered. "Asia would be my guess. It would be lonely, but with enough food and water, there would be much to enjoy in your last days, kind of Death Room scene from *Soylent Green*, but in reality."

"My bet is we'll die off sooner than we think," she said. "The medical systems we have will break down, and life expectancy will drop."

"How long do you give us?" he asked.

"Twenty to twenty-five years," she said. "By that time, we'll be just about 90, Courtney and Charlotte will be in their mid-60s, and about the youngest hereabouts. One good thing that I've heard about the visitors is that disused refineries, chemical factories and power stations are taken apart by them, and the land cleaned up. I just wish that whatever technologies they have to do that we had been able to use the same when we were running things."

"We did manage to make a mess of things, didn't we?" he said.

"We did," she agreed. "Consumerism and the emphasis on GNP growth just drove the demand for more and more resources, and a lack of population control meant exponential growth and, again, the demand for more resources. We were wrecking the planet; no wonder the visitors probably considered it a failed experiment. I wonder what the worlds that they considered a success did?"

"I guess we'll never know," he said. "I doubt that ET's going to tell us. Is there anywhere you'd really like to go before we die, anything you really want to see?"

"No," she said. "We've been to all the places on my list, you?"

"No, I'd just like to have enough to eat and drink and sit and watch the deer," he replied. "Given any thought to what may happen to us if we get some really bad disease or cancer?"

"I talked to the pharmacist in Bend and she gave me a supply of phenobarbital," Jane replied. "She told me a dozen of those and a glass of Scotch, and it's sayonara. Comfortable way to go, just fade out to sleep and don't wake up."

"I wonder how many of us will be doing that in later years?" he pondered.

"Probably more than you'd think," she said. "None of us wants to die, but it comes in the end, and why not be in control of how you go. I don't want to be on my deathbed in agony with some weird disease of advanced cancer."

"What was the Nevil Shute novel?" he asked.

"*On the Beach,*" she replied. "A post-nuclear war story about the slow spread of lethal radiation south and the trials and tribulations of the last group of people in New Zealand and their ultimate recognition that it was the end for them. What Shute didn't talk about was all the other species we took with us with our use of nuclear weapons, and as is a truism, there was no winner in that war, just death for everyone. At least in the current circumstances, all the other species get to live."

"I wonder how many post-apocalyptic novels have been written and movies made?" he said.

"The last count was well over 500 movies," she replied. "In some, we're just eking out an existence, in others, we've been replaced as the dominant species; novels, who knows how many."

"It's interesting when you think about it, how preoccupied we've been about the end of civilisation as we know it, and yet how little we actually did to prevent it from happening," he commented.

"I'm not sure what we would have done differently," she said. "There are things we could have done, like limiting the use of fossil fuels, limiting the number of children, like the Chinese did, but even that led to problems. No, I think the fundamental problem is in our nature, we have the innate desire to propagate, no matter the consequence, and the desire for ever better and better standard of living, which drove the need for and use of consumer goods and materials for infrastructure and housing, which drove the demand for raw materials. There was the Agricultural Revolution in Britain that increased the amount of food produced from the land, then the urbanisation of Britain and the higher cost of labour, which drove the necessity for innovation in producing what that population needed and wanted, so the Industrial Revolution, and after that the Electronic Revolution. After that, we were essentially doomed."

"That's a pretty negative view of things," he commented.

"I suppose it is," she agreed. "But, how else would it have gone?"

"I wonder how long it will be before there's no evidence that humans were here at all," he pondered.

"Studies I have seen suggest that cities start to really crumble and fall apart in a hundred years, but to eliminate all evidence will take thousands to millions of years," she commented. "Look at what our own archaeologists dig up, ancient remains from thousands of years ago and fossilised bones from millions of years."

"Do you think the visitors will repopulate the Earth?" he asked.

"I think this Hemsut will go back to the drawing board and try and work out what it is about our psychology that drives the aggression in us and the apparent need to conquer all around, being the neighbours or the natural world," she replied.

"Have we conquered the natural world?" he asked.

"We've certainly altered it and driven many species to extinction," she replied. "From the earliest times, man has messed with the environment, using fire, cutting the forest, changing the balance of things with the mass elimination of megafauna. We may not have conquered the natural world completely, but we've certainly made a mess of it."

"I wonder if reincarnation is real," he said. "I'd like to come back at some point, maybe a thousand years from now and see what the place looks like."

"Might be a *Planet of the Apes* thing where you see the Statue of Liberty poking up through the ground," she said.

"With intelligent apes?" he asked.

"Good question," she thought. "Somehow I doubt it; if it were going to happen, it would have done so already; they've been around as long as we have."

"God, who'd have thought it would come to this, living out our last days, hoping we stay healthy enough to not make those days painful, with no help coming from our government, and no help from our visitors," he lamented.

"Our own fault," she said. "We messed up the planet with no regard for all the other species that live here, and we had no idea that someone was watching and would take a dim view of what we'd done."

"And all appeals to them have fallen on deaf ears?" he asked.

"So I gather," she confirmed. "Reminds me of *Hitchhiker's Guide to the Galaxy*, where the plans for the hyperspace bypass have been on display in the local planning office of Alpha Centauri for 50 years, something like that."

"Not quite," he said. "We've not achieved the technological state to be able to travel outside our solar system, and live to tell about it."

"If this Hemsut makes minor alterations to our DNA, I wonder how they'll manage the fundamental fight or flight responses," she pondered. "We are what we are as an aggressive species largely through the need to survive in our earliest days, when we were at risk from other carnivores. If they are to repopulate the planet with humans, they'd have to make sure that they're not all wiped out quickly by competing species."

"I heard the other day that the last of the satellites that were up there have been removed, so now the skies are completely clear again," Tom said. "Travel has become a little more complicated now that all the GPS birds are gone, basic sextant navigation is back in vogue, and weather forecasters are back to more guesswork than analysis."

"I suppose that was inevitable," Jane said. "Better the Visitors remove all the satellites than have them sit up there and eventually come crashing down as orbital velocities decay. Anyway, enough philosophising, what are we going to eat tonight?"

"Venison stew," he said. "I used some of that venison John got last week, and it's cooking now, should be ready at any time."

"Red wine with that?" she asked.

"How much do we have left?" he asked.

"The last lot we liberated was forty cases," she said.

"Hope it doesn't go off on us," he said. "Imagine that, once a respected member of the government, now I'm consorting with a serial looter."

"I imagine that there's going to be quite a few who will just drink themselves into oblivion," she said. "For some, rather that than wait until they're infirm with age and can't manage all the bodily functions, they'll just decide to end it all in other ways."

"If they do, better make sure they do a good job, because there'll be precious little in the way of services to care for the aged and infirm," he commented.

"Are Courtney and Charlotte going to join us?" she asked.

"Courtney said she would, she and John will be over soon. Charlotte said that she and Brian were going off on a mission for three days," he replied. "I think they're going to barter some venison for cherries and wine."

"How long before fuel supplies run out?" she asked.

"Right now, there are some refineries on the West Coast that are still operating, but they're running out of staff who know how to run the places. As long as we can get vegetable oil, we can make our own diesel, and we won't be dependent on them," he replied.

"Better try and find as much as we can while we can," she said. "The infrastructure is breaking down, and roads are getting less usable."

"There's a fuel depot in Eugene, I heard about," he said. "I gather that for $5,000 cash, you can pick a tanker full. There's a disused 10,000-gallon tanker in the County Roads depot; we could borrow that and drive over and get a load. We've got the cash, might as well use it for something, we're not spending any."

"If you do that, get John to go with you and go well armed," she said.

"No other way," he said.

"Mom, Dad," Courtney greeted them when she and John arrived. "How are things?"

"We're fine," Jane replied. "Aches and pains associated with age, but nothing serious, you?"

"Same," Courtney replied. "We've got a good vegetable crop in right now, and if we can keep the deer out, we should do well."

"Your Dad was thinking of going over to Eugene and buying us a tanker load of diesel," Jane said.

"That'd be useful," John said. "I'll come with you. What are you going to do, take that tanker from the County Roads?"

"That was my idea," Tom confirmed.

"I suppose things are slowly going to disintegrate and we'll be more and more on our own," Courtney said. "We really did mess things up."

"Our generation did, not yours," Jane said. "Us plus generations before us who were intent on growth."

"Well, we've learned to be philosophical about it, and when the end comes, it comes," Courtney said. "Until then, I'm going to try and appreciate the natural world we tried so hard to wipe out."

"I suppose that's the best we can do," Jane said. "We have to accept what has happened, unpleasant as it is, and try and enjoy what time we have left on this Earth."

"So, that's going to be our epitaph, we tried to enjoy what time we had left on the planet, regretting that we and earlier generations had made an unholy mess of the place," Tom said.

"It's sad," Jane said. "That plus the fact that no one will see whatever memorial to us is placed, unless possibly some new colonisers or the latest Hemsut experiment finds our fossilised remains."

www.ingramcontent.com/pod-product-compliance
Lightning Source LLC
Chambersburg PA
CBHW070839250626
47159CB00003B/851